"Genevieve Lawr... the honor of being my fake bride?"

"You're being ridiculous."

"Don't ruin this special moment for me." He moved the hay ring back and forth for her to see. "It's not every day I get engaged."

"Fine," she said with an annoyed sigh as she held out her left ring finger. "I will be your fake bride, Knox. But only if you win the wager and show up tomorrow."

The cowboy stood up and slipped the makeshift ring made of hay onto her finger. Did she imagine it, or did a small shock pass between them when he took her hand in his? She looked at that ring encircling her ring finger; she had never thought to see any type of ring on that finger for years, if ever. Even a hay ring made her feel boxed in like a trapped wild animal. Genevieve swayed backward and put her hand on the door to steady her body. She was well-known for her nerves of steel when she was off-road racing or vaulting on the back of her horse—why were those nerves failing her now?

A PERFECT PLAN

JOANNA SIMS

&

USA TODAY Bestselling Author

TERI WILSON

2 Heartfelt Stories

The Maverick's Wedding Wager
and *The Maverick's Secret Baby*

 **HARLEQUIN**

Special thanks and acknowledgment are given to Joanna Sims and Teri Wilson for their contribution to the Montana Mavericks: Six Brides for Six Brothers continuity.

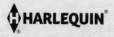

Recycling programs for this product may not exist in your area.

ISBN-13: 978-1-335-42735-9

A Perfect Plan

Copyright © 2022 by Harlequin Enterprises ULC

The Maverick's Wedding Wager
First published in 2019. This edition published in 2022.
Copyright © 2019 by Harlequin Enterprises ULC

The Maverick's Secret Baby
First published in 2019. This edition published in 2022.
Copyright © 2019 by Harlequin Enterprises ULC

For questions and comments about the quality of this book, please contact us at CustomerService@Harlequin.com.

Harlequin Enterprises ULC
22 Adelaide St. West, 41st Floor
Toronto, Ontario M5H 4E3, Canada
www.Harlequin.com

Printed in U.S.A.

CONTENTS

Joanna Sims is proud to pen contemporary romance for Harlequin Special Edition. Joanna's series, The Brands of Montana, features hardworking characters with hometown values. You are cordially invited to join the Brands of Montana as they wrangle their own happily-ever-afters. And, as always, Joanna welcomes you to visit her at her website, joannasimsromance.com.

Books by Joanna Sims

Harlequin Special Edition

The Brands of Montana

A Match Made in Montana
High Country Christmas
High Country Baby
Meet Me at the Chapel
Thankful for You
A Wedding to Remember
A Bride for Liam Brand
High Country Cowgirl
The Sergeant's Christmas Mission

The Montana Mavericks: Six Brides for Six Brothers

The Maverick's Wedding Wager

A Baby for Christmas
The One He's Been Looking For
Marry Me, Mackenzie!

Visit the Author Profile page
at Harlequin.com for more titles.

THE MAVERICK'S WEDDING WAGER

Joanna Sims

Dedicated to Sandie Weiss

I wanted you to know how much I love you,
so I dedicated this book to you!

I love you, Aunt Sandie, and I always will.

Chapter 1

"You are late."

"I *know*," horse farrier Genevieve Lawrence said to her phone as she stepped on the gas. She hated to be late and yet, here she was, running behind again on the way to her next client. Spotting one of her favorite off-road shortcuts ahead, Genevieve downshifted her four-wheel-drive Chevy Colorado, jerked the steering wheel to take a hard right and then floored it once the hind end of her truck stopped fishtailing. Laughing as she sped over a large bump in the road that sent her truck airborne for a split second, Genevieve knew she was taking a risk using this dirt road. It had been a rainy late August in Montana and there would be mud hole mine traps everywhere. But she'd been off-road racing since she was a teenager and knew this road like the back of her hand. If she didn't get stuck, she'd shave a good fifteen minutes off her time.

"What's life without a little risk?" Genevieve gave a rebel yell, fighting the steering wheel to keep it straight when the back tires hit a slick pocket of mud that sent her sliding sideways.

"Now you are really late," her phone gave her another verbal reminder.

"Nobody likes a know-it-all, Google!" Genevieve snapped as she went careening through a large puddle of standing water, splashing brown water onto her windshield and temporarily blinding her view.

Putting her wipers on high so she could see, she saw the end of the dirt road up ahead and, instead of slowing down, she floored it again. In Genevieve's mind, this was the best part. This was the most dangerous, and therefore, the most exhilarating, part of this shortcut. If she got up enough speed and momentum, she would really catch some air off a large mound of dirt right before she had to make a sharp left onto the main road.

"Woo-hoo!" she shouted, loving that wonderful sinking feeling in her stomach that she always got when all four wheels left the road.

A loud honk of a horn brought her smashing back into reality and made her tighten her grip on the steering wheel. She had successfully navigated the sharp left turn onto the highway, but miscalculated how close the next vehicle was to her entry point and she ended up cutting them off—just a little.

"Sorry!" She waved her hand out of the window with another laugh. She had cut that one a bit too close for comfort. But in her mind, no harm, no foul. This was what living was all about! Taking risks for big payoffs.

By the time she pulled into the driveway to the Crawford's cattle spread, the Ambling A, her heart was still pounding and her body was still crackling with adrenaline. She parked in front of the twenty-stall stable. When Maximilian Crawford, the patriarch of the Crawford family, purchased the ranch, the barn had been just a plain metal structure. Maximilian refurbished the barn, matching the exterior to the main house's log cabin design, and now the once plain barn was an impressive showpiece by anyone's standards. Everything about the updated stable wreaked of money—from the custom Ambling A windmill perched atop the cupola to the red brick rubber pavers in the long, wide aisle that provided a cushion for the horses' legs and joints. The Crawford cowboys had already begun to fill that fine stable with some of the highest pedigreed Montana-bred quarter horses money could buy.

Working with those horses was an honor Genevieve never thought to have. In fact, she had been completely shocked when Knox Crawford, one of Maximilian's six sons, had called to hire her as part of the Ambling A's horse care team. From her experience, most ranchers still had a mindset that being a horse farrier was a job for menfolk. And that mindset went double for her father.

As she was shutting off her engine, Genevieve spotted Knox up in the hayloft above the barn. The two large doors to the hayloft were open and Knox was restacking bales of hay, presumably getting ready for another shipment. The moment she spotted Maximilian's fifth-born son, she felt that same wonderful shot of adrenaline that she normally only experienced when she was bungee jumping from a bridge, off-road racing or winning a wager with some cowboy who thought that he couldn't ever lose to a chick.

Knox Crawford was tall and lean with intense brown-black eyes; his body appeared to be carved out of granite from years in the saddle. When Genevieve saw Knox as he was now, shirt unbuttoned with the glistening sweat from his muscular chest making an eye-catching trail down to the waistband of his snug-fitting, faded jeans, it made her almost change her mind about leaving Rust Creek Falls for more open-minded pastures in California.

Almost.

Knox heard the crunching sound of tires on the gravel drive and that got his heart pumping just a little bit faster. He'd been checking his watch, anticipating pretty Genevieve Lawrence's arrival. In fact, he'd found himself looking forward to seeing her all week. Knox hoisted one last bale of hay onto a tall stack nearby before he walked over to the wide opening of the hayloft to greet the horse farrier. Genevieve's truck, white with a colorful horse mural painted on the side, was covered in brown mud. The petite blonde got out of the driver's side door, looked up at him with an easy smile and waved.

"Sorry I'm late!" she called up to him and the sweetness in her voice rang some sort of bell in the deep recesses of his mind.

Ever since his father had tasked him with the job of finding a veterinarian and farrier for their horses, and Knox had stumbled upon Genevieve's Healing Hooves website, something in his soul seemed to hone in on this woman like a heat-seeking missile aimed at its target. Surprisingly for him, it wasn't the fact that she had long wavy, wheat-colored hair that framed her oval face in the most attractive way—even though he had always had a weakness for blondes. And it wasn't those wide cornflower blue eyes and full lips that seemed to always be turned up into a smile when she looked at him. It was more than just her looks. She fascinated him; she made him laugh. In his mind, that was a mighty potent combination.

"Not a problem." Knox took his cowboy hat off so he could wipe the sweat from his brow with his sleeve. "Did you get stuck in a mudhole?"

Genevieve had walked around to the back of her truck so she could get her tools as she always did. With a laugh and a cocky smile, she said, "I took a shortcut."

"Must've been one heck of a shortcut."

"It sure was," she said with another laugh.

While the farrier buckled on her scarred-up leather chaps that covered the front part of her thighs and knees, Knox tugged his gloves off his hands with his teeth so he could button his shirt. He never took his eyes off Genevieve. She was the sexiest darn tomboy he had ever met. Whenever he saw her, it made him sorely regret that he was dedicated to sticking to his self-imposed dating moratorium. His father was paying big bucks to a matchmaker to marry off his sons and Knox had no intention of going along with the plan quietly. If he had to give up dating for a good, long while, then that's what he was going to do—but he'd do it *his* way.

As she finished her task of putting on her chaps, she looked up to find him staring at her. There was no use trying to play it off—she had caught him dead to rights.

"How many do we have today?" Genevieve asked, all business. She was the one woman in his new hometown of Rust Creek Falls that he'd like to flirt a little with him, and yet she seemed to be the only one who *didn't.* When she came out to the Ambling A, she was friendly but always professional and on task.

"Four," he told her.

"You know," she said, "we could get all of these horses on the same trimming schedule. It'd be easier on you."

"Naw. Then I'd only get to see you once a month." He said with a smile. "I'll meet you down there."

Genevieve had a routine and he knew it well. She had a policy that the owner, or an owner's representative, had to be on site when she trimmed hooves, and from her very first visit back in June, Knox had been the one to greet her. There was something special about the time he spent with Genevieve while she worked; he could talk to her in a way he'd never been able to talk to another woman. In fact, he could talk to her like she was one of his brothers. She liked to do guy stuff and she wasn't overly concerned with her nails and her hair and she was as pretty as they came without makeup. Perhaps the confident, no-nonsense way Genevieve comported herself was why he felt, for the first time in his life, like he had begun a genuine friendship with a woman. The fact that she was easy on the eyes was just a bonus.

Knox slipped the halter on his big dappled gray gelding, Big Blue, and led him down the wide aisle of the barn to the cross ties where Genevieve had set up her hoof stand.

"How's Blue today?" The farrier ran her hand down the horse's neck as she always did, checking out the horse's body and stance before she moved to the hooves.

"No complaints." He hooked the cross tie onto Blue's halter to keep the horse standing in one place while Genevieve worked.

"He's got a good weight on him."

"He's fit, that's for sure."

Genevieve finished her inspection, circling back to the horse's left front hoof. Unlike any other farrier he had ever seen, she knelt down beside Blue's front left leg, lifted it and let it rest on her thigh while she took one of her tools from a pocket of her chaps. On the first day she'd come out to the ranch he'd asked her about her unusual trimming posture—kneeling instead of standing, which was the standard because it was safer for the farrier. Genevieve's answer had stuck with him—she had said that it was all about the comfort of the horse for her. Yes, it was more dangerous, but she trusted the horses and they trusted her. If she had to get out of the way, she knew how to do it. That night he had gone to his father, who was convinced that hiring a woman farrier was bad business, and told him that he had just met one of the most talented farriers he'd ever known. And to this day, he hadn't changed his mind about Genevieve.

"How's he looking?" Knox moved closer to Genevieve, liking the way she would flip her long, thick braid over her shoulder.

"He looks great." She glanced up from her work to nod at him. "The walls of the hoof are strong, the frog has got good give, and it's been so rainy and wet these last few weeks, I've been seeing a lot of thrush out there, but Blue's don't have any signs of that."

"All good news then."

"All good news."

After that brief exchange, Knox leaned back against a nearby wall and watched Genevieve work. She was fast and efficient, another trait he appreciated about her. She didn't smoke or spit tobacco, or take extended breaks in between horses to shoot the breeze about hunting or to recount worn-out rodeo stories like the past farriers he had hired. Genevieve kept her focus on the horse, even during the times when they had a conversation going.

"He's ready to go back to his stall." She unhooked Big Blue from the cross ties.

Knox had been so lost in thought that he hadn't even noticed that she had finished. Those moments when he had been brooding about the conflict he was having with the father had raced by without him noticing.

"He's already done?" He pushed away from the wall. "That was quick."

"Quick and competent." She handed him the lead rope with a smile. "Bring me my next victim, please."

Knox led Big Blue back to his stall before he grabbed a dun mare with a black mane and tail and a tan body his father had just purchased for breeding.

"Who's this beauty?" Genevieve's face lit up at the sight of the new addition to the stable.

"Honey."

Genevieve rubbed the mare between the eyes, and the mare, who had been head shy and skittish around most of the ranch hands at the Ambling A, lowered her head and nuzzled the farrier's hand.

"And, you're sweet like honey, aren't you?"

After her standard body and leg check of the mare, Genevieve went to work. The first order of business was pulling the mare's shoes; Genevieve had a reputation of being one of the best "barefoot" farriers and could often get a horse sound without shoes. Some horses required shoes, but it was best for the horse if they could have their hooves natural like God made them.

"Walk her forward for me so I can see her walk," Genevieve instructed once she pulled the last shoe off the mare. "Let's see how she does."

After a couple of cautious steps where the mare was trying to get used to the odd sensation of walking without metal attached to her hooves, she began to walk naturally without any signs of lameness.

With a pleased smile, Genevieve waved her hand. "Bring her on back. She's going to do just fine without shoes."

It didn't seem like any time at all that Genevieve handed the new mare off to him as she prepared for the third horse of the day. She was halfway done and he had wasted their time together lost in his own thoughts.

"I'm sorry I haven't been much company today." He didn't know why he felt like he owed her some sort of explanation. Most visits they had a lot to say to each other. But today he couldn't seem to get out of his own head.

Genevieve, in keeping with her easygoing manner, said, "Don't worry about it. There're plenty of days I don't feel like talking, trust me."

That was just the thing—he *wanted* to talk to somebody about his situation with his father. In fact, he felt like he *needed* to talk to somebody about it. It was eating him inside out keeping it all bottled up. Lately, he swung like an erratic pendulum from furious to just plain fed up and he was always thinking about a way to show his father, once and for all, that he couldn't meddle in his life. He was a full-grown man and he was dog tired of his father thinking that he could control him like a puppet on a string.

Knox had chafed under his father's rule for most

of his life. Even as a kid he had wanted to set his own
course, to make his own decisions. Max ruled the family with a proverbial iron fist—he was the boss and his
word was first, last and final. There had been plenty
of times when Knox thought to take a different path in
life and leave the family business behind but one of his
brothers would always reel him back in to the fold. In
fact, his decision to move to Montana in the first place
was touch and go. This move would have been the perfect excuse to start a new chapter in his life without having to always bend to his father's will. Yet, here he was,
in Montana, once again, doing it Maximilian's way.

And, perhaps that would have been okay for him.
The Ambling A had plenty of elbow room and he had
his own cabin. The town of Rust Creek Falls was nice
enough and the women sure were pretty. But, then his
father dishonored him, and his brothers, by offering
to pay a local matchmaker, Vivian Shuster, a million
bucks to find brides for his sons. Knox felt humiliated
and the wound was deeper because the source of that
humiliation was his own father. More than any time in
his life, Knox wanted to send his father a message: stop
meddling in my life!

In no time at all, Genevieve was finished with the
third horse and ready for the last one. Perhaps it was the
fact that their visit was about to be over—or perhaps
it was because he had grown so comfortable with this
woman. Either way, when Knox placed the last horse
in the cross ties for Genevieve, he broached a subject
with her that he had sworn he'd never broach with anyone other than family.

"I suppose you've heard all about the million-dollar deal my dad made with Viv Shuster." Knox had his

arms crossed in front of his body and he watched Genevieve's face carefully.

She was about to kneel down and begin working, but his words must have caught her off guard. Genevieve looked up at him with what could only be read as embarrassment—not for her, but for *him*. Of course the pretty farrier had heard all about the million-dollar deal Max had made to marry off his six sons. Of course she had.

Genevieve had hoped that the subject of the Viv Shuster deal would never come up between Knox and her. Everyone in Rust Creek Falls had heard about Maximilian's quest to marry off his six eligible bachelor sons. It was the talk of the town! Most of the townsfolk were rooting for Viv so she could keep her sagging wedding business afloat. And there was a good chance Viv could pull it off. There were a lot of single women in town who wanted in on the Crawford action. Because Knox had become a friend of sorts, Genevieve never wanted to bring up what might be a sore subject for him. After all, she knew too well what it was like to have an overbearing father determined to control the lives of his adult children.

"I heard," she said simply, not wanting to sugarcoat it. Knox didn't seem like the type to want things sugarcoated for him. She took a moment to look directly into his intense, deep brown eyes so he would know that she was sincere when she said, "And I'm sorry."

His heavy brown brows lifted slightly at her words. "Thank you."

She nodded her head. Perhaps she was the first to say that to him. Instead of starting right away on the last horse, Genevieve opened up to Knox in a way she hadn't before. "You know, I do understand how you feel. My dad's been trying to marry me off for years. He thinks that my profession is unladylike." She made quotation marks with her fingers when she said *unladylike*. "He thinks my expiration date for making babies is looming like an end-of-the-world scenario. As if that's the only thing I'm good for." She frowned at the thought. "I've gone out with every darn made-in-Montana cowboy within a fifty-mile radius—"

"You haven't gone out with me," the rancher interjected.

The way those words slipped past Knox's lips, like a lover's whisper full of promise of good things to come, made Genevieve's stomach tighten in the most annoying way. She did *not* need to get involved with anyone in Rust Creek Falls. That was not the plan.

Wanting to laugh off the suggestion in his words, she smiled. "Well, that's because you are a made-in-Texas cowboy. That doesn't count."

Knox took a step closer, his eyes pinned on her face in a way that had never happened before. This new line of conversation had seemed to open something up between them, and Genevieve wasn't all too sure that she shouldn't slam the lid shut real quick on what might turn out to be a giant Pandora's box.

"Well," the rancher said, his voice lowered in a way that sent a tingle right down her spine. "You know what people say about things from Texas—"

"I know, I know." She cut him off playfully. "Everything is bigger in Texas."

"Now, that's a dirty mind at work." Knox smiled at her, showing his straight white teeth. "I was going to say *better* but if you want to say bigger, then I'm not going to object."

The banter seemed to break the odd tension between them and they both laughed. And that's when she noticed that when Knox took a step toward her, she had mindlessly taken a step toward him. With a steadying hand on the neck of the horse patiently waiting in the cross ties, Genevieve said, still laughing, "Do you know that I even agreed to go out with your brother on a date, just to get my father off my back?"

In the rancher's eyes, there was a fleeting emotion that Genevieve could identify only as jealousy. It was brief, but she saw it.

"Not that anything happened between us," she was quick to add before she got to work on the final horse of the day. If she got lost in conversation with Knox, she would lose the time she had made up and then she would be late for her next client. "I knew that Logan had it bad for Sarah. As a matter of fact, I told him to quit being such a chicken on our date. It was just a one and done for me. I told Viv to take my name officially off the list and I told my dad I tried."

"So… Logan wasn't your type?"

Genevieve glanced up to see that same intense, focused, almost examining expression in Knox's eyes.

"No," she said with an easy laugh. "And obviously I wasn't his! He's married to Sarah and everyone in town knows how much he loves being a father to baby Sophia."

Genevieve gently moved the horse's hoof onto her stand so she could smooth out the rough edges left behind by her nippers. "My dad says I'm too picky, but is there really such a thing as being too picky when you're looking for your soul mate? I mean, unless I meet that exact right guy, I'm not even all that sure that I want to get married and have kids. I have my business and my career to build. I'm happy. Why fix what ain't broken, right? That's why I'm living in the apartment above my parents' garage—I'm saving money so I can move to California. There's a lot of really exciting stuff happening with holistic approaches to horse care there and I want to be a part of it."

"So, you're not even planning on hanging around Rust Creek Falls?"

"Nope."

"That might just be perfect, then."

The cryptic tone Knox used to say those words made an alarm bell go off in her head, but she didn't ask him about it. Some things, in her experience, were better left alone.

Genevieve finished her work and unhooked the last horse from the cross ties, hooked the lead rope to its halter and handed the horse off to Knox.

"You can tell your father that all the horses got a clean bill of health today. I can see these four again in four to six weeks."

Knox nodded rather absentmindedly. He led the horse back to its stall, and then he headed back to her, covering the distance quickly with his long-legged stride. There was a new determination in the way he walked, and there was a glint of mischief in his dark brown eyes that caught her attention and made her feel a little queasy in her stomach, like she had just gotten a mild case of food poisoning.

Instead of handing her a check as was typical, Knox stood in front of her, his hat tilted back a bit so she could see his eyes, and asked her, "How would you like to get your dad off your back while you're earning your way out of here?"

"How would I *like* that?" She shook her head with a laugh. "Are you kidding me? I'd *love* to get Lionel Lawrence off my back."

"Then you and I are in the same boat. Because I would love to get Max off my back and out of my business."

Genevieve heard, and understood, the frustration in Knox's voice. Having an overbearing, meddling parent as an adult could strain even the most solid of parent-child relationships.

She shrugged. "I hear you, Knox, but so far, nothing I've tried has worked. If I could find a guy who would just be a no-strings-attached boyfriend for a while, that would placate dad for a while I think. But, all the guys around here want a commitment. Something weird in the water around these parts, I think."

"I wasn't really thinking about a boyfriend," Knox said.

"Oh, no?" Her brow wrinkled curiously. "What were you thinking?"

Knox pinned her in place with those deep, dark eyes of his and his lips—very nice, firm, masculine lips—curled up into a little smirk. "I was thinking more along the lines of a husband."

Chapter 2

The idea that she would leap from single to married struck Genevieve as laughable.

"Giant fat chance of that!" She laughed as she swept up the leftover fragments of hoof that were scattered across the red rubber pavers. "Marriage? To a local guy? How would that get me closer to my goal of getting to California?"

When she finished cleaning up her area and dumping the hoof fragments into a nearby trash can, Knox still hadn't moved from his spot. Usually, as was their established routine, he would have gone to the office, written her a check, and by the time she was finished packing up her small cache of tools, the check would be in her hand. Genevieve slid her phone out of her back pocket and glanced down at the screen; she had gained a couple of minutes of time and if she left the Ambling

A shortly, she would actually be back on schedule for her next client.

"Well…?" she prompted, hoping the fact that she had her hoof stand in one hand would be a silent signal to Knox that, as enjoyable as his company was, it was time for her to move along.

As if it just dawned on him that he was holding her up, Knox gave a quick nod of his head. "Let's go to the office and I'll write you a check."

Fine. We'll do it this way.

Genevieve set her hoof stand down on the rubber pavers and followed Knox the short distance to an office space that had been incorporated into one of the tack rooms. Knox opened the door for her and let her walk in first. The room, which had rows of Western saddles and bridles lining the far wall, smelled of leather and soap, along with the sweet smell of hay from the small stack of bales just inside the door. Genevieve walked over to a black saddle with ornate designs carved into the leather and fancy-edged silver conches as accent pieces. From the smoothness of the leather on the seat, along with the craftsmanship, she knew that this was a classic saddle from the 1950s.

"That's my dad's saddle," Knox said as he closed the door. "Seen a lot of work over the years."

At the sound of the door closing, Genevieve's Cat Woman senses started setting off alarm bells in her brain and she spun around to face the rancher. Knox had a strange look on his classically handsome face. She didn't like the fact that he was blocking the door and she *especially* didn't like it when he reached behind his body and locked them in the tack room.

"Listen here, Knox Crawford." Genevieve scowled

at him, moving her body into a defensive stance. "I've had six weeks of self-defense training when I was in college and if you make so much as one wrong move, cowboy, I will hurt you!"

Knox lifted his hands as if he were surrendering, a slightly lopsided grin on his face that she hadn't seen him use before. "I promise you, I only want to talk business."

She pointed at the door. "We don't need a locked door to talk business, Knox. I trim the horses' hooves and you write me a check. Simple."

"The delivery of hay is here," Knox noted distractedly. Earlier she had heard the piercing sound of squeaking brakes on a large delivery truck backing up to the opening in the hayloft and the sound of deliverymen yelling to one another. But she didn't understand what the heck that had to do with the fact that Knox wanted her *alone* in the office.

"I have a proposal for you and I don't want us to be overheard or disturbed."

Her arms crossed in front of her body, Genevieve's interest was piqued in spite of herself. Even though he had locked the door, Knox wasn't giving off any creepy stalker vibes, so her defenses lowered ever so slightly. Knox had always been gentlemanly, kind, consistent and had never come on to her in all the months she had been working with him. It wasn't beyond reasonable to give him the benefit of the doubt.

"What proposal is that?"

Knox took his hat off and tossed it on the nearby desk, his dark brown eyes so serious.

"Marriage." He said it so plainly and simply she almost thought she had misunderstood.

Genevieve's arms tightened around her body, and her heart, without her permission, began to beat rapidly in her chest. This wasn't her first marriage proposal, but it certainly was the strangest.

"Gen." Hands in his pockets he took a small step toward her. "I want to propose marriage. Let's get married."

Today was the first day he had ever called her by a nickname, and she had to admit it sounded kind of nice when he said it in his raspy baritone voice.

Genevieve stared up at Knox and he stared right back at her. The only sound was the ambient noise of the scraping and stomping of men's feet as they moved bales of hay into the hayloft above them.

After a second or two, her arms fell away from her body as she laughed. "Very funny, Knox. Ha, ha. Yeah—let's get married. That makes total sense."

But Knox wasn't laughing.

"You're right. It does make perfect sense."

"You're serious?" She stopped laughing. "You want us to get *married*?"

"Yes."

Now she was frowning at him. They had started a friendship over the last several months and she liked him. But what in the world had possessed him to propose marriage out of the blue? He had never even so much as flirted with her!

"Are you going through some sort of mental crisis, Knox?" she asked seriously. "Because you can get help for that."

"I'm perfectly sane." He wasn't smiling but there was now a conspiratorial gleam in his eye. "Just hear me out."

"No." She scooted around him, unlocked the door and swung it open. In the open doorway, she held out her hand. "I'll take my check, please, and then I'll be on my way."

He didn't move to the desk to write her a check. "What if I told you I had a way for us to help each other get exactly what we want?"

Now that the door was open and any passing ranch hand could overhear their conversation, Knox had lowered his voice. She had to lean in slightly to hear his next words.

"You want to move to California." It was a statement of fact.

She nodded.

"How much does a move like that cost?"

His words touched a raw nerve in her body. From her calculations, to move her and her horse to California and get her business established it was going to take much deeper pockets than she currently had. In truth, as much as she hated admitting it, she was most likely years away from moving out of her parents' garage apartment.

"A king's ransom," she admitted gloomily.

"I just happened to know a king."

Everyone in town knew that the Texas Crawford cowboys were wealthy; if Knox wanted anything in his life, he just had to go out and buy it. It seemed to her, in this moment, that he was trying to buy himself a bride.

She wasn't for sale.

"Hear me out, Gen. If you don't like what I have to say—no harm, no foul." When he used one of her favorite expressions, her eyes moved back to his face. "We'll never speak of this again."

In spite of herself, she just couldn't say no to at least listening to a plan that could possibly shave off years of saving for her move to California. She would be crazy not to at least listen, wouldn't she?

Genevieve stepped back inside the tack room and closed the door behind her. "You've got five minutes."

"We elope," he told her in a no-nonsense manner. "Now that Logan is married to Sarah and Xander is happily married to Lily, my father will think he's three sons down with only three more to marry off. And when my other brothers get engaged, we'll get the marriage annulled."

"You really want to get back at your dad that much?"

She saw a shift in Knox's eyes, a flash of anger that disappeared as quickly as it had arrived, like a quick flash of light in the darkness.

"Nobody controls me. He needs to learn that lesson, yes." The rancher continued, "After the annulment, I'll make sure you get to California. All expenses paid. In the meantime, as a bonus, you'll be free to live your life without any hassle from your dad."

"As your wife." She scrunched up her face at the thought. She had never equated *marriage* with *freedom*.

"As my *fake* wife," he said. "A marriage in name only. You do your thing and I'll do mine."

"You know what, Knox? This is absolutely the most extreme way a man has tried to lure me into his bed. And there have been some doozies, let me tell you."

"I don't want to sleep with you, Gen. I want to marry you." He said it seriously, and then added as almost an unimportant aside, "Not that I don't think you're attractive."

"Gee thanks, Crawford." She rolled her eyes at the way he delivered the compliment. "You really know how to make a woman feel all girly inside. Am I blushing?"

As if the sarcasm didn't register, he asked, "So, what do you think?"

"What do I think?"

He nodded.

"I think," Genevieve said in a slow, thoughtful tone, "thank you, but no thank you." She gripped the door-knob. "Do me a favor, would you? Please put that check in the mail. My next client awaits."

Before she could open the door and walk out into the hall, she noted that Knox's expression was cloudy. He had his head tilted downward and he was tapping his finger on the top of the desk, as if that action would help him find a way to change her mind. Logan had told her that Knox didn't like to be wrong, he didn't like to lose and he didn't like to be told no. She and Knox had those three things in common.

He looked up and pinned her with eyes that looked more black than brown in the moment.

"I suppose all of those things I heard about you must've been a pretty big exaggeration then." Knox's words were laced with a challenge that made the small hairs on the back of her neck stand up.

"What's that supposed to mean?"

"I heard that Genevieve Lawrence never backs down from a challenge."

Knox caught her off guard by skillfully tapping into one of her weaknesses.

"I don't."

"I also heard that Genevieve Lawrence has never lost a wager in the town." This was said with a small challenging smile, as if he knew that he had just sunk the hook.

"You heard right." She found herself still standing there, gripping the doorknob. "I haven't."

She had always been a tomboy who felt more comfortable hanging out with the boys than the girls. And, for the most part, the boys had accepted her as one of their own. But they thought, wrongly, that because she was a girl she would be easy to beat. She wasn't. The boys in town had always made bets with her and they had always lost. When the boys grew into men, they still lost. What she lacked in strength, she more than made up for it with an innate desire to win. She had been competitive since she was a kid and that had never changed. Everyone knew Genevieve was the reigning champion for winning wagers in Rust Creek Falls; it was a title she wore with pride. And she planned on leaving this town undefeated.

There was a cockiness lurking behind Knox's dark eyes that made her jaw clench. This was the exact look cowboys gave her right before she beat them at tractor chicken. No matter how big or tough, the braggadocios all blinked and ended up driving their tractor into a ditch while she kept right on driving her tractor on the road. She *never* blinked.

"Then," Knox said as he took a step toward her, his tone steady and serious, "I dare you to marry me."

She'd always had a bit of a temper and it had gotten her in trouble more times than she could remember. She took a step toward Knox.

"You *dare* me?"

"That's what I said."

"You *dare* me?" she repeated, surprised that he had thrown down a gauntlet that he had to know she wouldn't be able to resist picking up.

"You'll be married by morning, Crawford, so you'd better watch who you're daring to do something." She jabbed her finger in his direction, her cheeks flushed.

"Naw, I doubt it. I bet you won't marry me." She hated the fact that there was smugness in his tone now. "You'll chicken out."

Chicken out? Did he actually know that those words were like waving the proverbial red flag in front of the meanest bull in Rust Creek Falls? "I *never* chicken out, Knox."

"Neither do I."

Genevieve slipped her phone out of her back pocket, typed in a search, and then scrolled through the information on the website she chose. She held out the phone for Knox to see. "We can drive to Kalispell tomorrow, get a license and get married the same day. No waiting."

"That doesn't scare me." He smiled at her. "Does it scare you?"

"Nothing scares me." She kept searching for information about getting married in nearby Kalispell. "There's a problem."

"What's that?"

"We need someone to officiate the wedding and it says here we need to book months in advance."

"That's not a problem. I know a guy I can call."

"You know a *guy*?"

"Yeah. I know a guy. I'm sure he'll be able to squeeze us into his schedule."

"How romantic." Genevieve slipped her phone back into her pocket. "Meet me tomorrow morning, eight o'clock outside of the Gold Rush Diner." Genevieve pushed open the door, bristling mad. "*If* you show up, we'll go get ourselves hitched."

"I like the sound of that." Knox held out his hand. "Shall we shake on it?"

Her hand slipped easily into his. "We enter into a *platonic* marriage and then when we get an annulment you pay all of my expenses to move to California—including moving my horse, Spartacus."

"My word is my bond as a man."

"My word is my bond as a woman," she countered as she tugged her fingers free.

She had meant to call his bluff, but it had backfired. Instead of backing down, he'd stepped up.

He picked up a long piece of greenish alfalfa hay off the floor, quickly tied it into a small circle and, with his straight white teeth showing in a genuine smile, he knelt down before her on one knee and extended the makeshift ring.

"Genevieve Lawrence, will you do me the honor of being my fake bride?"

"You're being ridiculous."

"Don't ruin this special moment for me." He moved the hay ring back and forth for her to see. "It's not every day I get engaged."

"Fine," she said with an annoyed sigh as she held out her left hand. "I will be your fake bride, Knox. But only if you show up tomorrow."

The cowboy stood up and slipped the crude ring onto her finger. Did she imagine it, or did a small shock pass between them when he took her hand in his? She looked at the ring encircling her finger; she had never thought to see any type of ring on that finger for years, if ever. Even a hay ring made her feel boxed in like a trapped wild animal.

Genevieve swayed backward and put her hand on

the door to steady her body. She pushed the door open quickly so she could get some air into her lungs. When she stepped out into the wide aisle of the barn, she took in a deep breath, wanting to fill her lungs with as much air as possible to fend off the dizziness that had sprung up out of nowhere. She forced her brain to will her body to get it together and calm down. She was well-known for her nerves of steel when she was off-road racing or vaulting on the back of her horse—why were those nerves failing her now? Perhaps because this was the most serious bet she had ever made in her life—and if she was wrong, and Knox actually showed up, Genevieve knew that she wouldn't be the one to back down. If she was wrong and he showed up, she would be married by sundown tomorrow.

Genevieve closed her eyes for the briefest of seconds; when she opened them, she had her game face firmly back in place. To Knox, she said in a clipped, no-nonsense tone, "Don't forget to put that check in the mail, Crawford. I've got bills to pay."

"No need, darlin'," Knox called out after her with a pleased laugh in his voice that made her shoulders stiffen as she walked away. "I'll just bring it to you tomorrow."

The next morning, thirty minutes before their planned meet time, Knox parked his truck in the crowded lot of the Gold Rush Diner. He spotted Genevieve's truck, still caked in mud from her off-road shortcut, parked nearby. He hadn't been able to sleep the night before, thinking about the moment he would arrive at the diner, not knowing if Genevieve would really show up. It surprised him that the sight of her truck didn't make him feel nervous in the least. In fact, his stomach had been churning all morning at the thought of her *not* showing up. Now that he knew she was here, all he felt was relieved. And hungry.

Knox pushed open the door to the diner and nodded his head in greeting to the folks he knew. Rust Creek was a small town; it was typical to run into folks he knew everywhere.

"Find a seat where you can," the waitress pouring coffee behind the counter called out to him.

Knox had already spotted his target. Genevieve was sitting in a booth in the back of the diner, her long, wavy blond hair freshly washed and cascading over her shoulders. She wasn't dressed for an elopement, but then again, neither was he. Just like him, Genevieve had on her work clothes—jeans, boots and a T-shirt. No doubt she assumed he was going to back out of the wager, just as he assumed she would. He couldn't explain it fully, but the moment he spotted her sitting alone in that booth, his spirits lifted and all of the nerves and anxiety he had been feeling slipped away.

"Mornin'." Knox sat down in the booth bench opposite his fiancée. He took off his hat and placed it on the table. From the pocket of his T-shirt he took out a folded check, unfolded it and slid it across the table.

Genevieve, who seemed to be stiff as a statue, her hands seemingly glued to the sides of her steaming coffee mug, stared at the check for a second before she snatched it off the table and put it in her jeans pocket.

"You're early." She stated the obvious in a harsh whisper.

"So are you."

"Do you really think that it's a good idea for us to be seen together like this?"

He caught her drift. There were some town gossips in the diner who stared curiously in their direction.

Feeling happy, Knox smiled at her. "May as well start giving them something to talk about."

"I can feel them staring at us," his bride-to-be said under her breath.

"They sure are."

The waitress swung by their table with her order pad and a pen. "What can I get you folks?"

"Are you hungry?" he asked Genevieve.

"No."

He took the menu out from behind the salt and pepper shakers. "Really? Suddenly I'm famished." He winked at the pretty, frowning blonde sitting across from him. With a teasing, private smile, he asked, "What do you suggest for a man who's about to eat his last meal?"

Chapter 3

They had decided to take his black decked-out GMC truck for the thirty-minute trip to Kalispell. Was Knox bluffing or was he truly pleased that they were on their way to get married? She had watched the man put away scrambled eggs, bacon, three biscuits with butter and honey, grits and two large glasses of orange juice. She had no idea how he could eat at a time like this! Her stomach felt like a washing machine on a spin cycle; the coffee she had drunk at the diner was just adding to the acid backing up in her throat. She felt miserable while he hummed contentedly behind the wheel.

"You played me pretty good, Knox. I have to admit it."

For two people who normally had a lot to say to each other, the first half of the ride to Kalispell had been a quiet one.

"How do you figure?"

"You knew I wouldn't be able to turn down a wager. You knew my weakness and you exploited it."

"That's true. I did."

"That's a move right out of my own playbook. I don't like it but I have to respect it," she admitted grudgingly.

After a moment of silence she added, "I've never lost a wager before." She had her arms crossed in front of her body as she stared out at the pastureland dotted with grazing cows on either side of the highway. "It galls me to lose to a Texan of all things."

"You didn't lose," Knox said with an easy smile turned her way. "I'd call this one a draw."

"Draws are for losers."

"That's not how I see it. We're both winners, as far as I can tell."

"The only way I win is if you back out. I can still win. There's still time."

He laughed. "I'm not backing out of this wedding wager, Gen. If someone's gonna back out of this deal, it's gonna have to be you."

Genevieve glanced over at Knox's profile; she took in the strong jawline and the straight nose. Had she finally met her match? Was this cowboy crazy enough to really elope today? Was she so pigheaded that her ego wouldn't let her back down for a bet? She suspected the answer to her first two questions, but she absolutely knew the answer to the last. Her ego wouldn't ever let her back down—not when she was racing, not when she was bungee jumping and not even when she was about to elope with one of the Crawford cowboys on a dare.

"Then," she said with a pensive frown, "I guess we're really going to get married today."

"Darlin', that's music to my ears."

"Quit being so darn cheerful," she snapped at him. "And quit calling me darlin'."

Genevieve had hoped for a long line to apply for their marriage license. There was a line, but it seemed to be the swiftest moving line she had ever seen. How did it even make sense that two people could just walk up to a counter and get a license to get married? But that's what they did. They went to the third floor of the Flathead County Justice Center, showed their driver's licenses, paid fifty-three dollars and left with a state sanctioned "permission slip" to become husband and wife.

"This is why there's so much divorce in this country," Genevieve complained as they stepped out into the sunshine with their marriage license in hand. "They make it too darn easy for just anyone to say *I do*."

"Lucky for us." Knox carefully folded up their marriage license and tucked it into his wallet.

Genevieve had stopped waiting for the cowboy to back out—she could see that he was full-steam ahead on this deal while her mind was whirling with a thousand consequences. What were her parents going to say? What was his family going to say? Of course, she could hear her mother now. *Genevieve, when will you ever learn to look before you leap?*

"We aren't exactly dressed for a wedding, are we?" Knox asked as they walked to the sidewalk outside of the Kalispell courthouse.

"I didn't expect you to show up," she admitted. In fact, she had only stuffed some things into a backpack at the last minute before she headed to the Gold Rush on the off chance he did show. In her backpack she had a toothbrush, a hairbrush, her laptop and a Swiss Army pocketknife. Not exactly the most practical of wedding trousseaus.

"Well, I did." He kept on smiling at her like the cat that ate the canary. "So, why don't we find some wedding duds? There's got to be a place where a man can get a suit and a bride-to-be can find a dress."

She wasn't quite sure why Knox wanted to make such an event of a civil ceremony for their marriage-in-name-only, but the thought crossed her mind that her family, particularly her two sisters and her mom, would want to see pictures. Her family would totally buy her eloping in her barn clothes—they almost expected that kind of behavior from her—but what about Knox's kin? Would they believe their elopement was the real deal if they didn't look like a head-over-heels couple sneaking off to make their secret romance official?

"I suppose," she said, looking up the main street of Kalispell to a row of shops. "If we're going to convince your father that we eloped because we're crazy in love, we had better look the part."

After a quick search on her phone, they headed toward the Kalispell Center Mall on North Main Street. They found their way to Herberger's department store for one-stop shopping. First, they purchased simple white gold wedding rings, just plain bands without any embellishment. After all, those rings were just costume props and would be discarded once Viv Shuster managed to get the last three Crawford cowboys engaged.

Knox hadn't wanted to scare Genevieve off, but it could take a while for Viv to make matches for the final three brothers. His brother Finn, older by only one year, might be the easiest to pin down with a bride. Finn didn't seem to mind their father's plan all that much and he was always falling in and out of love anyway. But, his one younger brother Wilder was going to prove extra challenging for Viv—he was a busy bee that loved to pollinate all the lovely flowers of Rust Creek Falls and it was going to be a neat trick to get Wilder to dedicate himself to one special rose. And, Hunter, well, he was a single father who wasn't focused on finding love in the least. Hunter's heart, mind, and soul were all wrapped up in six-year-old Wren.

Knox pocketed the wedding rings as they parted ways—he headed to the men's clothing section, while she headed for women's dresses. They agreed to meet back at the jewelry counter in one hour. Genevieve wasn't much of a shopper but she was quick to make decisions, so one hour suited her just fine.

"Hi! Welcome to Herberger's." A petite salesclerk with a blond bob and bangs popped out from behind a tall rack of dresses. "How may I help you?"

"I need a dress."

"Special occasion?"

"My wedding," Genevieve said. "I suppose."

"You suppose?" The salesclerk's name tag read Kimber. "That's a first. Don't you know?"

She didn't have any intention of sharing the details of her wedding wager to Knox Crawford with a stranger in Herberger's department store, so she ignored Kimber's question and focused on the dress.

"Do you have something you could show me? I'm in a bit of a time crunch."

"Of course, I do." Kimber beamed with pleasure. "I love dressing brides. White, off-white?"

"White." That was for her mom—it was a small token but it was the least she could do.

"Indoors or outdoors?"

Not wanting to say "I don't know," she just took a guess. "Outdoors."

Kimber marched her over to a section of white dresses that could be worn as a casual-ceremony wedding dress.

"You are short-waisted and petite like me," the sales-clerk said as they sifted through the rack. "If we aren't careful, we'll have you looking like you're a little girl playing dress-up in your mama's clothes. What size do you wear?"

"In a dress? I have no idea." She hadn't put a dress on her body since high school graduation. "A four maybe?"

"Ooooh, look at this!" Kimber pulled a gauzy white dress off the rack. It was a high-low dress with spaghetti straps and a sash at the waist. "What do you think?"

Genevieve felt the material—it was light and airy and it wasn't too fussy or girly. "I think, yes."

The moment she saw herself in the mirror with this flowing hippy-girl dress skimming over her body, she knew. This was her wedding dress. Kimber's beaming face was further confirmation that the first dress she had tried was the only dress she needed to try. They found a pair of cowgirl boots in white in the shoe de-partment, which worked perfectly with the gauzy dress. Kimber insisted that Genevieve go over to see her friend at the makeup counter just for a touch of mascara, blush and a light lip gloss. By the time she left the makeup counter in her new dress, her hair wavy and loose, Gen-evieve saw a bride in the full-length mirror.

"Thank you." She hugged Kimber. "I couldn't have done this without you."

"You look absolutely, positively gorgeous, Genevieve!" the salesclerk gushed. "Congratulations."

Knox was early to the jewelry counter, feeling slightly awkward in his new dark gray suit, crisp white shirt and a bolo tie. The suit wasn't a perfect fit—it was a little tight in the shoulders and the pants and the jacket sleeves were almost too short—but it was the best the store could do. He checked his watch before he tugged on his shirtsleeves and adjusted his bolo tie for the sixth time. He couldn't remember ever feeling this nervous to see a woman before, yet Genevieve wasn't just any woman. She was about to be his wife. At the moment, it didn't matter that it wasn't a genuine marriage—in the eyes of the State of Montana, their families and God above, they were about to be husband and wife.

One minute to the hour, Knox looked up from checking his watch and saw Genevieve round the corner in a filmy white dress with thin straps that showed off her tanned arms, toned from years of working with horses. Genevieve always presented herself as a confident, assured woman. Today, there was hesitancy in her cornflower blue eyes—a fleeting vulnerability that touched him. She wanted his approval; he could see it in her eyes. He didn't have to fake what he was feeling in the moment—he had never seen a more beautiful bride.

"Gen," Knox said, his eyes drinking her in. "You're a vision."

A pink blush stained her cheeks, so lovely and sweet that it made him want to reach out and touch her, but he resisted that urge.

"Thank you," she said. He had never seen this almost shy side to this woman and he had to admit that he liked it.

"I like that tie."

Knox looked down at the bolo tie. He hadn't been too sure about that fashion choice, but the salesman swore it was the item of choice for many Kalispell grooms.

"When in Kalispell…" he said, making yet another attempt to adjust the tie to make it less tight around his neck. Giving up, he held out his arm to his bride-to-be. "Shall we?"

Genevieve looked at his extended arm and he could almost see her thoughts as she stood there considering. A shift occurred on her pretty oval face. He witnessed the exact moment she decided, once and for all, to be his wife.

"Okay," she finally said. "Yes."

When Genevieve tucked her arm through his, a calm flooded his body. He had never felt so comfortable with a woman on his arm before. It was as if having this petite, strong-willed woman beside him made him feel more at home with himself. He didn't understand it exactly, but he knew that it meant something more than he could figure in this moment. All he knew was that Genevieve was special and she was going to be his bride.

"Where are we going to do the deed?" she asked him as they left the mall.

"It's a surprise."

"I have to tell you, I'm not a huge fan of surprises."

"This one you'll like."

"Lawrence Park." Genevieve read the sign at the public park entrance. She had been to Kalispell many times in her life, but she had never known that there was a park that shared her last name.

"There's a walking trail that leads to Stillwater River. I know you like the outdoors, so I thought that would be a good place to get married."

Knox's thoughtfulness caught her off guard. She had always gotten the impression that he was a hardworking man—a good man—but he had never really come across as an overly romantic or thoughtful man. This gesture showed her a different side of Knox Crawford— a side that she had to admit that she liked very much.

"There's Sonny." Knox nodded through the windshield at a heavyset man with a long white beard standing in faded overalls by an antique Ford truck. Beside Sonny was a woman in a long flowered dress and tennis shoes, her salt-and-pepper hair in a single thick braid down her back. In the woman's hands was a simple bouquet of Montana wildflowers.

"Is he officiating the wedding?"

Knox nodded. He came to her side of the truck and helped her out. "He goes way back with my dad. I knew he would be willing to help us out on short notice."

"Hello, young man!" Sonny raised his hand in greeting. "You picked a mighty fine day to get married."

Knox clasped hands with Sonny, then hugged his wife, Cora, before he introduced them to Genevieve.

"Knox wanted me to bring these for you." Cora handed her the flowers. "He's always been such a thoughtful boy."

Genevieve took the flowers, with a quick glance up at Knox who was watching her closely. She smiled down at the bouquet. Wildflowers were the perfect flowers for her.

"Young love is always in such a hurry." Cora smiled at her. "We were so surprised to get Knox's call."

"You're father's not gonna be too pleased with me, what with all of this secrecy," Sonny said as he thoughtfully tugged on his beard.

"I appreciate you doing this for us." Knox put his arm around her shoulder and she had to force herself to stand still and plaster a smile on her face. From this moment forward, she was Knox Crawford's blushing and loving bride and she had to act like it.

"Yes," she said. "Thank you. This all happened so fast for us." She met her fiancé's eyes. "We just want our first moments as husband and wife to be *ours*."

"My Cora and I eloped, so I can't really say I don't understand your thinkin'," Sonny said, still tugging on his beard. It seemed to Genevieve that there was a possibility that Sonny wouldn't agree to marry them after all. But, in the end, Cora gently persuaded her husband to go forward with the ceremony.

The four of them walked along the narrow path to the edge of the Stillwater River. They picked a spot where a small group of tall trees lined the bank of the river, shading them from the afternoon sun. With the sound of the water rushing over the rocks, Genevieve held her wildflowers tightly in her hands and stood before Knox, facing him, as Sonny began the intimate ceremony. Cora moved around them with her camera, capturing candid moments as her husband opened his bible to read a suitable verse from Corinthians on the patience and kindness of love.

It was difficult for Genevieve to keep her focus on Knox's eyes. It did not escape her that she was getting ready to commit herself to him on a dare—on a *wager*.

Her parents had been married for over thirty years and they took their marriage vows seriously. They would be so disappointed in her for taking a vow, saying that she intended to love Knox for life knowing full well that the marriage would end sooner rather than later. That thought of her parent's disappointment and the sad expression on her mother's face when she found out that she had missed the moment her daughter took her wedding vows almost made her turn away and bolt down the path back toward the truck.

Sonny closed his bible and added his own thoughts to the occasion. "The commitment you made here today will be the foundation upon which your marriage will be built. Don't ever go to bed mad. Forgive each other and move on. Say I love you every day and never get too old to hold each other's hands."

Sonny smiled at his wife for a brief moment before he continued. "You've got to give each other room to grow because, in the end, it will be the two of you, standing together, facing the challenges of everyday life. If you always remember this moment and the love you have for each other right now, this sacred union will last you a lifetime and beyond."

Cora stepped quietly forward and took the bouquet of flowers from Genevieve as Sonny prepared for the ring exchange. Knox took her hand in his and it flashed in her mind that she liked how strong, large and rough this man's hand was. It was the hand of a working man.

"With this ring, I thee wed." He slid the simple white gold band onto her ring finger. She detected the slightest tremble when he did so, and realized that, beneath the seemingly calm exterior he was presenting, Knox was feeling as uncertain, off balanced and flustered as she was. A split second later, it was her turn. She didn't look up at him as she slipped his wedding band over his knuckle until it was snugly seated on his ring finger. Then Knox squeezed her hand and when she looked up into his face, he was smiling at her kindly with his eyes.

"Knox and Genevieve, you have come to this beautiful place to vow to love each other for the rest of your lives. You have exchanged rings as a symbol of this commitment."

"Genevieve, do you take this man to be your husband? Do you promise to love him, comfort him, honor and keep him, in sickness and in health—and, forsaking all others, be faithful to him as long as you both shall live?"

It took Genevieve several seconds to make the words "I do" come out of her mouth. The moment the words finally did come out, Cora snapped a close-up photograph of her face and she hoped only that her internal turmoil wasn't captured for everyone to see.

"I do." When she said those words, there was a waver in her voice that she didn't recognize. It wasn't her way to be uncertain about anything in her life; she lived her life as she raced off-road vehicles—pedal to the metal and full steam ahead.

"Knox, do you take this beautiful woman to be your wife? Do you promise to love her, comfort her, honor and keep her, in sickness and in health—and, forsaking all others, be faithful to her as long as you both shall live?"

Knox lowered his head so she could see his eyes— eyes that were so steady and intent on her face. "I do."

"Well, then," Sonny said as he rolled back on his heels a bit, "by the power vested in me by the glorious

State of Montana, I am tickled pink to pronounce you husband and wife. Knox, my boy, you may kiss your lovely bride."

She couldn't get her heart to stop beating so fast. Her chest was rising and falling in the most annoying way as Knox, still holding on to her hands, with a question in his eyes that only she understood, leaned down and lightly kissed her on the lips.

It was their first kiss; it was their only kiss.

It occurred to her in that moment, as she stood there with her eyes closed, focusing her attention on the first feel of her husband's lips pressed gently upon hers, that she didn't want that kiss to end.

Chapter 4

"Well, we did it."

She looked over at Knox who was sitting in the driver's seat of his truck, his hands resting lightly on the steering wheel as he stared out the window.

They had just said their goodbyes to Sonny and Cora and now they were alone again, this time as husband and wife, when just the day before they had been employer and employee. Two people who were developing a friendship but who didn't really know each other all that well.

"Yes, we certainly did," Genevieve agreed, twisting the odd-feeling gold band around and around on her finger. She didn't wear jewelry—not even earrings. Now she had this ring on her finger that she was supposed to wear all the time?

Knox took a deep breath in through his nose and then

let it out slowly. Out of the corner of her eye, she saw him staring at the new ring on his finger.

"What now?" she asked him. The postnuptial euphoria, with Sonny and Cora and a small group of strangers walking the path by Stillwater River clapping and cheering for them, had subsided. When she had let her ego dictate her decisions, when she had thought this whole thing was a lark, this moment didn't feel like a real possibility. And yet, here she sat, in a wedding dress in Lawrence Park as Mrs. Knox Crawford.

In the quiet of the truck, with only the distant sound of children playing on a playground, her stomach rumbled. The loud sound made her laugh and it made Knox look over at her with a smile. She had felt too sick with nervous tension to eat when she was at the diner that morning, but now that the deed was done and she was officially wed, she was feeling famished. Hungrier perhaps than she had ever felt before in her life.

"Hungry?" Her husband—wow, that was weird— kept on smiling at her.

Her hands went to her stomach. "Starving. You?"

"I can always eat," he said. "What are you hungry for?"

"Barbecue."

"In that white dress?"

"Why not?" She made a face at him. "I'll put on a bib. I don't care."

Knox studied her face in a way that made heat come to her cheeks.

"I knew you were my kind of woman," he said as he turned the ignition key. "Any place in particular?"

"DeSoto Grill is my favorite."

"Then DeSoto Grill it shall be." Knox shifted into Drive. "A woman should have exactly what she wants on her wedding day."

Knox found a parking space on 1st Street and turned off the engine. But he didn't move right away to get out of the truck. Instead, he wanted to put Genevieve at ease. This whole marriage-by-bet, his idea to thwart his father and establish himself in his father's eyes as a full-grown man had been a whirlwind for both of them. Yesterday he came up with an outrageous plan and today they were married. It was enough to make anyone's head spin with crazy thoughts.

"Do you know what I think?" He turned his body toward his bride.

"Huh?"

"I think that I like you, Genevieve Lawrence."

"That's Genevieve Crawford to you," she said with a teasing tone.

Knox laughed. Gen had always made him laugh, from the first day they had met.

"My apologies. I think that I like you, Mrs. Crawford."

"Well, that's good, Knox, because you're stuck with me until Viv manages to hog-tie your last three brothers. And neither one of us knows how long that will be." Genevieve rolled her eyes and shook her head, and under her breath she added, "Leap before you look."

"What I'm trying to say is that I always liked your company when you came out to the Ambling A."

She sent him a small smile for his trouble.

"And you seemed to like mine…?"

That garnered him a nod.

"So, why don't we just have fun with this?" he asked

her. "Why not just keep on enjoying each other's company, keep on being friends?"

"Okay," Genevieve replied, her tanned exposed shoulders lifting up into a quick shrug.

"So you agree with me." He wasn't used to the women in his past being so easy to get along with.

"I just said so, didn't I?" She frowned. "Now, can I eat?"

"Yes." He laughed, wanting to reach out and squeeze her hand affectionately. He had wanted to ask Genevieve out on a date and now, oddly, he didn't have to ask her because he had married her.

When he came around to her side of the truck, Genevieve had already hopped down onto the sidewalk and was shaking out the skirt of her gauzy white dress. They walked together, side by side instead of hand in hand, to the door of the DeSoto Grill. At the entrance to the restaurant, it occurred to Knox that this was his wedding day, albeit a fake marriage, and he wanted to celebrate. Without even warning her, because he wanted to catch her off guard and get her laughing, Knox bent down and swung Genevieve into his arms.

"What the heck are you doing?" His bride's bright blue eyes, so close to his own now, were wide with surprise.

"I'm carrying you over the threshold."

She didn't struggle to get out of his arms; instead, she reached out so she could tug on the door handle to open it just enough that he could get his foot inside.

"This has been a very strange day." Genevieve tilted back her head and let her long blond hair fall over his arm.

"Do you mind?" Knox asked as he managed to open the door and then quickly carry her inside.

"Not at all. I like strange."

The barbecue joint was half-full and when Knox walked in carrying his bride in his arms, some of the patrons began to clap and hoot and holler.

"We just got hitched, y'all!" he called out to his fellow Montanans. "Drinks are on us!"

He held his bride in his arms a little while longer, liking the way her body felt pressed up close to his. Genevieve was a willing partner in the spectacle—her face was glowing with excitement and she was happily waving to the crowd. He had already begun to notice that Genevieve was at her best when she was performing for a crowd. It was making him feel more confident about how she would play her role as "blushing bride" in front of his family. Watching her now, Knox was pretty convinced that his family didn't stand a chance when it came to Genevieve Lawrence. Er, Genevieve Crawford.

The DeSoto Grill had a large selection of Montana beer and everyone in the bar got a free cold one on them. Sitting cross-legged in the chair with a napkin bib tucked into the front of her dress, Genevieve gulped down a second beer before she attacked a second rack of ribs.

"Oh, my goodness, this is soooo good." She grinned at him with a little barbecue sauce on the side of her mouth.

"I've never seen anyone other than my brothers eat that many ribs."

"Getting married must've made me hungry," Genevieve said between chewing, without a hint of self-consciousness. She didn't seem to care one way or another if he disapproved of her large appetite—and he just added that to the list of things that he already liked about her.

"Here's to us." Knox held out his glass after the waitress brought him water—because he had to drive them home—and a fresh beer for Genevieve.

"To us!" She clanked her glass with his. "Just two crazy kids in love."

"You know the next stop for us is the Ambling A."

"Uh-huh." She nodded. "I figured. First, your people and then I suppose we can go face the music with my folks tomorrow."

"Did you pack what you need to stay at my cabin tonight?"

They had gone through with this wager so quickly, so recklessly, that they hadn't even discussed the logistics. The truth was, he hadn't really expected to have a bride today—he figured she wasn't going to show.

His bride took a big napkin and swiped it over her mouth. "Not really. I mean what was I supposed to pack for a wedding night I really didn't expect to have? Let's see—what did I put in my backpack this morning? My toothbrush, a hairbrush, my laptop and my favorite Swiss Army knife."

"A knife? Why do you have that?"

"Are you kidding? Only for *everything*. I can fix a broken radiator hose or open a bottle of beer with one awesome tool. I think you're question should really be, why wouldn't *every* bride have one?" She laughed a big laugh. "Hey! Do you have a dollar? I want to get that jukebox going."

Now that Genevieve had cleaned her plate and had a few beers, her spirits were flying high from his perspective. She seemed to have shed the worry and the stress of their elopement and replaced it with good spirits and the desire to have a good time. He pulled a couple of dollar bills out of his wallet and handed them to her.

He watched Genevieve walk away, liking the way the material of her wedding dress hinted at the curve of her derrière and legs. No doubt, he was attracted to his bride—he always had been since the first time he had seen pictures of her on her website. He had agreed that this marriage was in name only—he had said it more to convince her to go along with his scheme—but would he really be able to keep it platonic between them? He hadn't ever acted on the physical attraction he had for Genevieve because he was on that self-imposed dating hiatus, but that physical attraction had always been there.

"Garth Brooks or Kenny Chesney?" His wife had spun around to ask him a question.

"Brooks!"

With a nod, Genevieve pushed a button and waited for the music to begin to play before she headed back his way. She gathered up the sides of her long skirt in her hands and began to sway the material back and forth to the rhythm of the music. When she arrived back at the table, Knox stood up.

"Do you want to have that first dance?" he asked her.

Her surprised smile reached those pretty eyes of hers. Genevieve craned her head so she could look up into his face. "You know how to dance? Really?"

"Darlin', I've been doin' the Texas Two-Step since I could walk."

"Well, all right then, cowboy. Let's do this." She gave him her hand.

There wasn't a real dance floor so he pushed a nearby table out of his way and pulled Genevieve into his arms. If he hadn't come up with this wager, how long, if ever, would it have taken him to be able to hold this woman as he was right now?

While the patrons looked on, they danced. They danced until they were both sweaty and out of breath and laughing. He had taken off his too-snug jacket and bolo tie, and he noticed the tendrils around her face had escaped from the sparkly hair clip and framed her face in the loveliest way. Several times while they danced Knox had to stop himself from kissing her. He wanted to kiss her. But they had made a deal and he was determined not to violate that agreement. This was to be a platonic marriage, no matter how hard it was on him.

"Kiss, kiss, kiss, kiss!" the crowd started to chant.

Her chest rising and falling from the exertion of dancing, her cheeks flushed pink, Genevieve looked around at the chanting crowd.

He leaned down, put his cheek next to hers, and asked in a voice that only she could hear, "It's your call."

"This won't be the last time people ask," she told him pragmatically and he knew she was probably right. The suddenness of their relationship would no doubt make people speculate about their sincerity. There would be times that they were going to have to be affectionate with each other because that was how most genuine newly-weds behaved. They may as well start practicing now.

Before he could respond, Genevieve threw her arms around his neck and planted a big kiss on his lips to gratified cheers in the background. Not thinking, only acting, Knox picked his bride up into the air and kissed her back, long and hard, before he let her slide down the length of his body until her toes touched the floor. Knox couldn't have known how he would feel about marrying a woman based on a wager—but he did know now. He felt more grounded today, in this moment, with this woman, than he had ever felt in his life. He'd always played the field and he had the reputation of never being in a hurry to settle down with just one woman. But the way he felt about Genevieve was already so different than he had ever felt for anyone else. He sensed that he could be himself around her—being around Genevieve was like being around a best friend that you really liked to kiss. And, even though Knox knew that this relationship wasn't meant to last, this petite firebrand of a woman had already changed how he felt as a man. And, maybe—just maybe—she had begun to change how he felt about settling down.

"Ugh!" Genevieve held her stomach, this time not because it was empty but because it was way too full.

She had eaten two racks of ribs on her own with a side of potato salad, corn bread and three beers. Their waitress had given them each a slice of cheesecake on the house in honor of their marriage and how could Genevieve say no to that?

"Am I waddling? I feel like I'm definitely waddling."

She was wearing Knox's jacket over her shoulders because the air conditioner had given her a bit of chill in her bones. She was also feeling a tad tipsy, so she naturally linked her arm with her husband's arm for support.

"You're not waddling," he reassured her. "You're weaving a bit, but not waddling."

"I knew I shouldn't have had that last beer."

Knox walked her over to the passenger side of the truck. When they had gone into the DeSoto, it had been bright and sunny outside. Now it was late afternoon. They had managed to laugh and dance and eat their way through several hours. Knox unlocked the truck door and opened it for her.

"You do know I'm perfectly capable of opening my own door, right?"

Knox, unfazed, held on to her hand while she swayed onto the seat.

"I was raised to be a gentleman and you're darn well going to enjoy it, Gen."

Genevieve groaned again as she closed her eyes. "Have it your way."

"Thank you. I will."

Her companion reached across her body, grasped hold of the seat belt and buckled her in. When he climbed behind the wheel, she could sense him looking over at her. She cracked open her eyes.

"What?"

"Next stop is the Ambling A."

"Uh-huh."

"You going to be okay to face the rest of the Crawfords?"

Genevieve pushed herself more upright in the seat. "I'm a pressure player, Knox."

"Meaning?" he asked as he backed out of the parking spot.

"I work better under pressure. In fact, that's when I'm at my best. I never crumble."

"That's good to hear because I'm giving you fair warning, Gen. They're gonna interrogate the heck out of us. Bugs under a microscope."

She closed her eyes again. "Trust me, hubby. I'll have your family believing that we are the most in-love couple they've ever seen. I'll have them wondering how we managed to put off the elopement as long as we did! And your dad?" She held up her pointer finger. "I'll have him wrapped around my little pinky in no time flat."

"Well, I'm certainly looking forward to seeing that,"

he said in response. "Of course, you do realize that's not your pinky, correct?"

"Smart-ass."

It was dusk when Knox pulled onto the long drive leading to the main house at his family's ranch. Throughout the day, they had both been texting periodically with their friends and family so no one would suspect that the day was anything other than ordinary. The sky behind the sprawling log cabin main house was glowing orange and pink and purple while the clouds were shadowy shapes drifting overhead. Knox parked the truck and turned off the lights. Genevieve was breathing deeply beside him; soon after he had buckled her in, she'd fallen asleep. He almost hated to awaken her, especially when he knew that they were about to be bombarded with questions and comments and, no doubt, suspicion from his brothers, his father, as well as Logan and Xander's new wives.

Knox reached out and put his hand on Genevieve's arm and gave it a gentle shake. His wife mumbled something in an irritated tone but she didn't open her eyes.

"Gen," he said quietly with another shake of her arm. "We're here."

That time she opened her eyes. She yawned loudly, stretched and then pushed herself upright, looking around groggily.

"I slept the whole way back?"

He nodded.

"Sorry about that." She wrapped her arms tightly in front of her body. "Not much company, huh?"

"I'm glad you slept. Hopefully that battery is recharged because behind that door is a roomful of crit-ics and skeptics."

"You sound worried."

"I am absolutely worried. If we don't convince them we're the real deal, this whole day was a waste of time."

Genevieve unbuckled her seat belt, tugged her arms free of his jacket and seemed to perk up quickly. She checked her reflection in the mirror on the back of the sun visor, gave her long blond wavy hair a quick brush through, and then declared, "I'm ready."

It was strange—he was about to bring his "bride" home for the first time and he appeared to be the more nervous of the two. Genevieve didn't seem nervous or anxious at the idea of facing his family. In fact, she seemed perfectly calm.

They walked up to the front door to the main house and Knox paused to take in a deep breath to calm his nerves. Genevieve reached over and took his hand in hers.

"Don't worry, Knox. We've got this."

He looked down at the top of her golden head. This petite woman seemed to have all the confidence in the world. And her confidence actually made him believe that they could pull this off. She had told him that she was a pressure player and now he was seeing that first-hand. His nerves were on the verge of getting the best of him but Genevieve was completely calm.

"They're a tough crowd." He felt the need to reiter-ate this point—to prepare her for what was to come.

Genevieve had a very serious expression on her face when she said, "Maybe they are. But they're not tougher than trying to shod a stallion with a stable full of mares in heat. If I can handle that, I bet I can handle them."

Chapter 5

"Here goes nothin'." Knox let out a long breath before he opened the heavy front door of the main house.

"Here goes everything," she countered.

With her arm firmly linked with Knox's arm, Genevieve didn't have to fake a smile. The idea of meeting Knox's family and pulling off the nearly impossible—convincing them that their whirlwind romance and sudden elopement was on the up-and-up—was a challenge. And she dearly loved a challenge.

Stepping into the foyer at the main house was like stepping into an architectural magazine for men who wanted rustic chic with a sophisticated flair. Yes, the inside of the log cabin mansion was full of dark wood and Western motif touches, but there was an overarching sophistication, from the paintings on the wall to the light fixtures, that gave a nod to the Crawfords' Dallas roots. On every other visit to the Ambling A she'd been the hired help. This was the first time that Genevieve had been invited into the main house.

"Sounds like a party," she noted as the sound of loud talking and laughter greeted them.

"We all try to get together at least one night a week for dinner," Knox explained. "So everyone's here."

She looked up into Knox's face, noting the tension in his jawline and his unsmiling lips.

"You don't look like a man who just married the love of your life, Knox," she whispered. "Smile."

Knox followed her instruction and smiled as he walked with her toward the sound of the voices. Gathered in an informal family room were her new in-laws. Standing by the window, holding an unlit cigar and a glass tumbler, was the man she immediately recognized as the patriarch of the family, Maximilian Crawford. The Crawford cowboys were famously handsome, Knox included, and it was easy to recognize that those six apples hadn't fallen far from the paternal tree. The Crawford patriarch was tall and solidly built with broad shoulders and a shock of silver hair combed straight back from his tanned, Hollywood-handsome face. Her eyes swept the rest of the room, taking inventory of all of the people in the room, and ending with Logan, the eldest Crawford brother, and his bride Sarah.

"Knox! Where the heck have you been?" Logan was the first to notice them standing in the entrance of the family room.

"Hey! Why do you have the hot farrier with you?" A brother with longish brown hair was lounging on a nearby couch, his hands behind his head, his booted feet propped up on the coffee table.

"What's with the get-up, Knox?" another brother, tall as Maximilian with mussed dark hair and his arm around a pretty petite redhead, asked. "Did you just come from a funeral or something?"

"No," Knox said with a slight waver in his voice that she hoped only she could hear. "A wedding."

Genevieve's eyes were on Knox's father. As far as she was concerned, he was the most important audience member. He sipped from his tumbler.

Logan, with his closely cropped dusty-brown hair and blue eyes, seemed to be catching on to the meaning behind Knox's words more quickly than the rest. The eldest Crawford brother, his eyes narrowed curiously, asked, "And whose wedding was that?"

Genevieve looked up at her husband and was gratified that he looked right back at her. When he winked at her, she laughed, genuinely laughed, which was perfect for the show they were presenting for the family.

Before he answered, Knox unhooked her arm from his, wrapped his arm possessively around her shoulders, dropped a quick kiss on the top of her head and then said, "Mine."

That one word was all it took. The entire crowd in the family room—one patriarch, five brothers, two women, a baby, and young girl playing with a chubby puppy in front of an unlit fireplace—who had pretty much ignored them when they'd walked in, now turned to them in silence. The only sound for a couple of heartbeats was the sound of the baby cooing in Sarah's arms.

"What did you just say, son?" The look on the patriarch's face said it all—he wasn't happy.

"I said," Knox, repeated loudly and clearly without

the waver in his voice, "I just got married. I would like to introduce you all to my wife, Genevieve."

She had never known what it felt like to be a celebrity, but Knox's announcement, made her feel like she was being mobbed by paparazzi. They were suddenly surrounded by the five brothers, all of them bombarding them with shocked questions interlaced with congratulations. Sarah wove her way through the throng of brothers, holding baby Sophia tightly in her arms, so she could give her a hug.

"Welcome to the family," Sarah said warmly. "It's so nice to have some more estrogen in this place."

Genevieve knew Sarah in passing and she had always liked her friendly, sweet personality. And it didn't seem that the fact that Viv Shuster had set Genevieve up on a date with Sarah's now-husband, Logan, bothered the young mother in the least.

"Thank you, Sarah." She smiled and reached out to touch baby Sophia's soft little hand.

Knox kept a protective arm around her shoulders while she said hello to her new brothers-in-law. Xander, the tallest and second oldest, had a skeptical look on his face. He pulled the petite redhead closer to his side.

"Logan and I just got married and now *you* turn up married out of the blue? Something smells to high heaven."

"So, what's the story, Knox?" Logan prodded. "None of us even knew the two of you were dating. How'd the two of you end up married?"

"Yes." Maximilian finally spoke, his tone rippling with anger. "I'd like an answer to that too."

Knox stiffened beside her and she instinctively pressed her body reassuringly into his. "I'd thought you'd be happy, Pop. Isn't this what you wanted? All of your sons married. Well, three down, three more to go, right?"

When Maximilian walked toward them, the rest of the family parted like when Moses parted the Red Sea. Perhaps the patriarch was accustomed to intimidating people with his stern, formidable, unsmiling countenance, but Genevieve had been facing tough male competitors ever since she was a teenager. She thrived on this kind of head-to-head matchup.

"Is this Viv Shuster's doing?" Maximilian now stood in front of them.

"No," Knox said with a satisfied rumble in his voice. "She can't claim credit for this one."

The older man's scowl deepened.

"Pop," Knox said, "I'd like to introduce you to my wife, Genevieve Lawrence Crawford."

"It's a pleasure to finally meet you, Mr. Crawford." She held out her hand, which he refused.

"That's real polite." Knox frowned at his father.

"Wait a minute." Maximilian stared down into her eyes and she stared right back at him. "Do you mean to tell me that you married that lady farrier I told you not to hire?"

"I wasn't aware that you had any objection to my services," Genevieve said before Knox could reply.

"You'd better know I did," Max snapped back at her.

"And you'd better know that you're talking to my wife." There was a heat behind Knox's black-brown eyes that she had never seen before. This power struggle between Knox and his father was real and it appeared to have very deep roots. Suddenly, the reason behind Knox's desire to break the grip his father had on his life with this fake elopement came into sharp focus for Genevieve. Knox had to win this one if he was ever going to truly be his own man.

There was a tense silence in the room, before Finn, one of Knox's older brothers, said, "Come on, guys! We can give Genevieve a better welcome than this, can't we? Knox is married! We need to drink to that!"

Finn, who seemed to always be brushing his scruffy bangs out of his eyes, grabbed her free hand and tugged her loose from Knox's side.

"We Crawfords can make a lousy first impression, sis," her new brother-in-law confessed. "But we aren't all that bad once you get to know us."

"I can handle it," she assured him.

Finn smiled down at her, his boyish hair in his eyes. "I just bet you can."

Hunter, the only brother who had been married before and who was now a single father to his daughter, Wren, had quietly retrieved a couple bottles of champagne from Maximilian's collection. Genevieve found herself standing beside her husband with a glass of champagne in her hand. All of the brothers and the two wives had glasses in their hands, ready to toast them. Maximilian was the only one who refused to participate in Hunter's toast.

"Here's to Knox and his beautiful wife, Genevieve! We had no idea the two of you were even dating, but who can argue with love? Congratulations!"

"Congratulations!" the rest of the family shouted.

"Why didn't any of us know you were dating?" Xander asked, his eyes still suspicious.

"I can keep a secret," Knox said with an easy shrug.

"As can I." She put her empty champagne glass on a coaster on the coffee table.

"Tell us the whole story." Xander's wife, Lily, leaned closer to her love.

Knox looked down and met her eyes. They had discussed their backstory over their postnuptial barbecue but this would be the easiest place for the family to find discrepancies if they didn't get it right. "Do you want to tell them, or should I?"

"I think you should tell them."

They sat together on a nearby love seat and Genevieve reminded herself to keep her body close to Knox's as any new bride would. She put her hand on his thigh and looked at her husband frequently while he told their story, making sure that her gaze was always admiring.

"All of you know that I first saw Genevieve's picture on her website when I was looking for a farrier." Their eyes met when he continued. "I liked the look of the website and the message—her mission statement was all about treating the whole horse, not just the hooves, with a holistic approach. And, without knowing her, I liked her. She was interesting…and beautiful."

The way his eyes roamed her face let her know that these were his true feelings. He was speaking from the heart in that moment.

"Did you hire her just so you could date her?" Knox's other brother Wilder asked in a booming, teasing voice.

Knox gave his brother a little wink. "I'd be lying if I said that the thought didn't cross my mind."

This was news to her, and with all the fibs they were telling, it was hard to know if Knox was telling the truth about that.

"The minute I met Genevieve, we hit it off."

That was true—they had.

"We became friends…" Knox put his hand over her hand.

That was also true.

"And then one day it hit me like one of those cartoon characters that gets hit over the head with a ton of bricks—I had found the woman I wanted to marry."

The way Knox had skillfully worded that last sentence was also the truth. He had all of a sudden decided she was the one he wanted to marry. But he left out the crucial part—the word *fake*.

"Why keep it a secret?" Xander pressed him.

"That was my idea, Xander," Genevieve piped up. "I knew that eventually we would be the talk of the town. I just wanted some time for us—to be *us* and to make sure that what we were feeling was real."

"It's so romantic." Lily's emerald green eyes were sparkling. "I love the fact that you eloped."

"We wanted to start our lives together in our own way, on our own terms," Knox added. "And we couldn't be happier with how things have turned out. Isn't that right, sweetheart?"

Genevieve scanned the faces of her new in-laws, noting that most appeared to be convinced that the marriage was the real deal. For extra effect, she put her head on Knox's shoulder. "We couldn't be any happier if we tried."

"What do you love about our brother?" Xander still wasn't thrown off the scent.

She lifted her head so she could look into her husband's face. In his deep brown eyes she saw a curious question about what she might say. The best way to get Xander to back off was to tell the truth.

"What's not to love?" This was her honest answer. "He's handsome and smart and talented. He shares my passion for horses. From the very beginning, he's made me feel like I belong in my career, that I have a right to be who I am."

The slow smile Knox gave her let her know that he liked what he was hearing.

"And," she added, "he's a cowboy and a gentleman."

There was sincerity in her words because they were the truth. Had she directly said that she was madly in love with Knox? No. But she had said enough to shift the suspicion in Xander's eyes. That was a step in the right direction. Now all she had to do was win over Maximilian.

Genevieve had a feeling that he was going to be a much tougher nut to crack.

Knox couldn't believe that they had really pulled it off. Genevieve had played the part of the loving new wife to perfection. By the time the family began to disband, everyone in the room, with the exception of his father, seemed accepting of the surprise relationship and elopement.

"Why is it that even when you get your way, you're miserable?" Knox had followed his father to his study.

Max shut the door to the study behind them and took a seat behind a heavily carved wooden desk.

"Sit, son."

Knox sat down in a chair opposite the desk, always aware of the power dynamic—the one behind the desk had the power, and that, as usual, was Max.

"I was expecting a bit more of a hero's welcome from you, Pop."

"Is that right?"

"Sure." He smiled broadly. "I gave you what you wanted."

"This isn't what I wanted." Max leaned his arms on top of the desk, his expression serious. "I don't know what kind of trick you're trying to pull."

"No trick." Knox took the marriage certificate out of his wallet and slid it across the desk. "I'm married."

Max studied the certificate, a muscle working in his jaw. Then he folded the certificate and shoved it back toward Knox.

"You've made a big mistake here, son."

"You're entitled to your opinion."

"What do you even really know about this girl?"

"I know that when you meet the right one you know."

Max's dark eyes were stormy as he said, "Marry in haste, repent in leisure."

Knox understood the reference. Max had been quick to marry their mother and his father had never made it a secret that he considered his marriage to be one of the biggest mistakes of his life. Years ago, their mother had run off with her lover, leaving Max a single father to six young boys. They never really talked about it, but Knox believed that Max had never fully recovered from his mother's betrayal.

"I'm not you," he said seriously. "I'm nothing like you."

"That's where you're wrong, son. You're exactly like me." Max stabbed the desk with his pointer finger. "Did you even bother to get a prenup?"

Knox stood up. "That's none of your business."

His father stood up and slammed his palms on the desk. "Everything about this is *my* business."

They stared each other down for several tense seconds before Knox gave an annoyed shake of his head. "Not this time. You disrespect my marriage, you disrespect my wife, you are disrespecting me. I don't want to hear one more word about a prenup."

While Knox went with his father for a one-on-one meeting, Genevieve made her way over to the rug in front of the fire where Hunter's six-year-old daughter, Wren, was sitting cross-legged.

"Hi," Genevieve said. "Do you mind if I join you?"

Wren nodded her blond head. She was a slight girl with lopsided pigtails and a pale complexion.

"Who's your friend?" Genevieve sat cross-legged as well, reaching out to pet the head of the sleeping puppy.

"Silver."

The chubby puppy opened its eyes sleepily, wagged its tail at Genevieve, before it yawned, rolled over onto its back and fell back asleep.

"I like your puppy," she told the quiet little girl.

"He's not mine," Wren said. "He's Uncle Knox's. I just get to play with him."

The young girl looked at her with the directness only a child could achieve. "How come you don't know that?"

Of course, out of everyone in the room, it took a six-year-old child to stump her. She didn't have a good explanation for that. She *should* know that her husband had a puppy.

Knox marched back into the family room with an unsmiling expression on his face. He walked directly over to her and held out his hand. "It's time for us to go."

Genevieve stood up quickly, glad that she didn't have to answer Wren's question. "Everything okay?"

"Everything's exactly as it should be."

"Can Silver stay with me tonight, Uncle Knox?"

Knox kissed his niece on the top of her head before he scooped the sleepy puppy up into his arms. "Not tonight, sweet pea."

Her husband held out his free hand to her and she accepted it. They said their quick goodbye to the family and then Knox made a beeline for the front door.

Once back in the privacy of the truck, Genevieve held Silver in her arms while Knox cranked the engine.

"What happened in there?" she asked about the meeting that took place between father and son.

"What happened?" Knox echoed with a big, pleased smile on his face. "We pulled it off, that's what happened. Every one of them bought it hook, line and sinker."

"Even your father?"

"Especially my father." Her husband winked conspiratorially at her. "You set the hook and I pulled him right into the boat."

Chapter 6

It was dark when they left the main house and took a gravel road to Knox's small log cabin located on the Ambling A ranch. Genevieve held the puppy tightly in her arms, her stomach twisting into an uncomfortable knot. The excitement of putting on a great show for the Crawford family had been an adventure—a challenge— and she had thrived under the spotlight. But now, on this pitch-black road with only the headlights to light their way, it was starting to sink in that she had just, at least for the short term, completely changed her life. She was now Knox Crawford's wife, and as such, would be living under the same roof with him.

"Here she is." Knox pulled up in front of his cabin, which had been built back in the woods with a small stream nearby. It was a mini version of the main house, fashioned out of rustic logs with rocking chairs on the front porch. If this had been a real marriage, Genevieve would have been pleased to call this her first home with her husband.

"Nice." The word came out of her mouth and it sounded hollow to her own ears. How could she swing so quickly from feeling triumphant to feeling horrified?

Genevieve opened the truck door and then repositioned the puppy in her arms. Dried leaves crunched beneath her feet as she slid out of the passenger seat onto the ground. The air was crisp and the familiar sound of field crickets singing all around them worked to settle her nerves. She followed her husband up the porch stairs, the wood creaking beneath their feet. Silver began to wiggle in her arms and whine, licking at her face to get her attention.

"I think he needs to go to the bathroom."

"I've got a fenced-in area out back."

Knox opened the door, flipped on a switch just inside the doorway and held the door open so she could walk through. In that moment, Genevieve realized that she had just walked into Knox's world—a world she had never thought to experience. The cabin, like Knox, was masculine and neatly appointed. From her experience, the cowboy was always well put together, even when he was working. In contrast, her garage apartment looked like a bomb had exploded inside. She was always just about to get around to cleaning it up but never quite got there.

"Make yourself at home," he said.

Silver finally wiggled free, ran over to Knox, stood up on his hind legs and began to paw at the rancher's leg.

"Hey, buddy. Let's go out."

Knox dropped her backpack on the couch in the small living room before he walked through the tiny kitchen to the back door. Silver bounded out the door, down the back porch steps and into a dimly lighted fenced-in area.

Genevieve followed them outside and stood on the back porch next to her husband. Her arms crossed in front of her body, she said, "This is just plain weird."

Knox looked over at her, his features in shadow. "You're right. It is."

They both laughed when Silver came galloping back toward them, his fat legs churning as he worked his way up the stairs.

"I didn't even know you had a dog. Wren caught me on that one."

"She's smart as a whip."

Genevieve nodded.

Back inside, she stood awkwardly in the living room, taking in the sparse decor. Knox, it seemed, was a no-frills kind of guy, which fit the picture she had always had of him. The cowboy shrugged out of his jacket and dropped it on the butcher-block counter top in the kitchen.

"What now?" she asked him.

He unbuttoned his white shirt exposing his tanned, corded neck and part of his chest. Knox then unbuttoned his cuffs.

"Now?" he asked. "I'm going to get some shut-eye. I get up before dawn. How 'bout you?"

She was exhausted and wired and disoriented.

"I meant, what's next?" she clarified. "For us."

"What do you mean?"

"What do you mean, what do I mean?" she snapped,

the exhaustion beginning to make it difficult to keep her tone friendly. "Are you prepared to face my family tomorrow?"

"Yes. I'm prepared. We've got to tell them before they hear it from someone else. Will they worry if you don't show up tonight?"

She shook her head. "No. I come and go as I please. Sometimes I don't get home until they've gone to bed and I can be gone before they awaken."

He joined her on the couch, lifting Silver up and putting him on the cushion between them. "Then we're covered for tonight."

She yawned with a nod. "A short reprieve."

When she opened her eyes, Knox was staring at her quietly.

"We actually did it."

She took a deep breath in through her nose and let it out. "Yes, we actually did."

"We haven't really discussed sleeping arrangements."

"We haven't discussed much of anything really," she interjected.

"I'll take the couch. You can have my bed."

"Thank you. Can I have your puppy too?"

She liked the way that the sides of Knox's eyes crinkled when he laughed. "I suppose, technically, he's your puppy now too."

"I may just ask for him in the divorce," she teased.

"Along with puppy support?"

"Absolutely."

Knox gave her the top to his pajamas and showed her where the toothpaste was kept in the medicine cabinet above the sink. The bathroom was cramped but clean and there was a claw-foot bathtub that would have been calling her name if she wasn't so weary. She quickly brushed her teeth and her hair, slipped on Knox's pajama top, which looked like a minidress on her, and then opened the door slowly.

"I'm coming out," she warned him.

"The coast is clear," he promised.

Genevieve quickly crossed the narrow hallway to the bedroom and closed the door partway so she could call Silver. Silver came bounding down the hall, squeezed his roly-poly body through the crack in the door and greeted her with unconditional love. The bed was made, of course, with dark blue–and–green-plaid linens. She got under the sheets and flopped back onto the pillows. The mattress was much softer than the one she slept on in the garage apartment, and surprisingly comfortable.

With the puppy curled up beside her, Genevieve switched off the lamp next to the bed and stared up at the ceiling. She had never really imagined herself married—but alone in a strange bed with a puppy wouldn't have made the short list of scenarios for a wedding night if she were to ever have one, that was for sure.

"Please," she said into the dark. "Let sleep come quickly."

Knox tried to sleep but he couldn't. Everything was going according to his plan, yet he couldn't have known what it would actually *feel* like to have a wife in his cabin. For the last hour, his mind had been fixated on the image of Genevieve wearing the top part of his pajamas. The fact that he hadn't seen her in the garment hadn't stopped his mind from imagining it. She was in his bed, in his pajamas, and he had promised not to touch her. He had given his word. What was he *think-*

ing? Now he had a beautiful, sexy wife with whom he had to maintain a hands-off policy. Living with Genevieve in such close quarters, it seemed like a monumental challenge he would have to fight to overcome every day.

"Wake up, lovebirds! It's time for your shivaree!"

Knox sat up at the sound of his brothers' voices. They were banging on what sounded like pots and pans, hooting and hollering at the top of their lungs. Knox threw off the blanket, stood up, switched on the light and stomped over to the front door. He yanked open the door and was greeted by Finn and Wilder.

"What are you doing?" he yelled at them, holding his hands over his ears.

"The shivaree, bro! From the movie Oklahoma." Finn laughed, banging his pot with enthusiasm.

"We're welcoming your bride to the family!" Wilder tipped his head back and hollered.

"Knock. It. Off!" Knox grabbed for the pots and pans but missed.

Wilder and Finn pushed their way into the cabin and it seemed that they all looked at the blanket on the couch at the same time. Knox turned back to his brothers, who now had a perplexed, wondering expression on their faces. At that moment, Genevieve came out of the bedroom in his pajama top. All three of them stared at her. Her long blond hair was mussed, her blue eyes blinking against the light and her tanned, muscular legs were exposed.

Instinctively, Knox stepped to her side and put his arm around her body. "My wife and I would like to spend our wedding night alone. Now take your *shivaree* and get the heck out of here."

Wilder lifted his eyebrows, his eyes shifting to the blanket on the couch. "It doesn't look like we were interrupting anything, bro."

If Finn and Wilder walked away thinking that they were having a platonic wedding night, the entire plan would be ruined. Knox couldn't let that happen. He took Genevieve's face in his hands and kissed her. He kissed her the way he had always thought about kissing her—slow, sweet and full of promise for good things to come. For a split second, she stiffened in his arms, but then she put her arms around his neck and kissed him back like a woman in love. By the time the kiss ended, his brothers were slamming the door behind them.

Knox let his arms fall away from Genevieve's body and took a step backward. "I'm sorry. I had to do something."

His wife looked a bit dazed, as dazed as he felt. That kiss—so unexpected and unplanned—had got his juices flowing and made his body stand at attention.

Genevieve touched her lips as if she were still feeling the kiss before she said, "You had to."

Knox tried not to notice the shape of her legs or the outline of her breasts beneath the thin material of his pajama top, but he couldn't avoid it. His wife was a beauty. How could he not notice?

"Were you able to sleep?" she asked him.

He shook his head.

"Do you think they'll come back?"

Knox took a glass out of the cupboard and got some water out of the tap. "Knowing them? It's possible."

"We can't let anyone see us sleeping apart," Genevieve said. "We can't risk it."

He brought her a glass of water, which she accepted with a thank you.

"What do you suggest?"

"We share the bedroom."

Knox's mind immediately went to the thought of sharing a bed with Genevieve and not being able to act on any desire that was surely to arise. Could he handle it? Would he ever be able to get any sleep with her just an arm's length away?

"Are you sure about that?" he asked.

Genevieve finished the water and put the glass in the sink. "I'm not sure about anything we've done, Knox. But we're here now, so we have to just find a way to make it work."

"Do you really think that you can share a bed with me and keep your hands to yourself?"

His wife laughed—a natural, sweet-sounding laugh that he enjoyed. "I will certainly give it my best shot."

"See that you do."

"Are you a right or a left?" Genevieve followed Knox back to the bedroom.

"Middle."

"Not tonight, you aren't," she said. "Silver is the middle."

The puppy's head popped up and he wagged his tail.

"Silver is our chaperone?"

"Yep. We'll keep the puppy between us like an adorable chastity belt."

Genevieve ended up getting the right side of the bed. She hurriedly slipped under the covers and pulled them up to her chin. Right before Finn and Wilder had barged in on their wedding night, Genevieve had just drifted to sleep surrounded by Knox's scent. The pillows and sheets and blanket all had the faint scent of Knox's body. Now that he was in bed next to her, the scent of his warm skin made it difficult for her to remember that this was a marriage in name only. The man was built for a woman's appreciative eyes and the sight of him naked from the waist up, the feel of his hard body and his soft lips on hers, awakened feelings in her that she had worked to push aside.

"Gen?" Knox said her name in the dark.

"Hmm?"

"If I had asked you out—you know—before we got married, would you have said yes?"

Genevieve hesitated to answer. "No."

The bed moved beneath him as he shifted his body toward her. "No?"

"No."

"Why not?"

"Are we really having this conversation now?"

"Why *not*?"

"Because, Knox," she said. "You're too young for me."

The bed wiggled because he sat upright. "Too *young*? You're thirty-two."

"Which you just learned today…"

"And I'm twenty-eight."

"Exactly."

"I'm only four years younger than you!"

"Which means that you're really ten years younger than me because men are about six years behind women as far as maturity. Hence why I don't date younger men."

"You just marry them."

Genevieve curled her body around Silver, rubbing his soft warm belly. "Touché, husband. Now go to sleep. Being your fake bride is exhausting."

Genevieve awakened to the smell of rich coffee and the feel of a wet puppy tongue licking her face. Giggling, she grabbed Silver and wrapped him up into her arms.

"How are you this morning, puppy breath?"

Silver barked and thumped his tail back and forth. Then he shimmied out of her arms, leaped off the bed and went racing out of the room. She pushed herself upright in the bed and checked her phone for the time.

"Oh, my goodness." She squinted at the screen, shocked. It was after eight! She never slept in like this.

"Good morning." Knox appeared in the door, freshly showered and shaved. He was wearing dark jeans and a button-down shirt tucked in neatly. "Coffee?"

"God, yes."

"If you want to jump in the shower, I put a fresh towel out for you and there's shampoo."

Knox had seen her in his pajama top the night before, but in the light of day, she suddenly felt self-conscious.

"Can I borrow your deodorant? Didn't think of that when I packed."

"What's mine is yours," he said. "Help yourself."

Genevieve quickly took a shower and changed into the jeans and T-shirt she had worn the day before. It seemed like a lifetime ago that she had been waiting for Knox at the diner. The simple gold band around her finger felt foreign but she knew that, at least for the time being, she would have to get accustomed to wearing it.

"You cook?" she asked as she walked barefoot out to the kitchen.

"Enough to survive." Knox handed her a cup of coffee. "Cream? Sugar?"

She shook her head and blew on the piping hot coffee.

"I can do scrambled or fried. Pick your poison."

"Scrambled."

Knox cracked an egg. With his back to her, she admired the way his jeans hugged his hips and his legs. He turned his head to look at her and caught her checking him out. He smiled at her with a wink.

"Enjoying the view?" he teased her.

"No. I was trying to read the label, that's all."

"If you say so," Knox said. "But I think this platonic marriage may just prove too difficult for you, Gen."

He brought two plates of scrambled eggs to the table and joined her.

"I can't believe how late I slept." She took a forkful of eggs. "How long have you been up?"

"A couple of hours."

"Did you sleep?"

"Like a rock once my two knucklehead brothers left."

"Do you think they bought the kiss?"

Knox caught her eye and held it. "It felt real to me."

Genevieve looked down at her plate and pretended to be preoccupied with moving the eggs from one spot to another. That kiss had felt real to her as well. It wasn't the kind of kiss that two platonic friends would share; it was a lover's kiss. Knox had felt it and so had she.

"How do you think your family's going to react?" Knox asked, bringing her eyes back to his handsome face.

Genevieve looked out the window for a moment, thinking. Then she gave a little shake of her head. "My mom will think it's typical. I've been impulsive since I was a kid. But my dad? I think he's going to freak out."

"Good to know. Looking forward to it." Knox stood up and took both of their plates to the sink. "I suppose we should go and face the freak-out then."

She had to agree. Putting off telling her parents was only making her stomach churn. And the thought of them finding out from anyone else was a serious concern. Rust Creek Falls was a small town with a big mouth. They had to get to the folks before the news of their elopement reached them by a gossip or a well-wisher.

Genevieve looked down at Silver who was on his back on the couch with his fat paws up in the air. "Let's take Silver. I mean, seriously. Who can stay mad when there's a puppy in the room?"

"Only a monster," Knox said.

"Exactly!" She nodded. "It's not the least bit cowardly to hide behind a puppy shield."

Chapter 7

Knox hadn't been in too many serious relationships in his life, so meeting-the-father moments had been far and few between. This was the first time he was meeting his in-laws and it didn't seem to matter that this was a marriage based on a wager. He was still nervous.

"You'd better fill me in more about your family," he said to his bride as he drove his truck to the Lawrences'. From their previous conversations, Knox knew that Genevieve was the oldest of three daughters and the only one who wasn't married with kids. He was well aware of the fact that Lionel, Genevieve's father, could be rigid, old-fashioned and didn't approve of his daughter's chosen profession.

"I don't know..." his wife said. "What can I really tell you in ten minutes?"

Their decision to elope without a plan had come back

to bite them several times and they weren't even a whole day in to the ruse.

"Just tell me what you think I should know."

"My mom, Jane, stayed at home with the kids. Lionel sold industrial farm equipment until he retired. The man was absolutely horrible at being retired, so we were all thrilled when he started going to farm equipment auctions with his friends, buying old equipment and refurbishing for resale. It keeps the man busy and out of my mom's kitchen," Genevieve said with a smile. "I have a sister Margo—married with four kids. I told you about her. And then there's Ella—she's my youngest sister—married, of course, with two kids and one on the way. I am the only Lawrence daughter who isn't married."

"Not the case anymore."

"Hey! That's true. I *am* married." Genevieve held up her hand to look at the gold band on her left hand. "One less thing for the folks to complain about."

The Lawrences owned a small homestead on the outskirts of town. The house was a classic two-story whitewashed farmhouse; there was a wraparound porch with a swing and the front door was decorated with heavy leaded glass. Next to the house was a two-car garage with a flight of stairs leading up to an apartment.

"This is home," she said as they pulled up and he detected the slightest catch in her voice. On the outside his new wife appeared calm, but she was, beneath the surface, understandably rattled.

"We're in this together." Knox wanted to reassure her.

She sent him the slightest of smiles but it disappeared quickly.

"Oh! Shoot! Let me get Oscar before he spots Silver." Genevieve hopped out of the truck and jogged over to the front porch where a giant orange tabby cat was sitting as still as a statue. Genevieve scooped up the massive cat, hugged it to her body and then disappeared inside the house.

Knox looked down at Silver, who looked up at him and then tried to lick him on the chin. "She is going to come back, isn't she?"

After a couple of minutes waiting, Genevieve reappeared on the porch and waved her hand for him to join her.

"All right," he said to his canine companion. "Here goes nothing."

With Silver cradled in his arms for extra protection, Knox walked up the porch stairs to meet his bride.

"You're going to meet my mom first. She's the easy one."

Knox stepped into the Lawrence home and it was like stepping into his grandmother's hug. The house was tidy and decorated with farmhouse decor—chickens and roosters and cows. The old wide-planked wood floors were dinged up from years of use, but an obviously recent coat of polish brought out their color and luster. There was something that smelled mighty good cooking in the kitchen at the back of the house. They walked past a stairwell leading to the second floor on their way to the kitchen and Knox noticed that there were framed pictures of family everywhere—on the walls, on the fireplace mantel, on every surface.

"Is that you?" He stopped to look at one of the framed pictures on the wall. The young blond girl was executing a perfect handstand on the back of a horse.

"Yes."

"You were a wild child even back then, weren't you?"

Genevieve laughed and he was glad to hear the sound. "Always, much to my mom's dismay."

As they approached the kitchen, Genevieve called out, "Mom!"

Knox had never met Mrs. Lawrence before, so he didn't really know what to expect. A heavyset woman appeared at the end of the hall wearing an apron covered in yellow flowers. She threw open her arms, a welcoming smile on her face.

"Ladybug! What are you doing home this time of day?"

"Ladybug?" Knox asked under his breath, loving the fact that his tough-as-any-cowboy wife had such a sweet nickname.

"Not one word, cowboy," Genevieve ordered.

"Oh!" Jane Lawrence noticed him but first enveloped her daughter in a tight hug. "This is such a wonderful surprise."

"Mom." His bride untangled herself from her mom's hug and turned to him. "I want you to meet Knox Crawford."

Genevieve had inherited her mother's lovely cornflower blue eyes; Jane's eyes twinkled with pleasure as she welcomed him into her home. Genevieve had also inherited her mother's smile. It was a smile he had always appreciated from the first time he'd met the pretty farrier in person. Knox was invited into a crisp white and cheerful yellow kitchen that was filled with refurbished 1950s appliances. Stepping into Jane Lawrence's kitchen was like stepping back in time.

Jane clasped her hands together, her eyes darting excitedly between her daughter and him. Knox got the distinct feeling that Genevieve didn't bring men home very often.

"I had no idea we were going to have company." Jane touched her short blond hair self-consciously. "I didn't even put on lipstick."

"It's fine, Mom." Genevieve scooped Silver out of his arms.

"It's a pleasure to meet you, ma'am."

"Oh, it's such a pleasure to meet *you*." Jane smiled. "You know, I saw your father at the post office once. He's so tall!"

Knox didn't think it was possible, but he felt immediately at home in Jane's kitchen. She offered him a cup of coffee and made a place for him at her small round kitchen table. Then she filled a bowl of water for Silver. He'd never experienced such a warm welcome as he received from Genevieve's mom; he only hoped it would continue once she found out that he had eloped with her daughter.

"Where's Dad?" Genevieve, who had been rummaging in the refrigerator, popped a couple of grapes in her mouth before she joined them at the table.

"He's outside tinkering with his toys," Jane said. "He brought a trailer heaping with rusty gold, as he calls it, from the auction yesterday."

Knox met Genevieve's gaze and he knew what she was thinking: When and how do we break the news? Jane was watching them closely, no doubt curious about this unusual morning visit.

"What do you think?" Genevieve asked him.

"No time like the present."

Jane clasped her hands on top of the table. "Is there something I should know before we get your father?"

"Ma'am, there really isn't any easy way to say this…" Knox stopped to clear his throat.

"We eloped," Genevieve said plainly and held up her hand so her mom could see her wedding ring.

There was silence at the table as Genevieve's mother took a moment to digest the news she had just received. Jane's expression changed from welcoming to confused to happy in a span of moments. She jumped out of her chair, embraced her daughter, kissed her once on the cheek and then quickly came around the table to embrace him. Jane clasped her hands together happily in front of her body, and Knox was shocked to see tears of joy glistening in her eyes.

"Oh, ladybug! You're married?!"

Genevieve's jaw was still set as if she was ready to deflect a bad reaction that wasn't coming. "I'm married. As of yesterday."

Jane rejoined them at the table, her face brightened from the news. She reached for her daughter's hand. "This means that you're going to stay in Rust Creek Falls!"

That was the moment when Knox understood why Jane had reacted so positively to the elopement. She didn't care that she had missed the ceremony, she only cared that her daughter wouldn't be moving away from home. When he first made this wedding wager with Genevieve, all he could think about was proving a point to his own controlling father. The impact of the fake marriage on someone as sweet and genuine as Jane Lawrence hadn't occurred to him in the least. When the marriage ended and Genevieve moved to California, Jane was going to be heartbroken. And, in part, it would be his fault.

Jane spent the next several minutes asking expected questions. She knew how they met because Genevieve had told her about servicing the horses of the Ambling A, but she wanted all the other details—the romantic bits.

"I can honestly say," Knox said to Jane, "that I have never met anyone like your daughter before, Mrs. Lawrence."

Jane reached over and took his hand in hers and squeezed it tightly. "I always knew that my ladybug would find a man who truly loves her just as she is."

Genevieve was squirming uncomfortably in her chair in a way he'd never seen before. Like him, he had a feeling Genevieve was just starting to fully appreciate the impact that their ruse would have on everyone in their lives.

"And 'Mrs. Lawrence' is too formal for family." Jane's eyes started to glisten with happy tears again. "Shouldn't you call me *Mom*?"

"Let's not rush into anything," Genevieve interrupted.

"Do you mean like a marriage?" Jane countered with a sweet, motherly smile.

Knox had to appreciate how quickly his mother-in-law had turned the table on Genevieve. He had a feeling it didn't happen very often.

"I'm actually kind of shocked you aren't upset that you weren't at the ceremony." Genevieve ran her finger along a groove carved into the top of the table. "I thought you would be."

"I never expect you to have a typical anything, ladybug. Why would your marriage be any different?"

"Point taken."

"I can throw you a reception!" Jane said, as if the

thought just occurred to her. "We can have it here and we can invite all of your friends and family. It will be the first time that the Crawfords and Lawrences come together. What do you say?"

Genevieve looked a little like a deer caught in the headlights. Knox was surprised too. Like Genevieve, he had never considered the idea that their families would want to celebrate their union. Still…

"I like the idea," Knox said, wanting to please Jane for some reason.

"You do?" Genevieve turned to him, her eyebrows raised in surprise.

"Sure." He nodded. "Why not?"

"Sure," she repeated slowly to her mom. "Why not?"

"Oh, that's so wonderful!" His mother-in-law's cheeks were flushed a happy shade of pink with excitement. "Now. I think it's time that we tell your father."

Genevieve started to get up but Knox stood up and held out his hand. "This is for me to do, Gen."

His wife resettled in her chair. "Hey, it's your funeral."

He winked at her. "Promise to take care of Silver if I don't make it back?"

Genevieve crossed her heart. "Girl Scouts honor."

Jane stood up and moved to the sink. "Genevieve was asked to leave the Girl Scouts for setting a tent on fire."

"A total accident!" his wife exclaimed.

Knox turned to his mother-in-law. "Mrs. Lawrence—"

Jane frowned at him for still using the formality.

He started again, this time correcting himself as he addressed her. "*Mom*…will you take care of Silver should I not make it back in one piece?"

"I would be honored to take care of my grandpuppy, yes." She nodded emphatically and gave him a smile.

"I find this whole conversation insulting," Genevieve said as she pointed to the back door. "You'll find Lionel out that'a way. God speed, young man."

Knox walked the short distance from the back porch to the shed in the backyard like a man walking the plank. He'd never met Lionel before and now he had to tell the man that he had eloped with his daughter? Not exactly starting off on the right foot.

"Hello, sir."

Lionel Lawrence was a man of average height, slender, with narrow shoulders and a ramrod straight back. He had deep-set blue eyes and about a day's worth of silver and brown whiskers on his long face. Lionel wore a faded green John Deere baseball cap and glasses with thick black frames.

"How do?" Lionel pulled a rag out of the back pocket of his jeans and wiped the sweat from the back of his neck.

Knox extended his hand. "I'm Knox Crawford."

Genevieve's father reached out his hand. "I've heard the name."

According to Genevieve, the Lawrences had been longtime friends of one of Rust Creek Falls's main families, the Traubs; even still, it wasn't a town secret that there had been a long-standing beef between the Traubs and the Crawfords. Knox was relieved that he didn't hear any carryover of that feud in Lionel's tone when he greeted him.

"What can I do for you, young man?"

Knox swallowed several times, finding that his tongue seemed to be stuck to the sides of his mouth.

"Well, sir…"

"While you're here, would you mind helping me move this aerator? Darn thing is too awkward for me to move myself."

Knox was grateful for the stay of execution. He grabbed one side of the piece of farm equipment while Lionel grabbed the other. Together, they moved the aerator out of the shed and into the yard. Lionel lifted up his hat, scratched the top of his head and then repositioned the ball cap so it shielded the sun from his eyes.

"That'll do for now," his father-in-law said. "I thank you."

"I was happy to help."

The two of them stood together for a moment, neither of them speaking until Lionel asked, "Your kin took up at the Ambling A, isn't that right?"

"Yes, sir." Knox nodded. "My father and my five brothers. By way of Dallas."

"It's a good piece of land."

"Yes, sir, it is."

"Good to have family all in one place."

Knox nodded his agreement.

"So…" Lionel rolled back on his heels a bit. "What brings you out to my neck of the woods?"

"Your daughter, sir."

Lionel's small eyes widened for a moment before they narrowed. "My daughter?"

"Yes, sir. Genevieve."

Genevieve's father didn't say anything, but the expression on his face said plenty. He was happy that a man might be coming to court his daughter.

"I don't know if you're aware that Genevieve has been coming out to the Ambling A for a while now. For the horses."

"I heard something 'bout it."

"Well, we've gotten to be pretty close."

Lionel's eyes were pinned on his face.

"And, well, sir…"

"Spit it out, son. I've only got so many good years left."

"…I married your daughter yesterday."

His father-in-law didn't blink for several seconds; he just stared at him, as if he were an old computer trying to process new information. Lionel stuck his finger in his ear and wiggled it around.

"I'm sorry, son. I don't think I heard you right. What did you say?"

"Genevieve and I got married yesterday."

For a moment, Knox actually thought that his father-in-law hadn't heard him because he just kept on staring at him. Then, Lionel put his hand over his heart, closed his eyes and pointed to the sky.

"Praise the lord," Lionel said. "My prayers have finally been answered."

Of all the responses Knox anticipated from Genevieve's father, this wasn't one of them.

Lionel opened his eyes and squinted up at him, "Do you love her?"

"I can honestly say that I've never met anyone like your daughter."

"She's as unique as they come." His father-in-law gave a big nod of agreement. "You can support a family should you be blessed with children."

It was a statement more than a question. Still, Knox felt compelled to answer.

"Yes, sir, I can." What else could he say?

"Do you want children?" Lionel pinned him with a pointed look.

They had already told so many lies, Knox couldn't bring himself to tell another. Instead, he told Lionel the truth. "Yes, sir, I do. When the time is right."

"Well, I hope your time is sooner rather than later." Lionel plopped his ball cap back onto his head. "I bet my Jane is tickled to pieces."

"Your wife's already planning the reception."

"That's my Jane! She never lets an opportunity to have a party pass her by." Lionel stuck out his hand, "Well, I suppose congratulations are in order. I don't know how you managed to get my daughter to that altar, but I'm mighty pleased you did. I've been worrying about her, I surely have."

Stunned, Knox shook his father-in-law's hand again. Neither of Genevieve's parents were upset about the elopement. In fact, they both seemed pretty pleased.

"Now, Knox, we Lawrences do have a strict no-return policy." Lionel looked at his face and then laughed loudly. "I'm just pulling your leg, son! Why would you want to give her back?"

Knox followed Lionel into the kitchen where Genevieve and Jane were awaiting their return with slightly anxious expressions on their faces. Lionel went straight over to his daughter and pulled her into a tight hug before he kissed her cheek.

"I've been waiting for years for you to find the right man to marry," Genevieve's father told her. "This is truly a blessing."

Knox caught Genevieve's eye and he could almost read her mind. *Lucky break.*

"Now, if only you can get her to quit that ridiculous job of hers and start working on some grandbabies, I could go gently into that good night a happy man."

"Dad…" Genevieve frowned at Lionel. Knox knew that the subject of her career was a sore spot for both daughter and father.

"Actually," Knox said, moving over to stand next to his wife, "Gen's career is what brought us together. I would never want her to give it up."

Chapter 8

Genevieve felt a bit catatonic as they drove away from her parents' house. The reaction she had expected and prepared for had *not* been the reaction they received. Jane was planning a reception and Lionel was planning for her uterus to be occupied by a strong Crawford baby. Their reactions had caught her off guard, that was true, but what had also caught her off guard was how terrible she felt by the deception of it all. Perhaps if Lionel and Jane had been upset about the elopement, as Genevieve had anticipated, then the inevitable divorce wouldn't be such a big deal to them. Based on their reaction to the news of her nuptials, the divorce was going to crush them.

"Your mom is a total sweetheart."

Knox's comment broke through her reverie. She looked over at him as he pulled his truck into a parking spot at the Gold Rush Diner. She hadn't seen her own truck since the day before but it seemed like a lifetime ago that she had parked in the lot behind the diner. So much had happened in a little more than a twenty-four-hour period it seemed a bit surreal to see her truck, so grounded in what used to be her old life.

"She's always been my biggest fan." Genevieve unbuckled her seat belt. "She really liked you."

"I like her."

All her life she had been acting out, getting in trouble, pushing the boundaries. Her motto had always been, *Why blend in when we were born to stand out?* For all of the trouble and angst she had caused her parents, she had never really felt guilty about it. Honestly, she had always been having too much fun. But this time was different. This time, she felt horribly guilty. She didn't like the feeling.

"She was so happy," she said quietly, pensively, hugging Silver to her body for comfort. "I didn't expect that. Did you?"

"No."

Genevieve caught Knox's eye. "This is a whole lot heavier than I thought it would be."

He nodded.

"I just didn't think…" Her voice trailed off. Then, again, wasn't that the point her mother tried to make with her again and again? Think before you act? Look before you leap? "We are going to hurt a lot of people, Knox."

"I see that now."

She had canceled her morning clients but her afternoon was full. She didn't have time to dwell on the monumental mistake she had made by going through with the bet. Her mom was the sweetest, kindest soul she had ever met. Genevieve would never want to do anything to deliberately hurt her.

"I am a horrible person," she said aloud even though the self-recriminating comment was really meant for her own ears.

Her husband reached over and squeezed her hand, and somehow, the strength and warmth of his fingers on hers, however brief, gave her temporary relief.

"You're not a horrible person," Knox said.

"Yes, I am," she said firmly. "And so are you."

She could feel Knox examining her profile before he turned to stare out the windshield, seemingly in thought. Finally, he said, hesitantly, "We can call this whole thing off now."

She breathed in and let it out. "Trust me, I've thought of that already. We go to all of our family and say, hey, it was all a big joke."

"And?"

"I don't think we can, Knox. Not now. Max knows the marriage is real—he's seen the certificate. If we tell them it was all just a hoax, we'll end up looking like the biggest jerks on the planet. Do you want that?" She asked the question but she didn't wait for him to respond. "Maybe we are the biggest jerks on the planet, but I'd rather not broadcast that to the planet. No. We've gotten our families involved and my mom is so excited to plan the reception. I think our only course of action is to plow forward. I think that we just have to keep going."

She looked at her husband who didn't seem to have anything to say in the moment. "People get divorced all the time, after all. We'll just be another statistic. No one has to know how this started. No one has to know that this was never real."

* * *

After he dropped Genevieve off at her truck, Knox returned to the Ambling A. Before they'd left the Lawrence homestead, Genevieve had gone up to her garage apartment and packed a few suitcases full of clothes and necessities. Knox carried the suitcases inside his cabin, realizing that this was the first time he'd ever moved a woman in with him. He'd never had any desire to live with the women he'd dated previously. Now, though, he was moving Genevieve into his life and he hardly knew her.

After he dropped off the suitcases in the living room, he went to work. In his mind, work was the only thing that was going to get his mind off his marriage. But that proved to be a false notion because by the time he got back to the ranch, the news of his elopement had spread like a fire on a windy day. Everywhere he went, ranch hands congratulated him or teased him about having a "ball and chain." It seemed that no matter how hard he tried, he couldn't escape thoughts of his wife.

Genevieve returned to the Ambling A, well after dark. "Hey," she called out as she entered the cabin.

"Hey," Knox said from the kitchen. "You hungry?"

His wife looked weary and dirty from a day of work. Genevieve shut the front door behind her and leaned back against it, closing her eyes for the briefest of moments. "Starving."

She opened her eyes and smiled down at Silver, who was jumping up and barking to get her attention. She scooped him up, hugged him tightly and then kissed him on the head before putting him down.

This was the first time Knox had experienced Genevieve returning home from work and he recognized, in himself, an odd happiness at seeing her walk through the door. He'd never thought that sharing his life full-time with a woman was a particularly appealing idea, which was why he'd always kept his relationships quick, light and uncomplicated. But, so far, in the short term, he liked sharing his life with Genevieve.

"That smells good." She leaned her elbows on the counter, her eyes drooping down as if she could fall asleep standing upright.

"Why don't you take a bath? Dinner will be done by the time you get out."

Genevieve smiled at him wearily. "Where have you been all my life, Knox?"

"Texas."

She left her truck keys on the kitchen counter and walked slowly, with Silver trailing behind her, toward the bedroom. A few minutes later he heard the bathroom door shut and the water in the tub running. All his life he had imagined who his wife would be, what she would look like, how many kids they would have. Perhaps that was why he was so offended when his father had tried to marry him off like he was part of a game show. Knox wanted to find a wife on his own terms, in his own time. It was true that one day, sooner rather than later, this marriage would end. One day, Genevieve would leave Rust Creek Falls for California as they had agreed. But for now, she was his friend and his wife and he may as well enjoy her company while he had it.

"How's married life treating you?" Finn asked him on the way to the local feed store.

"Pretty good, actually," Knox was surprised to say. It hadn't taken them long to form a pattern in their marriage—a rhythm of sorts—of how to cohabitate. Knox, who had learned to cook over campfires when he was a kid, didn't mind whipping up what he liked to call "cowboy cuisine" because, as it turned out, Genevieve was barely able to boil water. His meals were stick-to-your-ribs, everything cooked in one pot kind of food, but his wife never complained. And, Genevieve didn't mind doing the dishes, which suited him just fine.

After they ate, they would go out onto the porch and sit out in the rocking chairs, drink a beer and watch the sun set. It was the time when they shared the details of their days; it was a time when the early bond they had developed as friends seemed to grow deeper. It was a time in his day that he was really beginning to look forward to—his evenings with Genevieve. It was a bonus that, regardless of the strange circumstances of their current living arrangement, their friendship was the glue that allowed them to navigate the new strange waters in which they found themselves.

Knox pulled up to the feed store and shut off the engine. "How's Viv Shuster's dating service?"

Everyone in the family knew that Finn was fickle—he fell in and out of love as a hobby, it seemed. Knox had a feeling that the more women Viv sent Finn's way, the more women he was going to want.

Finn grinned at him. "There's a lot of beautiful fish in that sea, brother. A *lot*."

"I believe the point is for you to settle on just one."

His brother matched his pace as they entered the store. "This from the man who used to make chasing women an Olympic sport."

Knox stepped up to the counter. "That's not my game anymore."

He heard the seriousness in his own voice when he said those words to Finn. The marriage wasn't real, but his commitment to it was. For now, he was officially off the market. It was strange, but the thought of dating someone else after his divorce didn't appeal to him. The only woman in his mind—the only woman he wanted to date—was his wife.

"What can I do for you?" a young man named Jace asked them from behind the counter.

"We're gonna need 1000 pounds of alfalfa seed and 500 pounds of fertilizer," Finn said.

"Can you put that on our account?" Knox asked. "The name is Crawford."

The lanky cowboy behind the counter looked up from his task. "Oh, I know who you are."

The way the guy was looking at him with narrowed eyes, and the unfriendly tone of his voice, caught Knox's attention.

"Is that right?" Knox asked.

"That's right."

"What's your problem?" Finn stepped up so he was shoulder to shoulder with him.

"I heard you married Genevieve."

Genevieve had mentioned to him that her father had set her up on dates with just about every cowboy in a fifty-mile radius. It stood to reason that he was going to run into a couple of them now and again.

"That's right," he said, his tone was steady, his face unsmiling. He didn't know where this was heading.

"I've known Genevieve since we were kids," Jace told him.

"You don't say."

"I do say," Jace snapped back at him. "There were

a lot of guys around these parts who wanted to marry Genevieve."

It stood to reason that Jace was one of the "guys" that had wanted a shot at lassoing the elusive Genevieve Lawrence.

"It don't make no sense that Gen would go for a foreigner."

Finn laughed. "We're from Texas. You know that, right?"

"Like I said." Jace scowled at them. "Foreigners."

"Jace," the owner of the Sawmill Feed and Seed interrupted the conversation. "Go on to the back and help Ben with the shipment."

With one last scowl in his direction, Jace tossed his pen on the counter and headed to the back of the shop.

"Sorry about that," the owner, a heavyset man wearing tan overalls, said. "The young men around here can get mighty passionate about our womenfolk."

"No worries," Knox said with a quick shake of his head, his expression neutral. "I'd be upset if I lost out on a woman like Genevieve."

"Truer words have never been spoken, sir. Our Gen is the cream of the crop."

Knox didn't know why he felt compelled to do it, but he lifted up his left hand so the owner could see his wedding ring. "I suppose she's my Gen now."

"I suppose she is," the owner agreed. "I'll put this seed and fertilizer on your tab."

"Thank you." Knox tipped his hat to the man. "You have yourself a nice day."

"My friends are *still* blowing up my phone." Genevieve was sitting in the rocking chair next to him, Silver sitting in her lap and a half-drunk beer dangling in her fingertips. One leg was draped over the arm of the rocking chair, her cute bare toes within reaching distance of his hand.

Genevieve had decided the best way to announce their elopement to friends and extended family was en masse on social media. She had posted all of their wedding photos on her Instagram account and let the viral nature of social media do the rest of the work for them.

"Mine too." Knox had expected some interest in their elopement, but he couldn't go into town without someone stopping him to congratulate him or question him about his marriage to Genevieve. In the faces of some of the cowboys who approached him, he noted some downright jealousy that he, a Texas outsider, had managed to lasso the elusive Genevieve Lawrence.

"There are some pretty ticked-off people out there," Knox said before he took a swig of his own beer.

Genevieve sat upright, shifting a chubby, floppy Silver in her lap. "Tell me about it! I've gotten some pretty nasty looks out there. And the comments on my business Facebook page from anonymous women? Someone actually called me a gold digger. A *gold digger*! There are people I've known all my life who have actually convinced themselves that I must be pregnant. Pregnant! As if I would automatically race into a marriage just because I was pregnant. I mean what century are we living in?"

"I know," Knox agreed. "This whole thing has metastasized in a very strange direction."

"That's the truth. I didn't see any of this coming." She gave a little shake of her head. Their elopement had sent a shock wave through Rust Creek Falls. Genevieve nodded toward the wilderness that was their view. "Thank goodness for this."

Genevieve had shared with him that the only place she felt completely insulated from some of the negative reactions to their elopement was his cabin. It had become a sanctuary of sorts. There was no judgment—there was no suspicion or jealousy. It was just the three of them, the woods, cowboy chow and a rocking chair. It had made him feel good that she had called the cabin her little slice of heaven on Earth. He had noticed that Genevieve had begun to end her days a little earlier than was her norm just to get home in time to share a dinner with him. When they got divorced, Knox wondered if she would miss these moments with him. He had a feeling that he was going to miss it—perhaps even more than he even knew.

"I sure as heck hope that Viv can get one of your other brothers tied down soon so the spotlight can get off us," Genevieve said.

"Amen, Gen." Knox lifted up his bottle. "I'll drink to that."

"What are you doing?" Hunter's daughter, Wren, asked her.

Genevieve was standing on a step stool in the barn with an electric drill in her hand. "I'm getting these hooks into place so I can hang up my hammock."

"Why?"

She finished drilling the hole and turned slightly toward the little girl. "Do me a favor, will you? Hand me that silver hook right there by your foot."

Wren bent down and picked up the hook and held it out to her. "This one?"

Genevieve nodded. She slipped her drill into the tool belt on her waist and took the hook from Wren. "Thank you."

"Why are you putting a hammock up in the barn?" the young girl asked again.

"Because I can, for one." She leaned her body forward and twisted the hook into place. "And because I like to hang out with the horses and listen to them chew hay."

Once the hook was fully seated in the hole she had drilled, Genevieve climbed down off the step stool and grabbed one end of the hammock lying on the ground. She hooked one side to the hook she'd just drilled into the barn wall and then hooked the other side onto a hook on the opposite wall.

"This is perfect," she said, pleased. She now had a hammock that spanned the aisle of the barn. The Ambling A was her temporary home, she knew that even if the rest of the family didn't, and the only place that felt comfortable was the cabin. Genevieve wanted to change that. The only other place that made her happy on the Ambling A was the barn; when she wasn't at the cabin with Knox, she could spend some of her free time hanging out in the barn, relaxing in her hammock, listening to sound of the horses chewing their hay. That way, she would have two places on the Ambling A to call her own.

Wren watched her curiously as she leaned her hands on the hammock, testing to make sure that the hooks would hold.

"Seems stable enough." She removed her tool belt and put it off to the side.

With a happy smile on her face, Genevieve carefully sat down into the hammock, letting it slowly take her weight. When the whole thing didn't come crashing down, she leaned back, pushed her feet on the ground and then lifted her legs so the hammock would rock her back and forth.

"Oh, yes." She sighed. "This is the life right here."

"Can I get on?" Wren asked.

Genevieve sat up and stopped the hammock from rocking. "Sure."

Wren climbed onto the hammock and mirrored Genevieve's position. They both leaned back, legs dangling off the side of the hammock, their hands folded onto their stomachs. The hammock rocked gently back and forth and the only sound, other than the horses chewing their fresh pats of hay, was the creaking sound of the fabric rubbing against the metal hooks.

Genevieve sighed again, her eyes closed. She had always wanted to put a hammock up in a barn and this was her first real chance to do it.

"This is everything I ever thought it would be," she said to Wren. "What do you think?"

"I like it," her young companion said. "It's fun."

"It is fun."

The two of them swung together in silence, relaxing in the hammock and enjoying the company of the horses. Of course, all good things must come to an end and for Genevieve, that end came when Wren said, "My grandpa is coming."

Genevieve's eyes popped open and her head popped up; she saw Maximilian appear in the aisleway and the sight of him made her frown. She had made it her personal challenge to avoid her father-in-law and she had been pretty successful. As it always did when she saw Max, her stomach tightened like it was cramping and a rush of discomfort traveled through her body. He made her feel nauseated and nobody liked to feel that way.

"Do you like the hammock, Grandpa?" Wren asked Maximilian.

"No." There was that disapproving scowl Genevieve was accustomed to seeing. "I don't."

Her happy moment rudely interrupted by Knox's father, Genevieve helped Wren out of the hammock and then stood up as well.

"I'd like a moment of your time, young lady," Maximilian said to her as she took down the hammock.

The patriarch used the same tone as every school principal that had ever called her into their office, and every fiber of her being rebelled against that kind of tone.

"What can I do for you?" She stood with her hands on her hips, her eyes meeting his.

"Follow me."

Genevieve had to work to keep up the long-legged stride of her father-in-law as she followed him down the long aisleway. Max marched out of the barn to a nearby round pen where his newly acquired prized stallion was standing next to his trainer.

"Move him around a little, John," Max said to the trainer in a booming voice. "I want Miss Lawrence to see this."

No, the marriage wasn't actually *real*, but Max didn't know that. The fact that he insisted on referring to her as *Miss Lawrence* irked her but she kept her mouth shut about it. Her focus was on the stallion. She had been waiting—anticipating—the moment when Max tried to pin something on her with the horses. She knew that he doubted her ability as a farrier. Was this the moment she had been preparing for all along? Was this the moment he tried to blame her for an injury to one of his horses?

The trainer asked the stallion to move to the outside track of the round pen. The stallion, a tricolored tan, white-and-black paint with a black-and-white tail and blue eyes, was a magnificent horse—young and full of thick muscle and energy. But even though he had vet-checked sound, when he arrived at the Ambling A, he was lame. At the trot, the stallion was still exhibiting some telltale head bobbing that indicated that he still had some lameness problems.

"Just look at that," Maximilian said sternly. "John tells me you're responsible for this."

Genevieve bristled. "He was lame when he came off the trailer."

"I'm aware of that," her father-in-law was quick to retort.

"I didn't make him lame."

When Maximilian looked at her this time, Genevieve felt that he was seeing her for the first time. "I'm well aware of that, young lady."

"Then I'm afraid I'm missing your point."

Her father-in-law nodded toward the stallion. "He's better. He's not perfect, but he's better. How did you manage to do that?"

Genevieve wasn't often surprised, but this time she was caught completely off guard. She had been expecting, preparing for, an accusation. Not a compliment.

"His shoes were too tight, so I pulled them. He had

an infection in all four hooves and I've almost got that cleared up. If we keep on going in this direction, I think we can get him sound and keep him barefoot."

"You really think that you can get him sound?" Max asked her pointedly.

"Yes, sir. I do. It'll take time, but I've gotten a lot worse back to sound with some time, patience and some holistic approaches."

"Such as?"

"Acupuncture, for one."

"That's enough for now, John." Maximilian waved his hand to the trainer. Then he turned his attention back to her. "I've got a lot of money tied up in that horse. Can you get him sound or not?"

"I can get him back to sound," she told him.

"Then do whatever you need to do to get that done," Max said without an equivocation, and for the first time, she saw respect for her in his eyes. The man said his piece and then walked away without waiting for her response. A few feet away, he stopped and turned back to her.

"I expect you'll be at the family dinner tonight?"

Wren was listening, so Genevieve tempered her response. "I didn't get an invitation."

"Young lady, you don't need an invitation. You're family." Max looked her dead in the eye. "I'll expect you tonight. Come along, Wren."

Wren gave her a little wave before she trotted after her grandfather.

Genevieve was still rooted in her spot, a bit stunned by the interaction with her father-in-law. She was still standing there mulling over the interaction when Knox cantered up on Big Blue. The cowboy swung out of the saddle, ground tied his gelding and came to her side.

"What was that all about?" Her husband smelled of horse, and leather and sweat and she liked it.

"That was bizarre," she said. "Your father... He's given me carte blanche to do what I think is best to get the stallion sound."

Knox stared after his father, seeming as caught off guard as she felt.

"And he says he expects to see me at dinner tonight."

Knox adjusted his cowboy hat on his head. "Crap." They had both been happy to spend their dinners alone at the cabin in the woods—away from the spotlight— where they could be themselves and not pretend to be a crazy-in-love newlywed couple.

"My sentiments exactly," she agreed.

Chapter 9

"How do I look?"

How did she look? Like a petite, blonde goddess.

"Beautiful." Knox and Silver had been waiting on the couch for Genevieve to emerge from the bedroom. Max liked to have family dinner served at 6:00 p.m. on the nose, so they both rushed to finish their work in order to get home, get cleaned up and get to the main house for dinner.

Genevieve looked down at her simple aqua-blue sundress with spaghetti straps. The skirt fell just above the knees, clinging to her shapely thighs which were muscular from years of horseback riding. "Are you sure? I can change."

"No." He loved how the aqua-blue fabric matched the intense blue of her wide-set eyes. "It's nearly perfect."

Her wispy long blond hair floating over her shoulders, his wife put her hands on her narrow hips with a curious frown. "*Nearly* perfect?"

Knox smiled. In a short amount of time he had managed to figure out how to push several of Genevieve's buttons. "It's a little plain."

"Thanks a lot, Knox." Genevieve spun around and headed back to the bedroom. "Now I *do* have to change."

He jogged forward, grabbed her hand and stopped her. "Hold up, cowgirl!"

"Don't try to fix it now, Knox. You tell a woman her dress is plain and you may as well tell her that she's wearing a *rag*."

He didn't let go of her hand, coaxing her to face him. The honeysuckle scent of her hair enveloped his senses and he wanted to pull her close, bury his face in her neck and breathe her in. What would she do, how would she react, if he acted on his impulses to hold her, to kiss her, to make love to her? Would she push him away or pull him close?

"I was just trying to set the mood."

"Oh, you set the mood perfectly, Knox. I was in a good mood and now I'm not."

"I was trying to set the mood so I could give you this." He pulled a small box out of his pocket and held it out for her to see.

Genevieve stared at the box for a moment before she looked up at him. "What's that?"

"Something for you."

When she didn't take the box from him, he took her hand and placed it in her palm. "It won't bite you, Gen."

"Why did you get me a present?" she asked, not moving to open the box.

His eyebrows lifted. Did his wife have to stray from

the norm on absolutely everything? Why couldn't she just be a typical woman for once and be happy with a gift?

"Are you going to open it?"

"Fine." She tugged the ribbon loose from the box. "But I don't understand why you would get a present for me."

Knox smiled at her; he truly liked his wife. He truly did. Gen handed him the ribbon as she carefully unwrapped the giftwrap. He would have expected her to rip the paper off but she was taking her time, slowly peeling off the tape a little at a time.

"If I had known you were going to take this long, I would have just put it in a gift bag."

"Hush up," she snapped, but there was playfulness in her tone that kept him right on smiling.

Finally, she handed him the paper and opened the box. Knox watched her face carefully; he wanted to remember the expression on her sweet, pretty face once she realized what was inside the box.

"Where did you get this?" She looked up at him with such surprise that he knew he had chosen well.

"I had it made for you."

Gen was speechless as she took the custom white gold necklace out of the box. On the chain was a cluster of three farrier tool charms made of gold—a file, nippers and a horseshoe hammer. His wife held the charms in the palm of her hand, the necklace dangling down from her fingers.

"Do you like it?"

Gen slowly touched each charm. "I've never seen anything like it."

"It's one of a kind," Knox said, pleased to see how

much she liked his gift. He hesitated before he added, "Just like you."

He helped her put the necklace on. He stood behind her, enjoying the warmth of her body so close to his, lifted the necklace over her head, and then joined the clasp. Gen went into the bathroom to look at her reflection in the mirror. When she returned, her eyes were shiny with emotion.

"Thank you, Knox. I love it." She stood in front of him. "But you didn't need to do this for me."

Knox reached out and turned one of the charms so it was lying flush on her smooth, tanned skin. "I wanted you to always remember how we met."

They stared at each other for several long seconds. There was a sincerity, and honesty, in Genevieve's eyes when she said, "I'll never forget how we met, Knox. Not ever."

There was that urge again—to take her in his arms and kiss her breathless. Instead, he crossed his arms in front of his chest and smiled at her. With a nod toward the necklace, he said, "Well, since you don't need a reminder, I suppose I *could* just send that necklace back?"

His wife laughed, a sound he had become accustomed to quickly, and her hand naturally moved back to the charms. "Just try it, cowboy, and you'll draw back a nub!"

"How's married life?" Sarah asked her after the family had moved from the dining room to the outside patio after dinner.

Genevieve couldn't stop playing with the charms on her new necklace. Each tool had a round, brilliant diamond embedded in the gold. It was such a thoughtful gift that it made her wonder if Knox was beginning to have feelings for her that went deeper than friendship. Was her husband beginning to fall for her?

How would she feel if he did?

"I'm enjoying it," she answered honestly. She had enjoyed being married to Knox so far. Yes, it had been a bit strange to move into his cabin, but she had adjusted more quickly than she would have thought. Every night, they both climbed into bed, exhausted from their long day of work, and with Silver curled up between them, Genevieve was lulled to sleep by the comforting sound of Knox's breathing. She had never *slept* with any man—Knox was her first. She had never lived with any of her previous boyfriends and she didn't do overnights. If she had known how wonderful it would be to have a man's presence, a man's heat, a man's scent in bed with her, perhaps she would have signed up for overnights years ago.

"You look really happy," Lily said from a nearby chair.

Genevieve smiled wordlessly. Xander's wife wasn't the first to mention that. She looked at her husband who was on the other side of the patio deep in conversation with Hunter and Logan and felt an odd rush of emotion. Knox was so handsome—he stood so straight and tall. She loved the way his shoulders filled out his customary button-down shirts and the way his jeans hugged his thick thighs. In truth, Knox Crawford had always set her heart to fluttering but she had been careful to guard her heart from him. But it was getting harder and harder to keep her defenses up. She knew herself well enough to know that, in spite of her best efforts, her feelings for Knox were beginning to grow and take on a life of their own.

The adorable baby was a great distraction and Genevieve smiled at Sophia, making the little girl laugh and gurgle. Genevieve reached out so Sophia could wrap a chubby hand around her finger.

"You're so good with her." Sarah shifted the baby on her lap. "Any plans for children in the near future, or do you want to hold off for a while?"

Genevieve had been watching Wren playing with Silver in the grass just off the patio. She had never really wanted children. She'd just never had that motherly urge that her sisters seemed to have from the time they were little girls. While they were playing with baby dolls, she was racing the boys bareback on her pony. But sometimes, when she watched Knox with Wren, or saw him helping an elderly woman carry her groceries out to the car, Genevieve wondered what it would be like to have a child with Knox's good looks and her blue eyes. With his good heart and her daring do.

"We're not in a hurry," she told Sarah, preferring to keep her thoughts secret.

"The two of you are going to make beautiful babies together," Lily, ever the romantic, said with a dreamy smile.

As if realizing that she needed to be rescued, Wilder, the youngest Crawford brother, sauntered over to her, his longish brown hair acting as the perfect frame for his mischievous dark eyes, and grabbed her hands. "Dance with me, sis!"

Wilder was always ready for a party. He had turned on the surround sound system and was piping music onto the patio. Wanting to escape from the baby conversation, Genevieve jumped out of the chair and followed her brother-in-law to the middle of the patio. Just like Knox, Wilder knew how to dance. He led her in a small circle, dipping her, twirling her, and spinning her around so fast that she started to get dizzy. Laughing, she held on to his shoulder to keep from tipping sideways.

"Go get your own woman, Wilder." Knox showed up at their side and tapped his brother on the shoulder.

The younger brother rolled his eyes at her, spun her around a couple more times, and then let her go. Wilder held up his hands and backed away, but the grin on his face let her know that he felt good about getting Knox all riled up with jealousy. And Genevieve could see plainly on her husband's face—he *was* jealous.

"He was just playing around," she said in Wilder's defense.

"I know," Knox agreed easily. "But I still didn't like it.

Knox took her in his arms. His body swayed with hers and he pulled her close so that her breasts were pressed against him. Even though they were already married, it seemed to her that Knox was laying claim to her—letting his bachelor brothers to keep a hands-off policy where she was concerned. Genevieve wasn't usually impressed with masculine displays or gestures born out of male irrational jealousy. In fact, it was a total turn-off for her. When Knox acted jealous, it had the opposite effect on her. For Genevieve, it meant that he actually cared for her—something beyond the scope of their bet.

The night air was balmy and there wasn't much of a breeze, but it didn't stop her from pressing her body more closely to her husband. She loved the feel of his arms around her waist and the way his warm, strong hands were splayed possessively on her back. They had danced together the day of their wedding; this moment was different. There was a tension in Knox's body, in his arms, in his eyes, that made every fiber of her body crackle. His head was dipped down toward her and she had the distinct feeling that Knox was resisting the urge to kiss her with all of his family as witnesses. But, this time, it felt to her as if it wouldn't just be to give them a show. This time, it felt as if his lips were being drawn to hers.

Knox lowered his head until his lips were hovering near her ear.

"You look so beautiful tonight, Gen."

The sensual undertone in his voice, the feel of his breath on her skin, made her sway into his body. She titled her head up as he looked down at her face. She wanted her husband to kiss her—right there, right then. She was asking for it, not for the show, but because Genevieve wanted to feel his lips on her lips. And, for a moment, a split second really, she actually thought Knox was going to kiss her, but the song ended and her husband let her go. Even though Logan and Xander had joined them on the makeshift dance floor sometime during the song, Genevieve hadn't noticed. All of her attention, all of her focus, had been on being cocooned in her husband's arms. When he let her go, Genevieve wrapped her arms around her body, suddenly feeling cold when the night was so warm.

"Are you okay?" Knox asked her, his hands in his pockets.

Genevieve nodded her head silently, afraid that there

would be an emotional catch in her voice if she tried to say any words. No, she wasn't okay and she had no one to blame but herself for that.

Knox had watched all evening as his beautiful wife charmed his family without much effort at all. Even his father had begun to soften toward Genevieve, which was a miracle in its own right. His brothers—even Xander—seemed convinced that Genevieve was the best thing that had happened to him. All of them had said tonight that they'd never seen him so happy. But when he looked in the mirror, he looked exactly as he had a week ago. She fit in with Lily and Sarah and this had always been important to the brothers; they had always wanted their wives to be friends. So, everything was going according to plan. They were pulling off this fake marriage without much effort at all. He should feel triumphant. And yet, he didn't. In fact, he felt like he'd made a pretty big mess of things.

The one woman he had wanted to date in Rust Creek Falls was his wife—and he had promised not to touch her. Now, all he thought about was touching her. Morning, noon, night he thought about kissing Genevieve, he thought about holding Genevieve. He was exhausted from lack of sleep—while she seemed to easily fall asleep. She seemed completely unbothered by his presence in bed next to her, while he ached from wanting her. The scent of her hair, the warmth of her body, and the fact that he had only to reach over to touch her drove him wild with wanting. It seemed he spent every night with a mantra echoing in his head. *Forbidden. Forbidden.*

He found himself thinking it too when he'd held her

in his arms as they danced tonight. And again when he'd put his hand on the small of her back when he ushered her inside their cabin after the evening was over.

"That was so much fun!" Genevieve said as she opened the back door to let Silver outside. "I can't believe I dreaded that for a second."

His wife was a bit tipsy, so her body movements were broad and languid as if she were moving through Jell-O.

"I'm glad you had a good time." Knox took his hat off and hung it on the rack just inside of the front door.

Silver came bolting back inside, his tail wagging and his fat paws slapping on the wooden floor. Laughing, Genevieve scooped up the growing puppy, hugged him tightly and kissed him on the head. Silver licked Gen on the face and lips.

"How is it that my dog gets more action around here than I do?" Those words sounded more bitter than he had intended. He had intended to make a joke but it didn't exactly come out that way.

His wife set Silver down, walked directly over to him, took his face in her hands and planted a kiss on his lips. Genevieve pulled away and looked at him with a surprised look as if she were shocked at her own behavior.

"Don't be such a grouch, Knox." She spun away from him and headed to the bedroom.

Knox followed her into the bedroom and found her lying flat on her back, her legs dangling off the side of the bed.

"Is the room spinning?" Genevieve pressed her hands over her eyes to block out the light.

"No." Knox tugged her cowgirl boots off and then pulled off her socks.

"Are you sure?" Genevieve giggled and wiggled her toes.

"Yes," he said. "I'm sure." Her dress had slipped up to the tops of her thighs and a hint of her panties could be seen where her thighs met.

Everything in his body ached to touch this woman who was his bride. Every night he had spent lying next to her, enveloped in the scent of her hair, her beautiful body not even an arm's length away, had been torture for him. How could he avoid being aroused when Genevieve was in his bed?

Knox grit his teeth as he pulled down the hem of her dress before he turned to walk away, but Genevieve reached out and grabbed his hand to stop him.

"Hey. Where are you going?"

"You need to get undressed so you can go to bed."

"You're such a killjoy." His wife pouted at him in a more playful way than he had seen from her before. "Really and truly you are."

"Get some sleep, Gen."

Knox forced himself to walk to the door and leave his wife. She was throwing off some pretty flirty vibes but she was also a few bottles of beer past her limit. As much as he wanted to stay and take her up on this sexy invitation, it wouldn't be right. Of course, he had thought about making love to Genevieve. She was his wife and she was nearly naked beside him in his bed every night. But, that wasn't the deal. He had promised to keep his hands off and he'd been a man of his word, a man of honor, on that front. But, it had been damn difficult. *Damn* difficult.

"Hey!" she said, catching his attention and getting him to turn around. "Do you think that I have boy hips?"

Knox turned around to find that his wife had stripped

off her sundress and was standing on the bed in pretty white lacy panties and a matching strapless bra. With her strong curvy thighs, flat stomach and pert breasts, she was his youthful fantasy come to life. If he could have designed his perfect woman, he would have created Genevieve.

"No." He heard the growl in his own voice. The growl of a man who wanted more than just to look at his wife—the growl of a man whose body was already growing and hardening just at the sight of Genevieve's nearly naked body. "You don't have boy hips."

She had the hips of a woman—the type of hips a man could hold on to when he was deep inside of her.

Gen ran her hands over her stomach and hips. "I've heard that complaint before, you know."

Knox took a step forward and then forced himself to stop in his tracks. He wouldn't break their agreement. Not like this—not when her mind was fuzzy from alcohol.

"They were idiots," he told her. He couldn't seem to take his eyes off her nipples pressing against the thin, silky material of her bra. The desire—the need—to take those nipples into his mouth made Knox clench his teeth until it actually hurt.

She beamed at him and put her hands on her hips. "They *were* idiots."

Genevieve looked down at her own body, lost her balance and fell backwards onto the pillows with a laugh. She was still giggling when Knox came over, tugged on the comforter so she could get under the covers. Once he had his sexy wife tucked safely beneath the covers, he brushed her hair back away from her forehead.

"You're the most beautiful woman I've ever seen, Gen." Knox kissed her on the forehead. "Now go to sleep."

"Hey!" She reached out for his hand but missed. "Aren't you going to sleep in here with me tonight?"

Knox didn't trust himself to turn around when he shut off the light and closed the door firmly behind him. Without thought, Knox crossed the hall to the bathroom, turned on the cold water. This wasn't the first cold shower he had taken with Genevieve in the cabin and he knew it wouldn't be his last. With the icy water pelting his skin like tiny needles, Knox hit the shower wall in frustration.

Never in his life had he deprived himself of a woman's company—he'd never had to. If he wanted a woman, she had always wanted him in return. If he wanted a woman, he took her to bed. This hands-off policy with Genevieve was making him feel a little bit nuts. He wanted her—and maybe, just maybe, she wanted him. But, this time, for him at least, it was more than just the physical. He wanted to make love to her. He wanted to show her, with his lips, with his hands, with his body, what he was beginning to feel for her inside of his heart. Knox stepped out of the shower and stared at his reflection in the mirror. What he was starting to feel for Genevieve was different than anything he'd felt before for another woman. There was a deep, growing affection for his wife and he was beginning to wonder…was this what falling in love really felt like?

Genevieve awakened the next morning with a bad taste in her mouth and a roaring headache. She sat up, rubbed her hands over her face, yawned loudly and then flopped back onto the pillows. It was then that she noticed she was in her bra and panties and Knox's side of the bed hadn't been slept in. Even Silver was nowhere to be found.

"Silver!" she called out, only to realize that the sound of her own voice was making her head pound.

Silver came tearing around the corner, bounded onto the bed and then jumped into her lap, licking her face happily. Genevieve wrapped her arms around the puppy and kissed him on his head and face.

"Good morning, you stinky little puppy face."

Silver rolled over onto his back so she could pet his belly. She was in the middle of a very important belly rub when Knox appeared in the doorway of the bedroom holding a steaming cup of coffee in his hands.

"Mornin'." Knox looked crisp and clean and ready for his day of work. Not to mention handsome.

"Hi." Suddenly self-conscious of her lack of attire, she pulled the covers up and tucked them under her arms. She remembered every detail of the night before. Her inhibitions had been lowered and she had flirted shamelessly with her husband. And she had enjoyed it, every second. But for her trouble, it looked as if she had completely scared him away.

"Headache?" He handed her the coffee.

She nodded as she blew on the coffee. After taking a sip, she sighed. "Thank you."

"I've got to get on the road." Her husband seemed to be avoiding her eyes. She clutched the covers tighter to her body, wishing she had managed to at least put on a T-shirt before passing out. "I'll see you tonight."

"Knox?" She wanted to ask him why he had slept on the couch the night before. She wanted to apologize for shamelessly kissing him and stripping off her dress in front of him.

He turned back toward her.

"Never mind," she said. All the words she wanted

to say, all the questions she wanted to ask, got jammed up in her throat. She didn't want to sound desperate.

Knox waved his hand without meeting her eyes and headed out the door. She wasn't imagining it—something had changed between them. Knox usually lingered with her in the morning and shared a meal. Today, it seemed as if he couldn't get away from her fast enough. Genevieve slumped down onto the mattress, turned onto her side and grabbed Silver for a cuddle. She had come on to her husband and he was sprinting away from her.

"Great," she muttered. "Just great."

Then she remembered that they had both agreed to a platonic relationship. Knox had been the one to hold up his end of the bargain. What had she been doing going around kissing him and stripping in front of him? And why did it hurt her so much to awaken to an empty bed?

Before she could ponder those questions, the phone on the nightstand was chiming, signaling that she had several texts coming in. She stretched her arm back, grabbed her phone and looked at the messages. All of them were from her mother and sisters about the plans for the reception. Genevieve groaned and pushed her phone away. The last thing that she wanted to think about right now was the reception. How could she think about a wedding reception when she was in the midst of a very real emotional crisis?

Genevieve buried her head under her pillow with another mournful groan. "Of all the men in the world, you had to go and fall for your husband."

Chapter 10

"Why don't you come with us to the picnic?" Hunter asked Knox as they walked toward the barn.

"I'm not much of a picnic kind of guy, brother."

"Neither am I," Hunter agreed. "But just wait until you have your own little girl one day. You'll find yourself doing all kinds of things you never thought you would do, just to put a smile on her face."

"I'll have to take your word for it," Knox said noncommittally. Not surprising, his brothers had all begun to ask him about when he was going to start a family with Genevieve. None of them could know that he had agreed to a platonic marriage with his sexy wife. None of them could know how frustrating it was to answer the baby question over and over again when he knew the truth—he hadn't consummated his marriage!

"It could happen sooner than you think," Hunter mused aloud.

They rounded the corner and spotted Wren with Genevieve. Knox had noticed how frequently he found Wren tagging along after Genevieve in the barn and he didn't like it. One day soon Genevieve was going to be gone and that little girl was going to get hurt. Wren didn't deserve that. And, deep down, he knew it would be his fault.

"I don't think it's such a good idea for Wren to be getting so attached to Genevieve." Knox spoke the words he had been thinking aloud.

Hunter's surprised expression made Knox regret having giving voice to his concern.

"Why not?" his brother asked. "She's your wife. I would think she's the perfect person for Wren to attach herself to. Why would you say that?"

It took Knox a split second to figure out what he could say to backtrack. "This thing with Genevieve and me is still new. Nothing is guaranteed in this life."

Hunter, who had always been the brother that seemed to have the best advice, clapped him on the shoulder. "You guys are going to make it, Knox. Everyone in the family can see that she's in love with you. A woman can't fake that."

A woman couldn't fake that? His wife had been faking it the whole time! Was Genevieve that good of an actress or was his family just that naive and blind? Genevieve didn't love him. In fact, hadn't she been the one who said she wouldn't have even dated him if he had asked?

"Are you ready, Wren?" Hunter asked his daughter

who was watching Genevieve trim one of the horse's hooves.

Wren spun around at the sound of her father's voice, ran toward him and then leaped up into his arms for a hug.

"Can Genevieve come with us?"

Knox's throat tightened uncomfortably to stop himself from saying no. His attempt to keep Wren and Genevieve apart was failing miserably.

"If she wants." Hunter kept his arms around his daughter's shoulders. "Are you up for a back-to-school picnic, Genevieve?"

"Genevieve might have more horses to trim, Wren," Knox interjected quickly.

"Nope." His wife shook her head. "This was the last for today. Besides, I haven't eaten lunch and there's always really good food at picnics."

"I'm trying to convince Knox to go with us." Hunter looked at him. "Viv Shuster is still hard at work trying to get the last three Crawford bachelors married off. I'm telling you, a woman hurled herself at me at the feed store the other day."

"I was there and *hurled* is a pretty big exaggeration of the facts," Knox interjected.

"She *hurled* herself at me. She had the first button of my shirt undone before I knew what was happening! Thank goodness Wren wasn't with me." Hunter assured Genevieve. "I need a bodyguard."

Genevieve laughed. "A single father is pretty powerful catnip."

"See?" His brother nodded his head toward Genevieve. "She gets it. How can you abandon me in my time of need, Knox? I need someone I can trust to run interference for me."

"Come on, Uncle Knox." Wren turned that sweet smile on him. "It'll be fun."

"Why did you agree to go to this picnic?" Knox asked her as he opened the passenger door to his truck for her. "I thought we were trying to keep a low profile."

"It would be weird if we were reclusive all the time, right? If we want to silence our critics—of which there are many—trust me, just look at my social media! Then we've got to put on a show every now and again. Besides," Genevieve added as she swept her hair into a ponytail at the nape of her neck, "I'm hungry."

"You didn't have to rope me into going to this picnic just to get a hot dog on a stick, Gen."

Knox's tone caught her attention. She looked at his profile, his unsmiling lips, and tried to figure out what was going on with her husband. The first week of their marriage had gone more smoothly than either of them could have expected. But the second week had been a bit rocky, starting with Knox's reaction to his father's expectation that they would attend the weekly family dinners together at the main house. It seemed that whenever she did her part of convincing their friends and family that they were a real and legitimate couple, the more irritated Knox became. Genevieve would have thought that he would be excited that they were pulling off the impossible. Instead, he was getting grumpier by the day.

"You know what, Knox?" Genevieve said, her tone sugary sweet and laced heavily with sarcasm. "Maybe this picnic will be just the thing that will help you turn that frown upside down. We'll get you a balloon and have your face painted. And if you're a really good boy, we'll get you some cotton candy!"

He just *harrumphed.*

Realizing that Knox was determined to stay in a bad mood, Genevieve ignored her husband for the rest of the short ride to Rust Creek Falls Park. When they pulled up to the already-crowded picnic, her husband still had that ridiculous scowl on his handsome face.

"Hey," she said, a hint of irritation creeping into her tone. "Put your game face on, cowboy. It's showtime."

Knox looked over at her as he unclipped his seat belt and her words must have at least resonated a bit because his features softened. He wasn't smiling but at least he didn't look like a man who was itching to pick a fight.

Genevieve met him in front of the truck and slipped her hand into his. This would be their first official town event that they attended as a couple and she was determined to give the whole town a show they wouldn't soon forget. By the time they left the picnic, the doubters and the haters would be silenced. But only if Knox cooperated!

"Lean down and kiss me," she said with a sunny smile plastered on her face.

Knox obliged but the kiss was flat and felt more like a platonic peck from a distant relative. She wanted to kick him—really kick him hard—but instead, she tossed her head back and laughed as if he had said something amazingly funny and held on to his arm like a woman who wanted to let every other female within fifty paces know that Knox was *hers.*

"Aunt Gen! Uncle Knox!" Wren raced toward them through the throng of people.

Was it her imagination or had Knox stiffened next to her when his niece had called her *aunt*?

"Hi, sweet pea." Her husband always had warmth in his eyes and a smile on his lips for his slight, fair-haired niece. "What do you want to do first?"

"I want to get my face painted." Wren began to count on her fingers. "I want to go on the Ferris wheel, ride on the bumper cars and go in the bouncy house."

"And consume copious amounts of sugar," Hunter added as he joined them. "I can't thank you guys enough for coming. Walking through that crowd was like navigating my way through a deadly gauntlet."

Hunter lowered his voice so Wren wouldn't hear his next words. "Remember the woman from the feed store I was just telling you about? She's here selling cotton candy. I'm terrified she's going to spot me!"

"We'll protect you, Hunter." Genevieve smiled at her brother-in-law. She liked Hunter; he was a nice man and a wonderful, doting father. In fact, she was beginning to warm up to all of Knox's brothers. She had never thought about what it was going to feel like to walk away from the Crawford family once this sham marriage ended. In her heart, she knew now that it was going to hurt. When she went to California, a piece of her was going to be left behind at the Ambling A.

Holding on to Knox's arm, Genevieve could feel so many eyes on them as they wound their way through the picnic crowd toward the face-painting booth. By the time they made it there, they had been inundated with congratulations, kisses and hugs from the townsfolk. There were also some people who greeted them with sour expressions and their congratulations rang hollow; some of them were no doubt the anonymous people on social media who had accused her of being a gold digger or pregnant. Genevieve's head spinning from all of the attention and, when she finally had a chance to look up at Knox's face, she saw that he was scowling again.

"Smile." She squeezed his arm. "You look miserable."

Knox forced a smile while she waited in line with Wren to get their faces painted. Her husband's demeanor and attitude at the picnic was really starting to get under her skin. As far as she could tell, she was working overtime trying to convince everyone that their marriage was legit, while he was busy undermining all of her effort.

"What are you going to get?" Wren asked her excitedly while they waited for their turn.

"Hmm," she mused aloud. "I think I'll get a unicorn."

"Me too! I'll get a unicorn too!"

When they returned to Hunter and Knox, Genevieve and Wren had matching unicorns on the right cheeks of their faces. Hunter swept his daughter up into his arms and admired her face. "That's a mighty pretty unicorn for a mighty pretty little girl."

Wren giggled happily in her father's arms while Knox examined Genevieve in a strange way that made her neck suddenly feel hot. But before she could ask him why he was looking at her in such an odd way, schoolteachers Paige Traub and Marina Dalton, and Josselyn Strickland, the school librarian, joined their small group.

"Genevieve!" Paige hugged her tightly. "We're so happy to see you here! We've been meaning to get in touch with you to say congratulations, haven't we, Marina?"

Marina was the next to hug her. "We have! But you know how the beginning of school year is for us. We've been so swamped."

After congratulating them on their marriage, Marina and Josselyn were quick to make a big fuss over Wren. It could be tough for a child to go to a new school, but Wren seemed to have taken a liking to her teacher and she was beginning to make some friends.

"Oh, Hunter," Josselyn said. "I've been meaning to ask you. Is it true that your family found an old diary in the floorboards at the Ambling A?"

"It's true," Hunter said. "Found it when we were refurbishing the wood floors."

"I just love Rust Creek Falls history and folklore." Josselyn's eyes lit up with the news. "I would love to see it."

"What's this about?" Genevieve hadn't heard anything about a diary.

"We found this jewel-encrusted diary in the floorboards of the main house," Knox explained. "It's got to be at least sixty or seventy years old."

"Fantastic." Josselyn clasped her hands together. "Is there a name?"

"We're assuming it was written by one of the Abernathys, the previous owners of the Ambling A. We searched on the internet for information on the family, but that was a dry well. Xander did manage to open the diary with a screwdriver and found some love letters written by someone with the initial W. Other than that, we've still got a lot of missing holes in that story."

"An unsolved mystery." Genevieve rubbed the palms of her hands together with a smile. "How can we figure this out, Josselyn?"

"Well," the librarian drawled, her brow wrinkled in thought, "if I were the one looking, I would go straight to the *Rust Creek Falls Gazette*. The town newspaper will have a cache of historical records that can't be found on the internet."

"We'll have to try that, Josselyn." Hunter smiled his gratitude. "Thank you for the tip."

"Oh, you are so welcome. Please, please, *please* keep me in the loop. I am just dying to know more about this diary!"

After the face painting, Genevieve insisted on heading straight for the area where the food vendors were selling their wares. Three corn dogs and a large cola later, she was beginning to feel full. But she left a small amount of room for some homemade pie. What would a picnic be without a piece of pie?

"Are you sure three corn dogs were enough? Why not go for four?" Knox was sitting across from her with a genuine smile in his eyes. It was the first she had seen during their time at the picnic.

"I thought you liked a woman with a healthy appetite?" she teased him.

"I do." He leaned forward and rested his elbows on the table. "I never cottoned to women who picked at their food like chickens pecking at seed on the ground."

It was moments like these that made Genevieve glad that she had agreed to Knox's crazy scheme—when her husband, so handsome and rugged, was smiling at her in a way that made her feel like she was truly appreciated for who she was. Instinctively, she reached across the table and squeezed his hand.

"I like it when you smile at me, Knox."

This entire fake marriage had blurred so many lines that it was difficult to know when they were being real with each other and when they were just putting on a show. This time, her words weren't for anyone other than Knox and she hoped he knew that.

"Welcome, everyone, to the Back to School Picnic!"

Genevieve's attention was drawn away from her husband to Mayor Collin Traub who had just stepped behind the microphone on the main stage.

"That man dearly loves a microphone." She laughed. The Traubs and the Lawrences had been friends for years and years. In fact, she kept her horse, Spartacus, out at the Traubs' Triple T Ranch.

The mayor made several announcements, including some raffle ticket winners. Then Collin seemed to be scanning the crowd for something, or someone, and when his eyes landed on her, Genevieve realized that *she* was the someone the mayor had been looking for.

"Ladies and gentlemen, we have some newlyweds with us today!" Collin said loudly into the microphone. "Come on up here, Knox and Genevieve!"

"Damn it!" Knox cursed under his breath but loudly enough for people sitting around them at the other picnic tables to overhear. "If I have to hear one more person tell me congratulations!"

With a smile plastered on her face, Genevieve kicked her husband under the table. She stood up quickly, acutely aware of the stares they were drawing, and grabbed Knox's hand. She was relieved when he stood up, held on to her hand and led her through the crowd toward the stage. Once on stage, Knox stood stiff as petrified wood next to her with an equally stiff, unconvincing smile on his face. He looked like a hostage and she couldn't do anything about it. Instead, she kept right on smiling and waving to the crowd. She leaned her head on Knox's shoulder several times for effect and gazed up at him adoringly.

"Congratulations to Mr. and Mrs. Knox Crawford!" the mayor announced and led the crowd in loud clapping.

"Kiss her, man!" someone in the crowd called out and others followed.

Without a moment's notice, Knox hooked his arm around her, drew her into his body, bent her back over his arm and kissed her like he'd never kissed her before. The kiss was deep, and long, and as his tongue danced across hers, the sound of catcalls from the crowd faded into the background and the only sound she could hear was the sound of her own beating heart.

Genevieve wasn't speaking to him and he couldn't muster the strength to care. Soon after being forced up on stage in front of the entire town, Knox insisted that they leave the picnic. All the way home, his wife was giving him the silent treatment and it was for the best. Yes, this whole scheme had been his idea, but now he was convinced it was the worst idea he'd ever had in his life. And for that, he had no one else to blame other than himself. This was *his* fault.

When they got home, Knox couldn't help it. His eyes touched on every pile of paper, every shoe left near the door, everything that was out of place, because he had brought Genevieve into his home. "Why do you have to leave your bra on the couch, Gen?"

"Really?" Genevieve looked at him like she was looking at a misbehaving toddler in a grocery store. "That's your big problem? Your sensibilities are offended by my bra on your couch?"

"No." He took off his cowboy hat and slammed it down on the kitchen counter. "My sensibilities are offended when you walk around here without your bra on!"

Genevieve stared at him for a second and then laughed. "I live here, Knox. Every now and then you're going to accidentally see me crossing the hall to the bathroom in, *God forbid*, my underwear."

He leaned back against the counter, his eyes stormy, his arms crossed in front of his body. "You prance around here in your underwear and your tank top and what, I'm not supposed to notice?"

Genevieve rolled her eyes. "Get over it! I'm not going to wear a muumuu to go to the bathroom. Besides," she said, waving her hands at his chest, "you walk around here without your shirt on all the time. You don't see me having a cow about it, do you?"

"That's not the same thing," Knox said, rubbing his neck which was sore from restless nights spent out on the couch.

"So says you," she retorted.

There was a moment of silence between them and then Knox said quietly, seriously, "This isn't working for me anymore."

He hated to see the flash of hurt and confusion that he saw on Genevieve's pretty face. "If that's how you feel, then let's get an annulment."

That very thought had crossed his mind but when the words came out of Genevieve's mouth Knox knew it wasn't what he really wanted. He didn't want an annulment; he wanted more of his wife, not less.

"I don't want an annulment," he said, honestly.

"Then *what* do you want, Knox? Are you so much like your father that you can't be happy when you actually get what you want? The whole town thinks we're really and truly married!" And then she added, "No thanks to you."

Knox pushed his hands into his jeans pockets to keep from hauling Genevieve into his arms. What would she say when he told her the truth? What would she do when she found out that he couldn't go on wanting her, needing her, dreaming of making love to her? He was completely eaten up with desire for his wife—a woman he had promised not to touch. Knox knew, one way or another, something had to change between them.

"Tell me, Knox." Genevieve walked over to stand in front of him. "What do you want?"

Knox's eyes focused on the softness of Gen's lips and the honeysuckle scent of her wispy blond hair. He didn't have any words for her; he could only show her.

He pulled her into his arms and kissed her. Not a kiss for show—this was a kiss that was all about them. His arms tightened around her slender body as he deepened the kiss, encouraged by the fact that his wife had melted in his arms. Knox kissed a trail from his lips to her neck.

"I want you," he whispered harshly. "I want *this*."

"I want you too, Knox."

Surprise mixed with relief registered on his handsome face. "Are you sure, Gen?"

She locked gazes with him so he could see how serious she was. "I'm sure." She slowly unbuttoned one button on his shirt. "Now…in keeping with our tradition, I dare you to take me, Knox."

"You dare me?" A playful glint flashed in his dark eyes.

"I dare you."

"Be careful who you're daring, Gen," Knox echoed her own words that seemed so far in their past. "You'll be my wife in every way a woman can be a wife before the sun goes down."

Genevieve unbuttoned a second button. "That doesn't scare me, Knox. Does it scare you?"

"Nothing scares me, Mrs. Crawford." Knox swung her up into his arms as he had on their wedding day and carried her across the threshold of his bedroom. "You should know that by now."

Knox carried his bride into the bedroom and kicked the door shut behind them. She was light in his arms; the sweet smell of his hair intoxicating to his senses, and the curve of her breast pressed into his body, were tantalizing reminders of all good things to come. Genevieve dropped little, butterfly kisses on his neck as he lowered her down to the mattress. He loved the feel of her lips on his skin and could only imagine what it would feel like to have her kiss him in other, more private parts of his body.

His wife smiled up at him welcomingly, letting him know that this moment was what they both wanted. Knox shut the blinds, darkening the room, before he quickly unbuttoned and shrugged out of his shirt. Genevieve knelt on the edge of the bed, hooked her finger into his bell loop, and pulled him toward her.

"I think this moment was inevitable." She unsnapped his pants.

He knew that he was looking at her like a hungry lion looks at its prey as her hand lingered at his groin.

"Don't you?" she asked, her fingers sliding the zipper down.

Genevieve slipped her hand inside of his underwear and wrapped her fingers around him. Knox closed his eyes, his head tilted back, and groaned at the feel of his wife's cool fingers touching his hot skin. This moment, played out so many times in his head, was so much better than his imagination had conjured.

Knox opened his eyes and looked down at his wife's lovely face; there was an impish, teasing expression in her cornflower blue eyes. He quickly disrobed. He wanted her to see all of him, to touch all of him.

The expression on her face told him all he wanted to know—she wasn't disappointed. His wife ran her hands over his chest, down his stomach and back to his hard shaft.

"Hmm," she said with a sexy smile in her voice. "You are handsome, cowboy."

Unable to wait a moment longer to see her naked, Knox lifted Genevieve so she was standing on the bed in front of him. He rid her of her shirt and her bra, a routine he had perfected over the years. But, this time it was different. This time it was his lovely Genevieve.

Those nipples, so taut and rosy, were too tempting to ignore. Knox took one into his mouth, suckled it lightly, while his large hand covered the other breast, massaging it gently. He was rewarded with a sensual gasp as Genevieve raked her fingers through his hair.

"My beautiful wife," Knox murmured against her body.

Her fingers still buried in his hair, Knox quickly unzipped her jeans and pushed them down over her hips. He couldn't wait to slip his hand inside of her simple white cotton panties to cup her. Genevieve arched her back and pressed herself down into his hand begging him to slide his fingers into her slick, tight warmth.

"Don't wait." Genevieve's fingernails were digging into his shoulders as she held on to him. "Please, don't wait."

It was clear that she wanted him to be inside of her as much as he did. Knox stripped her jeans and panties from her body and tossed them on the floor. Genevieve was waiting for him, her hair spread out on the pillows, her arms open to welcome him. Knox grabbed a condom from the nightstand, rolled it on, and then rolled into her arms.

"Yes, my beauty," Knox said, watching the expression of pure pleasure on her face as he joined their bodies together.

Knox buried his face into her neck and he buried himself more deeply into her body. Theirs was a rhythm of two like-minded souls—two pieces from the same puzzle—working in natural harmony. They didn't need to "figure each other out." They just knew how to move together.

Genevieve clung to him, her fingers flexing on his biceps, her breathing shallow and quick. He could feel her tightening around him and it made him thrust deeper and harder. He wanted her to come apart in his arms.

"Oh, Knox." Gen lifted her hips to meet him.

"Yes, baby." He kissed her lips. "Come for me."

One hard thrust and he broke the dam; Genevieve cried out as she bucked up against him, demanding more—taking more. She was slicker now and so hot that Knox couldn't wait another minute. Bracing his arms on either side of her body, Knox drove into her one last time and exploded. Shocked by his own body's reaction to this woman, Knox lowered himself down and wrapped Genevieve tightly in his arms. He kissed her lips, her cheeks, and her forehead, wanting to savor the aftermath in a way he'd never desired before. Knox had taken countless women to bed, but he was certain that this was the first time he'd ever made love.

Chapter 11

Genevieve awakened after dark. She blinked her eyes and yawned, taking a minute to realize that she had become the middle of the sandwich—she was spooning Silver and Knox was spooning her. By the sound of her husband's breathing, he was still asleep after they had made love for the third time. Not wanting to awaken them, Genevieve tried to readjust her body ever so slightly so the moment wouldn't end. Usually the first time making love was a bit awkward for her—not with Knox. Making love with Knox had been like coming home; he seemed to know her body in a way that didn't make sense. The way he held her, the way her touched her, the way he kissed her—it was everything she had always wanted and thought impossible to have. When he made love to her, with such gentle intensity, Knox gave her everything she had ever needed. And then he gave it to her again and again.

Genevieve closed her eyes and reveled in the feeling of her husband's warm skin and his hard chest muscles pressed against her back. She reveled in the feel of his arms holding on to her so tightly and the feel of his breath on the back of her neck. There was part of her that wanted to dwell on the negative side—the impending, inevitable divorce—yet the part of her that wanted to bask in the afterglow of their lovemaking won out when Knox tightened his arm around her body and kissed the nape of her neck.

"Are you awake?" he asked groggily.

"Yes."

Knox's large hand moved down to her bare stomach and pulled her back into his body. "Any regrets?"

"No." There were no regrets. Maybe one day there would be, but for now, she was happy they had consummated their marriage.

"Good," her husband murmured behind her.

Genevieve threaded her fingers with his and kissed his hand. "Well, maybe one regret."

She felt Knox lift his head up off the pillow and it made her smile as she continued. "I do regret that we missed dinner."

Her husband dropped his head back onto the pillow with a groan. "I've never known another woman to be so driven by her stomach."

She spun around in his arms so she was lying on her back. Silver sprang upright, barked and then used both of their bodies as a springboard to jump off the bed.

"Feed us," Genevieve demanded playfully.

Knox yawned again and rubbed his hand over his face and eyes. "Fine. I'm getting up."

Like two teenagers left alone in their parents' house, Genevieve and Knox raided the refrigerator. Genevieve pulled on a T-shirt and her underwear while Knox opted to wear only his boxer briefs. They gathered their snacks and headed for the couch. After Silver gobbled up the food in his bowl, he jumped up onto the couch, and sat down on a bag of chips.

"Silver!" Genevieve scolded him. "You have no manners!"

Knox pulled the bag of chips out from underneath the puppy.

"I'm serious, Knox. Your puppy needs some training."

"*Our* puppy," he corrected, dipping a chip into the salsa. "Don't try to shirk your responsibility to the family."

"Fine. *Our* puppy needs to be trained. We can't just keep on carrying him around. He needs to learn to walk on a leash, heel and sit."

"He's sitting now," Knox said before he popped the chip into his mouth. "Aren't you, boy?"

Silver wagged his tail at Knox happily, looking between the both of them, hoping that someone would take mercy on him and pass a treat his way.

"I'm going to enroll him in a puppy class." Genevieve took a swig of her beer. She couldn't imagine a better post-lovemaking snack than chips, salsa and a cold bottle of beer.

"I will leave the education of our puppy to you." Her husband raised his bottle up to her.

"Talk about shirking your duties." She smiled at him.

They finished eating their snack and then headed back to the bedroom. It was unspoken, but they both wanted to get back into each other's arms. It felt as if they were truly newlyweds on their honeymoon—they couldn't get enough of each other. Genevieve stripped out of her scant clothing and slipped under the covers into Knox's awaiting arms. She curled her body into his, draping her leg over his thickly muscled thigh. Her hand on his chest, Genevieve sighed happily. Knox rested his chin on the top of her head, his free hand petting her hair.

"An annulment is off the table now." She felt his voice as much as she heard it in the dark.

Genevieve tried not to stiffen her body when his words registered. She felt his words like a cut on her skin. Why would he bring up the end of their relationship at a moment like this? She pushed away from him and turned over.

"Hey, what's wrong?" Knox tried to bring her back into his arms.

She didn't answer him. If she needed to explain it to him, then he wasn't as smart as she had originally given him credit for. She heard him sigh.

"That was a stupid thing to say," he acknowledged.

She didn't respond because she was fighting to keep tears at bay. She so rarely cried that, much like these new feelings for Knox, this well of emotion caught her completely off guard. Genevieve bit her lip hard to keep the tears in her eyes from falling.

"Gen." He said her name again. "I'm sorry. I just…" He paused for a second and then restarted. "I broke a promise to you. I told you this was going to be a marriage in name only and I let us both down.

"Please," he added. "Don't turn away from me."

When she felt that she could speak again, Genevieve turned back to her husband. "I wanted this to happen."

Knox tucked wayward strands of hair behind her ear and then put his hand gently on her face. "I don't want you to have any regrets, Genevieve."

"My regrets are mine. If I have them, I own them." She reached out to put her hand over his heart. "Besides, this was bound to happen, Knox. You've been walking around without your shirt on, bare chested. A red-blooded American woman can only be expected to have so much willpower."

That made her husband laugh and it broke the tension between. He took her hand and kissed it.

"If memory serves, *you* were the one teasing *me*." He tugged her closer to his body.

"Oh, trust me." She tucked her head into the crook of his neck so she could listen to his beating heart. "I was."

Knox put his finger beneath her chin and brought her lips up to his for a sweet, lingering kiss.

"Hmm." She ran her hand over his tensed, bulging biceps. "I love the way you kiss."

As if on cue, Silver climbed on top of them like he was climbing a hill, flopped down in between their bodies and began to lick their faces.

"See?" Genevieve laughed. "No manners!"

Silver started to scratch an itch on his neck, smacking Genevieve in the face with his foot.

"Okay, brat." Knox scooped up Silver. "Out of the bedroom with you."

In the sparse light coming in the bedroom window, Genevieve admired the sheer beauty of her husband's naked body as he walked back toward her. The man was a leaner version of Michelangelo's David and for the time being at least, he was all hers. Knox returned to her and wordlessly began to love her with his mouth and his hands. Genevieve closed her eyes and clung to her husband, giving him control, knowing that he would take care of her, knowing that he was about to take her on another glorious ride.

Making love to his wife had become Knox's new favorite pastime. What he had truly grown to love about Genevieve was her sense of adventure, which, as it turned out, was just as present when it came to the physical side of their marriage. Their desire for each other made them act like two horny teenagers and when they could sneak away to make love, they did. When they weren't making love, they were finding excuses to touch each other, to hold hands, as if they were afraid that the other one would suddenly disappear. And there was a part of him, like a little warning bell ringing in the back of his mind, that reminded him that, like it or not, Genevieve was going to leave him. That was the deal. Yet, that knowledge didn't stop him from wanting his wife in every way he could possibly want her. As a companion, as a friend, and now, as his lover.

He simply couldn't stop thinking about her.

As if his thoughts conjured her up, she appeared on the ladder to the hayloft where he was working.

"What are you doing up here?" Genevieve asked as she climbed up into the hayloft. "Aren't you supposed to be fixing fences with Logan and Xander?"

He put his finger to his lips and winked at her as he took her hand in his. He led her through a maze of hay bales stacked to the roof until he reached a small clearing tucked away from prying eyes. On a small bed of loose hay, Knox had put down a soft flannel blanket. Knox studied his wife's pretty face to see her reaction to his secret hideaway in the hayloft. Without a word, Genevieve nodded her head in agreement. She was game to make love in the hay loft with him. Knox was eager to join his body to hers; it was all he had been thinking about since he'd had the idea to make love to her in the loft. There was going to be something so sexy about being seated between his wife's thighs, his lips on hers, his world standing still in a moment of ecstasy while the work of the ranch continued all around them.

When her husband sent her a text asking her to meet him in the hayloft, she had assumed that he wanted to discuss some sort of change in the hay they were feeding some of the higher-end horses. A sexy afternoon rendezvous hadn't even been on the radar! But, she couldn't deny that she loved the idea. She had always wanted to make love in a hayloft and this was her chance. What better person than the man who had turned out to be her most incredible lover?

"You can't be noisy," she warned him with a lover's smile as she shimmied out of her jeans.

"Me?" he asked in a loud whisper. "You!"

"Shhhh." She put her fingers to her lips. "Someone will hear you."

Knox had his jeans unzipped and she was immediately drawn to the outline of his erection pressed against his boxer briefs. She tugged his briefs down and wrapped her lips around his hard shaft.

"Oh, God." If Knox had tried to speak those words in a lowered tone, it hadn't worked.

Laughing quietly, Genevieve lay back on the blanket and opened her arms to him. Instead of taking her invitation, Knox knelt down between her thighs and kissed her on that most sensitive spot. Biting her lip hard to stop herself from crying, Genevieve slipped her fingers into Knox's hair and arched her back. Turnabout was fair play and he was making it nearly impossible for her to keep their location a secret.

"Knox." She whispered his name over and over again while his tongue slipped in and out of her body.

She was panting and aching when he sat up so he could look at her with a Cheshire cat smile. She reached out her arms to him.

"Please," she said under her breath. "Hurry."

With his smile in place, Knox searched his pocket and then the look on his face changed.

"What's wrong?"

"The condom." Her husband checked his other pockets. "It must have fallen out of my pocket."

Genevieve covered her face and groaned in frustration. *"No."*

Her body was so revved up that she ached with wanting. She *needed* to feel Knox inside of her now—she needed him to relieve this gnawing ache he had created in her.

"I need you." She grabbed the blanket in her fists and squeezed tightly.

"I need you," he said, the expression on his face pained—they were both so ready for each other that it seemed impossible to stop now. She held out her arms to him and he covered her body with his, but he was careful not to enter her.

Knowing it was a risk, and not caring in the moment,

Genevieve reached between them and guided him to her slick opening.

"Are you sure?" Knox asked through gritted teeth.

"I mean it, Knox," she demanded, her body demanding relief.

He slid his thick shaft inside of her, so deep, so hard, making her forget about everything except for Knox. He moved inside of her, slow and steady, knowing what she liked—giving her exactly what she needed.

"Yes, my beauty." Knox nibbled on her ear, cupping her bottom and seating himself so deeply inside of her that it brought her to climax.

Gasping and shuddering in his arms, Genevieve clung to Knox tightly, her breath mingling with his as buried his face in her neck to stifle the sounds that he just couldn't contain.

"God, I love you." The words seemed to be wrenched out of his throat, unplanned and unexpected.

Not trusting her own ears, Genevieve held her husband tightly, kissing his chest, and admiring his pure masculine appeal at the moment of his release. The muscles of his biceps bulging and sweat dripping down his chest, Knox threw back his head, his eyes closed with a stifled growl on his lips.

Both of them spent and satiated, Knox rolled over onto his back, taking her with him. Genevieve draped her leg over thighs and rested her head on his chest, listening to his beating heart. Many times during their lovemaking, Knox had said that he *loved to be with her*, but this was the first time it had been boiled down to just "I love you." Had he been too overcome with passion to get the rest of the words out or had this been a true declaration? Nestled in her husband's arms, the scent of sweet alfalfa hay in the air, Genevieve genuinely wished she knew the answer to that question. It was clear in her mind that she had fallen for her husband, but it was not at all clear to her if Knox had, indeed, fallen for her.

"What do you think of the menu?" Jane Lawrence was bustling around her cheerful yellow kitchen.

"If you're happy, I'm happy," Genevieve said noncommittally. Her mother and sisters had all been driving her nuts with the plans for the wedding reception shindig. Party planning was not her activity of choice and she wished that her family would just make all the arrangements and leave her out of it.

"What do you think, Knox?" Jane turned her attention to her son-in-law, who was busy stuffing his face with a bowlful of Jane's homemade beef stew.

Seemingly perfectly at home in her parents' house, Knox took a quick break from the stew. "I think you have a really good variety, Mom. Something for everyone."

"Thank you, Knox." Her mom hugged him and sent her daughter a disapproving glance. "At least one of you is involved in the planning."

"Seriously? Mom, he hasn't even looked at the menu and somehow he's the good one?"

"I've looked at the menu," Knox told her. "Margo emailed it to me."

"How did *Margo* get your email?"

"Ella gave it to her," her husband said.

Genevieve lifted up her hands in the air. "Since when are you in contact with Ella? What the heck is going on around here?"

Before he could reply, her mother said, "Since you wouldn't respond to any of my emails about the reception, I got in touch with Knox…"

"And we've been texting ever since," Knox finished as he smiled at Jane fondly.

Genevieve turned to Knox. "You're texting with my mom and emailing with my sisters? I feel like there's a whole lot of stuff going on behind my back."

"Going on right in front of your face." Her husband scooped up the last spoonful of beef stew.

Genevieve sat back in her chair and watched her mother interact like a giddy schoolgirl with Knox. There was no doubt that the two of them had hit it off. It pained Genevieve to think about how hurt her mom was going to be when the marriage ended. She had asked Knox to not call Jane "Mom" but whenever he tried to call her by her given name, her mom corrected him. What a tangled mess they had created.

"Did you see the beautiful picture Knox had framed for us?" Jane asked, picking up Knox's empty bowl.

"No."

"Oh! It's so lovely." Her mom disappeared into the formal living room and came back with a framed picture of them in Lawrence Park on their wedding day.

Knox did look a bit sheepish when he said to her, "I was over here helping your father with the tractor."

"Honestly!" Genevieve crossed her arms in front of her body. "Am I literally the last person to know anything that's going on in my own family?"

"Ladybug." Her mom hugged her tightly around the neck and planted rapid-fire kisses on her cheek. "I know it's difficult to discover that the world doesn't actually revolve around you."

Genevieve just groaned.

She knew it would get only worse when her sisters arrived for dinner.

Dinner at the Lawrence house was a less formal affair than at the Ambling A, but it was just as loud and raucous when the entire family was present. And minutes later, they were.

Ella, the youngest of the three Lawrence daughters, arrived first with her twin boy toddlers, her husband, Jason, and a very pregnant belly. Once Margo arrived with her brood of four children, the noise volume in the house doubled.

"Outside! Outside! Outside!" Margo shuttled her four children through the kitchen and out into the backyard with their grandfather. Her sister shut the door with a happy sigh. "Thank goodness it's not raining so they can run off all that energy."

The Lawrence sisters all looked very similar, with blond hair and blue eyes. Both of her sisters were taller and leaner, and out of the three of them, Margo had always had the curves.

Her youngest sister put her hands low on her back and leaned backward with a wince. "Take the boys outside will you, honey? It'll be good for them to play with their cousins."

Once her husband and the twins were on their way outside, Ella joined them at the table. "Phew. I am ready for this girl to come on out."

Margo lifted up the paper towel covering the fried chicken their mom had made earlier and snitched a small piece of the skin before she took the last seat at the round kitchen table.

"I really appreciated your feedback on the decorations, Knox."

"Yes," Ella agreed. "You've been so helpful. Unlike some people who shall remain nameless."

Genevieve caught Knox's eye. "I can't believe you're so interested in the reception."

"Of course I'm interested." Her husband said it so convincingly that she would have believed it if she didn't know the truth. "I only intend to get married once."

Chapter 12

Three weeks into the marriage and it felt to Knox like Genevieve had always been an integral part of his life. They had developed a rhythm; they had developed a way of moving in each other's lives that made sense. Not only did he have a lover now, his friendship had deepened. Between their busy work schedules, they had found time to play together. Genevieve, as it turned out, was a skilled fisherwoman and one of their first afternoon getaways was to his newfound favorite fishing spot. That night, they served their freshly caught bounty to the family. When it was his wife's turn to pick their next outing, she chose rock climbing. Everything Genevieve liked to do for fun involved some sort of risk to life and limb. In spite of the fact that he was not the biggest fan of heights, Knox had allowed her to strap him into the safety gear and he managed to climb his way up the sheer face of a mountain. Once he got to the top, he was rewarded with a kiss from his beautiful wife, but the family jewels were still sore from the safety straps and there wasn't a snowball's chance in hades that Genevieve was going to convince him to rock climb again.

They were on their way to another outing this afternoon, albeit a tamer, less risky one.

"I can't wait for you to meet Spartacus!" his wife said excitedly from the passenger seat. They had both finished their work early because Genevieve wanted to take him out to the Triple T Ranch, the sprawling Traub family cattle spread.

Knox found that when it came to Genevieve, he could muster enthusiasm for just about anything. The wedding reception was a perfect example. He wouldn't typically be interested in menus and decorations, but it was Gen's family and he wanted to make a good impression on them. He wanted them to like him; he wanted them to accept him.

"Look!" She pointed out of the window as they turned onto Triple T land. "There he is!"

"Holy monster horse," Knox exclaimed. "What the heck is he?"

"Stop here." She was already opening the door and he hadn't stopped the truck. "He's a Percheron, of course."

With a halter and an apple in her hands, Genevieve climbed up to the top of the fence and straddled it. She whistled at Spartacus, who lifted his large black head, snorted and then began to gallop at full speed toward the fence. Gen laughed, her cheeks flushed with happiness, her blue eyes shining in the most enchanting way. Spartacus bucked several times, his muscular black body glistening in the sun and his thick black mane and tail dancing in the wind.

"You're gorgeous!" Genevieve called out to her horse.

Spartacus was so big and so powerful that Knox worried that he might try to jump the fence. Gen stood up on the fence, her boots balanced precariously on the planks, to greet the Percheron. Spartacus slid to a halt in front of her, snorting and tossing his head and pawing at the ground.

"Yes, my beautiful boy." Gen offered him the apple before putting the halter on his head. "I'm happy to see you too."

"What are you doing?" Knox leaned over so his voice would reach her through the open truck window.

"I'll meet you at the barn." Genevieve climbed on the horse's back. Spartacus kicked up his hind leg in protest, but Gen just gently chided him. "Knock that off, grump."

Without any warning to him, his wife squeezed her legs on the horse's side and Spartacus took off at a full gallop.

"Darn it, Gen." Knox fumbled to get the truck out of Park. He stepped on the gas and tried to keep his eyes on his wife as she galloped bareback on the giant Percheron. With her blond hair loose around her shoulders, Genevieve reminded him of a warrior goddess racing into battle. Had he ever seen anything more incredible than his wife, his lover, riding bareback on this magnificent black horse?

Knox quickly found a place to park his truck near the barn, grabbed his keys, jumped out and ran to the fence. He had lost sight of Gen as she rode into the woods and he was anxious to see her emerge in one piece.

"Howdy, Knox." Collin Traub walked out of the barn and headed toward him.

Knox gave the town mayor a quick nod but his eyes were laser focused on the spot where Genevieve should appear any moment.

"She's riding Spartacus bareback again, I take it?" Collin asked.

"No bit, no bridle," Knox said.

"That's about right," the mayor said. "I'd better open that gate for her or she'll try to jump it."

Collin walked quickly over to the gate that led from the field to a riding arena adjacent to the barn. Knox didn't realize that he was holding his breath until he let it out when Genevieve appeared. Still galloping, his wife headed straight for the open gate.

"Watch this." Collin rejoined him at the fence.

One hand holding on to Spartacus's thick mane, once she guided the gelding into the arena, Genevieve leaned her weight back and the draft horse halted. Laughing, his wife patted the horse on his neck and then smiled at Knox.

"Has she always been like this?" Knox heard himself asking the question aloud.

"Yes, sir." Collin chuckled. "You've got a tiger by the tail, my friend."

All Knox wanted Genevieve to do was get off of the horse. Yes, she was an accomplished horsewoman but for some reason this horse seemed riskier than the quarter horses he was used to riding at the ranch. Spartacus was nearly eighteen hands tall; Big Blue was only sixteen hands.

"Now what's she doing?" Knox muttered.

"What she always does," Collin responded with another chuckle.

Genevieve pulled off her boots and socks and tossed them toward the fence. Now barefoot, she slowly stood up on Spartacus's broad back. The horse stood stock still for his mistress while Knox's heart started to beat faster in his chest. The thought of Genevieve getting hurt made his stomach knot. And yet, she wasn't the type of woman who would ever be hemmed in. He was just going to have to get used to watching his wife take risks with her life and limb.

Once she was balanced on Spartacus's back, she leaned forward, pressed her palms on the horse's rump and then lifted her legs into the air.

"Have you ever seen anything like that before?" Collin asked him.

"No," he said. "I can honestly say I haven't."

No one in his or her right mind would think to do a handstand on the back of a horse—at least no one he knew in Texas. This was a first.

Genevieve executed a perfect handstand on Spartacus's back before she carefully lowered her legs and carefully slid into a seated position. Once seated, his wife clucked her tongue and asked the horse to move over to the fence where Knox and Collin were waiting for her.

"Hi, Collin." Genevieve held out her hand to high-five the mayor.

"Howdy, Genevieve."

Knox's wife smiled and held out her hand to him. "Get on."

The last thing Knox wanted to do was get on Spartacus bareback. Honestly, he wasn't too sure he'd be all that jazzed to ride the draft horse with a saddle and bridle. Collin was staring at him with an amused look on his face, as if he knew that Genevieve had him between a rock and a hard place. Not wanting to look like a coward in front of the mayor or Genevieve, Knox climbed up the fence and onto Spartacus's back.

"Wrap your arms around me," Genevieve said. "You're about to go on the ride of your life."

That was exactly what he was afraid of.

"Have fun, you two." Collin gave a wave of his hand.

"Have you done this before?" Knox asked the mayor.

"Oh, yes." Collin grinned at him. "I have. All I can say is hold on tight, my friend. Hold on *real* tight."

As it turned out, that was the best advice anyone had given him in a long time.

Genevieve turned the Percheron toward the open field and the next thing he knew, he was working overtime to stay on the back of the draft horse. His wife was laughing like she was having the time of her life while his legs were on fire from gripping the horse. Genevieve had only one speed and that was full-steam ahead. She pointed the gelding toward the woods and all Knox could see was a maze of tree limbs just ripe for taking off their heads.

"This is the best part," Genevieve said as she leaned forward.

Knox instinctively tightened his hold on his wife's waist. If she thought something was the "best part" he had a feeling he wasn't going to like what was about to happen next. Over the top of Genevieve's head, he spotted a creek without a bridge.

"No, Gen!"

"Yes, Knox!"

The next thing he knew, his body was lifting off the back of the horse as Spartacus jumped over the creek. When the horse's hooves touched the ground, Knox landed hard and he felt his private parts get smashed in the process. All the way back to the riding arena, he was gritting his teeth against the pain he was feeling between his legs. He'd never been so happy to get off a horse in his life.

"Wasn't that the best time ever?" Gen slid off her horse, gave him a kiss on his nose, took off the halter and let the horse run back through the gate and into the field.

Knox took a step and winced in pain. He would be walking a bit more bowlegged for a while, thanks to that ride. And not for nothing, there might be a question of his ability to procreate. Once his brothers saw him limping around and riding tender in the saddle, they were never going to let him hear the end of it.

His wife, oblivious to his distress, linked her arm with his. "I'm so glad I got to share that with you."

"Oh, yeah." He shook his leg to reposition himself. "Me too."

After their amazing ride on Spartacus, Knox had insisted that they go straight home. Disappointed, Genevieve couldn't figure out why they had to cut their afternoon short until Knox made a beeline for the kitchen, stuffed some ice into a Ziploc bag and stripped down to his boxer briefs.

Sitting on the couch with a bag of ice on his private area, a clearer picture began to form in her mind.

"I thought you might've landed a bit hard on the other side of the creek," Genevieve said contritely.

Knox frowned at her. "Why does every activity you pick for us to do end with me needing an ice pack?"

She sat cross-legged on the couch next to him and called Silver up to sit beside her. "Not *everything*."

"Rock climbing," he recounted. "I couldn't sit in the saddle for two days after that little episode."

"Sorry." She giggled. She couldn't help it. Knox was as masculine a man as they made and it was cute to see him show some vulnerability.

"Now this." He held up two fingers. "And what? Next week you want us to go bungee jumping?"

Her face lit up. "Yes! Let's do it. You'll love it."

"No." He shook his head. "I won't *love* it. You'll love it and I'll end up sitting on the couch with another ice pack. No. Thank. You."

She frowned at him playfully. "Spoilsport."

"Look, woman." Knox repositioned his ice pack. "If you want to have children one day, you're gonna have to pick activities that don't involve crushing the family jewels."

Genevieve stopped smiling. It wasn't the first time Knox had talked about their marriage as if it didn't have an expiration date. Now that they had been intimate, all of the lines had been blurred and it was difficult to know what was real and what was fantasy. Sometimes she felt that Knox was in her same boat—that he was falling for her in the same way she couldn't help but be falling for him. But nothing tangible had been said. And no promises—other than a promise of a divorce—had been made.

"You know what?" She reached out and patted him affectionately on the arm. "I'm going to make you dinner."

"Do you know how to cook?"

She sprang up off the couch. "I know enough to get by. You're always making dinner for me, so now it's my turn to spoil you."

A short while later Genevieve had to admit that she had oversold her ability in the kitchen. They ended up eating turkey sandwiches with a side of potato chips on the front porch. But one of the many things that she liked about Knox was his willingness to appreciate her smallest effort. Like the day she'd done their laundry. Knox had acted like she had done something really special for him. Out of every man she'd ever known, Genevieve was beginning to believe that Knox understood her in a way that no one else ever had.

"It's so beautiful here, Knox," she said, looking out at the setting sun. "I'm really going to miss it."

Knox turned his head and she could feel him staring at her profile. She found herself giving him opportunities to talk her into staying, but no matter how many times she opened that door, Knox never walked through it. He never said, "I don't want you to go."

"I saw that you got some literature in the mail from some stables in California."

She nodded. "It's not easy to find a place suitable for a horse like Spartacus."

"That's an understatement."

"His size can be intimidating and he does have food aggression in the stall, so I have to be careful where I stable him."

"Did you find any good prospects?"

"No. Not yet."

For a minute or two, they sat in silence, each in their own thoughts.

"So, California is still the dream?" Knox asked.

California had been her dream for so long it was hard to imagine her life without that goal in mind. And yet, the time she had spent with Knox had begun to make her imagine a different kind of life. A life with a family, a husband and a dog—not in California, but right here in Rust Creek Falls.

When she didn't respond, Knox filled in his own blanks. "California is the right place for you, Gen. I want you to be happy."

Maybe California was right for her. Maybe she would be happy there. But would she be happier than she was right now, sitting on the front porch of Knox's cabin in the woods?

No. That was the answer that floated into her mind. No. She wouldn't be happier. Being Knox Crawford's wife had brought a new level of happiness into her life. But she couldn't be so sure that Knox shared her desire to stay married. Yes, he was an eager and passionate lover—the best she'd ever had—but physical chemistry didn't automatically translate to happily-ever-after. She had never been a chicken before in her life until now. She just couldn't bring herself to build up the nerve to tell her husband that she had fallen in love with him.

That night, Knox made love to Genevieve slow and long. He didn't want the moment to end. Perhaps he was afraid of what it was going to feel like when she was gone from his life. The day he had found information from California in their PO Box, he had actually been contemplating asking Genevieve to give their marriage a chance. There had been moments when he was sure that Gen returned his feelings. It certainly felt that way when they made love. And it was more than just the physical. It was all of the little things she did for him that made him believe she cared—like doing his laundry or picking up his favorite barbecue sandwich on her way home. She noticed every little thing about him and tried to make his life more comfortable. What she didn't realize was that just her being in his life, being his friend, had made his life so much better.

Knox curled his body around Genevieve's body, holding her tightly as they both were drifting off to sleep.

"Knox?"

"Hmm?"

"I had a wonderful time with you today."

He smiled, his eyes still closed. He pulled her just a little bit closer. "I'm glad."

"Knox?"

"Hmm?"

"Do you want to have children?"

Knox's eyes opened in the dark. When he had mentioned giving Genevieve children earlier in the day, he had regretted those words the second they came out of his mouth. Sometimes it was difficult for him to remember that this thing between them wasn't the real deal. It felt like the real deal to him.

"Yes." He stared at her flaxen hair that was spread out across the pillow. He had imagined a little girl with Genevieve's blond hair, blue eyes and tomboy fearlessness. "I do."

Several seconds passed before she responded. "I've seen you with Wren and my nieces and nephews. I think you are going to be an amazing father one day, Knox. I really mean it."

He hadn't ever voiced it aloud, but he had often imagined Genevieve in the role of mother. Yes, she was tough and fiercely independent, but she had a nurturing side. He had seen it particularly in her kindness to Wren. Genevieve saw that Wren needed extra attention and she gave her exactly that.

"I think you'll be a wonderful mother."

He felt her hand tighten in his at the compliment. "I never thought that I wanted to be a mother."

He heard an unspoken "but" dangling off the end of that sentence.

"Has that changed?"

His wife snuggled more deeply into his arms. "Yes. I think it has."

Chapter 13

"Happy one month anniversary."

After a long day of work, Genevieve had put up her barn hammock and was swinging gently, listening to the horses chewing their early evening hay. At the sound of her husband's voice, she opened her eyes. Knox was holding out a small bouquet of wildflowers.

Genevieve took the flowers and held them up to her nose. "Thank you. Happy anniversary."

"I can't believe that Dad has let you get away with this hammock idea."

She held up her pinky. "I told you. Totally wrapped. Care to join me?"

Knox didn't move to get in the hammock, but she could tell that he was tempted. She scooted over just a bit, not enough to tip the hammock over. "Come on. Live a little, cowboy."

"Why do I let you talk me into all kinds of odd things?"

"I don't know." She held on to the edge of the hammock while Knox sat down. "But I'm glad I do."

Knox took his hat off, leaned back slowly until his head was next to hers. She leaned forward so he could put his arm under her head. Resting her head on his shoulder, Genevieve curled into his body. She rocked the hammock back and forth a bit to make it swing them gently. Knox placed his cowboy hat on his stomach and at first the muscles in his arms and legs were stiff.

"Relax," she whispered.

"I feel ridiculous."

"Relax," she repeated. "Just listen to the horses and ignore everything else."

It took him a minute or two, but she felt Knox's body begin to relax next to her. She glanced up and he had closed his eyes. She loved to be in this hammock, listening to the horses. It had never occurred to her that she would be able to lure Knox into the hammock with her.

"Hmm," she murmured. "This is nice."

"Only for you," Knox said, but this time his voice had a languid quality that let her know that the magic of the hammock was working on him too.

"You have to admit—this is relaxing."

Instead of answering, Genevieve heard Knox's breathing change. Her husband could fall asleep faster than any other person she knew. Five short minutes in the hammock and Knox had drifted off. With a happy smile, Genevieve wrapped her arm around Knox's body, nuzzled her head down into his shoulder, and closed her eyes. In her mind, this was heaven on Earth.

"Why aren't you moving the herd with Finn and Wilder?"

Crap. The sound of Maximilian's stern, distinctive voice made her eyes pop wide open. It was like being caught skipping class by the principal. It was her fault that Knox was sleeping on the job in a hammock.

Her husband surprised her. Instead of sitting up at the sound of his father's voice, Knox stayed where he was in the hammock, his arm still tightly around her.

"They've got it handled," he said. "I wanted to wish my wife a happy anniversary. One month today."

Genevieve was very curious about Maximilian's re-action to the news of their one-month anniversary. Her father-in-law didn't have any response, which in her opinion was an improvement.

Maximilian pointed at her. "I'd like a moment of your time, Genevieve."

Huh. She had graduated from "young lady" to "Gen-evieve." Nice.

It took some doing, and some laughing, but they both managed to roll out of the hammock while Max looked on. Genevieve had never seen Knox allow himself to be so silly in front of his father, nor had she ever seen her father-in-law so silent in the face of so much silliness.

"Did you receive your invitation for the reception?" she asked her father-in-law as she worked double time to keep up with his long stride.

"I'll be there."

It would be strange to have Maximilian in their farm-house—it didn't seem natural to encounter him any-where other than the Ambling A. But Jane was giddy with excitement about the party and because of the guilt she felt over the fact that the whole marriage was based on a wager, Genevieve wouldn't deny her mother anything. She tried to not dwell on how her mother would react once she knew the truth.

Knox walked out to the corral with them. He caught her hand as they walked beside Max. Genevieve looked over at him, once again surprised. Her husband was growing into being his own man, unafraid to be who he was in front of his father. That was the whole reason why he wanted to elope in the first place and now she was seeing that unfold right before her eyes. Knox Crawford was his own man, full stop. And it was plain to see that, however grudgingly, Maximilian was beginning to respect his son's autonomy.

As they rounded the corner, Genevieve saw her father-in-law's prized paint stallion in the round pen. Per Maximilian's instructions, she had contacted a veterinarian trained in advanced acupuncture and laser therapy. It had cost a pretty penny to fly the vet in from out of state, but Maximilian had said he wanted no expense spared to improve the Stallion's health. The three of them stopped outside of the round pen.

"Make him move a bit, John," Max said.

The trainer asked the stallion to move to the outside track and trot. Genevieve had been working hard to get this stallion sound. She cared about all of her clients, but this stallion in particular was her way of proving herself to her father-in-law. His opinion of her mattered. After all, he was Knox's father.

"Look at that," Max said in a quieter voice than she'd ever heard him use. "Will you look at that?"

Knox put his arm around her shoulder and kissed her on the top of the head. "You've got a gift, Gen. A real gift."

"I didn't do that by myself."

"No," Max agreed. "You didn't. But you knew what to do."

It was moments like this when Genevieve thought that maybe, just maybe, she could make a life as a farrier in Montana. If she could change the mind of a man like Maximilian, there was hope for others to follow.

Her father-in-law turned to her. "I thought Knox was damn crazy hiring you."

Knox kept his hand on her shoulder as if to lend her extra support.

"I thought he was doing some hippy-dippy millennial equality-of-the-sexes garbage."

Genevieve had to bite her lip to stop herself from arguing that equality of the sexes was not *garbage*, but decided to let these baby steps for Maximilian play out.

"But I wasn't exactly right about that."

An odd way to admit that he was wrong, Genevieve had to admit.

Finished with what he had to say, Maximilian simply turned on his heel and left.

"That's the closest I've ever heard him come to admitting that he was wrong," Knox said to her and she heard the amazement in his voice.

Genevieve looked after her towering father-in-law. "Your father is a very odd man."

Her husband laughed in that hearty way she had come to love. "I can't really argue with that."

"Happy anniversary." Genevieve surprised him with a plate of homemade cookies when they arrived back at their cabin.

"Did you make these?" He took a bite of one of

the cookies which was chock-full of white chocolate chips—his favorite.

"I stopped by mom's yesterday and baked them. I don't bake for just anyone." She smiled. "Okay—let me rephrase that. I've never baked for *anyone* before. I hope you like them."

He leaned over and kissed her on the lips. "They're delicious."

"I'm glad." She smiled at him. "And that's not your only surprise."

Genevieve put her anniversary wildflowers in a small vase by the sink and then hooked a leash onto Silver's collar. Knox grabbed two more cookies before he followed her out back.

"Watch this."

His wife proceeded to take Silver through some basic training sequences, asking him to heel, sit and stay. The puppy performed on command.

"Did you see that?" she asked excitedly. "He's so smart!"

"When did you have time to do this?"

"I worked with him a little here and there." She leaned down and took the leash off and gave Silver a big rub on his head. "Didn't I, handsome?"

Silver pranced around her legs, wagging his tail and barking loudly. It never failed to amaze him how talented his wife was. If a man didn't feel confident in himself, a woman like Genevieve could be too intimidating for him.

"Thank you." He wrapped his arms around her shoulders and kissed her again.

"You're welcome."

"We should do something for our anniversary. Don't you think?"

"What did you have in mind?"

"I'm up for suggestions."

They all went inside and Genevieve curled up next to him on the couch in a way he enjoyed. Silver, who was growing like a weed, sprawled out on the other end of the couch.

"How about we go to the Ace in the Hole?" she suggested.

"Heck no."

"Why not?"

"Because it's my anniversary and I don't want to share my wife with a bunch of sweaty, dirty, drunk cowpokes, that's why."

Genevieve wrinkled her nose at him. "Fine."

"Don't sound so disappointed."

"I like the Ace in the Hole."

Knox ran his fingers through his wife's hair, loving how silky it felt in his fingers. "How about we go camping? We could find a romantic spot to pitch a tent in the Flathead National Forest."

Genevieve spun around so she was facing him more fully. "I love that idea! We could cook by campfire…"

"Sleep under the stars…"

She wiggled her eyebrows at him suggestively. "Make love in a sleeping bag."

He put his hand on her face, tipping her head up gently so he could kiss her again. Those lips, so soft and willing, made him want to forget camping and just move into the bedroom. But this was a special night— an anniversary night—and they both seemed to want to celebrate it.

"Have I told you lately how much I love spending time with you?" he asked.

It was rare to see her blush and he felt pleased that he had managed to pull that feminine side of Genevieve out into the open.

"I love spending time with you too, Knox."

He gave her another quick kiss before he got up. "I'll throw the camping gear in the truck if you want to grab some supplies in here."

She nodded. "We'll probably have to stop by the general store on the way out of town."

"Good idea," he agreed before he went out the front door to prep for their impromptu overnight anniversary camping trip.

Genevieve made quick work of packing some essentials for them. She had camped all of her life, so it was second nature to gather up things that they would need. In the bathroom, she threw some toiletries they could share into a bag. When she was rummaging for a small bottle of mouthwash under the sink, she noticed a box of tampons, unopened, in the back corner. For some reason, that unopened box struck her as odd. Sitting on the side of the tub, Genevieve looked at the calendar on her phone and tried to remember when she had her last period. She had been married to Knox for a month today and she hadn't had a period. This meant that her last period was *before* the wedding.

"Oh." She stared at the calendar on her phone. "No."

She wasn't irregular. Never had been. And she and Knox had not always been careful during some of their more adventurous, passionate moments. The roll in the hay was just one of many careless moments they had shared.

Genevieve dropped her head into her hands and sat on the edge of that tub for several minutes. It was a biological fact that she could be pregnant. She lifted up her head and stared at the wall. If she were pregnant, what in the world would she say to Knox? No promises had been made other than the promise of a quickie divorce. Yes, Knox had said he wanted to be a father, but not *this* way. And this wasn't how she wanted to become a mother either. She wanted much better for herself and any child she brought into the world.

"Gen?" Knox knocked on the door. "You okay in there?"

She cleared her throat. "Yes! I'll be out in just a minute."

Genevieve stood up and looked at her reflection in the mirror. In a whisper, she told herself, "Remain calm and carry on."

She put a smile on her face and swung the door open.

"Ready?" Knox was waiting for her at the front door.

"Let me just grab something in the bedroom and I'll be ready to go." She ran into the bedroom, opened the top drawer of the nightstand, took a handful of condoms out and stuffed them into her overnight bag.

"Okay. I've got a change of clothes for both of us, supplies for Silver and for us. We definitely need to stop by the general store and get some food for dinner and breakfast."

They made a quick stop at Crawford's General Store for food and some other staples before they headed out of town toward Kalispell.

"The last time we were on this road, we were heading toward our wedding," Genevieve reminisced.

"It seems like a lifetime ago."

She looked out the window, her hand on her stomach. "It was a lifetime ago."

As much as she tried to put the missed period out of her mind, she couldn't. It seemed unfair not to tell Knox what was going on, but then again, she could get him upset for absolutely no reason. He was so excited about their anniversary, as was she—why ruin it for them both? After the wedding reception tomorrow she would find a way to get her hands on a pregnancy test. Of course, the last thing she was going to do was buy a pregnancy test in Rust Creek Falls. The whole town would know she missed her period before she even had a chance to get the pregnancy test out of the box.

"Are you okay?" Knox looked over at her.

"Yes," she said with a small smile. "I'm just a little tired, I suppose."

He reached for her hand. "We'll go to bed early tonight. Tomorrow is a big day."

"I know. My mom has been driving me nuts!"

Knox found them the perfect place to make camp. Flathead National Forest was right outside of Kalispell and it felt fitting that they should return to the place where they had been wed. For Genevieve, every moment of the marriage had been filled with so many mixed emotions. She was certain now that she was deeply in love with her husband—and there was a part of her that sincerely felt that Knox returned her feelings. But he had said that he loved her only once, when they were making love. Any other time he mentioned the word *love*, it was framed more in friendship than romance. It had always been push me/pull me with Knox. He would celebrate their one-month anniversary today and then bring up her moving to California tomorrow.

Perhaps it was time that she confronted him. Was he just enjoying the ride while it lasted—enjoying their physical chemistry and friendship—while not caring that it would end? Or did he, like her, want something more?

"Come here." Knox opened his arms to her. They had just finished cleaning up after their meal and the campfire was dying down.

Genevieve sat between his legs, careful to keep a hold of Silver's leash, and let Knox wrap her up in his arms.

"I've never had a friend like you, Gen."

She cringed at the word *friend*. Yes, she wanted to be Knox's friend—of course she did. But was that all she really was for him? A friend with benefits?

"I'm tired," she said with a sigh. "Would you mind if we went to bed?"

They doused the fire and went inside the tent. Silver curled up in a bed of blankets they created for him while they slipped inside a sleeping bag designed for two. She turned her back to Knox and let him put his arms around her as he liked to do. He started to kiss her neck but she couldn't concentrate on lovemaking. Her brain was too filled with worries about being pregnant.

"I'm sorry, Knox," she said in the dark. "I'm so tired."

He was quiet for a moment. This was the first time she had ever begged off lovemaking with him. Knox kissed her again, this time more platonically.

"You don't need to apologize," he told her. "I'm just happy we're here together, Gen."

"Me too."

She said the words but she wasn't so sure she meant them. She had been happy until she got the scare of her life. An unplanned pregnancy would be a disaster for them now. Knox would be tied to her for the rest of his life when all he'd ever really said out loud was that he wanted things to end in divorce when the time was right.

The whole marriage was a careless decision made by two impulsive people. They'd done something serious based on a frivolous wedding wager. And to make matters worse, they had involved their families, innocent bystanders who would be collateral damage. Genevieve couldn't stomach the idea of bringing an innocent baby into the bargain and she prayed over and over again for it not to be true until she finally fell into a fitful sleep.

Chapter 14

Genevieve drove herself to her parents' house ahead of the wedding reception. When she arrived at the farmhouse, she slowed down to admire the decorations. Her mom had outdone herself. The large oak trees lining the drive were decorated with lace and ribbon and flowers. The house was also decorated in that same white-and-silver theme, including the porch railing, which was wrapped with garlands of flowers.

"Oh, Mom." Genevieve sat in the truck with the engine off, just staring at the house. "I am so sorry."

Before she could get to the top of the porch stairs, her mom threw open the door and rushed out to greet her.

"What do you think?" Jane was aflutter. Her pretty blue eyes were shining and her fleshy cheeks were flushed pink. Her mom always died her hair at home, but for the party, she had gone into Kalispell for a new hairstyle and a professional coloring.

"Mom." She felt her eyes well up with tears—tears because she was touched by the work her family had put into this party on her behalf and because this whole party was based on a lie. "It's more beautiful than I could have ever imagined."

Her mom took Genevieve's face in her hands and kissed her on the cheek. "We love you so much, lady-bug. We just want you to be happy."

The moment she entered the house the sweet and spicy aroma of barbecue coming from the kitchen made her stomach growl. Her mom, dad and sisters had invited nearly the entire town and there would be food enough for people to take home leftovers. That was the Rust Creek Falls way.

"I'm going to change my clothes." Genevieve carried her dress over her arm as she went upstairs to her old bedroom.

"Take your time, sweetheart. This is your special day with Knox."

Knox. He had been texting her for the last hour and she hadn't responded. He had thought that they would come to the party together, but she had grabbed her dress and makeup and had come alone.

Genevieve peeked outside of her bedroom window, remembering how many times she had climbed out of that window when she was a kid. Watching her father setting up the long tables for the buffet-style service, Genevieve wondered why she was still causing her family so much heartache. Why hadn't she learned more from her childhood mistakes?

Her phone rang and it was Knox. "Hello?"

"Gen! Where are you?"

"I'm at Mom and Dad's."

There was a pause on the other end of the line. "I thought we'd go together."

"I know. But I wanted to get here early just in case Mom needed help."

Another pause.

"Okay," Knox said slowly as if he didn't fully believe her. "Are you sure everything's all right?"

It was strange. Knox knew her better than she realized. He had picked up on a change in her behavior even when she had tried to hide the fact that something was wrong. Now that it had occurred to her that she had missed a period, it was all she could think about.

"I'm good." It was a lie, but it was a necessity. More than anything, she did not want to ruin this day for their families. They deserved to have this day after what Knox and she had put them through needlessly and thoughtlessly.

"Okay." He was still speaking in that slow, unconvinced voice. "Then I'll see you later."

"Of course. It's our wedding reception."

Genevieve took her time getting ready. She left her hair long and loose, just like the day she married Knox. Her wedding dress had been dry-cleaned for this party and when she put it back on, all of the feelings she had when she had married Knox—fear, excitement and exhilaration—came flooding back. Once she was dressed, Genevieve lay down on top of the covers of her bed and hugged her pillows. She stayed there even when she heard guests beginning to arrive. She stayed there even when she knew that she should go down to greet the people who had come to celebrate her union to Knox Crawford.

A rapid banging on the wall next to the stairs let her know that her time sequestering herself in her bedroom was over. "Ladybug! Your husband is here."

With a heavy sigh, she pushed herself upright, swung her legs off the bed and walked slowly to her door. The moment she left this bedroom she was going to have to play a part—the part of the happy, carefree bride. She had done it before and she had played her part well. But her heart wasn't in it anymore. The fun—the thrill— was gone. And the only thing she had left now was regret and a pain in the pit of her stomach.

At the top of the stairs, Genevieve paused. At the bottom of the stairs, Knox awaited. Her heart, as it always did when she saw him, gave a little jump. He was dressed in a suit—not the ill-fitting suit in which he was married—but a dapper dark gray suit that fit his broad shoulders and long legs.

"Gen." He said her name with awe, with reverence, and it made her breath catch. He did have feelings for her. He must. He couldn't possibly look at her that way if he didn't feel something for her.

As she descended the stairs, their eyes remained locked. Guests milled past Knox, but they faded into the background the closer she came to her husband. Those dark, enigmatic eyes drank her in as she landed on the last step.

"You're wearing your wedding dress." His eyes swept down the full length of her.

"My mom wanted to see me in it."

"You look…" He paused with a shake of his head. "More beautiful now than the day I married you."

He held out his hand for her and she took it. How easily her hand slipped into his larger, stronger one. Hand in hand, they greeted their guests. It was a whirlwind of hugs and congratulations and well wishes for a long and happy marriage. Even though her mother specified "no gifts," there was a growing cache of prettily wrapped presents in the formal living room. They would all have to be returned.

"I need some fresh air." Genevieve felt hot all over her body and beads of sweat were rolling down the back of her neck.

Together, they went outside to the backyard where her father was holding an impromptu revival, preaching the word of God to anyone who would listen.

"Are you hungry?"

Oddly, she wasn't. She had been starving earlier but somewhere along the way, she had lost her appetite.

"I think I'll wait." Genevieve begged off the food. "But you go."

"I'm not leaving your side."

"It's okay, Knox. Truly. I just need to sit down and cool off."

It took some convincing, but she finally got Knox to head off to the food tables. Genevieve moved into the shadows and watched the townsfolk laughing and talking. Everyone seemed to be having a wonderful time. Even Maximilian who seemed to have difficulty enjoying life in general had cracked a smile or two.

"Hey, sis!" Finn popped up out of nowhere, making her jump. He sat down next to her and bumped her with his shoulder. She punched him on the arm in retaliation.

"Don't sneak up on me like that, Finn!"

"What are you doing over here moping in the dark? Isn't this your party?"

"I'm just taking a breather."

"Your mom throws a great party." Finn stretched out his long legs in front of him. "So many pretty girls."

"I've heard Viv is keeping you busy."

Finn laughed. His laugh was so similar to Knox's that she couldn't help but smile. "I've been dating a new girl every week. One gets off the carousel and another one gets on. I don't ever want this ride to stop."

"The point is for you to get married, Finn, not date for the rest of your life."

Finn stood up, distracted by another pretty girl. "Life's too short to settle down, sis."

Her brother-in-law disappeared into the crowd and then Knox appeared at her side. He handed her a plate. "I brought you some food just in case you changed your mind."

The man could be so thoughtful. Not wanting to give him a reason to be suspicious, Genevieve decided just to acquiesce and eat a bit. Once she got started eating the barbecue and potato salad and coleslaw, she couldn't stop until she was completely stuffed.

"Now that's the Genevieve I know." Knox was watching her clean her plate. "I was beginning to wonder where she went."

"She's still here."

Together they milled through the crowd and Knox reached out to grab ahold of her hand.

"I want to dance with you." He said it loud enough for her to hear over the din of the crowd. "Like we did the night we were married."

If she were honest with herself, she would admit

that she wanted to dance with Knox too. "Let me just go check on Mom. When I get back, I promise you we'll dance."

Knox held on to her fingers until the very last second as if he were afraid to let her go. She walked away, but glanced back over her shoulder to find him still watching her. Genevieve found her mom in the kitchen checking on her pies.

"Mom."

"Yes, ladybug?" Jane untied her apron and hung it on a hook on the wall. "Are you having the time of your life?"

"It's your best party yet." It was the truth, so Genevieve didn't hesitate to say it.

"Mom?"

"Yes, sweetheart?"

"Why is there a goat in the kitchen?"

In the corner of the kitchen, a baby pygmy goat, the color of ginger and cream, was curled up in one of her mother's good comforters.

Jane ran her hand gently over her hair to smooth it down. "Oh! Well, that's Old Gene and Melba's goat."

"Why do they have a goat?"

"I can't say that I know," her mother said with a quick shrug.

"You didn't think to ask why they brought a goat to a wedding reception?"

"No. I didn't want to be rude about it. Besides, I figure if they wanted to tell me why they had a goat they would tell me. Otherwise, I don't think it's any of my business really."

"Except that it's in your kitchen."

"You go tend to your husband and let me tend to the goat."

Her mom shooed her out of the kitchen and Genevieve decided to take her mom's advice. After all, this was her wedding reception. Why not push any thoughts of pregnancy out of her mind and focus on having some fun?

"Do you want to dance, cowboy?" Genevieve asked as she walked up to Knox and put her hand on his arm.

"Just don't tell my wife." Knox winked at her as he took her hand in his.

He led her onto the makeshift dance floor and, just like the first night, they danced as a married couple, Genevieve relaxed into his strong, capable arms and let herself get totally lost in the silky, dark depths of his soulful eyes.

The Lawrence family had organized one heck of a wedding reception. Knox had eaten his way through the buffet table, danced with his wife until they were both too tired for one more dance and he had laughed with friends and family for hours. It was one of the best nights he had had in recent memory. When he had watched Genevieve descend the stairs in her wedding dress, all thoughts had vanished from his mind and it felt as if he had been frozen in his spot. For him, she was the most beautiful woman. He loved her bright blue eyes, the way she threw her head back when she laughed and her sharp intelligence. Perhaps more than any other moment since he had married her on a bet, Knox realized that he loved Genevieve. He loved her as a friend. He loved her as a partner and a lover. He loved her as the woman he wanted to spend the rest of his life with.

The party was winding down and many of the guests had already left. Knox had been standing alone watching Genevieve talking with her sisters and holding one of her twin nephews in her arms.

"She's been good for you."

At the sound of his father's voice, Knox turned toward him. "I love her."

It was strange to admit it out loud to his father, the man who had begun this entire chain of events because of his bargain with Viv Shuster. Knox's plan to marry Genevieve had begun out of a desire to prove something to his father and in the end, it had taken on a life of its own. His feelings for Genevieve—his relationship with his wife—had absolutely nothing to do with his father and everything to do with falling in love. Now all he had to do was convince Genevieve that her life was here with him and not in California. She loved him—he could feel it. But did she love him enough to give their marriage an honest try? Did she love him enough to give up on her lifelong dream of making a life in California?

It was difficult to admit that he didn't know the answers to those questions. Every day that he left things unsaid between himself and Genevieve was a day closer to losing the woman he loved. It was time to propose real marriage to his wife. It was past time.

"Congratulations, son." Max held out his hand to him.

It was a moment that Knox never thought to have with his father. Yes, they loved each other. They were family. But the two of them had always butted heads, beginning when he was a teenager. Perhaps it would always be a complicated relationship, but his father's acceptance of his marriage to Genevieve went a long way to heal some old wounds.

"Thank you, Dad." Knox shook his father's hand. In truth, Max had brought him Genevieve and he needed to be grateful to him for that.

After his family took their leave, Knox ran into Collin Traub as the mayor was heading out of the front door.

"Hey, Collin, let me bend your ear for a minute."

The mayor paused just outside of the front door of the Lawrence home.

"I'd like to arrange to move Spartacus to the Ambling A," he told Collin. "As a surprise."

The mayor raised his eyebrows and the look on his face wasn't encouraging. "Genevieve isn't all that keen on surprises. I'm sure you know that."

"I'm aware." Knox felt his jaw tense. "But she lives at the Ambling A now and I want her to have access to her horse. It makes sense that Spartacus should be with us."

Collin gave a quick nod of his head. "I get that it makes sense, Knox. The question is, will it make sense to Genevieve."

Knox didn't like the fact that the mayor was debating this idea with him. There had been a long-standing family feud between the Crawford and the Traub families going back generations. But because the two families had marriages between them, the feud had been squashed. Despite the fact that most of the new generation couldn't remember what started the feud, perhaps there was some lingering animosity bubbling up in this conversation.

"This is a wedding gift from me to my wife," Knox said in a tone that brooked no argument. "I've got to find a trailer big enough to haul him and once I do, I'll be in touch with the details."

Gen joined them then, interrupting the conversation. "Collin, I just wanted to thank you so much for coming."

The mayor hugged Genevieve, gave Knox a little salute and then headed down the porch stairs. Genevieve had pulled her hair back into a ponytail and her cheeks were still flushed from all the dancing they had done.

"Did I interrupt something?" His wife had a keen eye.

Knox had a bad feeling in his gut that Collin was going to tell Genevieve about his plan to move Spartacus. The Traub and Lawrence families went way back and his loyalty would be to Genevieve.

"I was talking to Collin about moving Spartacus to the Ambling A," Knox told her, deciding maybe a total surprise wasn't the way to go. "As a wedding gift to you."

The expression on Genevieve's face changed. She stood stock still while she stared up at him, then came the unexpected flash of anger in her eyes. His wife spun on her heel, marched down the steps and then waved her hand for him to follow her. They walked along the driveway and away from the house. When they were far enough away from prying eyes and listening ears, Genevieve said, "Why would you *do* that? Why would you talk to Collin about my horse? *My* horse?"

"I wanted to do it for you," Knox said. "Why are you getting so upset, Gen?"

"Why am I so upset? Because Spartacus is off-limits, that's why. He's the only thing in this world that's truly mine. *I* make the decisions about his life. No one but me."

They stopped walking and he turned to face his wife. This wasn't at all how he expected their night to end. He was hoping to continue the celebration at home, take her to bed, make love to her and propose real marriage. A fight hadn't been in the plan.

"Okay, I get it. I wasn't trying to make you upset, Gen. I was just trying to surprise my wife."

"I don't like surprises." Her words echoed Collin's and it only served to irritate him.

"I know," Knox acknowledged. "But now that we're talking about it, it makes sense that Spartacus move to the Ambling A. We're just going to have to find a trailer big enough for a giant, is all."

Gen shook her head. "It doesn't make a bit of sense to move him."

Perhaps in his own way he was giving his wife a test. He knew how much she loved Spartacus and if she agreed to move him to the Ambling A, it would be a signal to him that she thought of his family's ranch as home.

"It doesn't make a bit of sense to move him," she reiterated.

"Ambling A is your home," he reminded her.

"For now," she snapped. "But for how much longer? Until Viv finds wives for the rest of your brothers? Why would I go through the trouble of moving him, upsetting his routine, only to have to move him again when this whole thing between us falls apart?"

Chapter 15

Knox was blindsided but maybe he shouldn't have been. Nothing between them had been solidified and that was his fault. Their relationship had been such a whirlwind, he hadn't been able to figure out his own feelings fast enough. But the fact that Gen didn't want to move her horse to the Ambling A spoke volumes. In her mind, the Ambling A wasn't her home. Now it was his job to convince her otherwise.

"Why do things between us have to fall apart, Gen?"

Hurt, pure hurt, entered her eyes. It was an emotion he'd never seen there before and hoped to never see again.

"That's a cruel thing to say, Knox." His wife crossed her arms tightly in front of her body. "Divorce was always in the cards for us. That was the deal, right?"

"Gen." He tried to reach for her hand but she turned

away from him. "What I'm trying to say to you—clumsily I admit—is that I—"

His wife interrupted him and pointed back at the house. "Look at what we've done, Knox! Just look at what we've done! We've involved the whole blasted town in this ridiculous lie!"

"I thought we were having a good time tonight, Gen. Was that part of the lie?"

"Of course we were having a good time. That's all you and I do. We do what feels good and damn the consequences! We're so…irresponsible. And selfish."

Suddenly, Knox felt in his gut that Genevieve was saying one thing but talking about something entirely different. There was something deeper going on and he was certain he didn't know what it was.

"Tell me what's going on, Genevieve. What's wrong?"

Her arms still crossed tightly in front of her body and her expression grim, Gen said, "I'm done with this game."

Knox's hands tightened reflexively into fists at his side. He wanted to grab her, hold her and stop her from leaving him. And she was leaving him—he could feel it in his gut. And yet, all he could ask was, "What do you mean?"

"I mean I'm not going home with you tonight."

"Gen, please."

"No." She shook her head. "I'm serious, Knox. I'm staying here tonight and I'm telling my mom everything—the whole truth. After all of this—" she nodded her head back toward the house "—she deserves the truth."

There was a long silence between them before he asked his next question. "And then what?"

"Then we get a divorce. Sooner or later, that was always going to happen. Now I want it to happen sooner rather than later."

The morning after the wedding reception, Genevieve awakened in her garage apartment with Oscar the cat sleeping half on her pillow and half on her face. For some reason, Knox speaking to Collin about moving Spartacus had been the proverbial straw that had broken the camel's back. Had she meant to end her marriage behind an oak tree on her parents' driveway? No. But it had happened and now she needed to go forward. She still had to confess to her mom and then she needed to find a pregnancy test ASAP so she could find out if this fake marriage was going to be with her for the rest of her life in the form of a child.

"I love you." She hugged the round fluffy feline tightly and kissed him on the head. Oscar, as he always did, began to purr loudly for her.

Genevieve slowly extracted herself from beneath the weight of the cat and sat upright on the edge of the bed. Her mom was well aware that she hadn't gone home with Knox after the party, but she didn't know why. Now it was time for Genevieve to pay the piper. Knox had been calling and texting regularly; she had ignored all of his attempts to talk. What was there to say? At this point, she wasn't so sure of her own feelings anymore and she certainly wasn't convinced of his. Either way, the two of them had made a royal mess of things.

Genevieve pulled her hair back into a quick ponytail, threw on some old jeans and a T-shirt and walked barefoot down the stairs, across the yard and up to the front door. Inside the house, the remnants of the party lingered—half-inflated balloons hanging from the stair-well railing and the large pile of unsolicited gifts in the formal living room that she was going to have to re-turn. From the kitchen, she could hear her mother hum-ming. As it always did, the thought of her mother in that cheerful yellow kitchen gave her a sense of security, of well-being—even when there wasn't any reason to feel those things. Her mother had always been her comfort.

"Good morning." Genevieve walked into the kitchen and was greeted by the scent of coffee brewing.

Jane turned toward the sound of her voice and there was such kindness and care in her mother's eyes that Genevieve had to stop herself from immediately burst-ing into tears.

"You don't look like you had a good night, ladybug." Jane enveloped her in a hug. "Sit down and I'll get you a cup of coffee."

Genevieve rested her head in her hands, dreading the conversation to come. Her poor mother had been put through the ringer while Genevieve was in high school. This table had seen more than its fair share of "what has Genevieve gotten into now" conversations. Now that she was in her early thirties, it was getting through her thick skull that she needed to grow up and start taking her adult responsibilities more seriously. Not everything in life needed to be approached like a death-defying, adrenaline-producing adventure. And she didn't have to win every time.

Jane set the cup of coffee down in front of her and then joined her at the table. Her mother's cool hand felt good on her arm. She lifted up her head out of her hands and looked into her mother's kind eyes.

"What's wrong, ladybug? Why didn't you go home with your husband last night?"

"Does Dad know I'm here?"

"No." Jane shook her head. "He left before dawn to go to that farm supply auction. He won't be back until late this evening."

That was a lucky break. She knew that everyone in town would soon know that her marriage to Knox was over, but it was going to be particularly difficult to tell her father. The man was beside himself with happiness that she was finally married to someone he considered to be a "good, solid, God-fearing man." For all she knew, that grandchild he had always wanted from her might very well be on the way. Then she would be a single, divorced mother.

"I've really screwed up, Mom."

"Nothing is so bad that it can't be fixed."

Genevieve wrapped her hands around the warm coffee cup, her eyes focused on a scratch on the table.

"Holding it in only makes it worse," her mother said in a gentle tone. "Light is the best disinfectant. Speak it and heal it, sweetheart."

"I don't even know where to begin." She sighed. "I never meant to hurt anybody, especially you."

"Genevieve." Her mother said her name in a way that made her lift her eyes up. "You are my daughter, my firstborn. You have given me a run for my money, that is the God's honest truth. But I love you more than any person has a right to love another. No matter what, that is never going to change."

Genevieve took in a deep, calming breath and then let it out very slowly. "My marriage to Knox isn't real."

Saying those words aloud to her mother—speaking

that truth—hurt. For the first time, tears of sadness and anguish formed in her eyes and she didn't try to stop them. She had wanted to cry over Knox for weeks, but she hadn't allowed herself to acknowledge—truly acknowledge—that this relationship wasn't going to work out for her. If he loved her, he would have told her.

Jane stared at her, stunned. Of all the things her mother might have imagined to be wrong, this obviously wasn't on her radar. Her mother stood up, grabbed a box of tissues and brought them over to the table. She pulled a couple of tissues free from the box and handed them to her.

Genevieve wiped the tears from her face before she blew her nose. The tissues crumpled up into a ball on the table as she waited for the questions from her mother that were bound to come.

"Your marriage isn't real?" Jane's words came out very slowly. "What do you mean? You aren't really married to Knox?"

"No." She frowned. "I'm really married."

"Then, I don't understand, Genevieve. You need to spell this out for me."

Once she started talking, recounting the whole story, from the initial wager to the elopement to the layers of lies they had told in order to make the whole plan work, she couldn't seem to stop. She told her mother everything, including that they had consummated the marriage and that she feared she was pregnant. It took her a long while to finish confessing, and when she did, her mom didn't say a word. She just sat at the table, her round face unsmiling, her finger tapping on the tabletop while she mulled over what her daughter had just told her.

"Oh, Genevieve," Jane finally said with deep sadness laced in her voice. "When are you ever going to learn to look before you leap?"

"Hopefully I've learned that lesson now. I'm so sorry, Mom. I'm sorry I hurt you. I'm sorry I had you go through all of this planning and expense for the wedding reception."

"Don't you be sorry for a thing. I'm not. I had the time of my life and don't have a bit of regret."

"But the money—"

"Ladybug, when you were born, your father and I started a college fund and a wedding fund. I spent your wedding fund to throw this party."

"Well, at least I don't have to feel guilty about the money anymore."

"No. And there's no sense feeling guilty about anything. It's a complete waste of energy." Her mother reached for her hand and squeezed it. "And do you know what else I think? I think your husband is crazy about you. I think he's head over heels for you, I really do. Everyone sees it. Everyone. Even your father sees it and that man is blind as a bat when it comes to just about everything. As a matter of fact, even Maximilian Crawford sees it. He told me so himself last night. So maybe this marriage isn't as fake as you believe."

"I don't see it," Genevieve muttered. "He's never said it to me."

With the exception of that one time in the loft when they were making love. In her mind, coming as it did in a moment of passion, that didn't count.

"Some men are just slow to come to their senses," Jane said. "Your father loved me for months before it occurred to him to speak the words aloud. I remember he actually thought he told me that he loved me and he hadn't. He'd thought it in his mind and didn't bother to get the words out of his mouth. If Knox loves you, he'll break down the door looking for you and then you'll know."

"Maybe. But that's not my biggest problem right now. A baby wasn't part of our bargain, Mom."

"Life is what happens when you're busy making other plans, ladybug. I think it's time we find out if there's even anything to worry about."

"I'm not going to buy a pregnancy test at the general store."

"Oh, no," Jane agreed. "Absolutely not."

Her mother got up and walked over to the phone on the wall and dialed a number. "Darling, do you happen to have any pregnancy tests in your medicine cabinet?"

Of course. As often as her sisters got pregnant, no doubt they had a stockpile of pregnancy tests in their bathrooms.

"Thank you, love," Jane said into the phone. "We'll see you in a minute."

Her mother hung up the phone.

"There. Problem solved. Ella is coming over and we'll have our answer right quick. Better to know than sit around worrying and wondering."

As usual, her mom was right. If she *was* pregnant, she needed to know. And if she did have a Crawford bun in the oven, then that was going to take the next conversation she had with her husband in a whole different direction. In fact, it was going to take her whole *life* in a different direction.

* * *

Knox took his hammer and smashed into the hinge, banging it again and again even though it didn't budge.

"Are you trying to fix that or break it more, Knox?" Hunter was holding the gate up so he could try to unseat the rusted hinge.

Knox gave the stuck hinge a few more hard whacks before he cursed and threw his hammer on the ground. Frustrated, he kicked the gate several times. With a concerned look on his face, Hunter let go of the gate and focused his attention on Knox.

"What's going on? You've been off all day."

If it had been any other brother than Hunter asking, Knox would have made an excuse, any excuse, just to end the conversation. But Hunter was different. He had been married, and he had a daughter for whom he was responsible. It made Hunter more grounded and Knox trusted his counsel.

Knox wiped the sweat off his brow with his sleeve. "Genevieve left me."

He hadn't spoken those words aloud. It felt like a punch in the gut to give them a voice.

Hunter stared at him for a second or two and then waved his hand with a smile. "If that's a joke, brother, it ain't funny."

"It's not a joke. She left me. She didn't come home with me last night. As far as I know, she's planning on moving back into that garage apartment at her parents' house."

Now he had Hunter's full attention.

"I don't understand," Hunter said. "The party…"

Knox kicked the gate again. "It was a lie. All of it was a damn lie."

Perhaps he shouldn't have begun to tell Hunter the

truth, but once he told him one part of the problem with Genevieve, his brother wasn't satisfied until he knew the whole truth of the matter. When he was done explaining his elopement scheme, the disbelieving, disappointed look on his brother's face spoke volumes.

"You and Dad are cut from the same bolt of cloth, Knox," Hunter said with a shake of his head. "The same darn bolt of cloth."

Knox hated to hear that, yet there was a ring of truth in his brother's words. Both he and his father would go to any lengths to get their way, to be in control—to be right.

"You need to go and fight for her," Hunter said plainly. "If you love her, then don't let her go."

"I tried to tell her how I felt last night."

"You tried," his brother scoffed. "Please."

"I did," Knox said. "Now she won't answer my calls. My texts."

"I know you can't possibly be as dense as you're sounding right now, Knox. A woman wants her man to fight for her. Genevieve is begging for you to step up and be a man and *claim* her, to prove to her that this marriage might have started out as a wager but it ended up as the real deal. Instead of going over there and fighting for her, you're standing here and kicking a fence! That woman is the best darn thing that has ever happened to you. We all see it. And you're a better man for having married her, no matter the circumstances. If you let her go, then all I can say is that I love you but you're not the man that I believed you were."

Genevieve sat on the side of her garage apartment bed and stared at the pregnancy test. Never in her life had she experienced such mixed emotions. One minute she was happy and the next she was incredibly sad, like a giant grandfather clock pendulum swinging back and forth. With a heavy sigh, she slid the pregnancy test back into the box, walked into the bathroom and put it on the edge of the sink. All she wanted to do with the rest of her day was hide under her covers. The confession to her mother and then her sister had exhausted her. It was going to take a full day of sleeping just to prepare her for the next round—dealing with her father and then with Knox.

With a heavy heart, Genevieve climbed under the covers and rested her head on the pillow next to Oscar, who had easily slept right through her traumatic morning. Genevieve rubbed Oscar's fat belly, causing the cat to roll on his back and purr loudly. Why couldn't her life be a simple as Oscar's life? She pulled the covers over her head to block out the light and wished for sleep. She had deliberately turned off her phone because she didn't want to be disturbed. For now, she wanted her life and everyone in it to just go away.

Sleep had thankfully come and Genevieve had no idea how long she had slept when a loud knock on the door jolted her awake.

"Go away!" she grumbled, turning over and burying her head back under the covers.

"Gen!" Knox's strong, determined voice penetrated the door. "Open up, please. We need to talk."

"Go away!" she yelled. She wasn't ready to speak to him.

When he didn't respond, didn't fight her on it, it only confirmed her suspicions that her feelings for Knox were one-sided. It really had been just a game to that Crawford cowboy.

A sound like a key in the door made her pop her head out from underneath the covers. The door opened and suddenly Knox, as handsome and put together as always, was standing inside of her sanctuary.

"Mom gave you a key."

Knox shut the door behind him. "She did."

"I'm not in the mood to talk to you." Genevieve pushed her mussed hair out of her eyes.

Her husband sat on the edge of the bed, his eyes steady, his face more somber than she had ever seen.

"You don't have to talk if you don't want to, Genevieve. I just need you to hear me out. I just need you to listen."

Chapter 16

Knox had never truly been in love before. Perhaps that was why he hadn't been able to pinpoint the exact moment he had fallen in love with Genevieve. But he certainly knew it when she walked away from him. That moment was burned into his brain and his heart. The night of the wedding reception, he had returned home to Silver and an empty bed. Yes, he had known that Genevieve had quickly become an integral part of his life, but it wasn't until she was no longer filling the cabin with her laughter and her sweet smile that he realized how important she had become to the very fabric of his happiness. He had never been so happy as he was when he opened the door to the garage apartment to find a groggy, grumpy Genevieve scowling at him. Even a disgruntled Gen was better than no Gen at all.

"This is all my fault," he said for openers.

Gen looked up at him with narrowed eyes. "You know, I've been thinking about that a lot. And, you're absolutely right. This *is* all your fault. If you hadn't bet me to marry you, we wouldn't be in this mess."

"I know." Knox turned his body so he was able to look her in the eye. "But if I hadn't convinced you to elope with me, would we have ever fallen in love?"

His wife's eyes widened for a moment before they narrowed. "Who says we did?"

Knox reached for her hand; he was encouraged that she didn't pull her hand away from him.

"You know we did, Gen." He looked at her with an open and steady gaze. He wanted her to see what was inside of his heart. "Do you remember when I told you that I wasn't afraid of anything?"

His wife nodded.

"That wasn't true. I am afraid of something. I'm afraid of losing the best thing that's ever happened to me. I'm afraid of losing you."

A single tear slipped onto her cheek and the sight of that tear crushed him. He reached out and wiped it away with his thumb. "I'm so sorry I didn't tell you this before, Gen. I love you. I *love* you. With everything that I am, and with everything I have, I love you. I believe I've loved you from the first moment I saw your picture on your website."

"Why didn't you tell me?" she asked with an emotional crack in her voice.

He couldn't wait a moment longer—he gathered his wife up in his arms and hugged her so tightly. "I don't know. I'm a man. I'm an idiot. I'm a slow learner."

Through her freshly shed tears, Genevieve laughed. "You are all of those things."

He leaned back so he could see her face. "Yes. I am all of those things. But I'm also the man who loves you, Genevieve. I'm the man who wants to spend the rest of his life with you."

Knox kissed his wife, tasting the salt from her tears on his lips. He kissed her tears from her cheeks and then took both of her hands in his.

"Tell me that you love me."

"I love you, Knox."

Knox noticed the engagement ring made of hay he had given her sitting on the nightstand. He reached for it and held it out for her to see. "I want you to be my wife, Genevieve."

With a little laugh she took the ring and held it gently in her hand, as if it were made of precious metal. "I am your wife, Knox."

"Then promise to be my wife for the rest of my life, Gen. Promise me."

"I promise you."

"Thank God." Knox pulled her back into his arms.

During the hug, Knox felt Genevieve rub her face on his shoulder. He sat back with a suspicious smile. "Did you just dry your face on my shirt?"

His wife grinned at him guiltily. "Maybe just a little."

Knox stood up and looked around for a box of tissues. Genevieve pointed to the bathroom. "Toilet paper in there."

He walked over to the bathroom and when he was bending over to pull some toilet paper off the roll, something caught his attention on the bathroom sink. Squares of toilet paper crumpled in his hand, he reached out to pick up the pregnancy test. He stared at the box and then, with legs that didn't seem to want to move, he looked in the direction of his wife.

* * *

Genevieve was still reeling from the sudden appearance of Knox in her garage apartment and his profession of love. It took a minute for it to register that he was in the bathroom with the pregnancy test. Careful not to disturb Oscar, who had managed to keep on sleeping, Genevieve got out of bed. She was heading toward the bathroom when Knox emerged holding the box.

"Are you?" he asked quietly.

Feeling sadder than she could express in words, she shook her head. Genevieve took the box from his hand and threw it in the trash. When she turned around, she turned into Knox's waiting arms.

"Are you okay?"

She buried her head into his chest and nodded. He kissed the top of her head so sweetly that it almost made her start crying all over again. It was the strangest feeling. She was actually mourning a baby that never was. When she'd seen that the pregnancy test was negative, it had driven home how much she had begun to like the idea of being a mom. No, it wouldn't have been easy to be a single mother, and no, she wouldn't have wanted to trap Knox with an unplanned pregnancy. But in the end, she had *wanted* to be pregnant and now she knew she wasn't.

"Why didn't you tell me?" He rested his chin on her head.

"I didn't know for sure." She put her hand over his heart. "I missed my period but I wasn't sure."

He handed her the balled-up toilet paper so she could blow her nose and then they sat down on the end of the bed together.

"Are you sad that you aren't pregnant? Is that it?" He held her hands in his.

"Actually," she admitted, "I am sad. I don't even know why."

Knox put his arm tightly around her. "Maybe because you're ready to be a mom now."

"Are you ready to be a dad?"

Her husband looked down at her and met her eyes. "With you? Absolutely."

"A woman's fertility drops off a cliff after thirty-five," she told him after she blew her nose again. "That's only a couple of years away."

Knox got off the bed, kneeled down on one knee before her, and held her hands in his. "Why don't we go on a honeymoon, Genevieve? I'll take you anywhere in the world you want to go."

"Anywhere?"

"Anywhere."

The one place in the whole entire world that popped into her mind was the one place she had always wanted to go.

"Paris," she told him. "I want to go to Paris."

"Paris?"

She nodded.

"A cowgirl in Paris? I didn't expect that."

"You said that you would take me anywhere in the world I wanted to go."

"I did. And I meant it." Knox stood up and coaxed her up as well. "If you want to go to Paris for our honeymoon, then that's where we'll go."

Genevieve had never felt more safe or loved as she did when she was being held in Knox's arms. Knox kissed her again—a kiss filled with the promise of so much love to come.

"Maybe we could try for a baby on our honeymoon?"

"My beautiful wife, I'll give you as many babies as you want." Knox pulled her into his body. "And we don't have to wait until Paris. We can start trying for that baby right now."

As good as his word, Knox made all the arrangements for their honeymoon. The first leg of the trip was made by private jet to Paris and they couldn't resist making love over the Atlantic Ocean. After a quick shower, Genevieve slipped back into bed while Knox went to talk to the stewardess about a late-night snack.

"How does chocolate and champagne sound?" Knox opened the door carrying a silver tray.

"Amazing." She smiled at him warmly. "I would say we worked up an appetite."

Knox put the tray on the small table just inside of the bedroom door.

"Would you grab my robe out of the suitcase?" Genevieve climbed out of bed, her arms wrapped around her body. "I'm cold for some reason."

Her husband unzipped the suitcase while she sat at the table and took a bite out of juicy, chocolate-covered strawberry.

"Hmm. This is delicious."

Knox joined her at the table, kissed some strawberry juice from her chin and handed her the robe.

"Look what Xander put in our suitcase." Knox put the old Abernathy diary on the table.

Genevieve slipped her arms into the robe quickly so she could get her hands on the antique diary.

"Why would he do that?" She sat down, holding on to the diary as if it were precious.

"Here's the note he put with it."

Gen took the note and read it. According to Xander, the romantic passages in the diary acted as an aphrodisiac.

With a laugh, she said, "Xander thinks that we help in the lovemaking department."

"Do we?" Knox asked teasingly.

"Not hardly," she reassured him, even though she knew he was teasing. Genevieve carefully ran her fingers over the yellowed and tattered pages of the diary. Holding this diary was like reaching back into the past and touching someone's heart. These were someone's private thoughts—their most heartfelt desires.

"Find anything interesting?" Knox put a glass of champagne on the table near her.

"Yes! As a matter of fact." Genevieve looked up from the pages. "It says here that W's girlfriend was pregnant! That's a huge clue if I've ever seen one, don't you think?"

Knox drained his glass, stood up and took her hand. "I think that I'd rather worry about getting you pregnant."

With a happy laugh, Genevieve abandoned the diary and let her husband take her back to bed.

Knox was a very enthusiastic partner in their attempt to conceive. Genevieve didn't care if they conceived in a private jet or a hotel in Paris or under the stars in a national park. All she cared about was having a healthy baby with the man she loved.

"Have you ever seen anything so beautiful?" Genevieve was sitting on a window seat in their hotel room.

Knox had found them the perfect room with a view of the Eiffel Tower. At night, with the Eiffel Tower lit brightly, Genevieve would sit in the window seat and gaze at that amazing iconic structure.

Her husband sat behind her and pulled her back so she was leaning against his chest. "As a matter of fact, I have seen something that beautiful."

She hugged his arms into her body, so happy to be with this man in the most romantic city in the world.

"I think we should come back here every year," Genevieve mused aloud. "Every year on our anniversary."

"Whatever you want, my love."

She had everything she wanted. It was everything she hadn't even known that she wanted. Genevieve had been so focused on her career that she hadn't considered how fulfilling finding true love with a man could be. Yes, she would always have her career—that was a given—but now she had so much more. She had this man who adored her—and hopefully, someday very soon, she would have a child—a child created from so much love.

Genevieve snuggled more deeply into Knox's arms, her eyes drinking in the lights from the Eiffel Tower. "You've made my dream come true."

"It's only fair that I return the favor."

Knox moved to stand up and she shifted her weight toward the window, wanting to burn the image of the Paris skyline in her brain. Her husband returned and put a small box on the window seat next to her.

"What is this?" She looked up at him in surprise.

"I know you don't like surprises." He smiled at her. "But maybe you'll let me have just this one."

"You didn't have to get me anything, Knox. You've already given me so much."

Carefully, Genevieve unwrapped the paper from the box. Her heart was pounding in the most ridiculous way when she opened the lid. Inside of the box, nestled in black velvet, was a sparkling diamond ring.

"Oh, Knox. It's beautiful."

Her husband took the ring out of the box, bent down on one knee with the lights from the Eiffel Tower in the background.

"Genevieve Lawrence Crawford, would you do me the honor of being my wife?"

She took his handsome face in her hands and kissed him. "Yes, Knox. It would be my honor to continue to be your wife."

Knox slipped the ring onto her finger and they stood up together to embrace. "I wanted you to have a real proposal and a real engagement ring. You deserve that."

"I never expected to have a Paris proposal." She twisted her hand back and forth to make her ring sparkle.

"Now you have."

In their elegant hotel room in the heart of Paris, they danced together. Knox played his country music playlist so they could have a touch of home with them.

"Do you think they've ever had anyone dance the Texas Two-Step in this room?" Knox moved her across the carpet.

She laughed the laugh of a woman who was happy and in love. "I don't think so, cowboy."

They danced until they were both tired and thirsty

for more champagne. Knox poured her a glass and they toasted each other. Once her glass was empty, her husband went back to kissing her. He couldn't seem to get enough of her lips and she had no complaints. Knox slipped his hands beneath her blouse, his hands so warm on her skin. He kissed her neck, his breath sending chills of anticipation down her spine. She knew where this was leading. Knox wanted her again and she wanted him. It didn't take him much effort to undress her, and soon she was standing in the middle of their hotel room wearing nothing but her new engagement ring.

He lifted her into his arms and carried her to the bed, kissing her all along the way. She lay back in a mountain of soft overstuffed pillows, feeling languid and decadent while Knox disrobed. It was her pleasure to watch her husband, so lean and muscular, in the sparse light.

"You are so handsome." She held out her arms to him.

The moment his hot skin pressed against hers, she moaned with delight. His biceps tightened as he wrapped her up so snuggly into his arms. With his lips on her neck, his hands on her body, it was easy to lose herself in the feeling of this man. Knox pressed her back into the mattress, the weight of his body such an odd relief. She wanted to be joined with him, no waiting, no fanfare—just two bodies becoming one.

He captured her face in his hands. "I love you, Genevieve."

"Oh, Knox," she gasped. "I love you."

Their bodies joined so tightly, their breath mingled, their hands clasped together, it was as if they were making love for the very first time. Every movement, every touch, every whisper of love took Genevieve to a whole new level of joy. Knox took them on a delicious ride, so slow, so sweet, until they were both crying out each other's names. Trying to catch her breath, Genevieve curled her body into her husband's, her head resting atop his rapidly beating heart. They looked at each other and began to laugh at their own incredible luck to have found each other.

"We are so very good at that." She kissed his chest affectionately.

"Yes. We are." Knox rubbed his hand over her arm, his eyes closed contentedly. "I might have just given you a child, Mrs. Crawford."

"Hmmm," she murmured sleepily. "That would be the most wonderful souvenir."

They fell asleep in each other's arms then, both of them spent from a night of eating and dancing and lovemaking. In the early morning light, Knox awakened her with butterfly kisses on her neck. After they made love, they ordered room service and began to plan their day of sightseeing.

"When we get back to Rust Creek Falls, we're going to have to move the rest of my things from the garage apartment to the cabin."

Barefoot and shirtless, Knox joined her on the window seat wearing faded jeans. Her husband had to be the sexiest cowboy to ever visit France.

"And you need to move Spartacus to the Ambling A," he reminded her as he pulled her pajama top down her arm so he could kiss her shoulder.

"Yes." She admired his persistence. For him, if her horse was at the Ambling A, that meant she was officially at the Ambling A to stay. "I will move Spartacus. As soon as we get back."

"Good."

Sitting wrapped up in Knox Crawford's arms, Genevieve realized that for the first time she had managed to win big by losing a wager.

"What do you want to do today?" she asked her husband. "Paris awaits."

"First, I'm going to take you back to bed," Knox whispered lovingly in her ear.

"And then?"

"I'm going to keep you there for the rest of the day."

With a delighted laugh, Genevieve decided it was time to make another wager with her husband. "I bet you can't get me pregnant before we leave Paris."

Always up for a friendly wager, Knox picked her up in his arms and carried her back to bed. "Oh, my lovely wife, I'll just bet you I can."

* * * * *

Teri Wilson is a *Publishers Weekly* bestselling author of romance and romantic comedy. Several of Teri's books have been adapted into Hallmark Channel Original Movies, most notably *Unleashing Mr. Darcy*. She is also a recipient of the prestigious RITA® Award for excellence in romance fiction for her novel *The Bachelor's Baby Surprise*. Teri has a major weakness for cute animals and pretty dresses, and she loves following the British royal family. Visit her at teriwilson.net.

Books by Teri Wilson

Harlequin Special Edition

Lovestruck, Vermont

Baby Lessons
Firehouse Christmas Baby
The Trouble with Picket Fences

Wilde Hearts

The Ballerina's Secret
How to Romance a Runaway Bride
The Bachelor's Baby Surprise
A Daddy by Christmas

Montana Mavericks: Six Brides for Six Brothers

The Maverick's Secret Baby

HQN

Unmasking Juliet
Unleashing Mr. Darcy

Visit the Author Profile page
at Harlequin.com for more titles.

THE MAVERICK'S
SECRET BABY

Teri Wilson

This book is dedicated to my writing friends from the Leakey, Texas, writing retreat. From the small-town shop with the meat cleaver door handles to the house on the river and the nighttime campfires, it was the perfect inspiration for writing a Montana romance with a cowboy hero. I love you all.

Chapter 1

Finn Crawford was living the dream.

Granted, his father, Maximilian, had gone a little crazy. The old man was intent on paying a matchmaker to marry off all six of his sons. If that wasn't nuts, Finn didn't know what was.

This wasn't the 1800s. It was modern-day Montana, and the Crawfords were...*comfortable*. If that sounded like something a rich man might say about his family, then it was probably because it was true. Finn's family was indeed wealthy, and Finn himself wasn't exactly terrible-looking. Quite the opposite, if the women who'd been ringing Viv Dalton—the matchmaker in question— were to be believed. More important, he was a decent guy. He tried, anyway.

Plus, Finn loved women. Women were typically much more open than men. Kinder and more authentic. He loved their softness and the way they committed so much to everything, whether it was caring for a stray puppy or running a business. Show him a woman who wore a deep red lipstick and her heart on her sleeve, and he was a goner. At the ripe old age of twenty-nine, Finn had already fallen in love more times than he could count.

So the very notion that he'd need any help in the marriage department would have been completely laughable, if he'd had any intention of tying the knot. Which he did *not*.

Why would he, when Viv Dalton was being paid to toss women in his direction? His dad had picked up the entire Crawford ranch—all six of his sons and over a thousand head of cattle—and moved them from Dallas to Rust Creek Falls, Montana, for this asinine pretend version of *The Bachelor*. The way Finn saw it, he'd be a fool not to enjoy the ride.

And enjoying it, he had been. A little too much, according to Viv.

"Finn, honestly. You've dated a different woman nearly every week for the past three months." The wedding planner eyed him from across her desk, which was piled high with bridal magazines and puffy white tulle. Sitting inside her wedding shop was like being in the middle of a cupcake.

"And they've all been lovely." Finn stretched his denim-clad legs out in front of him and crossed his cowboy boots at the ankle. "I have zero complaints."

Beside him, Maximilian sighed. "I have a lot of complaints. Specifically, a million of them where you're concerned, son."

Finn let the words roll right off him. After all, paying someone a million dollars to find wives for all six Crawford brothers hadn't been his genius idea. Maximilian had no one to blame but himself.

"Mr. Crawford, I assure you I'm doing my best to find Finn a bride." Viv tucked a wayward strand of blond hair behind her ear and folded her hands neatly on the surface of her desk. All business. "In fact, I believe I've set him up with every eligible woman in Rust Creek Falls."

"All of them?" Finn arched a brow. This town was even smaller than he'd thought it was. It would have taken him a lifetime to go through the entire dating pool back in Dallas. He should know—he'd tried.

Vivienne gave him a tight smile. "Every. Last. One."

"Okay, then I guess we're done here. You gave it your best shot." Finn stood. He'd miss the girlfriend-of-the-week club, but at least his father would be forced to accept the fact that he wasn't about to get engaged to any of the fine female residents of Rust Creek Falls.

Finn placed his Stetson on his head, set to go. "Thank you, ma'am."

"Sit back down, son." Maximilian didn't raise his voice, but his tone had an edge to it that Finn hadn't heard since the time he'd "borrowed" his father's truck to go mudding with his high school buddies back in tenth grade.

That little escapade had ended with Maximilian's luxury F-150 stuck in a ditch and Finn mucking out stalls every weekend for the rest of the school year.

Of course Finn was an adult now, not a stupid teenager. He made his own choices, certainly when it came to his love life. But he loved his dad, and since the Crawfords were all business partners in addition to family, he didn't want to rock the boat. Not over something as ridiculous as this.

"Sure thing, Dad." He lowered himself back into the frilly white chair with its frilly lace cushion.

Maximilian sat a little straighter and narrowed his gaze at Viv Dalton. "Are you forgetting what's at stake?"

She cleared her throat. "No, sir. I'm not."

A look of warning passed from Finn's father toward the wedding planner, and she gave him a tiny, almost imperceptible nod.

Finn's gut churned. What the hell was that about?

Damn it.

Knowing his dad, he'd gone and upped the ante behind Finn's back. When Maximilian ran into problems, he had a tendency to write a bigger check to make them go away.

Finn sighed. "I'm no longer sure entirely what's going on here, but I think it might be time for this little matchmaking project to end. Half of us are already married."

One by one, Finn's brothers Logan, Xander and Knox had become attached. It was uncanny, really. None of them had ended up with women of Viv's choosing, but they'd coupled up all the same. The way he saw it, his dad should be thrilled. The Crawford legacy would live on, Finn's bachelor status notwithstanding.

Maximilian shook his head. "Absolutely not. We need Viv's help now more than ever. It's not going to be easy to make matches for you, Hunter and Wilder. Hunter hasn't so much as looked at another woman since his wife died. Wilder is just…well, Wilder. And you can't seem to focus on one woman to save your life. If you're not careful, son, you're going to wind up old, alone and lonely. Just like me."

A bark of laugher escaped Finn before he could stop it.

"Please." He rolled his eyes. "You're far from lonely."

His father was rarely, if ever, alone. The business and living arrangements at their sprawling Ambling A Ranch pretty much assured that Maximilian saw each of his six sons on a daily basis. Plus, he was the biggest flirt Finn had ever set eyes on.

His dad had been single for decades. Finn's mother had abandoned the family when all six of her sons had been young. Maximilian might have remained single, but that hardly meant he lacked female companionship. His wallet alone was an aphrodisiac—plus he was something of a silver fox. Being in his sixties didn't stop him from dating nearly as much as Finn did.

Like father, like son.

"Point taken." Maximilian shrugged one shoulder. The corner of his mouth inched up into a half grin. "In any case, we're not here to talk about me. We're here to find you a bride."

"Your son might need to adjust his standards," Viv said, as if Finn wasn't sitting right there in the room. "The sheer number of women he's dated in the past three months should have guaranteed a good match."

"I guess you'll just have to dredge up more women. It seems like the only solution." Finn aimed his best sardonic smile directly at the wedding planner. She was really beginning to annoy him.

Adjust his standards? What the hell was that supposed to mean?

"I've been calling around town to see if I've overlooked any single ladies. This morning alone I've tried all the day-care centers, the veterinary clinic, the medical center and Maverick Manor." Viv tapped a polished fingernail on the pink notepad in front of her. "I thought maybe I could find a few datable, single women working in one of these locations whom I might not be acquainted with, some ladies living in one of the surrounding counties."

So now she was going to import women into town to date him? This whole ordeal was getting more absurd by the minute.

"Any luck?" Maximilian said.

"Not yet. But there's still one place left on my list—Strickland's Boarding House."

An ache took up residence in Finn's temples. "That ramshackle Victorian mansion by the fire station?"

Viv's lips pursed. "It's a town landmark."

"It's purple," Finn retorted.

"Lavender gray, technically." She smiled brightly at him. Jeez, this woman never gave up, did she? *Maybe because your father is offering her a million dollars to marry you off...possibly more.* "Just the sort of place a lovely single woman might choose to stay."

"That actually makes sense, son." Maximilian waved a hand toward Viv's list. "Go ahead and call over to the boarding house. We'll wait."

Finn was on the verge of pulling his Stetson low over his eyes and taking a nap. No one here seemed to care much what he thought, anyway. But once Viv dialed the number, she put her phone on speaker mode, which made napping pretty much impossible.

After two rings, an older man's voice rattled on the other end. "Howdy, Strickland's Boarding House."

Viv smiled. "Hello there, Gene. It's Vivienne Dalton calling."

"Hi there, darlin'. What can Melba and I do for you today?" he said.

In the background, Finn heard a woman—Melba, presumably—asking who'd called. When Old Gene supplied her with the information, she yelled out a greeting to Viv.

Viv and Old Gene exchanged a few more pleasantries. Gene asked about her husband, and she inquired as to the well-being of the baby pygmy goat Gene and Melba were caring for.

Of course there's a baby pygmy goat. Finn suppressed a grin. Maximilian, however, was less charmed. He cleared his throat, prompting Viv to get on with the matter at hand.

She took the hint. "Actually, Gene, I have a rather odd question for you. Do you happen to have any single young women staying at the boarding house who might be interested in a date with a handsome cowboy named Finn Crawford? I'm trying to help out a friend who's new in town."

"Funny you should mention single young women," Old Gene said. "We've had a darling young lady staying with us for a couple weeks now. A bit on the shy side, but sweet as pie."

Viv's eyes lit up. "Really? What's her name?"

"Avery."

Finn narrowed his gaze at Viv's phone.

Avery?

The only Avery he knew would never fit into a place like Rust Creek Falls. She couldn't possibly be talking about...

"Avery who?" Maximilian growled. "Please tell me you're not talking about the daughter of that rat bas—"

"Dad." Finn shook his head. "Chill out."

As usual, Maximilian had a harsh word at the ready for anyone related to his old nemesis, Oscar Ellington.

Finn was certain he didn't need to worry. It just wasn't possible. Oscar Ellington's daughter lived over a thousand miles away, in Texas. Plus, with her pencil skirts, red-soled stilettos and designer handbags, she wasn't exactly what Finn would describe as sweet. Considering they'd only shared one night together, she wasn't exactly *his*, either.

Still, what a night it had been.

"Gene! Stop talking right this minute!" Melba's voice boomed in the background again.

Viv frowned down at her phone. "Is everything okay over there?"

"Fine and dandy," Gene said.

Melba issued a simultaneous "No, it is not. Gene seems to have forgotten we shouldn't be giving out guests' private information."

"But she seems a little lonely," Old Gene countered while Melba continued to balk.

Again, Finn's memory snagged on a sweet, sultry night on an Oklahoma business trip and the most electric kiss he'd ever experienced. The power had gone down, bathing the city in darkness. But when his lips touched Avery Ellington's, they'd created enough sparks to light up the sky.

How long had it been?

Months.

"Excuse me." Finn leaned forward in his chair. He knew he was supposed to be a quiet observer at the moment, but he had to ask. "What exactly does this Avery woman look like?"

The glare Viv aimed his way shot daggers at him.

"Never mind," she said primly. "Sorry to bother you, Gene. We'll chat soon. Give that baby goat a kiss for me. Bye now."

She ended the call, and for a minute, Finn was seriously worried she might throw the phone at his head. "What does she *look like*? You can't be serious."

Maximilian shrugged. "It's a legitimate question."

Finn held up a hand. "Wait. That's not what—"

But Viv wasn't having it. She cut him off before he could explain. "There are far more important things than looks when it comes to a potential life partner."

Agreed.

Finn wasn't looking for a life partner, though. He doubted he'd be looking for one for another decade or so. Besides, he'd simply been trying to figure out if they'd been talking about the same Avery. All Old Gene needed to say was long, lush brown hair and dark, expressive eyes. Then he would have known.

Give it up. This is the opposite end of the country from Texas.

Or Oklahoma, for that matter.

Besides, Avery Ellington would stick out like a sore thumb in Rust Creek Falls. Surely he'd have run into her by now.

"You've found all of Viv's picks attractive so far, son. I'm sure this Avery girl wouldn't be any different," Maximilian said.

Finn let out a long exhale. How shallow could his father possibly make him sound? Maybe it was time to stop humoring the old man and dating every woman Viv Dalton threw at him.

"Thank you for everything, Ms. Dalton, but I think it's time to go." Finn stood and turned toward Maximilian. "Dad?"

His father didn't budge.

Fine. He could waste all the time and money he desired, but Finn was out of there. He tipped his hat to Viv and waded through all the pastel cupcake fluff toward the exit. All the while, his father's words echoed in his head.

I'm sure this Avery girl wouldn't be any different.

That's where he was wrong.

Finn had never met a woman quite like Avery Ellington.

Avery Ellington tucked her yoga mat under her arm and made her way down the curved staircase of the old Victorian house where she'd been living for the past few weeks.

Living? Ha. Hiding is more like it.

Her grip on the banister tightened. She didn't want to dwell on her reasons for tucking herself away at Strickland's Boarding House in Nowheresville, Montana. She had more pressing problems at the moment—like the fact that her Lululemons were practically bursting at the seams.

Even so, instead of heading to the back porch for her early-morning yoga session when she reached the foot of the stairs, she veered toward the kitchen to see what smelled so good in there.

Her appetite had never been so active back in Dallas. She hardly recognized herself. Before, breakfast consisted of a skinny triple latte consumed en route to a business meeting. Then again, her entire life had been different *before*. This new *after* was strange…different.

And scary as heck.

"Ah, good morning, dear." Melba wiped her hands on her apron and smiled as Avery entered the boarding house's huge kitchen. "Claire just left to take Bekkah to school, but she made a fresh batch of muffins earlier. Would you like some?"

Claire, the Stricklands' granddaughter, was the official cook for the boarding house. She and her family used to live with the Stricklands, but according to Old Gene, they'd recently moved out, leaving Melba a little out of sorts. Claire still came by regularly to cook, but Melba's empty nest meant Avery got more than her fair share of the older woman's attention.

Not that being doted on was a bad thing, necessarily. Truth be told, Avery was accustomed to it. She'd been doted on her entire life.

"Good morning. And thank you." Avery bit into a muffin and nodded toward her mat. "I'm about to do a little yoga out back. It's such a nice, crisp day."

God, who was she? She sounded like Gwyneth Paltrow on a spa weekend instead of the Avery Ellington she'd been since graduating with honors from the University of Texas and stepping up as the vice president of Ellington Meats.

You're still the same person. This is only temporary. Mostly, anyway.

Right. As soon as she did what she'd come to Rust Creek Falls to do, she'd go straight home and get back to her regular life in Dallas. Her *charmed* life. The life that she loved.

"Here you go." Melba handed her a steaming mug of something that smelled wonderful—nutmeg, brown sugar and warm apple pie. Autumn in a cup. "We've had hot apple cider simmering all morning. This will get you nice and warmed up before you go outside."

"Thank you." Avery took a deep inhale of the fragrant cider and had a sudden urge to curl up and knit by the fire in the boarding house's cozy hearth instead of practicing her downward dog.

Never mind that she'd never held a knitting needle in her life. Clearly she'd been in Montana too long.

She took a sip and glanced at Old Gene, sitting at the kitchen table with a live goat in his lap. "How's the baby this morning?"

Baby.

Her throat went dry, and she took another gulp of cider.

"She's settling in." Old Gene nodded and offered the adorable animal a large baby bottle. The goat wasted no time latching on.

Melba rolled her eyes. "If you call waking up every two hours 'settling in.' Honestly, I don't know what possessed you to bring that thing home."

"My cousin is in the hospital with a broken hip, and he's got a barn full of animals that need tending. What was I supposed to do? Bring home a pig?"

Melba tossed a handful of cinnamon sticks into the pot of cider. "Lord, help me."

Old Gene winked at Avery behind Melba's back, and she smiled into her mug. The morning goat wars had become a regular thing since Gene had returned from his rescue mission to his cousin's farm a week or so ago, goat in hand. Melba was antigoat, particularly indoors, whereas Old Gene doted on the animal like it was a child.

Avery had yet to go anywhere near it. She didn't know a thing about goats. Or baby bottles, for that matter.

"You're really doing your best to get on my last nerve this morning." Melba sighed.

"I was simply trying to do something nice," Old Gene muttered. "You never know. Avery might enjoy going on a date with a nice young man."

"Wait…what?" She blinked.

How had the conversation moved seamlessly and at lightning speed from the goat to her love life?

"Gene." Melba looked like she might hit him over the head with her ladle.

"Can I ask what you two are talking about?" Avery set her mug down on the counter with a *thunk*.

Old Gene shrugged. "Viv Dalton just called. Apparently she knows a lonely cowboy."

"Don't you worry, dear." Melba reached for her hand and gave it a pat. "I made sure Viv knows you're not interested in meeting a man right now. Old Gene had no business even giving her your name."

Avery had no idea who Viv Dalton was, nor did she care. But she cared *very much* about her name floating around town. She might be new to Rust Creek Falls, but she was well aware of how swiftly the rumor mill worked. Case in point: Melba knew her husband was bringing home a goat before he'd even walked through the door. Old Gene had stopped by the general store for supplies on the way back to the boarding house and before his truck had pulled into the driveway, Melba had already gotten half a dozen texts and calls about the furry little kid.

"You gave my name to a stranger?" Avery felt sick.

The goat let loose with a pitiful bleat that perfectly mirrored the panic swirling in her consciousness.

Old Gene and Melba exchanged a worried glance.

"Only your first name." Melba reached for Avery's empty cup and refilled it with another ladleful of fragrant apple cider. A peace offering. "I'm sorry, dear. Old Gene was just trying to help, but I set him straight."

Avery nodded.

She wasn't sure what to say at this point. The day she arrived, she'd made it very clear to Melba that she was in town for a little respite. She'd been in desperate need of peace and quiet.

Avery had a feeling Melba assumed she was on the run from a bad boyfriend—maybe even a not-so-nice husband. She was somewhat ashamed to admit that she'd done nothing to correct this assumption. But it had been the only way to prevent her arrival in Rust Creek Falls from hitting the rumor circuit.

Her time had run out, apparently.

"Apologize to Avery, Gene." Melba pointed at her husband with a wooden spoon.

"I'm sorry," he said.

Avery smiled in return, because it was impossible to be angry at a man bottle-feeding a baby goat. "You're forgiven."

Melba let out a relieved exhale and turned back to the stove. "Go on now and do your yoga in peace. Gene and I both know you're not one bit interested in meeting that Crawford boy, no matter how charming and handsome Viv Dalton says he is."

Avery almost dropped her yoga mat.

That Crawford boy?

She couldn't be talking about Finn. Absolutely not. *Please, please no.*

And yet somehow she knew it was true.

Charming? Check.

Handsome? Double check.

She swallowed hard, but bile rose up the back of her throat before she could stop it. She felt like she might be sick to her stomach…again. But that was pretty much par for the course now, just like her crazy new insatiable food cravings and the broken zipper on her favorite pencil skirt.

The goat slurped at the baby bottle, and Avery stared at the tiny animal. So utterly helpless. So sweet.

Tears pricked her eyes, and she blinked them away. *Get a grip.*

She had more important things to dwell on than an orphaned goat. *Far* more important, like how on earth she could possibly explain to Melba and Old Gene that the last thing she wanted was to be set up with Finn Crawford when she was already four months pregnant with his child.

Chapter 2

No amount of downward dogs could calm the frantic beating of Avery's heart. She tried. She really did. But after an hour on her yoga mat, she felt more unsettled than ever.

Probably because every time she closed her eyes, she saw Finn Crawford's handsome face and his tilted, cocky smirk that never failed to make her weak in the knees.

She huffed out a distinctly nonyogi breath, scrambled to her feet and rolled up her mat. So much for the quiet, peaceful space she'd managed to carve out for herself in Rust Creek Falls. Her little time-out was over. She could no longer ignore the fact that she'd come here to find her baby's father—not when fate had nearly thrown her right back into his path.

"Finished already, dear?" Melba said when Avery pushed through the screen door and back into the kitchen of the boarding house. She shook her head. "I don't understand why you young girls enjoy twisting yourselves into pretzels."

Melba's apron was dotted with flour, and a fresh platter of homemade biscuits sat on the kitchen island. The baby goat snoozed quietly on a dog bed in the corner by the window.

"Yes. I think I'm getting a little stir-crazy." She needed a nice distraction, something to completely rid her mind of Finn Crawford until she worked out exactly how to tell him he was going to be a daddy. "Maybe I could help clean some of the guest rooms again?"

Back home in Dallas, Avery typically put in a sixty-hour workweek. Fifty, minimum. She couldn't remember having so much free time on her hands. *Ever.* When she'd first arrived in Montana, all the unprecedented free time had been a dream come true. Pregnancy hormones had been wreaking havoc on her work schedule. The day before she'd left town, she'd actually nodded off in the middle of a marketing meeting. She'd needed a respite. A work cleanse.

Staying at the boarding house had given her just that. And it was lovely…

Until the morning she couldn't force the zipper closed on her favorite jeans—the boyfriend-cut ones that were always so soft and baggy. Faced with such painful evidence of the life growing inside her, Avery had experienced a sudden longing for her old life. She didn't know the first thing about babies or being pregnant, so she'd thrown herself into helping out around the boarding house in an effort to rid herself of her anxiety. Unfortunately, she knew as much about cleaning as she knew about caring for an infant.

"Oh. Well. That's certainly a kind offer." Melba picked up a dishcloth and scrubbed at an invisible spot on the counter. "But I'm not sure that's such a good idea. Old Gene is upstairs, still trying to unclog the toilet in the big corner room."

Avery's face bloomed with heat. The clogged toilet had been her doing. But what were the odds she'd accidentally flush another sponge?

The baby goat let out a long, warbly bleat. *Meeeeeeehh-hhhhhh.*

Avery narrowed her gaze at its little ginger head. Was the animal taunting her now?

Melba cleared her throat. "Don't look so sad, dear. If you really want to help out around here, I'm sure we can figure something out."

"I do. Honestly, I'll try anything." Except maybe bottle-feeding the goat. That was a hard no.

Melba consulted the to-do list tacked to the refrigerator with a Fall Mountain magnet. "I need to make a run to the general store. Would you like to come along?"

Avery's heart gave a little leap. She was much better at shopping than cleaning toilets. She *excelled* at it, quite frankly. A closetful of Louboutins didn't lie. "Shopping? Yes, count me in."

"You're sure?" Melba gave her one of the gentle, sympathetic glances that had convinced Avery the older woman thought she was running from some kind of danger. "You haven't wanted to get out much."

Avery nodded. She was going to have to leave the boarding house at some point. Besides, the odds of running into Finn Crawford or his notorious father at the general store were zero. Not a chance. They weren't the sort of men who ran errands. They had employees for that kind of thing. How else would Finn have time to wine and dine every eligible woman in town?

"We're just going to the general store, right? No-where else? I have a…um…conference call later, so I shouldn't stay out too long." There was no conference call. At least not that Avery knew of. She hadn't checked in to the office for days. Another first.

If she called in, her father would surely pick up the phone. She'd been a daddy's girl all her life, through and through. That would change once he found out she was carrying Finn's baby. Oscar Ellington would rather she have a child with the devil himself.

"Straight to the general store and back." Melba made a cross-my-heart gesture with her fingertips over the pinafore of her apron.

"Super! I'll run upstairs and change." Avery beamed and scurried up to her corner room on the third floor of the rambling mansion.

Along the way, she heard Old Gene cursing at the clogged toilet, and she winced. The wincing continued as she tried—and failed—to find something presentable that she could still manage to zip or button at the waist.

It was no use—she was going to have to stick with her yoga pants and slip into the oversize light blue button-down shirt she'd borrowed from Old Gene. Lovely. If by some strange twist of fate Finn did turn up at the general store, he probably wouldn't even recognize her.

Any lingering worries she had about running into him were instantly kicked into high gear when she and Melba reached the redbrick building on the corner of Main and Cedar Streets. Melba said something about the amber and gold autumnal window display, but Avery couldn't form a response. She was too busy gaping at the sign above the front door.

Crawford's General Store.

Did Finn's family *own* this place?

"Avery?" Melba rested gentle fingertips on her forearm. "Are you okay?"

"Yes. Yes, of course." She pasted on a smile. "I just noticed the name of the store—Crawford's. Does it belong to the family you mentioned earlier?"

"Heavens, no. The general store has been here for generations. The Montana Crawfords have lived in Rust Creek Falls for as long as I can remember. The new family is from Texas."

I'm aware.

Seriously, though. Finn's family was huge, and Rust Creek Falls was very small. Quaint and cozy, but rural in every way. Their addition to the population must mean that half the town had the same last name all of a sudden.

"I see," Avery said.

She tore her gaze away from the store's signage long enough to finally take in the window display, with its garland of oak and maple leaves and towering pile of pumpkins. They'd walked a grand total of two blocks, and already she'd seen enough hay bales, woven baskets and gourds to make her wonder if the entire town was drunk on pumpkin spice lattes.

Autumn wasn't such a big thing in Texas. The warm weather back home meant no apple picking, no fall foliage and definitely no need for snuggly oversize sweaters. It was kind of a shame, really.

But here in Montana, fall was ushered in with a lovely and luminous harvest moon, smoky breezes that smelled of wood fire and the crunch of leaves underfoot. Avery had never experienced anything like it.

"Maybe we should get some ingredients for caramel

apples and make them for my great-granddaughter Bek-kah's kindergarten class. I always bring some to the big Halloween dance, but the children might like an early taste." Melba glanced over her shoulder at Avery as she pushed through the general store's entrance. "What do you think?"

"I think that's a marvelous idea." Avery had never made caramel apples before, but there was a first time for everything.

Apples…autumn…*babies*.

She glanced past the dry goods section near the front of the store and spotted a rack of flannel shirts, quilted jackets and cable-knit cardigans. It wasn't exactly Neiman Marcus, but she was going to have to bite the bullet and invest in a few things that actually fit her changing body.

"Good morning, ladies. Is there anything I can help you with?" A slim woman with dark wavy hair, big brown eyes and a Crawford's General Store bib apron greeted them with a wide smile.

"Yes, please." Melba pulled a lengthy shopping list out of her handbag and plopped it onto the counter. Then she gestured toward Avery. "Nina, I'd like you to meet Avery. She's one of our boarders."

Nina offered Avery her hand. "Welcome to Rust Creek Falls. I'm Nina Crawford Traub."

Seriously. Did *everyone* in this town have the same last name?

"Hello." Avery shook Nina's hand, then dashed off to grab a few warm, roomy items of clothing while the other women tackled Melba's list of supplies.

By the time she returned, the counter was piled high. It looked like Melba was buying out the entire store.

"Wow." Avery's eye widened. She clutched her new

flannels close to her chest, because there wasn't enough space to set them down. "This is…"

"Impressive," someone behind her said. There was a smile in his voice, a delicious drawl that Avery felt deep in the pit of her stomach. "Here's hoping you've left some stuff for the rest of us."

Don't turn around, her thoughts screamed. She knew that voice. It was as velvety smooth as hot buttered rum and oh, so familiar.

But just like the last time she'd been in the same room with the bearer of that soulful Texas accent, her body reacted before her brain could kick into gear. Sure enough, when she spun around, she found herself face-to-face with the very man she so desperately needed to speak to—Finn Crawford, the father-to-be, looking hotter than ever wearing a black Stetson and an utterly shocked expression on his handsome face.

Avery realized a second too late what was about to happen. Trouble.

So.

Very.

Much.

Trouble.

Avery?

Finn blinked. Hard.

No way… No possible way.

He was hallucinating. Or more likely, simply mistaken. After all, the brunette beauty who'd just spun around to stare at him might bear more than a passing resemblance to Avery Ellington, but she was hugging a stack of flannel shirts like it was some kind of security blanket. The Avery he knew wouldn't be caught dead in plaid flannel. She might even be allergic to it.

It had to be her, though. On some visceral level, he just *knew*. Plus he'd recognize those big doe eyes anywhere.

Avery Ellington. Warmth filled his chest. *Well, isn't this a fine surprise*.

Finn glanced at the older woman beside her— Melba… Melba *Strickland*, as in the owner of Strickland's Boarding House. So Old Gene's "darling young lady" that Viv Dalton wanted to set him up with was indeed the Avery he knew so well.

He burst out laughing.

Avery's soft brown eyes narrowed. She looked like she might be contemplating dropping the flannel and using her hands to strangle him. "What's so funny?"

"This." He gestured back and forth between Avery and Melba. "I'm not sure you're aware, but an hour or so ago, we were almost set up on a blind date."

"I might have heard something about that," Avery said, clearly failing to find the humor in the situation.

She seemed a little rattled. If Finn didn't know better, he would have thought she was unhappy to run into him. But that couldn't be right. The last time they'd seen one another had been immensely pleasurable.

For both of them.

Finn was certain of it. Plus, they'd parted on good terms.

"It's incredibly good to see you. What on earth are you doing in Rust Creek Falls?" He arched a brow. She was awfully far away from her daddy's ranch in Texas.

Melba interjected before Avery could respond, "Avery is a guest at the boarding house."

Finn nodded, even though they'd already covered

Avery's local living arrangements. It still didn't explain what she was doing clear across the country from home.

He swiveled his gaze back to Avery. She looked beautiful, but different somehow. He couldn't quite put his finger on what had changed. Maybe it was the casual clothes or her wind-tossed hair, but her usual cool elegance had been replaced with a warmth that made him acutely aware of his own heartbeat all of a sudden.

"How's the little one?" he said with a smile.

"Um." Avery blinked like an owl. "How did you—"

Finn shrugged. "Everyone in town is talking about it. There's nothing quite as cute as a baby goat."

"The goat. Right." Avery swallowed, and he traced the movement up and down the graceful column of her throat.

Was it his imagination, or did she seem nervous?

"The goat's cute, but she's a handful. I don't know what Old Gene was thinking." Melba rolled her eyes. "She has to be bottle-fed every four to five hours, round the clock. It's almost like having a real baby again, but maybe a little less noisy."

Avery turned toward Melba with an incredulous stare. "*Less* noisy?"

Melba shrugged. "Sure. You know how babies are."

Avery shifted from one foot to the other as she glanced at Finn and then quickly looked away.

Melba's eyes narrowed. "How exactly do you two know each other?"

Why did the question feel like a test of some sort?

Finn gave her an easy smile. He had nothing to hide. "Avery and I are both in the beef business."

"Really?" Melba looked him and up down.

"Absolutely. Our paths used to cross every so often,

but we haven't bumped into each other since my family relocated to Montana." A pity, really. "I'd love to take you out while you're in town, Avery."

She bit the swell of her lush bottom lip. "Oh…um, well…"

Not exactly the reaction he was going for. Avery looked as scared as a rabbit, and Melba was once again scrutinizing him as if he were giving off serial killer vibes.

Was he missing something?

His thoughts drifted back to the night they'd spent together in Oklahoma City. It didn't take much effort. The entire encounter was seared in his memory—every perfect, porcelain inch of Avery's skin, every tender brush of her lips.

They'd been in town for a gala dinner of cattle executives, and Finn would be lying if he'd said he hadn't been hoping to run into her. Through their overlapping business connections and a handful of mutual friends, Finn and Avery had been moving in the same orbit for quite a few years. He'd wanted her for every single one of them. How could he not? She was lovely. And smart, too. It took a special kind of woman to hold her own as the vice president of a major company in a business dominated by men. Finn considered himself a Southern gentleman, but that wasn't true of everyone in the beef business. Avery had run into her fair share of chauvinists and good old boys, but she never failed to rise above their nonsense with her head held high.

As much as she fascinated him, he'd respected her too much to make a real move. Their interactions had been limited to a low-key flirtation that he found immensely enjoyable, if somewhat torturous.

But the night in Oklahoma had been different. June in the Sooner State was always a nightmare of blazing heat and suffocating humidity, but that particular weekend had been especially brutal. A heat wave swept through the area, causing widespread power outages as the temperature soared. The gala's luxury hotel was plunged into darkness. Even after they got the generator up and running, the crystal chandeliers were barely illuminated, and heady, scented candles were scattered over every available surface.

He remembered Avery saying something about the animosity between their families, and true, his father had never uttered a kind word about Oscar Ellington. Quite the opposite, actually. There was definitely bad blood between the Crawford and Ellington patriarchs. But Finn and Avery had always managed to get along. And something about the darkness made their little flirtation seem not so low-key anymore, so over laugher and dry martinis at the bar, they'd agreed to set aside any familial difficulty.

She'd looked so damned beautiful in the candlelight, all soft curves and wide, luminous eyes. He'd taken a chance and leaned in…

He swallowed hard at the memory of what came next. It had been like something out of a dream. A perfect night—so perfect he hadn't taken another woman to bed since, despite his popularity in Montana. And now Avery was right here, less than an arm's length away, when he'd thought he'd never see her again.

"Please," he said. "Dinner, or even just coffee? For old times' sake."

He'd been neck-deep in women for the past three

months, and now he was begging for an hour of Avery Ellington's time. Wonderful.

Melba cut in again before she could give him an answer. "Look at the time! Sorry to interrupt, but we simply must be going. Avery, how could you let me forget? We have to stop over at the Dalton Law Office to pick up those papers for Gene."

Avery's expression went blank. "What papers?"

"Those very important papers. You know the ones." Melba took the flannel shirts from Avery and handed them to Nina, who shoved them into a bag.

Avery crossed her arms, uncrossed them and crossed them again. Finn's gaze snagged on her oversize blue button-down. Was that a *man's* shirt she was wearing?

His jaw clenched. They hadn't even spoken since that simmering night in June, but Finn didn't like the thought of her with another man. Not one bit.

Overreacting much? It was one night, not an actual relationship. Maybe he wasn't such a fine Southern gentleman, after all.

"Come on, now. We don't want to keep Ben Dalton waiting." Melba shoved one of her five shopping bags at Avery and then linked elbows with her.

"Right. Of course we don't." Avery glanced at him one last time as Melba practically dragged her out of the store. "It was good seeing you, Finn. Goodbye."

He stared after them, wondering what in the hell had just happened.

"Can I help you find anything, Mr. Crawford?" Nina said from behind the counter.

Finn dragged his gaze away from the scene beyond the shop window and Avery's chocolate-hued hair, whipping around her angelic face in the wind like a dark halo.

He smiled, but his heart wasn't in it. "No, thank you."

For some strange reason, he almost felt like he'd already found what he needed. And now he'd just watched her walk away.

Again.

"Where are we going, exactly?" Avery gripped her shopping bag until her knuckles turned white and did her best to resist the overwhelming urge to glance over her shoulder for another glimpse of the general store.

Of Finn.

She almost wanted to believe she'd imagined their entire awkward encounter just now. Since the moment she'd first spotted the two tiny pink lines on the drugstore pregnancy test she'd taken in her posh executive washroom at Ellington Meats, she'd tried to imagine what she'd say to Finn the next time she saw him. Somehow she always imagined she'd be able to utter more than two stuttered words.

Had she managed to string a whole sentence together at all? Nope, she was pretty sure she hadn't. So much for being a strong, independent woman and facing the situation head-on.

"We're not going anywhere, dear. I thought you were going to faint when you saw Finn Crawford. I made something up to get you out of there." Melba gave her hand a comforting pat.

So her panic had been that obvious? Fabulous.

"Oh, thank you. But I was surprised, that's all." Shocked to her core was more like it.

Which was really kind of ridiculous, since the whole reason she'd come to Rust Creek Falls was to tell him about the baby. Get in, drop the baby bomb and get out.

That had been the plan. It was just so much harder than she'd imagined. And now here she was, a couple weeks later, still secretly pregnant.

"Finn is an old friend." She stared straight ahead as they walked back to the boarding house. What had just transpired at the general store was a minor setback, not a total disaster. It's not like she could have told him she was pregnant right then and there.

Hey, so great to see you. FYI, I'm having your baby, and I'm planning to raise it on my own. Just wanted to let you know. I've got to pay for my pile of flannel now. Have a nice life.

Beside her, Melba snorted. "Well. He seems to have a lot of friends, if you know what I mean."

Avery's steps slowed as her heart pounded hard in her chest. "I don't, actually."

"It seems pretty obvious that you aren't ready to jump into a relationship. In any event, from what I've heard, Finn Crawford wouldn't be a great candidate."

Avery concentrated hard on putting one foot in front of the other as she turned Melba's words over in her mind. She was almost afraid to ask for more information, but she had to, didn't she? If the father of her baby was an ax murderer or something, that seemed like vital information to have. "Melba, what exactly have you heard?"

The older woman shook her head. "Don't get me wrong. He's a right charming fellow—possibly *too* charming. He's dated practically everyone in Rust Creek Falls since his family moved to town. It's sweet that he asked you to dinner, but Finn isn't right for a nice girl like you."

A nice girl like you.

What on earth would Melba think if she knew the real story?

Avery took a deep breath. The air smelled like cinnamon and nutmeg, courtesy of the decorative cinnamon brooms so many of the local business included in the fall pumpkin displays decorating the sidewalk. But the cozy atmosphere couldn't get her mind off a troubling truth—Finn might not be a serial killer, but apparently, he was a serial *flirt*. Somehow she didn't think a baby would fit neatly into a carefree lifestyle like the one Melba had just described.

But that was fine. More than fine, really. She didn't need Finn's help. If she could run the business division of a Fortune 500 company, she could certainly raise a baby. Her father would blow a gasket once he found out his first grandchild was going to be a Crawford, but he'd get over it. Having Finn out of the picture might even make things easier, where the whole family feud matter was concerned.

She obviously needed to let Finn know it was happening, though. That just seemed like the right thing to do. His reputation around Rust Creek Falls didn't change a thing. It wasn't as if she'd thought she could actually build a life with the man.

Still, the fact that he'd been acting as if Montana was the set of *Bachelor in Paradise* while she was battling morning sickness and freaking out about starting a family with the son of her father's sworn enemy stung a little bit.

Who am I kidding? Avery climbed the steps of Strickland's Boarding House alongside Melba and thought about all the nights she'd spent in this house, secretly wishing Finn would call or text out of the blue so she'd feel less awkward about their situation. Less lonely.

It stings a lot.

Chapter 3

"Mr. Crawford." Melba Strickland stood on the front steps of her big purple house and looked Finn up and down. "This is a surprise."

Was it?

Finn got the feeling she wasn't shocked to see him in the least. The furrow in her brow told him she wasn't pleased about his impromptu visit, either.

"Good morning, Mrs. Strickland." He tipped his hat and smiled, but her frown only deepened.

Once Finn had recovered from the shock of running into Avery at the general store the day before, he'd realized she'd never given his invitation a straight answer. Granted, she hadn't exactly jumped for joy when he'd told her he wanted to take her out while she was in town, but she hadn't turned him down, either. Melba hadn't given her a chance.

After he'd finally collected what he needed at the store, he'd returned to the Ambling A and spent the afternoon making repairs to the ranch's barbed-wire fence. One of the things Finn liked best about Montana was its vast and sweeping sky. He'd always loved the deep blue of the heavens in Texas, but here it almost felt like the sky was stacked on top of itself like a layered cake. A man could do a lot of thinking under a sky like that, and while he'd pounded new fence posts into the rich red earth, he'd managed to convince himself things with Avery hadn't been as awkward as he'd imagined. Old Gene probably had papers waiting to be picked up at the Dalton Law Office, just like Melba said. There was no legitimate reason why Avery should be trying to avoid him.

Now, in the fresh light of day, he wasn't so sure. Melba was definitely giving him the side-eye as he shifted his weight from one foot to the other and tried to see past her to the inside of the boarding house.

Was she even going to let him in?

"I stopped by to see Avery." He nodded toward the bouquet in his hand—sunflowers and velvety wine-colored roses tied with a smooth satin ribbon. "And to give her these."

Melba glanced at the flowers. Her resistance wavered, ever so slightly.

"I'll have to see if Avery is available." She held up a hand. "Wait here."

"Yes, ma'am." He winced as she shut the door in his face.

Finn felt like a teenager again, trying to get permission to take a pretty girl to the school dance. Even back then, he wasn't sure he'd ever run into a protective parent as steadfast as Melba Strickland.

At long last, the door swung open to reveal Avery with her thick brunette waves piled on top of her head and her lips painted red, just like she'd looked that fateful night in Oklahoma. But instead of her usual business attire, she was wearing faded jeans and an oversize cable-knit sweater that slipped off one shoulder as she gripped the doorknob. Finn's attention snagged briefly on the flash of her smooth, bare skin, and when he met her gaze again, her mouth curved into a bashful smile.

"Finn Crawford, whatever are you doing here?" She tilted her head, and a lock of hair curled against her exposed collarbone.

It took every ounce of Finn's willpower not to reach out and wind it around his fingertips. "Shouldn't I be asking you that question?"

What *was* she doing in Montana…in Rust Creek Falls, of all places?

"I had business nearby, and since I was a bit intrigued by the charming town you'd told me all about, I thought I'd check it out while I was in the area." That's right—the last time they'd seen each other, he'd told her all about the plans to relocate the ranch. "It seemed like a nice place to escape for a few days."

Finn nodded, even though her answer raised more questions than it answered, such as what exactly did she need to escape from?

"I actually thought about looking you up, but I wasn't sure if I should," she said.

He arched a brow. "Why not?"

Avery took a deep breath, and for a long, loaded moment, the space between them felt swollen with meaning. But then she just bit her lip and shrugged.

"Are those for me?" She smiled at the bouquet in his hand.

A wave of pleasure surged through him. Whatever her reason for being here, it was great to see her again. "They sure are."

"How very gentlemanly of you. Thank you." She took the flowers and held them close to her chest. Her soft brown eyes seemed lovelier than ever, mirroring the rich, dark centers of the sunflowers. "Do you want to come in while I put these in some water?"

She gestured toward the interior of the boarding house, which was the last place Finn wanted to be while Melba was around.

"Actually, since you seem so interested in the area, why don't I show you around town for a bit? I can even give you a tour of the ranch if you like."

"A tour of the ranch," she echoed. The flowers in her grip trembled. "*Your* ranch?"

Finn paused, remembering what she'd told him in Oklahoma about the supposed feud between their families. Once upon a time, Oscar Ellington and Maximilian Crawford had been friends. Best friends, according to Avery's father. They'd roomed together in college, both majoring in agriculture and ranch management. After graduation, they'd planned to go into business together, but at the last minute, Finn's father had changed his mind. He pulled out of the deal, and the friendship came to its tumultuous end.

"Sure," Finn said. He and Avery weren't their parents. He saw no reason why he couldn't take her to the Ambling A and walk the land with her, show her how the fall colors made the mountainside look as if it were aflame.

Although, if Oscar and Maximilian had turned their youthful dreams into a reality, the ranch wouldn't be his. It would be theirs—his and Avery's both.

Imagine that, he thought. *Being tied to Avery Ellington for life.*

He could think of worse fates.

But that would never happen. Ever. He wasn't even sure why he was entertaining the notion, other than the fact that his dad and Viv Dalton were dead set on putting an end to his independence.

"All right, then," Avery said, but her smile turned bittersweet. "Let's go."

Copper and gold leaves crunched beneath Avery's feet as she and Finn walked from his truck to the grand log cabin overlooking acres and acres of ranch land and glittering sunlit pastures where horses flicked their tails and grazed on shimmering emerald grass.

Calling it a cabin was a bit of a stretch. It looked more like a mansion made of Lincoln Logs, surrounded by a sprawling patio fashioned from artistically arranged river stones. The Rocky Mountains loomed in the background, rugged and golden. Enemy territory was quite lovely, it seemed.

Finn slipped his hand onto the small of her back as he led her toward the main house, and she tried her best to relax. An impossible task, considering that her father would probably disown her if he had any idea where she was right now. Finding out about the baby was going to kill him.

But she couldn't worry about that now. First, she had

to figure out how to tell Finn, and that seemed more difficult than ever now that this little outing was beginning to feel like a date.

Does he have to be so charming?

It was the flowers—they'd completely thrown her off her game. Which was pathetic, considering how active Finn's Montana social life had become. He probably got a bulk discount at the nearest florist.

"This place is gorgeous," she said. "Do all your brothers live out here?"

Finn nodded. "Logan, Knox and Hunter have cottages on the property. Xander and his family just moved into their own ranch house in town. Wilder and I live in the main house with my dad."

His dad.

So Maximilian Crawford was *here* somewhere. Great.

"You look a million miles away all of a sudden." Finn paused on the threshold to study her. "Everything okay?"

No, nothing was okay. She felt huge and overly emotional, and he was still the same ridiculously handsome man, perfectly dashing in all his clueless daddy-to-be glory.

"Actually…" Her mouth went dry. She couldn't swallow, much less form the words she so desperately needed to say.

Tell him. Do it now.

"Yes?" He tilted his head, dark eyes glittering beneath the rim of his black Stetson.

Meeting his gaze felt impossible all of a sudden, so she glanced at his plain black T-shirt instead. But the way it hugged the solid wall of his chest was distracting to say the least.

"I, um…" She let out a lungful of air.

"You're beautiful, that's what you are. A sight for sore eyes. Do you have any idea how glad I am to see you?" Finn reached up and ran his hand along her jaw, caressing her cheek with the pad of his thumb.

It took every ounce of Avery's willpower not to lean into his touch and purr like a kitten. Her body was more than ready to just go with the flow, but her thoughts were screaming.

Tell him, you coward!

"I'm relieved to hear you say that." Butterflies took flight deep in Avery's belly—or maybe it was their baby doing backflips at the sound of its daddy's voice. She swallowed hard. "Because…"

Then all of a sudden, the front door swung open and she was rendered utterly speechless by the sight of her father's mortal enemy standing on the threshold with an enormous orange pumpkin tucked under one arm.

She recognized him in an instant. His picture appeared every year in the Crawford Meats annual report, and he looked exactly the same as his slick corporate portrait. Same deep tan and lined face, same devil-may-care expression.

Maximilian Crawford stared at her for a surprised beat. Then he glanced back and forth between her and Finn until his eyes narrowed into slits. "Well, well. Howdy, you two."

"Dad," Finn said. There was a hint of a warning in his voice, but Maximilian seemed to ignore it.

"Aren't you going to tell me what you're doing keeping company with Avery Ellington?" The older man smiled, but it didn't quite reach his eyes.

Maximilian Crawford had just smiled at her. She was surprised lightning didn't strike her on the spot. If her father were dead, he'd be spinning in his grave.

"Avery's just here for a friendly visit." Finn's hand moved to the small of her back again, and a shiver snaked its way up her spine. "I'm not sure you two have officially met. Avery, meet my dad, Maximilian."

"Hello, sir." She offered her hand.

He gave it a shake, but instead of letting go, he kept her hand clasped in his. "You're Oscar's little girl."

He was going there. *Okaaaay.*

"One and the same," she said, reminding herself that this man wasn't just her father's nemesis. He was also the grandfather of her unborn child.

"Right." He gave her hand a light squeeze and then finally released it. "I'm not sure if your daddy ever mentioned me, but he and I go way back."

Avery nodded. "I'm aware."

She shot a quick glance at Finn. The night they'd slept together in Oklahoma, he didn't seem to care much about any animosity between their families, but she'd wondered if he'd simply been downplaying things in order to avoid any awkwardness between them.

Not that she'd cared. She'd been more than ready to forget about anything that got in the way of their ongoing flirtation. Besides, they'd been miles away from Dallas. Just like the famous saying—what happens in Oklahoma stays in Oklahoma.

Unless it results in an accidental pregnancy.

"Interesting man, your father." Maximilian's expression turned vaguely nostalgic. "We were roommates back in the day. Almost went into business together. Truth be told, I occasionally miss those times."

Finn sneaked Avery a reassuring grin as his father's attitude softened somewhat.

"How's he doing? And your mom?" Maximilian shifted his pumpkin from one arm to the other. "Good, I hope."

Avery nodded. "They're great."

For now, anyway. Once she started showing, all bets were off.

"Avery's in town for a few days, so I thought I'd show her around a little bit." Finn eyed the pumpkin. "Tell me you're not on the way out here to try to carve that thing into a jack-o'-lantern."

"It's October. Of course that's what I'm going to do."

"Dad, this isn't Dallas. Halloween isn't for a few weeks. If you leave a carved pumpkin outside, it's going to get eaten up long before the thirty-first. The coyotes will probably get it before sunup." Finn shrugged. "If the elk don't get to it first."

"Fine. I'll take it inside after it's done. I've got five more to carve after this one. We can line them up by the fireplace. I just thought the place could use some holiday flair." Maximilian grinned. "Especially since we're welcoming a new little one to the family."

Avery coughed, and both men turned to look at her. "Excuse me. Little one?"

They couldn't possibly know. Could they?

"My brother Logan is a new stepdad. He and his wife have a nine-month-old little girl, and my father suddenly wants us to believe he's transformed from a cattle baron into a doting grandfather." Finn narrowed his gaze at his dad.

"Oh." This seemed promising. It almost made her wish she planned on raising the baby closer to Montana, but that would be insane. She had a job back in Dallas. A family. A life. "How sweet."

Finn held out his hands to his father. "Why don't you leave the pumpkin carving to us? Manual labor of any kind isn't exactly your strong suit."

Maximilian glanced at Avery and lifted a brow. "You're willing to stick around long enough to help Finn with my mini pumpkin patch?"

Avery couldn't help but smile. She wasn't naive enough to believe Maximilian was just a harmless grandpa. He was a far more complicated man than that. On more than one occasion, she'd heard Finn refer to him as manipulative.

Even so, she had a difficult time reconciling the man standing in front of her—the one who wanted to carve half a dozen jack-o'-lanterns for his new baby granddaughter's first Halloween—with the backstabbing monster her father had been describing to her for as long as she could remember.

"I think that can be arranged," she said.

She still planned to tell Finn about the baby today. Of course she did. But what different could a few more hours make?

"I like her," Maximilian said as he handed the pumpkin over to Finn and slapped him hard on the back. "She seems like a keeper, son."

What on earth was she doing here?

A keeper.

Nope. No way, no how. She could have a dozen babies with Finn, but she'd never, ever be a Crawford—not if her daddy had anything to do with it.

* * *

Avery set down her paring knife and wiped her hands on a dish towel so she could inspect the pumpkin she'd been attempting to carve. Its triangle-shaped eyes were uneven, and its wide, toothy grin was definitely lopsided. Overall, though, it was a decent effort.

Or at least she though it was until she took a closer look at what Finn had managed to produce in the same amount of time.

"Wait a minute." She frowned at twin jack-o'-lanterns on the table in front of him. "When did you start on the second one?"

He glanced at her pumpkin and stifled a grin. "Somewhere around the time you decided to give yours a square nose."

She swatted at him with the dish towel. The nose had started out as a triangle—she wasn't quite sure how it had ended up as a square.

Finn laughed, ducking out of the way. He managed to catch the towel and snatch it away from her before it made contact with his head. His grin was triumphant, but it softened as he met her gaze.

"You've got a little something." He gestured toward the side of his face. "Right there."

Shocker. Avery wouldn't have been surprised to discover she was covered head to toe in pumpkin guts. The jack-o'-lantern struggle had been very real.

She wiped her cheek, and Finn shook his head, laughter dancing in his eyes.

"I just made it worse, didn't I?" she said, looking down at her orange hands.

"Afraid so. Here, let me." He cupped her face with

irritatingly clean fingertips and dabbed at her cheek with the towel.

It was a perfectly innocent gesture. Sweet, really. But Avery's heart felt like it was going to pound right out of her chest, and she had the completely inappropriate urge to kiss him as his gaze collided with hers.

She cleared her throat and backed away. She blamed pregnancy hormones…and the insanely gorgeous surroundings. Finn had set up their pumpkin-carving station on one of the log mansion's covered porches. It had a lovely, unobstructed view of the mountains, plus an enormous outdoor fireplace crafted from stone with a weathered wooden mantel. Any woman would have melted under the circumstances.

Avery kept having to remind herself that half the female population of Rust Creek Falls likely already had.

"You're shockingly good at this." She arched a brow at his two perfectly carved pumpkins in an effort to get her thoughts—and sensitive libido—back under control. "Do you have a degree in festive fall decorating I don't know about?"

"No, but I suppose it's fair to say there are indeed things you don't know about me. After all, our interactions have been pretty limited to business gatherings." Avery waited for Finn to crack a joke about their night together being the exception, but he didn't.

She wasn't altogether sure why that made her happy, but it did. "True."

He seemed different here than he'd been back in Dallas, and it was more than just a switch from tailored business suits to worn jeans and cowboy boots.

"So you like it here in Montana?" she asked.

"I do." Finn nodded and stared thoughtfully at the

horizon, where a mist had gathered at the base of the mountain, creating a swirl of smoky autumn colors. "Life is different here. Richer, somehow. I always liked spending time on our ranch back in Texas, but somehow I never got out there much. I spent more time in boardrooms than I did with the herd. Does that make sense?"

Her face grew warm as he glanced at her. "It does."

Avery couldn't remember the last time she'd been to her own family ranch, much less spent any time with the herd. She'd spent more hours with Excel spreadsheets than she ever had with actual cattle.

Finn's gaze narrowed, and as if he could see straight inside her head, he said, "When was the last time you hand-fed a cow?"

Laughter bubbled up her throat. "Seriously? Never."

"Never?" He clutched his chest. "You're killing me, Princess."

Princess.

She usually hated it when he called her that, but she decided to ignore Finn's pet name for her for the time being, mainly because it sort of fit, as much as she was loath to admit it.

He stood and offered her his hand. "Come on."

She placed her hand in his as if it were the most natural thing in the world, and he hauled her to her feet. "Where are we going?"

"You'll see." He winked, and it seemed to float right through her on butterfly wings. "You trust me, don't you, Princess?"

That was a loaded question if she'd ever heard one. "Should I?"

He gave her hand a squeeze in lieu of an actual answer, then shot her a lazy grin and tugged her in the direction of the barn.

Right. That's what I thought.

Of course she couldn't trust him. He might seem at home here on the farm in a way that made her think there was more to Finn Crawford than met the eye, but just because a man could carve a jack-o'-lantern and went all soft around the edges when he talked about animals didn't mean he was ready for a family.

Avery slipped her hand from his and crossed her arms. "What about the pumpkins? Won't coyotes come and devour them if we leave?"

Her mind had snagged on Finn's casual reference to coyotes earlier, probably because the biggest threat to jack-o'-lanterns in her Dallas neighborhood were mischievous teens.

He glanced over her shoulder toward the porch, where Maximilian had begun cleaning up their mess and hauling the pumpkins inside.

Avery rolled her eyes. "And you call *me* a princess."

He flashed a grin. "Touché."

He took hold of her hand again, and she let him, because his rakish smile and down-home charm were getting to her. And honestly, considering she was pregnant with the man's baby, it was a little late to be worried about hand-holding.

The barn was cool and sweet-smelling, like hay and sunshine. It reminded Avery of the horseback riding lessons she'd had as a little girl. She'd ridden English, of course. No rodeos or trail rides for the daughter of Oscar Ellington. Her childhood and teen years had been about posh country club horse shows and debutante balls.

Her thoughts snagged briefly on what might be in

store for her unborn child. If she raised the baby by herself, in Dallas, she'd be setting her son or daughter up for the same type of upbringing she'd had. Her father would see to it.

But was that really what Avery wanted?

She wasn't so sure, and suddenly she couldn't seem to focus on the many difficult decisions she needed to address. She couldn't seem to focus on *anything* except Finn's cocky, lopsided grin and the cozy hayloft in the barn's shady rafters. Wouldn't it be nice to be kissed in a place like that?

For the last time, calm down, pregnancy hormones!

"It's really lovely here," she said, glancing around the sun-dappled space. Horses poked their heads over the tops of stable doors and whinnied as they walked past.

"It's nice. We've got a lot more space than we had in Texas."

"So your move here is permanent, then." She held her breath. What was she saying?

Of course it was permanent. This was Finn's new home.

"Oh, yeah." He nodded and guided her toward the corner of the barn, where a few barrels were lined up along the wall.

Avery wondered how much of his enthusiasm for Rust Creek Falls had to do with his overactive dating life…and just how many women he'd brought out to the Ambling A for this quaint little tour. On second thought, maybe she was better off without that information.

"Here we go." Finn reached into one of the barrels and pulled out a few ears of colorful calico corn— sapphire blues, deep burgundies and ruby reds. It almost looked like he was holding a handful of gemstones.

He offered her a few ears, and she took them. "Pretty. Are we adding a little harvest decor to the jack-o'-lantern display for your niece?"

"No, my dad donated a big batch of harvest corn to the town for the autumn festival, and we've got a few barrels left over. So now what you've got there is a treat for the cattle."

She glanced down at the corn and back up at Finn. He'd been dead serious about spending hands-on time with the herd. "You mean cow treats are a thing?"

"Everyone deserves a little something special now and then, don't you think?" His eyes gleamed.

Avery was a firm believer in this sentiment. It was precisely how she ended up with her most recent Louis Vuitton handbag. It's also how she'd ended up in bed with Finn Crawford on her last business trip.

She blinked up at him and prayed he couldn't read her mind. "Absolutely."

Finn couldn't shake the feeling that there was something different about Avery. When he couldn't figure out exactly what it was, he realized the difference wasn't just one thing. *Everything* about her seemed different somehow.

Then again, he'd never seen her this way before. Finn knew the proper, corporate Avery—Princess Avery, as he liked to call her, much to her irritation. He'd never seen the coppery highlights that fresh sunshine brought out in her tumbling waves of hair. He'd certainly never wrapped his arms around her from behind and held her close in a pasture while she tried to feed an overeager cow an ear of calico corn.

Every time the Hereford's big head got close to her

hand, she pulled it back and squealed. The poor confused cow glanced back and forth between Avery and Finn and then stared longingly at the ear of corn.

"Cows seems significantly bigger up close," Avery said.

"This one's harmless, I promise. She's a gentle giant, wouldn't hurt a fly." He took hold of Avery's hand and guided the corn toward the cow's mouth.

The Hereford snorted in gratitude and wrapped her wide tongue around the corncob.

"Ahh! I'm doing it." Avery laughed, and the cow's ears swiveled to and fro.

The corn was gone within a matter of minutes, and Avery beamed at Finn over her shoulder. "Can I give her another one?"

"Sure." He handed her another ear of the colorful corn.

Avery fed it to the cow all on her own this time, giggling in delight when the animal made happy slurping sounds.

"This is the most hands-on I've ever gotten with cattle." She turned in his arms so she was facing him and shot him a conciliatory look. "You were right. It gives me a whole new appreciation for what we do."

Finn had been a rancher all his life, and he'd never seen anyone take such sheer delight in feeding cattle before. It was a shame Avery's father had never taken the time to teach her the ins and outs of hands-on ranch management in addition to crunching numbers and networking. But he wasn't about to bring up Oscar Ellington and spoil the mood. The man hated him, apparently, although Finn probably never would have known as much if Avery hadn't mentioned it over martinis in the darkened bar in Oklahoma.

"Then it's a good thing I dragged you away from the boarding house," he said.

Avery's hands found their way to his chest, and their eyes met for a beat until she seemed to realize she was touching him.

"Right, but I should probably be getting back." She took a backward step and collided with the cow.

She let out a loud moo, and Avery jumped back into his arms.

He couldn't help but laugh. "Relax, Princess. Everything's fine."

"It's really not." She shook her head, but at the same time melted into him. And this time, when her hands landed on his pecs, they stayed.

Finn could feel her heart beating hard against his chest, and her eyes grew dark...dreamy...as her lips parted ever so slightly.

He'd never wanted to kiss a woman more in his life, but he was still a little thrown by her words.

It's really not.

He had no clue what she meant. Everything certainly seemed fine. She felt so good in his arms. So soft. So warm. And he especially liked the way she was suddenly focusing intently on his mouth.

But he wasn't about to kiss her if it wasn't what she wanted. He inhaled a ragged breath and cast her a questioning glance.

"Honestly, I should go." She lifted her arms and wound them around his neck.

"Avery." He half groaned her name.

If he couldn't kiss her, he was going to have to take

her arms and unwind them himself. He wasn't going to last another minute with her pressed against him, looking up at him like she wanted to devour him. He was only human.

But just as his fingers slipped around her wrists, she rose up on her tiptoes and kissed him so hard that she nearly knocked him over. Her mouth was warm and ready, and before he fully grasped what was happening, her fingertips slid into his hair, knocking his Stetson to the ground.

Finn didn't give a damn about the hat. He didn't give a damn about much of anything except the woman in his arms and the way she was murmuring his name against his lips, as if they were suddenly right back in the middle of that surreal, sublime night in Oklahoma.

He'd been thinking about that night for four long months, convinced their paths would never cross again. And now here she was, as beautiful and maddening as ever.

He nipped softly at her bottom lip and she let out a breathy sigh, and somewhere in the back of his mind, he wondered again what exactly she was doing in Montana, so far off the beaten path. He wasn't altogether sure he bought her business trip explanation. No one had business this far out. He didn't dare ask, lest he ruin the moment.

But he didn't have to, because the moment came to an abrupt end, thanks to an earsplitting chorus of hungry moos.

Their eyes flew open, and Avery blinked, horrified. Whether she was more shaken by the sight of half a dozen cows suddenly surrounding them in the pasture or the fact that she'd thrown herself at him, he wasn't entirely sure. He hoped it was the former, but he wouldn't bet his life on it.

"I, um…" She bit her lip. "I'm sorry about that."

"Avery, talk to me. Tell me what's wrong."

One of the cows nudged her, and she shook her head. "Nothing. Nothing's wrong. I'm just… I'm sorry. I should really…"

"It's okay." He nodded, still thoroughly baffled but getting nowhere amid a sea of cattle and half-eaten harvest corn. "I'll take you home."

The look of relief on her face was almost enough to make him think he'd imagined the fact that she'd just kissed him silly. Not quite, though.

Not quite.

Chapter 4

"Tell me again why we're doing this?" Melba's gaze cut toward Avery as she slid one foot to rest alongside her opposite ankle in a wobbly modified version of tree pose. The baby goat bleated in her arms.

Avery had to give Melba credit. She was really being a good sport about the whole goat yoga thing.

"People pay good money to do this in the city. I promise," Avery said as she settled into her own tree pose.

Thanks in part to yoga with animals being all the rage on Instagram, her yoga studio in Dallas had held a special goat yoga fund-raiser after the most recent Texas hurricane and ended up raising thousands for storm relief. How a private fitness boutique in the luxury Highland Park neighborhood procured a dozen tiny goats for the day was a mystery Avery couldn't begin to fathom. But her life in Rust Creek Falls seemed to be teeming with farm animals.

Avery placed her hands in prayer position and closed her eyes. "Think of it as pet therapy and yoga all rolled into one. It's supposed to clear the mind and release loads of feel-good endorphins."

Plus Avery just needed the company. Since her visit to the Ambling A with Finn two days ago, she'd practically been a hermit. She'd shut herself up in her room, poking her head out only for meals and a few speed-yoga sessions, lest Finn turn up at the front door again.

She wasn't ready to see him—not after that kiss. Making out with the father of her baby before he even knew she was pregnant was definitely *not* part of the plan. Nor was making out with him afterward. Her mission was pretty straightforward: face her moral responsibility to tell Finn about the baby, then hightail it back to Dallas and get on with her life as a single-mom-to-be.

The plan involved zero kissing whatsoever.

The trouble was, when Finn dropped her off at the boarding house after she threw herself at him in the pasture, he'd asked if he could see her again and she'd said yes. How could she not? They still needed to have a very important conversation. But she needed some time to get her bearings first, and she definitely didn't need to go back to the Ambling A. It was far too cozy over there, with all the pumpkin carving and the cows munching on harvest corn. What would happen next time? A moonlit hayride?

No.

Because there wouldn't be a next time. She should have never set foot on Crawford property in the first place. Telling him about the pregnancy needed to take place on neutral territory. Someplace safe.

"Is your mind clear yet?" Avery cracked her eyes open to check on Melba.

The older woman gave her a blank look. The baby goat in her arms let out a warbly bleat, and Melba bit back a smile. "Afraid not, dear."

That made two of them.

"Melba!" someone called from inside the house, and before either of them could respond, the door flew open and Old Gene strode onto the porch.

He took in the yoga mats, then glanced back and forth between their tree poses. "What in the world is going on out here?"

"What does it look like?" Melba sniffed. "Avery is teaching me some of her fancy yoga moves."

"You're doing yoga?" He gaped at her as if she'd just sprouted another head. "With the goat?"

"Avery says it's a thing." Melba glanced at her for confirmation.

"Indeed it is." Avery nodded. "Very on trend."

"I'm old, but I'm not dead. I can still learn new things. Besides, you've been gone all morning. Someone had to watch the wee thing." Melba scratched the baby goat behind the ears. When she appeared to realize what she was doing, she stopped.

Her resistance was crumbling where the goat was concerned, much to Avery's amusement. Not that she was surprised. Melba was a natural caretaker. It was what made the boarding house such a nice place to stay.

Avery, however, was still avoiding any and all hands-on interaction with the tiny creature. She knew next to nothing the about farm animals, her recent cattle experience notwithstanding. The one thing she did know, though, was that it should probably have a name by now.

"Have you thought of what you want to call the poor goat yet?" she asked Old Gene.

His gaze darted to his wife. "I thought Melba might want to do the honors."

"Oh, no, you don't." She dumped the baby goat in Gene's arms, where it landed in a heap of tiny hooves, soft bleats and furry orange coat. "If I name her, that means we're keeping her. Nice try, but no."

Melba gave her eyes a mighty roll and huffed off in the direction of the kitchen.

Okay, then. Namaste.

Avery smiled to herself as she bent down to roll up the yoga mats. "Give it a few more days, Gene. I think the little kid is growing on her. Where were you off to this morning?"

Old Gene had been notably absent at breakfast. For once, Claire's homemade cinnamon rolls had lasted past 9:00 a.m. Avery had indulged in seconds, since she was eating for two.

"I was at a planning meeting for the upcoming autumn festival over at the high school, but then the delivery of hay for the hay maze arrived and needed unloading. The last time I tossed a hay bale around, I threw my back out. So I left that to the younger folks and scooted on home." He set the goat on the ground, and the animal teetered toward the grass beyond Avery's makeshift yoga area on the porch.

"That sounds like a wise choice," Avery said. The thought of Melba taking care of an incapacitated Old Gene on top of the boarding house and an orphaned goat was too unnerving to contemplate. "So is this autumn festival a big thing around here?"

Finn had mentioned the festival, and her curiosity was definitely piqued.

Old Gene nodded and crossed his arms as he watched

the baby goat bounce around the yard. "Yes, ma'am. It certainly is."

"What's it like?"

"Let's see. The festival starts off with two weeks of fall-themed activities in the evenings and then ends with a Halloween party in the school gym. It's a big family event. The kids dress up in costumes, there are always a lot of Halloween-themed games and Melba brings her famous caramel apples. You'd love it."

Avery grinned.

She'd never been to a small-town festival before. And the last Halloween party she'd attended had been a stuffy masquerade ball at the country club. Adults only. The costumes had all been extravagant rentals and the guests dined on delicate hors d'oeuvres and cocktails. A quaint small-town Halloween did indeed sound lovely.

Old Gene dragged his gaze away from the goat and studied her for a moment. "You'll still be here in two weeks, right?"

"Oh." She straightened and hugged her yoga mat to her chest. "I'm not sure. It kind of depends…"

On how much longer I put off the inevitable.

"I doubt it," she added.

She'd already been away from the office far too long. Her parents thought she was off on a spa getaway with friends. That excuse would wear thin eventually— sooner rather than later.

Old Gene refocused his attention on the goat, and Avery noticed his shoulders sag a little bit. "That's too bad. Melba is going to worry about you when you're gone. She has a soft spot for you, you know."

Guilt nagged at Avery's conscience. She'd known for weeks that Melba suspected she was on the run from a bad relationship, and she'd done nothing to alleviate such worries. Letting her believe in some fictional ex-boyfriend seemed so much easier than trying to explain the truth.

"I know." An ache knotted in her throat.

She liked it here. She liked Melba and Old Gene. She even sort of liked the goat. She would have, anyway, if its very presence didn't remind her of her complete and total lack of maternal instincts. The real reason she'd yet to try to bottle-feed it was because she was afraid she'd mess everything up and the goat would reject her.

How sad was that?

"My wife wouldn't try yoga for just anyone, especially not with this troublemaker." Old Gene scooped the goat into his arms and stuck a foot out in front of him as if he were trying to kick an imaginary soccer ball. "What about me? Am I doing it right?"

Avery snorted with laughter. "You're nailing it, Gene."

"Who says you can't teach an old dog new tricks?" He flashed a triumphant smile and carried the goat inside.

Its little head rested on Old Gene's shoulder, and the animal fluttered its long eyelashes at Avery as they disappeared from view.

She wondered if the sentiment applied to herself, as well. She wasn't exactly old, but aside from the fact that she wasn't in a relationship with her baby's father, she was woefully unprepared for motherhood. She'd never once changed a diaper. As an only child, she'd never spent much time around children, either. She hadn't even babysat for extra money as a teenager. She hadn't needed to. Her parents had always been more than happy to give her everything she wanted, including a job.

There was more truth to Finn's nickname for her than she wanted to admit.

Princess.

She took a shaky inhale of crisp autumn air and tried to ignore the nagging feeling that her charmed existence was about to come to an abrupt end. Maximilian Crawford might have fond memories of her father, but the feeling definitely wasn't mutual. Oscar Ellington was going to hit the roof when he found out she'd slept with Finn.

Ready or not, life as Avery knew it was about to change.

Finn leaned against the vast kitchen counter in the main house of the Ambling A while he stared at the screen of his iPhone and frowned. Four missed calls showed on his display, and not one of them was Avery.

He sighed, put the phone down and then picked it back up again just in case.

Still nothing. Damn it.

He did his best to ignore the fact that he was acting like a lovesick teenager and jabbed at the power button of the high-end espresso machine his father had imported from Europe. You could take Maximilian Crawford out of the big city, but you couldn't take the big city out of Maximilian.

"There you are," the older man said as he strolled into view.

Speak of the devil. "Hello, Dad."

Finn flipped a switch, and dark, aromatic liquid began to fill his cup. Black, like his mood.

"Where have you been, son?" Maximilian jammed his hands on his hips. "Viv Dalton has been trying to get ahold of you all day."

Finn was well aware of the fact that the matchmaker/wedding planner had been trying to reach him. She'd been blowing his phone up all morning, hence the missed call notifications.

"I had meetings all day in Billings. I have a job, remember?" He sipped his coffee, then arched a brow at his father. "And contrary to whatever you've started to believe, it doesn't involve carrying on the family name."

That's what his five brothers were for.

Maximilian glared at Finn's phone, sitting quietly on the marble countertop. "You need to call her back. She's set up a date for you this evening."

Just as Finn suspected. Ordinarily, this bit of news would have taken the edge off his stormy mood. Now, not so much.

"No." Finn shook his head.

"What do you mean, no?" Maximilian looked at him as if he'd just sprouted two heads.

Finn didn't really blame him. He'd nearly surprised himself, as well. "I mean, no. I can't."

Can't was a stretch. *Won't* was more like it. After recently spending the day with Avery, he just didn't have it in him for another date with another total stranger. Frankly, the idea didn't sound appealing at all.

What the heck had gotten into him?

Avery's spur-of-the-moment kiss, that's what.

Finn cleared his throat and took another scalding gulp of coffee.

"Balderdash." Maximilian waved a dismissive hand. "Viv has been going the extra mile to line up these dates for you. Unless you have other plans, you'll go."

Much to his dismay, Finn had zero plans. Avery had agreed to see him again, but he'd been trying to give her some space, since she'd seemed so rattled by the kiss. He thought it best to let her contact him instead of the other way around.

He just hadn't bargained on it taking so long…or that waiting for her call would make him feel like an insecure kid hoping for an invitation to prom.

"I do have other plans, actually." He set down his coffee cup with a little too much force, picked up his phone and tucked it into his pocket as he strode toward the door.

"Since when?" a disbelieving Maximilian said to his back.

Since now.

"Finn." Avery wrapped her arms around her middle and glanced back and forth between the father of her baby and Old Gene, sitting across from one another at the big farm table in the kitchen of the boarding house. "I didn't realize you were here."

"I gave Melba a shout upstairs and asked her to send you down." Old Gene shrugged.

The baby goat was snuggled in his lap with its spindly legs tucked beneath itself. What must Finn think? He lived on that massive log cabin estate out at the Ambling A, and their kitchen looked like a scene out of *Green Acres*.

She blinked.

Their kitchen?

You don't actually live *here, remember. This is temporary.*

"Yes, you did holler for me to send Avery to the kitchen." Melba bustled into the room behind Avery and paused, hands on her sturdy hips. "But you didn't mention we had company."

Finn pushed back from the table and stood. "Hello, Mrs. Strickland." He set amused eyes on Avery. "Hi."

"Hi." Her face went warm, suddenly bashful to be interacting with Finn in front of the Stricklands, which was patently ridiculous. They weren't kids, after all.

But Melba and Old Gene were nurturing in a way that Avery's parents had never been. Not only was it making her think long and hard about what sort of mother she hoped to be, but it was also making her fall more in love with Rust Creek Falls every day.

Of course the fact that there was currently a handsome cowboy smiling at her didn't hurt, either.

"What brings you by, Mr. Crawford?" Melba, apparently the only woman in Montana impervious to Finn's charms, crossed her arms.

"I thought Avery might like to take a ride out to the maple syrup farm." He winked at Avery—just a quick, nearly imperceptible flutter of his lashes, but all the air in the room seemed to gather in her lungs. She was breathless all of a sudden. "If that's okay with you folks, of course."

Avery bit back a smile. He was asking Melba and Old Gene for permission to take her on a date, which was kind of adorable. Too adorable to resist, actually.

"Well, I don't know," Melba said.

"Don't be silly, dear." Old Gene stood. "It's fine. Avery would probably love it out there. It's so colorful this time of year."

The goat bleated its agreement. Melba, outnumbered, sighed.

"I'll go get changed." Avery pulled her T-shirt down in an effort to more fully cover her midsection. She was still wearing yoga pants, and chances were they showed off an entirely different body than the one Finn had seen naked a few months ago.

"It's a farm." Finn tilted his head and looked Avery up and down. "You're not planning on slipping into one of your pencil skirts, are you?"

She laughed a little too loud. Her days of fitting into a pencil skirt were over. For five months, minimum. "No, just something cozy."

Translation: something baggy enough to hide her rapidly expanding baby bump.

She slipped into one of her new flannel purchases, a soft pair of leggings and bouncy sneakers. Melba seemed a little less hostile when she returned to the kitchen. Finn must have really turned on the charm, because when they left for the maple syrup farm, Melba sent them off with a thermos of her special apple cider.

"The Stricklands really seem to enjoy having you around," Finn said as they passed the Welcome to Rust Creek Falls sign on the outskirts of town.

The smells of cinnamon and spice swirled in the cab of Finn's truck, wrapping around them like a plush blanket. Avery closed her eyes and took a deep inhale. "Mmm. Melba and Old Gene are the best, aren't they?"

"They are, but I'm not sure the feeling is mutual, especially where Melba is concerned."

"She's just a little protective, that's all." Avery nearly gasped at how colorful the trees looked as they moved deeper and deeper into the countryside and farther away from Rust Creek Falls.

Finn shot her a mischievous glance. "Do you think you need protecting from me, Princess?"

Avery thought about the warning Melba had given

her about Finn after they'd bumped into him at the general store.

Finn isn't right for a nice girl like you.

She arched a brow. "You tell me. Do I?"

Finn responded with a wide grin that told her he definitely hadn't forgotten about the way she thrown herself at him in the pasture at the Ambling A. Maybe Melba had it wrong and he was the one who needed protecting.

Avery straightened in her seat. Finn could smile all he wanted. She intended to take this time together to have a serious discussion with him. There would be no more kissing. Not today, anyway.

Except there was.

Once again, Avery fell completely under the spell of Finn in his natural habitat. Why did he suddenly seem like he belonged on the pages of a hot cowboys calendar rather than in the boardrooms where she usually ran into him back in Texas?

The maple syrup farm was much quieter than she anticipated. She'd expected trees with sap buckets attached and the hum of boilers in the nearby sugarhouse. But as Finn explained, the sapping season usually ran from February until mid-April or so. The farms still had a good number of visitors during autumn, though, due to the spectacular fall colors of the sugar maple trees.

Avery could hardly believe her eyes. After they'd stopped by the farm's quaint little gift shop and Avery purchased glass bottles of syrup in varying colors of amber, they went for a walk in the sugar bush. The deeper into the woods they wandered, the closer together the trees grew, until she and Finn were surrounded by nothing but blazing red. Crimson leaves floated through the air like radiant snowflakes, and when they came upon a tiny white chapel nestled far into the cluster of maples, Avery was completely and utterly enchanted.

That was her only explanation for what happened next. It was as if the beautiful surroundings had indeed made her fall under a magical spell, because when she looked at Finn in the dappled sunlight of the fiery woods, her canvas bag of maple syrup slipped from her hand and fell to the ground with a soft thud. She wrapped her arms around the father of her baby and kissed him, long and deep. She kissed him so hard that the force of it seemed to shake loose the leaves from the surrounding sugar maples, until at last she had to pull away to catch her breath.

What was happening to her? Why did she keep losing her head like this?

"I'm so sorry," she said, backing away against the solid trunk of a maple tree. Good. Maybe it would knock some sense into her. "I don't know why I keep doing that."

Finn gave her a tender smile that slowly built into a full-wattage grin. Avery's cheeks burned with heat, and she suspected her face had gone as red as the surrounding foliage.

But like the gentleman that he was, her Texas-businessman-turned-Montana-cowboy spared her the embarrassment of saying anything. He simply bent to pick up her discarded bag, then took her by the hand and walked her back down the forest trail, leaving the kiss behind.

Just another of their secrets.

Chapter 5

Finn returned to the Ambling A after taking Avery back to the boarding house to find his dad and his brother Hunter fully immersed in a craft project with Hunter's six-year-old daughter, Wren.

The two men looked woefully out of place in their ranch attire while doing something with paper plates full of paint. Finn wasn't entirely sure what they were trying to accomplish, but Wren seemed as pleased as punch, which he supposed was the objective of the messy affair.

He took it all in with bemused interest and cocked an eyebrow at his father. "This is a surprise. For some reason, I thought you had plans tonight with one of your lady friends."

It was a logical assumption. On any given Friday night, Maximilian typically had a date. Sometimes two.

When he wasn't preoccupied with meddling into his sons' love lives, of course.

"I do." Maximilian ruffled Wren's fair blond hair. "With this little lady right here."

Wren gigged and made jazz hands at Finn, her palms and fingers dripping orange paint onto the copies of the Rust Creek Falls *Gazette* that provided a protective covering for the table. "We're making handprint leaves, Uncle Finn. Do you want to make one, too?"

Large sheets of manila paper were scattered in front of her, decorated with yellow, orange and red handprints that had been fashioned into leaves with the help of stems and leafy veins drawn in brown magic marker.

"It looks like the three of you have got it covered." Finn eyed his brother. "Where on earth did you come up with this?"

Hunter shrugged. "Pinterest."

"Pinterest?" Finn bit back a smile. If anyone actually needed Viv Dalton's dating service, it was Hunter. Most definitely.

"What?" Hunter said, as if perusing Pinterest for kids' craft projects was something all of the Crawford brothers did on a daily basis.

"Nothing." Finn shook his head. It was actually really sweet how his brother had immersed himself into being both a father and mother to Wren. Not that he'd had much of a choice.

Still, it was pretty amusing seeing his rough-and-tumble brother and father sitting around doing arts and crafts on a Friday night. He was used to them doing things like roping calves and cutting hay, not finger-painting.

"I'm going up to bed. See you all in the morning."

Finn faked a yawn and headed toward the stairs, eager to shut himself in his room before Maximilian had a chance to question him about his whereabouts.

"Hold up there, son."

Too late.

"Where have you been off to tonight?" Maximilian frowned down at the mess of paint in front of him. Clearly he'd skipped the Pinterest tutorial. "The young woman Viv wanted to introduce you to called here a little while ago and said she hadn't heard from you."

Finn's jaw clenched shut tight. *Give it a rest, old man. I'm handling my own love life just fine these days.*

And since when had Viv started giving out his phone number?

"I was with Avery Ellington," he said.

There. Maybe if he threw Maximilian a bone, his father would leave him alone for once.

"Is that right?" Maximilian's eyebrows furrowed and then released. "Glad to hear it. The Ellington apple seems to have fallen quite far from the tree. You two make a fine couple."

"Right." Hunter let out a snort as he drew another stem onto one of Wren's handprint leaves. "As if Finn is actually serious about her."

Hunter's casual dismissal of Finn's feelings about Avery rubbed him the wrong way, although he wasn't entirely sure why. She was only in town temporarily, and as Finn himself had reiterated time and again, he wasn't looking for anything serious.

"He's seen her more than once. For your brother, that's serious," Maximilian said.

Hunter nodded. "Point taken."

Finn's chest grew tight. Why had he thought it was

ever a good idea to live under the same roof as his family? "Are you two enjoying yourselves?"

"I am." Wren wiggled in her chair.

"Yes. You are, sweetheart. And I'm glad." Finn narrowed his gaze at his father. "But you need to calm down. Avery and I are just casually seeing each other until she goes back to Texas. It doesn't even qualify as a relationship."

Right... That's why you can't stop thinking about her.

He shifted his weight from one foot to the other, suddenly acutely uncomfortable with the direction this conversation was headed.

"Would it be so awful if she stayed in Montana?" Maximilian pressed his palm into a paper plate full of yellow paint.

Finn couldn't help wishing he'd accidentally spill it down the front of his snap-button Western shirt. "I'm surprised you're pressing the issue. Aren't you and her father are supposed to be mortal enemies?"

"Ellington or not, Avery seems good for you." Maximilian waved a hand, sending yellow paint splatters flying, much to Wren's amusement. "Her daddy and I haven't spoken in years. Maybe all that mess is simply water under the bridge."

Finn somehow doubted Avery's dad saw it that way.

"Regardless, I'm not in a relationship with his daughter." Finn's head hurt all of a sudden. He sighed. "We're just…"

Words failed him.

What *were* they doing? Hell if he knew. Nor did he have any idea why he was still standing around trying to explain it to his meddling father and smart-ass brother.

"You're just what, exactly?" The twinkle in Maximilian's eyes was as brilliant as a three-carat diamond engagement ring from Tiffany.

"Never mind. I'm going to bed." Finn ignored the suggestive smirks aimed his way and headed to his suite.

He didn't have the first clue what he and Avery were doing. One minute she was throwing herself at him, and the next she was knocking her head into a tree. It should have been making him crazy. And it was…

But in a good way—a way that had him counting the minutes until he could see her again. The warmth of Avery's sultry mouth had suddenly become the last thing he thought about before he drifted off to sleep and his first memory upon waking. Because whatever was really going on between them, Finn liked it.

He liked it a whole heck of a lot.

The third time Finn showed up unannounced at Strickland's, Avery was ready.

Call it intuition, or chalk it up to wishful thinking— Avery greatly preferred to think of it as the former. Either way, when he showed up bright and early the morning following their trip to the maple syrup farm, no one was surprised. Not her, not Melba, not Old Gene.

Not even the baby goat. The tiny animal woke from her nap on her dog bed by the back door and kicked her little hooves as Melba escorted Finn into the kitchen.

"Look who's here," she said, wiping her hands on her apron. "Again."

Melba seemed to be doing her best to keep up her general dislike of Finn, but the sparkle in her eye told Avery he was wearing her down. The tote bag full of maple syrup in his hands probably didn't hurt.

"Who wants pancakes?" Finn said, winking at Avery.

The baby goat bleated, and Avery couldn't help but smile.

Melba narrowed her gaze at Finn. "Pancakes aren't on the menu this morning."

Claire had whipped up her famous ham biscuits, which were up for grabs in the dining room. Avery had already eaten one, but she wouldn't turn down pancakes with real maple syrup. Not when she was eating for two.

"I thought I'd make them." Finn reached into his bag and extracted a box of organic pancake mix. "Pumpkin spice. Who's in?"

Had Finn Crawford just waltzed into Melba Strickland's home and announced he was going to cook? Oh, this was going to be good. Such a bold move was sure to either win her over or make her an enemy for life.

Old Gene's eyebrows shot clear to his hairline. Avery had to the bite the inside of her cheek to keep from laughing.

"What do you say, Mrs. Strickland?" Finn shot the older woman his most devastating bad-boy grin, and against all odds, it worked.

"Fine." She untied her apron and handed it to Finn. "If you insist. But you'll need to clean up after yourself. Claire and I won't abide a messy kitchen."

She paused a beat, then added, "And call me Melba."

"Yes, ma'am." Finn's grin widened as he tied the frilly apron around his waist.

He looked utterly ridiculous in his boots, jeans and Melba's lacy kitchen attire, but then again, Avery was still snug in her flannel pajamas.

"Come on, dear." Old Gene folded the newspaper he'd been reading into a neat square and pushed back from the kitchen table. "Let's leave these two young things alone for a spell."

Melba cast a questioning glance at Avery, and she nodded. "Go put your feet up. We'll let you know when the pancakes are ready."

The thought of Melba actually putting her feet up was almost laughable, but with a little added encouragement from Gene, she finally vacated the kitchen.

"I think she's starting to like you," Avery said after the swinging door closed behind the Stricklands.

"Good." Finn cocked his head. "Should I be worried about why she didn't like me to begin with?"

That would be due to your reputation as a serial womanizer.

Avery picked up the box of pancake mix and stared intently at the directions. She wasn't about to comment on Finn's overactive social life. Although, since she'd run into him at the general store, he hadn't had time to go on any dates. He seemed to be spending all of his free time with her.

Not that she was complaining. She'd definitely been enjoying his company. Truth be told, she enjoyed it far too much—hence the rather embarrassing habit she'd developed of kissing him whenever the mood struck her. Which was often.

But Avery had to give Finn credit. He still hadn't tried to get her into bed again, which she considered a major point in his favor. Instead of assuming they'd take up right where they'd left off in Oklahoma, he was wooing her.

And it was working. Melba wasn't the only one around the boarding house who'd developed a soft spot for Finn.

You're not supposed to be dating *him. It's a little late for that, isn't it?*

The box of pancake mix slipped through Avery's fingers, and Finn caught it before it hit the floor.

"Whoa there, butterfingers," he said, but affection glowed in his eyes. He gave her a lopsided grin, and her heart pounded with such force that she wondered if he could hear it beneath the thick layer of her flannel pajama top.

If she wasn't careful, she was going to kiss him again, right there in the boarding house kitchen.

She grabbed the first thing she could get her hands on—Claire's favorite cast-iron skillet—and held it in front of her. A shield. "You need some help with those pancakes, cowboy?"

"Not really." He reached toward her and tucked a wayward lock of hair behind her ear. "But I'd never turn down a beautiful woman in pj's."

So I've heard.

She forced a smile. "All right, then. Let's do this."

Even though Finn's hands were occupied pouring batter and flipping pancakes, he was having serious trouble keeping them to himself.

Avery danced around him in her plaid pajamas, giving the batter an extra stir here and there, and there was something about her high, swinging ponytail and slippered feet he found adorably irresistible. He even found himself fantasizing that his mornings could start like this every day if he and Avery were a real couple.

If they were married, for example.

"Oops." Avery winced. "I think you're burning that one."

Finn blinked and refocused his attention on the cast-iron skillet in front of him, where smoke had begun rising from the lopsided circle of batter in its center. Oops indeed.

He scooped up the smoldering remains with a spatula and dumped them in the trash. "We've still got a pretty good stack going."

"Good, because I think there's only enough batter for a few more." She handed him a semi-full measuring cup.

Finn took it, emptied it into the pan and handed it back to her, arching a brow when her fingertips brushed against his. Did she feel it, too? That little jolt of electricity that happened every time they touched?

The sudden flush of color in her peaches-and-cream complexion told him that indeed she did. "If you keep looking at me like that, cowboy, you're going to burn the next one, too."

He didn't much care. He wasn't even hungry, and there was already a towering stack of pumpkin-spiced goodness for Avery and the Stricklands.

The pancakes had been an excuse to see her again. That, and an attempt to get on Melba's good side, since she apparently had decided he wasn't good enough for Avery. When it came right down to it, he tended to agree. Avery was out of his league. She was the kind of woman who deserved to be wined and dined, whisked off to Paris for a romantic weekend getaway, swept off her feet with a surprise proposal.

Finn frowned down at the frying pan. For a man who had absolutely no interest in marriage, the antiquated institution certainly seemed to be occupying a large portion of his thoughts all of a sudden. He blamed his father. And Viv Dalton. And his brothers, three of whom had already fallen like dominoes. Being surrounded by so much marital bliss was messing with his head in a major way.

Things with Avery were exactly as he'd described them to Maximilian earlier. Casual. They were just enjoying each other's company until she went back to Texas.

Sure you are. Because playing house like this is just the sort of thing you usually do with women you're dating.

He flipped the last pancake on top of the stack and tried not to think about what the other Crawford men would say if they could see him now. Truthfully, he didn't much care what they thought. He was enjoying getting to know Avery better.

That didn't mean he wasn't counting down the minutes until she was back in his bed. He definitely was, and the minutes felt like they were getting longer and longer. But he and Avery were under the watchful gaze of Rust Creek Falls now, not on their own in the middle of Oklahoma. The Stricklands were old-fashioned folks, and as much as he wanted to, scooping Avery into his arms and carrying her upstairs to bed simply wasn't an option. Neither was asking her to spend the night at the Ambling A, for obvious reasons.

He wiped his hands on Melba's apron, and before he could stop himself, he said, "Will you go away with me next weekend?"

"Um. You want to go away together?" Avery's eyes went wide. Perhaps he should have removed the frilly apron before suggesting a romantic getaway. "Where?"

Anywhere, damn it.

"A nice B&B someplace. I can take a look around

and find someplace special." He ditched the spatula, took a step closer and planted a hand on the counter on either side of her, hemming her in. "What do you say, Princess?"

She narrowed her gaze at him, but he could see the pulse booming at the base of her throat. Could hear the hitch in her breath when his attention strayed to her mouth—so perfectly pink.

"You weren't kidding about the pj's, were you?" she said, her voice suddenly unsteady. "You really do like them."

He ran his fingertips over her cheek. "Princess, where we're going, you won't need flannel."

He leaned closer, so close that her breath fanned across his lips and a surge of heat shot through him, so intense, so molten that he nearly groaned. What the hell was he doing? They were in the Stricklands' kitchen and he was on the verge of kissing her so hard and so deep that she'd forget all about the silly grudge her daddy had against his family.

"Is that a promise?" She lifted her chin ever so slightly, an invitation.

Finn's body hardened instantly. He didn't need to be asked twice. He could practically taste her already— perfectly tempting, perfectly sweet. All sugar and spice and everything nice.

She made a breathy little sound and it was nearly his undoing, but in the instant before his mouth came crashing down on hers, the door to the kitchen flew open.

"It smells delightful in here. Is breakfast ready?" Melba said.

Finn and Avery sprang apart like they were teenagers who'd just been caught behind the bleachers in high school.

"Yes. We were just about to come find you," Finn said, a blatant lie if he'd ever told one.

"That's exactly what it looked like you were about to do," Old Gene deadpanned.

Melba elbowed her husband in the ribs, and he flinched but shot Avery and Finn a wink when she wasn't looking.

Chapter 6

On Friday, Melba sat in the rocking chair on the shaded porch of the boarding house with the baby goat in her lap and eyed Avery's overnight bag.

"You're sure about going off alone for the weekend with Finn?" she said, looking mildly disapproving, as if she suspected that Avery's pajamas were still folded neatly in her dresser upstairs.

"Not the whole weekend." Avery held up a finger. "Just one night."

She had, in fact, packed her pajamas. Because her night away with Finn at the B&B wasn't going to be about sex…not *all* about sex, anyway. The main reason she'd agreed to spend the night with him in the nearby town of Great Gulch was so she could finally tell him she was pregnant.

The secrecy had gone on long enough. It was past

time she told him the truth, and she definitely couldn't go to bed with him until he knew about the baby...no matter how very badly she wanted to.

"Your room will be right here waiting for you when you come back." Melba shifted, and the goat let out one of her loud, warbly bleats.

"The little one sounds hungry," Avery said.

The little one.

Her throat grew dry.

"Doesn't she always?" Melba stood, and the tiny animal's cries grew louder. "Hold on to her while I go get a bottle warmed up, will you, dear?"

"What? I... No..." Avery held up her hands in protest, but before she could come up with a reasonable excuse, she suddenly had an armful of kicking, squirming goat.

"I'll be right back." Melba pushed through the door into the boarding house, seemingly oblivious to Avery's distress.

She stared at the goat, and it stared back.

Meeeeeehhhhhhh.

"Shhh," Avery murmured. "Everything's fine, I promise. Or it will be as soon as Melba gets back."

The goat blinked its long eyelashes as if it was really listening to what she was saying. Its little ears twitched.

"You like it when I talk to you?" Avery smiled tentatively.

This wasn't so bad, really. It was sort of like holding a puppy.

Meeeeeehhhhhhh.

"I know. I heard you the first time," she said, then turned at the sound of a car door slamming shut.

Finn grinned as he strode from his truck toward the

front steps of the porch, a dimple flashing in his left cheek. "Now here's a sight I never thought I'd witness."

"What's that?" she asked, rocking slightly from side to side as the goat relaxed into her arms.

Finn arched a challenging eyebrow. "Corporate princess Avery Ellington holding a goat."

Right. The only thing that might be less likely was the sight of her holding a baby.

Oh, God.

She didn't even know what to do with a baby farm animal. How was she going to succeed as a single mother?

"You should take her." She thrust the animal toward Finn. "I don't think she likes me."

"Don't be silly. Sure she does." He reached to scratch the goat behind one of her ears.

"You think so?"

"Yeah. You just need to relax a little bit." Finn shrugged, as if he'd just suggested the easiest thing in the world.

Relax…while holding a goat and pretending not to be secretly pregnant. No problem.

She took a deep breath. If a goat didn't like her, what hope would she have with a baby? Since the animal seemed to enjoy being rocked, she swayed softly from side to side. Seconds later, she was rewarded with a yawn and then some really sweet snuffling sounds.

"See? There's nothing to it," Finn whispered as the goat's eyes drifted closed.

To her embarrassment, Avery realized she was blinking back tears. She sniffed. "Of course. Easy peasy."

Finn regarded her more closely. "Princess?"

She staunchly avoided his gaze, focusing intently on

the goat's soft, ginger-colored fur with a swirl of white on its forehead. "Hmm?"

"Hey, talk to me." Finn brushed her hair from her eyes, the pad of his thumb coming to rest gently on the side of her face. "What's wrong? Are you having second thoughts about going to Great Gulch?"

"No, not at all." She shook her head. Second thoughts? God, no. She couldn't wait to spend time alone with him, except for the part where she needed to tell him he was going to be a father. But maybe that could wait just a tiny bit longer. "Nothing's wrong, I promise."

Liar.

No more waiting. She was getting weepy over bonding with a goat. Finn clearly knew something was going on.

"Actually…" She cleared her throat. Maybe she should go ahead and tell him right here and right now. Just get it out. "I…"

"Oh, hello, Finn." Melba bustled out onto the porch with a bottle in her hand. She glanced back and forth between them. "I suppose you two are ready to head off on your…adventure."

Finn's lips tugged into a half grin. "Yes, ma'am. But do you want some help with that first?"

Avery went still as he reached for the bottle. What was he doing? She knew he was trying to stay in Melba's good graces, but surely she wasn't going to have to try to operate a baby bottle for the very first time while Finn and Melba watched.

"Be my guest." Melba handed him the bottle and reclaimed her place in the rocking chair. "Gene should be doing this himself, but as usual, he's found something else to do and left me in charge of this troublemaker."

"Do you want to do the honors, or should I?" Finn jiggled the bottle in Avery's direction.

Her heart jumped straight to her throat. She hadn't been this nervous since she'd taken her admissions exam before applying to graduate schools for her MBA.

Her panic must have been obvious, because Finn gently prodded the bottle's nipple toward the baby goat's mouth. "Like this, see?"

Within seconds, the goat was happily sucking at the bottle. Finn winked at her over the animal's fuzzy little head, and slowly, carefully he transitioned the bottle to her hand. Avery held her breath, but the switch didn't seem to bother the goat in the slightest. She felt herself grinning from ear to ear as the kid slurped up the rest of her formula.

"You're a natural," Finn said, and something about the sparkle in his warm brown eyes made her blush.

"That you are." Melba slipped her a curious glance. "You know what, dear? I think you're right. It's high time that wee one had a name."

"Oh, good." Avery handed Finn the empty bottle so she could set the goat down. Her hooves clip-clopped on the wooden planks of the porch. "What name did you choose?"

"I didn't." Melba shook her head. "I thought you might like to pick one."

"Me?" Avery's hand flew to her throat.

Melba shrugged. "If you'd rather not…"

"Pumpkin." It flew out of Avery's mouth almost before she knew what she was going to say.

"Pumpkin?" Finn laughed.

"It fits. Look at her." Avery gestured toward the tiny

animal, kicking and bucking up and down the porch steps on her little orange legs.

"I think it's perfect." Melba nodded. "Pumpkin, it is."

An hour later, Avery stood beside Finn as he slipped the key into their room at the bed-and-breakfast cottage in Great Gulch.

The tiny town was only about thirty miles from Rust Creek Falls, but it may as well have been in a different hemisphere. Avery hadn't spotted a familiar face since they'd crossed the county line, and after spending weeks in a place where everyone knew your name—and a fair amount of your personal business—it was a welcome relief.

She loved Rust Creek Falls. She loved Melba and Old Gene. She'd even developed a soft spot for Pumpkin, much to her own astonishment. But giving Finn such private news in a town where gossip was one of the local pastimes only added to her sense of dread about the whole thing. At least here if he reacted badly to the revelation that he was about to be a father, the only witnesses to his meltdown would be strangers.

But that wouldn't happen. Surely not. He'd been so sweet bottle-feeding the little goat. Avery could suddenly see him helping care for a newborn baby... loving his child.

Maybe even loving her.

"Here we are." Finn smiled down at her as held the door open.

Avery stepped into the room and gasped. A fireplace glowed in the corner of the room, bathing the space in glimmering gold light. The antique furniture was all crafted from dark cherry, the most spectacular piece being the four-poster bed covered in delicate lace bedding. Fairy lights were strung along the canopy, and an array of scented candles covered every available surface.

"Finn, this is lovely." She turned to face him, her head swimming with the rich, dreamy aroma of cinnamon and cloves mixed with something she couldn't quite put her finger on. Vanilla, perhaps.

"So you like it?" He dropped their overnight bags on a luggage rack beside a beautifully crafted armoire that looked like it might hold handmade quilts or chunky knit blankets.

"I love it. It's like something out of fairy tale," she said, suddenly wistful.

"Good." He studied her for a moment, and then his lips curved into a slow smile that gradually built into an expression that took Avery's breath away. "I've wanted to be alone with you, really alone, since the second I spotted you in the general store."

She let out a shuddering breath, and suddenly the air in the room felt thick with promise. Or maybe the intimate hush that had fallen between them was the memory of the night they'd spent in Oklahoma City.

"Avery." Finn held out his hand, and the subtext was clear. He wasn't just offering her his hand—he was offering her himself, body and soul.

But for how long?

She couldn't seem to move a muscle. Even breathing seemed difficult. Her heart was pounding so hard she thought she might choke.

Finn's face fell, and he dropped his hand. "Did I presume too much? If you don't want this…"

"I *do* want this. I want *you*…more than I can possibly

say. This place, this room…it's all so beautiful. I don't want anything to mar our perfect night together." She inhaled a steadying breath before she hyperventilated. Why was this so hard? "I should have been straight with you from the start."

Finn closed the distance between them, wove his fingers through hers and kissed the backs of her hands. First one, then the other. Tenderly. Reverently. "Princess, there's nothing you can tell me that will change the way I feel about you."

She didn't deserve this kind of blind faith—not when she'd been hiding such an enormous secret from him.

"You can't know that," she said, shaking her head from side to side.

"I think I know what you're trying to say." He lifted a hand to her face, drawing his fingertips slowly across her cheek. She closed her eyes and fought the urge to lean into him. Because he couldn't possibly know, could he? "You came here on purpose looking for me."

She opened her eyes and nodded slowly. It was the truth, but not all of it. It was barely even the tip of the iceberg.

"That's great! I'm glad you did. Now come here." He wrapped an arm around her waist and pulled her close until she was pressed flush against him.

Then his mouth was suddenly on hers, and she was opening for him, wanting the warm, wet heat of his kiss—wanting it so badly she could have wept, because she could feel the crash of his heartbeat against hers. Frenzied. Desperate. And she could feel the way his body hardened as the kiss grew deeper, hotter.

Her fists curled around the soft material of his T-shirt, and in one swift move, Finn pulled back, slid the shirt over his head and tossed it onto the floor. In a heartbeat, he was kissing her again, cupping her face and groaning his pleasure into her mouth.

Avery's hands went instantly to the solid, muscular wall of his chest, and he felt so good, so right that she felt like she might die if he didn't take her to bed again. She'd wanted him since Oklahoma…since before she'd even known about the baby.

The baby.

Her eyes flew open and she pulled away, ending their kiss. Her palms, however, stubbornly remained pressed against his pectoral muscles. Was it her imagination, or had he gotten in even better shape since she'd last seen him shirtless? It must be all of the ranch work out at the Ambling A. It hardly seemed fair. He'd gone and made himself hotter while she'd been bursting out of her pencil skirts.

"Finn, wait."

He gave her one of his lazy, seductive smiles that she loved so much and glanced down at her hands, which seemed to be making an exploratory trail over the sculpted ridges of his abdomen. "We'll take it slow, baby. It will be good. So good."

She had no doubt that it would—better than the last time, even.

"We can't." She shook her head, somehow forced herself to stop touching him and crossed her arms.

Finn's gaze flitted to the bed and then back to her. "Why the heck not?"

She couldn't bring herself to say it. How could she? She couldn't even think straight while she was looking at that bare chest of his, much less form a coherent sentence.

But this was it—the moment of truth. One way or another, he was about to find out she was pregnant. He'd see the change in her body the second she undressed.

Slowly, she took his hand and rested it on her belly, telling him the only way she knew how.

His expression went blank for a moment, and then he stared down at his hand covering the slight swell of her tummy. The wait for understanding to fully dawn on him was agonizing. Avery lived and died a thousand deaths in that fraction of a second, until at last he lifted his gaze to hers. A whole array of emotions passed over his face, a lifetime of feelings all at once.

She took a deep breath. Then she let the rest of her secret unravel and laid it at his feet.

"It's yours."

Chapter 7

Finn's ears rang.

The noise in his head started out as a faint roar—like listening to the inside of a seashell—but it multiplied by the second, drowning out all other sound. Avery's lips were moving, so he knew she hadn't stopped talking. But he couldn't make sense of the sounds coming out of her mouth. Nor could he hear the crackle of the fire in the old stone fireplace, even after he forced his gaze away from Avery and stared at its dancing flame.

He blinked, half tempted to stick his hand in the hearth to jolt himself back to life.

It's yours.

Avery was pregnant…with *his* child. He was going to be a father.

He didn't know whether to be furious or ecstatic. Somewhere beyond the scathing sense of betrayal, he was delighted at the news. A baby…with *Avery*.

That night in Oklahoma had changed him. Finn had realized that the moment he'd run into her at the general store. All the nonsense he'd put himself through since he'd moved to Montana—all the casual dates with women he didn't even know—reminded him what he was missing without Avery Ellington in his life. It was as if that Oklahoma City blackout had somehow split his life into two parts, before and after. Only now did he fully comprehend why it had felt that way.

But she should have told him sooner. She'd been in town for *weeks* and hadn't said a word.

"It's mine," he said in an aching whisper. And with those two quiet words, the fog in his head cleared.

"Yes." Avery nodded, tears streaming down her face. "Yes, of course it's yours. There hasn't been anyone else. Not for a long, long time."

In the mirror hanging on the calico-papered wall, he saw himself shake his head. She didn't get it. Couldn't she understand? He wasn't questioning her assertion. He was stating a fact. The baby was his. *Theirs.*

Which meant he had a right to know of its existence.

"How could you have kept this from me all this time?" He closed his eyes and thought about all the times in the past few days he'd sensed that something was off. He'd *known*, damn it. He'd asked her time and again to tell him what was on her mind, and she'd refused. Every damn time.

"I tried to tell you. I really did. I just couldn't find the words. Please, you have to understand." She pressed her fingertips to her quivering mouth.

She stood stoically, awaiting his response. But he could see the hint of tension in her wide brown eyes, then he saw her bite her lip. And even in his fury, Finn hated himself for making her feel that way.

"I asked you to talk to me," he said with measured calmness. But his voice sounded cold and distant, even to his own ears. "I asked you what was wrong, and you looked me straight in the eye and said 'nothing.'"

He sat down on the edge of the bed and dropped his head in his hands.

"There were cows! And your father. And then I couldn't even bottle-feed the goat…and then…" The words caught. A sob escaped her, and when Finn looked up, Avery had wrapped her arms around her middle as if it took every bit of her strength to simply hold herself together. "Finn, I'm sorry. I didn't know how to tell you. I knew it would be a shock. It was for me, too."

He narrowed his gaze. What on earth was she rambling on about? Old Gene's orphaned goat?

She'd been so happy when the tiny thing took a liking to her. She'd beamed like she'd just won a shiny blue ribbon at the state fair. Was this what all that excitement had really been about? The baby?

Not the *baby.* Our *baby.*

"Look, I didn't even realize I was pregnant myself for quite some time. For *months.* I missed my period, and I was so tired all the time, I fell asleep at my desk! But I'd been working such long hours and I just thought…"

Finn flew to his feet. "Are you okay? Is the baby healthy?"

Avery nodded, her eyes still wet with tears.

What had he done? His first thought should have been about the baby, not how long it had taken her to tell him about the pregnancy.

He reached a trembling hand toward her belly and

then pulled it back. He had no right to touch her. Not after the way he'd just spoken to her.

"Okay." He swallowed, shame settling in his gut. He couldn't turn back time and change his initial reaction, but he could still make this right. He *had* to make it right. "In the morning we will make the arrangements."

"The arrangements?" The color drained slowly from Avery's crestfallen face. "Surely you're not suggesting I have a…um…procedure?"

Over his dead body. She thought that much of him, did she?

"Princess, you really don't know me very well. Absolutely not." His gaze dropped to her belly again, and he had to ball his hands into fists to stop himself from reaching for her so he could feel the swell of life growing inside her.

The life they'd made *together*.

When he lifted his gaze back to hers, she regarded him with what looked like a cautious mixture of hope and shame. And he hated himself just a little bit more.

He was thoroughly botching this. It was time to make himself clear.

"You and I are getting married," he said flatly.

Avery's jaw dropped. She stared at him for a beat and then had the audacity to laugh in his face. "You can't be serious."

"As a heart attack," he said evenly.

No child of his was going to grow up without a father. Finn knew all too well what it was like to be brought up without two present, supportive parents.

Maximilian was no saint. Finn wasn't fool enough to overlook the fact that his father could be manipulative and somewhat domineering. But he could count on one hand the number of times he'd seen his mother since she'd filed for divorce. She hadn't just walked away from her husband—she'd walked away from her six sons, too. An absence like that left its mark on a boy. A soul-deep wound that took a lifetime to heal.

Possibly longer.

Finn wouldn't do that to an innocent child. He would be there every step of the way, come hell or high water.

"Finn, what you said a few seconds ago is the truth. I don't really know you, and you don't know me, either. Certainly not well enough to entertain the idea of marriage." She shook her head and looked at him like he was as mad as a wet hen.

The only thing his impulsive proposal had accomplished was putting an end to her tears. That was something, at least.

"I won't be shut out of my child's life," he said. His voice broke, and something inside him seemed to break right along with it.

How had he and Avery come to this? They should be in bed together right now, but instead they were suddenly standing on opposite sides of the room as if the past few days hadn't happened at all.

Spending time with Avery in Rust Creek Falls had been fantastic, like something out of a dream. Finn had gone to bed every night thanking his lucky stars that she'd somehow found her way back into his life. He hadn't thought about his dad's ridiculous arrangement with Viv Dalton in days. He'd been too busy figuring out how to see more of Avery before she left town to think about the bounty on his head.

Oh, the irony.

Maximilian was going to be happier than a pig in slop when he heard about this. Avery's dad, not so much.

Just how much did her father despise the Crawfords? Finn hadn't given the matter much thought since he and Avery had agreed to put their family differences aside, but that would no longer be possible.

"I would never prevent you from seeing your child. You know how much I love it in Rust Creek Falls. I'll come visit, and you can come see the baby in Texas as often as you like," Avery said.

She took a step toward him, her hand resting protectively on the slight swell of her abdomen. She looked more beautiful than Finn had ever seen her before— already so attached to the baby they'd made together.

It seemed crazy, but Finn felt that way, too. Even though he'd only known about the pregnancy for a matter of minutes, an intimacy he'd never experienced before drew him closer to both Avery and their unborn child. Despite her words of assurance, a raw panic was clawing its way up his throat, so thick he almost choked on it.

He couldn't be just a visitor in their baby's life. He *wouldn't*.

"Can I ask you a question?" His jaw tightened, because he had a definite feeling he knew why Avery was so dead set on raising the baby on her own.

She blinked. "Of course."

He lifted a brow and fixed his gaze with hers. "How do your parents feel about the fact that you're carrying a Crawford heir?"

Because that's precisely what their child would be— an heir, not only to the Ellington fortune, but to everything the Crawfords had built, as well. The two empires their fathers had created from the ground up would be forever intertwined in a way that neither of them had ever anticipated.

"Um." Avery looked away, and that's all it took for Finn to know the rest of the story.

Oscar Ellington had no idea that his darling princess of a daughter was pregnant with Finn Crawford's baby.

Avery felt sick, and for once, the slight dizziness and nausea that had her sinking onto the B&B's lovely four-poster bed had nothing to do with morning sickness.

She should have told Finn about the baby sooner. That much was obvious. If she could rewind the clock and go back to the very first time she'd seen him in Rust Creek Falls, she would blurt out the news right there in the middle of the general store. Melba would have fainted, and the news would have been all over town faster than she could max out her credit card during a Kate Spade sample sale, but that would have been just fine…because at least Finn would never have looked at her the way he was regarding her right now.

The look of betrayal in his dark eyes was almost enough to bring her to her knees. Her legs wobbled as she sat down, and a coldness settled into her bones, so raw and deep that a shiver ran up and down her spine. She felt more alone than she'd ever been in her entire life.

He wants to marry you, remember?

Weirdly, Finn's abrupt proposal—if you could even call it that, since it was more of a command than a question—only exacerbated the aching loneliness that had swept over her the minute he'd begun looking at her as if she'd inflicted the most terrible pain in the world on him. Probably because she knew his desire to get married had nothing to do with her. He wanted to be close to their baby.

Not her.

"My parents don't know I'm pregnant," she said, heart drumming hard in her chest.

She couldn't even look at Finn as she admitted the truth. When had she become such a coward? It was pathetic. Her baby deserved a mother who could face challenges head-on, like an adult. Not a spoiled princess who'd had everything handed to her on a silver platter.

She squared her shoulders and forced herself to meet Finn's gaze. "I'm going to tell them, obviously. But I wanted to tell you first."

The set of Finn's jaw softened, ever so slightly. But the hurt in his eyes remained.

Avery swallowed hard. "You deserved to know before anyone else. You're the baby's father."

He took a deep breath, and she wondered what would happen if she went to him and wrapped her arms around him. Pressed her lips to his and kissed him with all the aching want she felt every time she looked at him.

Because she did still want him, and a part of her always would. They were tied together for life now. And as scary as that probably should have been, knowing her attraction to him was part of something bigger— something as meaningful as another life—gave her a strange sense of peace.

The only thing keeping her a chaste three feet away from him was stone-cold fear of what he would say or do next. He wanted to *marry* her, for crying out loud.

That was a hard no. This wasn't the 1950s. Besides,

Avery wasn't about to marry a man who wasn't in love with her.

"Where do they think you are? You've been out of the office for weeks. I'm guessing you didn't actually have meetings in the area at all." Finn's brow furrowed, and he looked like he was mentally scrolling through all the little white lies she'd told since she'd rolled into town. She wanted to crawl under the bed's beautiful lace coverlet and hide.

He pinned her with a glare. She wasn't going anywhere.

No more hiding.

"There were no meetings." She shook her head. "Everyone—my mom and dad, the office—thinks I'm at a spa."

She waited for him to make a crack about what a completely believable lie that had been. Was there a soul on earth who would believe Princess Avery had been bottle-feeding a goat and carving pumpkins instead of munching on kale salad and getting daily massages at Canyon Ranch?

For once, he didn't poke fun at her, and for that, she was profoundly grateful. When he came and sat down beside her, she almost wept with relief.

But the feeling was fleeting, because he wasn't finished asking questions.

"I think it's high time your parents, especially your father, know what's going on. Don't you?" He turned to face her, and he was so close that she couldn't help but stare at him and wonder if her baby would have those same features.

Would he or she have those brown eyes with tiny

gold flecks that she loved so much? The same nose? The same dimple that Finn had in his left cheek?

Her face went warm and she nodded. "Yes, I do."

If she was going to come clean, she might as well do a thorough job of it. Besides, telling Finn he was going to be a father had been the most difficult thing she'd ever done. As crazy as it seemed, the prospect of telling her parents seemed easy in comparison. Even talking to her father seemed manageable, especially with Finn sitting beside her.

They weren't an actual couple, and they *certainly* weren't getting married, but was it too much to think they could be something of a team where their baby was concerned?

He crossed the room to collect her handbag from the pile of their untouched luggage and handed it to her. "I'm assuming your phone is in here?"

She nodded. So this was happening now…as in, *right* now.

She could do this. She was a grown woman. Having a baby was a perfectly normal thing to do.

The phone trembled in her hand as she pulled up her parents' contact information, and Finn's gaze seemed to burn straight into her. She knew he fully expected her to chicken out, so she gave the send button a defiant tap of her finger.

The line started ringing, and she glanced at Finn for a little silent encouragement, but he stood in front of her with his arms crossed, stone-faced. Having him tower over her like that made her heart flutter even more rapidly, so she got up so they could stand eye to eye. Technically, they were eye to chest since he was so much taller than she was, but still. It helped.

The phone rang once, twice, three times. Then at last her father picked up. "Hello?"

"Daddy, hi," she said a little too brightly.

"Hello, sweetheart. Are you on your way back from the spa? I was beginning to wonder if you were ever coming home."

"No, not exactly," Avery said. Her gaze flitted again to Finn's serious expression, and she knew the time had come for the truth. All of it. "I actually haven't been to the spa. I've been in Montana."

There was a long stretch of silence before her dad responded.

"Montana," he said. "I don't understand."

"I'm in Rust Creek Falls." She didn't need to elaborate. Her father was well aware the Crawford ranch had picked up and moved away from Texas. He'd practically thrown a party.

Now his voice shifted from daddy mode to CEO mode in an instant. "Avery, what's going on?"

Before she could say anything, her mom picked up the other extension. "Avery? Hello? Are you okay? What's happened?"

Everything. *Everything* had happened. "I'm fine. I'm in Montana with Finn Crawford and, well, I have something I need to tell you."

Her eyes fixed with Finn's, and he took her hand. It was the smallest possible indication that they were a united front, but she seized on it as if it were a lifeline.

"We're having a baby," she blurted.

"Oh, dear," her mother said.

"What?" Oscar Ellington boomed. His voice was so loud that Avery had to hold the phone away from her ear.

"Daddy, calm down," she said, and Finn's brows drew together in concern.

"I don't understand." Avery's mother sounded mystified. "How did this happen?"

The usual way, Mom. Avery wasn't about to get into the details. Her father was already breathing loud enough to make her wonder if he was on the verge of a heart attack. "I'm four months along, and I came up here to let Finn know."

"Is the Crawford boy there right now? Put him on the phone," her father demanded.

The Crawford boy. What were they, twelve years old? She gripped the phone tighter. "No."

Now wasn't the time for Finn and her dad to have a heart-to-heart, but this was probably the first time Avery had ever willfully refused her father...with the notable exception of sleeping with the enemy.

"Avery, I'm sending a private jet to collect you first thing in the morning. Be on it," her father said. Then he spat, "Alone."

"I can't leave so soon, Daddy. There are things I need to figure out here. But I'll be home soon."

"The hell you will," Finn said with deadly calm. "We're getting married, remember?"

Avery froze. Why in the world would he bring that up now?

She shushed him, but it was too late.

"Honey, I'm not sure getting married is the best idea," her mother said.

Her father was far more insistent. "Avery, I forbid you to marry that man. I won't have a Crawford anywhere near my business. The Ellingtons have the financial means to take care of a child without any help from him."

She wanted to explain that Finn wasn't the horrible person her parents thought he was, despite the fact that he was trying to strong-arm her into marrying him. He was decent. He was kind. Under different circumstances, he might have even been the love of her life.

But she couldn't say any of those things—not while Finn was right there listening to every word she said. She wasn't ready to put her heart on the line like that. Today had been a big enough disaster already. First and foremost, she needed to build a future for her baby. Love was a luxury she couldn't worry about now.

Maybe not ever.

One thing was certain, though. She'd had enough of stubborn men telling her what to do. "Daddy, what exactly are you saying?"

He wanted her to hightail it back to Dallas, but somehow she sensed there was more.

She closed her eyes and concentrated on breathing in and out. No matter what her dad said, she couldn't board a private jet first thing in the morning. She and Finn still needed to hammer out custody arrangements. That might take a while, since he still seemed to think there was a wedding in their future, although she was sure Finn would change his mind once he had time to sleep on it. After all, he'd never much seemed like the marrying type.

Plus, Avery couldn't leave without telling Melba and Old Gene a proper goodbye. The thought of moving out of the boarding house suddenly left her with a lump in her throat. The Stricklands had been so kind to her for weeks now. And what about Pumpkin? She'd miss the sweet little goat.

Once you name an animal, it's yours.

Somehow she doubted her parents would welcome a baby goat any more than they'd welcome the news of her pregnancy.

"I'm telling you to come on home, Avery," her father said.

Just as she'd expected...

Almost.

"But only after you cut Finn Crawford out of your life entirely."

Chapter 8

Finn felt his throat closing up as he watched Avery's eyes go wide and fill with tears again.

"Daddy, you don't mean that." Her voice was a shaky whisper.

Why had he insisted on the phone call with her parents? Oscar Ellington's disdain for Finn's family was clearly far worse than he'd imagined. So far Avery had done a remarkable job of standing her ground, but something had just changed. Finn wished he knew what.

"I can't deprive my baby of his father." Avery's gaze flew toward his. "It wouldn't be right."

Finn held out his hand. "Give me the phone, Avery."

He couldn't let this continue. She was getting too upset, too shaken. What if it somehow harmed the baby?

Finn wouldn't be able to live with himself if something terrible happened to either Avery or their unborn child all because he'd forced her to confront her parents.

"Avery, please," Finn said, working hard to keep his voice even and failing spectacularly.

At last she dropped the phone in his outstretched hand. "Too late. They hung up."

"Good." He tossed the phone onto the bed and jammed his hands on his hips.

"Good? Are you kidding?" She let out a hysterical laugh. "I just told my parents I'm having a baby and they hung up on me."

We, he wanted to say. *We* are having a baby.

Somehow he managed to bite his tongue. "The important thing is that it's done. They know."

She bit her lip, nodding slowly. "You're right. The worst is over. I'm sure my father will calm down after the news sinks in."

She didn't look sure. The fairy lights wrapped around the delicately carved frame of the romantic four-poster bed brought out the copper highlights in her hair, and Finn fought the urge to bury his hands in her dark waves.

He had the absurd wish that he could kiss her and make everything better. He wanted to lie beside her, take her into his arms and whisper promises that he knew good and well he couldn't keep.

It will all be okay.

Your parents will come around.

We're in this together.

He sat down beside her again, this time close enough for his thigh to press softly against hers. When she didn't pull away, he reached for her hand and wove their fingers together. Progress.

He gave her hand a gentle squeeze and dropped a tender kiss on her shoulder. She turned wide, frightened eyes toward him, but her lips curved into a wobbly smile. Maybe they really were in this together, after all.

He took a calming inhale and said, "We can start planning the wedding as soon as we get back to Rust Creek Falls."

Avery rolled her eyes and dropped his hand abruptly. "Would you stop with the wedding talk?"

And just like that, they were back at square one.

"It's not talk. I'm serious." He stood and started pacing from the bed to the fireplace and back again. "You're going to start showing soon, and everyone in town knows we've been seeing each other. I'll be damned if people start whispering that Finn Crawford has a bastard child. I won't do that to my baby. You shouldn't want that, either."

"You have no right to tell me what I should or shouldn't want. From what I hear, you've never been in any kind of committed relationship." She looked him up and down. "What makes you think you're so ready to jump into marriage?"

"What makes you think I'm not?" he countered.

"Oh, I don't know. Maybe the dozens of women you've dated since our night together in Oklahoma." She marched toward her suitcase while Finn stood, paralyzed.

Of course she knew about all those silly dates Viv Dalton had set him up on. No one could keep a secret in a town as small as Rust Creek Falls.

But it wasn't as if he'd been trying to hide anything. When he and Avery had parted ways in Oklahoma, they'd both thought they'd never see each other again—other than in the normal course of business. He'd done nothing wrong.

Then why did he suddenly feel like the biggest jerk in the world?

"Those women meant nothing," he said to her back as she gathered her luggage together. "I promise. If I told you the truth about why I'd been going on so many dates, you'd laugh."

She couldn't leave. If she walked out the door, she could be on the next plane to Dallas and he'd never know. He willed her to turn around and stay until they figured things out.

Together.

She dropped her suitcase with a thud and spun around, arms crossed. "Try me. I could use a good laugh."

Finn drew in a long breath. "My dad wants all six of his sons married off. He's offered a matchmaker in town a million dollars—possibly more—to find wives for each of us. Those were all just meaningless setups."

Avery didn't laugh, but she didn't grab her suitcase again, either. A small victory.

Her eyes narrowed. "Because you didn't intend to marry any of them?"

"Exactly. I wasn't looking for a relationship. I was just…"

Having fun.

He couldn't say it, because he could suddenly see how the entire arrangement looked through Avery's eyes, and it certainly didn't seem like the actions of a man who was ready to marry anyone. Not even the mother of his child.

"Things are different now." He held up his hands, either in an effort to stop her from fleeing or as a gesture of surrender. He wasn't sure which.

"Because I'm pregnant," she said flatly.

Was that the entire reason?

He wasn't sure, so he refrained from answering her. His head was spinning so fast that he couldn't make sense of his thoughts. Avery…a baby…a wedding. Was he ready for all of it?

"Right. That's what I thought." Avery nodded, taking his silence as an admission. "Let's table the marriage talk for now, okay?"

For now.

Finn's jaw clenched. Powerless to press the marriage issue again so soon, he felt an overwhelming emptiness gnaw at him as she continued.

"We can work out a generous visitation schedule while you and I get to know each other better." Avery smiled, but it didn't quite reach her eyes.

Where was that beautiful carefree woman who'd thrown her head back and laughed while one of his cows ate from her outstretched hand? Where was the light that always seemed to shine from somewhere deep within her soul?

Was the prospect of having a baby with him really so awful?

Perhaps, if they did it the way she was describing. She rattled off days of the week and alternating holidays in some crazy, mixed-up fashion that would require a spreadsheet to keep track of. She didn't bother mentioning the fact that if she went back to Dallas, a shared custody arrangement would require multiple flights across the country on a monthly, if not weekly, basis. Maybe it was a good thing her father had a private jet at his disposal.

The thought of Oscar Ellington made Finn grind his teeth so hard that he was in danger of cracking a molar.

"Avery, I…"

Before he could tell her he had no intention of shuttling an infant back and forth between time zones, her cell phone blared to life on the center of the bed. One word lit up the tiny screen: Daddy.

Avery scrambled to pick it up while Finn let out a relieved exhale. Thank God. Surely her parents had come to their senses and Oscar was calling to take back whatever awful things he'd said that had left Avery so shaken. She was the apple of her father's eye. His approval meant a lot to her, and once her dad had gotten over the initial shock, Finn and Avery could stop discussing the baby as if they were two complete strangers and get back to who they'd been in recent days.

And who's that exactly? The future Mr. and Mrs. Finn Crawford?

The thought did seem oddly appealing, despite the fact that he'd been doing everything in his power lately to avoid the altar.

"Daddy," Avery said, smiling faintly as she gripped her phone to her ear. "I'm so glad you called back."

Finn took a tense inhale and reminded himself that the supposed feud between their families wasn't an actual thing.

But apparently hatred was a powerful emotion, even when it was one-sided. Avery's face fell the moment her father started speaking. Finn couldn't make out what was being said, but whatever it was seemed to suck the life right out of her.

Avery's beautiful brown eyes settled into a dull, glassy stare.

"Daddy, be reasonable," she said. Then, in a voice choked with tears, "Daddy, that's not fair."

This time, when her father hung up on her again, she didn't appear panicked or angry or even sad. There was no spark of life in her expression whatsoever. Her hands dropped to her sides, and the phone slipped from her grasp. It bounced off the toe of Finn's left cowboy boot and then skidded beneath the bed.

His gaze snagged on it as it disappeared from view, and when he looked back up, Avery's delicate face had gone ashen.

She shook her head as she blinked back a fresh wave of tears. "I've just been disinherited."

Avery lay in the dark, too exhausted to sleep. Too exhausted to do much of anything, really. Especially too exhausted to keep turning down Finn's marriage proposals.

What had gotten into him? It was as if finding out he was going to be a father had flipped a switch and transported him back to the 1950s. Hadn't he gotten the memo about modern families? Single mothers weren't unheard-of. Families took all shapes and forms nowadays. Just because she was pregnant didn't mean she needed a ring on her finger. She was perfectly capable of raising a baby on her own.

Or she would be, if she wasn't suddenly unemployed.

And homeless.

And alone.

Except she wasn't technically alone. Not entirely. Finn's long, lean form was stretched out beside her, looking more masculine than ever beneath the bed's gauzy white canopy. He'd kicked off his boots but otherwise remained fully dressed on top of the covers. After her big announcement, what was supposed to be a romantic getaway had turned into something much more somber. Any lingering flicker of romance had been fully doused by the most recent phone call from her father.

Now there might as well have been a line drawn straight down the middle of the bed.

She and Finn hadn't discussed the fact that they wouldn't be sleeping together tonight. It had sort of been a given, though. Since she'd told him about the baby, that seemed to be the only thing they'd managed to agree on. Plus, nothing killed the mood like turning down a marriage proposal.

Avery bit the inside of her cheek to stop herself from crying again. Meanwhile, the father of her child was sleeping like a baby. Ugh, it was infuriating.

How could he rest so soundly while her whole world was falling apart? Probably because she was officially stuck in Montana.

He let out a soft snore, and she jabbed him with her elbow. The sharp poke managed to quiet Finn down, but he still didn't crack an eyelid. Avery briefly considered filling the ice bucket with cold water and dousing him with it, but honestly, a wide-awake Finn would be even worse than a snoring Finn at the moment.

She needed time to think. Time to figure out what to do now that she had nothing to return to in Dallas. In the span of one phone call, her entire life had gone up in smoke.

After she'd told Finn her parents had cut her off, they'd agreed to postpone any more baby talk until tomorrow morning. They'd eaten dinner in silence at a charming little bistro in Great Gulch and then returned to their gorgeous room in the B&B, where they'd been forced to deal with the awkwardness of sleeping in the same bed.

This isn't the way tonight was supposed to turn out.

Avery pulled the lacy comforter up to her neck and sneaked another glance at Finn. Was it possible to be thoroughly angry with a man and yet still want to curl up beside him and burrow against his shoulder? Because she sort of did.

She couldn't help it. It was ridiculous, she knew. But she'd spent the past week and a half wanting him like she'd never wanted another man, and those feelings were impossible to just turn off in an instant. She wished she could. Standing her ground on the whole marriage thing would be so much easier if her heart didn't give a little tug every time he mentioned it.

If she wasn't careful, she might make the critical mistake of falling for the father of her baby. That couldn't happen. She'd lost enough already—losing her heart to Rust Creek Falls' biggest playboy wasn't an option.

She took a deep breath and stared up at the ceiling. The twinkle lights draped from the bedposts bathed the pretty room in glittering starlight. Even in her despair, Avery got a lump in her throat at the beauty of it all.

Finn had chosen well. This would have been the perfect place to rekindle their physical relationship. It was like something out of a fairy tale, except instead of a happily-ever-after ending, she'd just been stripped of everything she'd always known and loved.

Disinherited.

She couldn't wrap her head around the concept. Never in her wildest dreams had she thought her family would turn its back on her under any circumstances, least of all these. She knew her father might be upset to find out she'd been intimate with a Crawford, but cutting her out of his life seemed especially cruel. And the fact that her mother was going along with it was wholly inconceivable.

Avery wasn't technically a mother yet, but she felt like one. In five short months, she'd be able to hold her baby in her arms. Right now, she didn't even know if she was having a boy or a girl, but that didn't matter. She loved her baby, sight unseen. She couldn't imagine ever shunning her child, no matter what. Wasn't that what love was all about—accepting someone unconditionally?

Maybe Avery had it coming, though. She'd been keeping such a big secret for far too long. Finn deserved to feel like a father every bit as much as she felt like a mother. Maybe getting disinherited was some cosmic form of punishment for failing to tell him the truth right away. It was probably a miracle that he wanted to have anything to do with her, much less marry her.

She swallowed around the lump in her throat. Finn wasn't such a terrible person. She knew that. He was a good man, just not exactly marriage material. He went through women like water, and his crazy explanation about why he'd been dating so much was no comfort whatsoever. It made him seem more like a contestant on *The Bachelor* than ever.

And yet…

He was still there, right beside her, when everyone else she knew and loved had disappeared.

Which was why when the sun came up the following morning, casting soft pink light over the lacy white bedding and bathing the room with all the hope of a new day, Finn turned his face toward hers and Avery whispered the precious words he'd been waiting to hear.

"I'll marry you."

* * *

They were getting married.

After months of running away from the altar as fast as he could, Finn was elated. He, Avery and their child were going to be a family. His baby would grow up with a real father, one who was there for him or her, every step of the way.

His relief was so palpable that it felt almost like something else. Joy. Maybe even…love.

He swept a lock of hair from Avery's face and pressed his mouth to hers. It was a tender kiss. Gentle and reverent, full of all the things he didn't know how to say. But while his eyes were still closed and his lips still sweet with Avery's warmth and softness, she laid a palm on his chest, covering his heart.

She didn't push him away, though. She didn't have to. He got the message all the same.

"I have a few conditions," she said.

Conditions?

His gut churned, and the sick feeling that had come over him last night as he'd watched Avery's agonizing phone calls with her parents made a rapid return.

He sat up. "Such as?"

Avery propped herself against the headboard next to him and crossed her arms. "For starters, I'd like to keep the pregnancy quiet for a while. Just between us, as long as I can continue getting away with baggy clothes."

He could live with that.

Finn nodded. "Fine. We can tell my family after the wedding. I'm not sure how quickly we can get the church, but once my dad hears we're engaged, I'm sure he'll be more than willing to pull a few strings and—"

She shook her head. Hard. "No."

"I'm not talking about an out-and-out bribe." Although Maximilian wasn't exactly a stranger to that type of behavior. "But we know people in town, and—"

She cut him off again. "I mean no church wedding. I'd like to keep things as simple as possible. A ceremony at the justice of the peace, maybe."

How romantic.

Finn suppressed the urge to sigh. After all, they were getting married for the baby. Why did he keep forgetting that?

He reached for her hand and wove his fingers through hers. "Are you sure that's what you really want?"

"Yes, which brings me to my second condition." She glanced at their intertwined hands and then promptly looked away, taking a deep inhale. "Given the circumstances, I think a marriage of convenience is the best idea."

She let go of his hand and scrambled out of the bed, darting around the room as if she could somehow escape the remainder of the conversation.

No such luck, sweetheart.

"Avery," he said as calmly as he could manage. "What are you talking about?"

She began pulling things out of her suitcase, refusing to make eye contact with him. "I'm just saying that since this marriage is about the baby, we shouldn't muddy the waters by making it personal."

What could possibly be more personal than having a child together?

He arched a brow. "And by personal, I'm guessing you mean sex."

Avery's face went as red as a candy apple. "Exactly. I'm glad you agree."

He did not agree. In fact, he disagreed quite vehemently, but he wasn't about to push the matter.

She was scared.

Scratch that—she was terrified. And Finn couldn't really blame her. He'd always thought Maximilian Crawford was as tough a nut as they came, but clearly he'd been wrong. Avery's father made Maximilian look like a teddy bear.

"I want you to feel safe and secure," he said quietly. "I want that for our baby, too. And if that means no sex for the time being, that's fine."

"Actually, I—"

He held up a hand. "Let's take things one day at a time, okay?"

Surely she didn't think they were going to remain married for the rest of their lives and never make love. They were good together. So good. Once everything calmed down and they were living together as husband and wife, she'd realize he was in this for the long haul. She had to.

"One day at a time." She nodded and shoved her refolded items back into her suitcase. The poor thing was a nervous wreck.

Finn stood, raking a hand through his hair. "Why don't I go get us some coffee? Then we can get ready and head on down to the courthouse."

Her eyes grew wide. *"Today?"*

"Today." His voice was firm. "You have your conditions. This one's mine. There's no waiting period to get married in Montana. We just have to stop by a county office for a license and then we can go straight to the justice of the peace."

Thanks to his father's hobby as matchmaker extraordinaire, Finn knew more about getting married than he'd ever wanted to. For once, all the knowledge he'd picked up in Viv Dalton's wedding boutique was finally coming in handy.

Avery sighed. "Fine."

He crossed the room, intent on getting the coffee he'd mentioned. This conversation was really stretching the limits of his uncaffeinated early-morning state.

But as his hand twisted the doorknob, he paused. "Of course if you'd rather wait and have a church wedding in Rust Creek Falls, we can do that instead."

He could already see it—the little chapel at the corner of Cedar and Main all decked out in tulle and roses. A big fancy dress for Avery and all five of his brothers standing up for him at the altar. Maximilian with a triumphant smile on his face. Funny how the thought of such a spectacle would have made him ill a month ago. Now, it actually sounded nice.

Maybe Avery was right. Maybe he didn't really know what he wanted.

"Nice try, but no." She let out a nervous little laugh and shook her head.

"All right, then. It's settled." He shoved his Stetson on his head and went out in search of coffee, bypassing the free stuff in the lobby in favor of something better.

He thought he remembered seeing a fancy coffee-house a few blocks away as they'd driven into town. From the looks of the exterior, it had been the sort of place that served frothy, creamy drinks—lattes and cappuccinos with hearts swirled into the foam. Not his usual preference, but this morning it sounded about right.

After all, this was their wedding day.

Chapter 9

It was all happening so fast.

Just a few hours ago, Avery had been sipping the cinnamon maple latte Finn had brought back for her—decaf, obviously—and now she was sitting in Great Gulch's justice of the peace court, waiting to officially become a Crawford.

The district clerk's office was situated just below them, in the building's basement. They'd been able to get their marriage license and then headed straight upstairs—one-stop shopping, so to speak. With its rough-hewn wooden posts and quaint clock tower, the small-town Montana courthouse looked like something out of an old Western movie. The judge wore Wranglers and a cowboy hat, while the bailiff's boots jangled with actual spurs, as if he'd arrived at work on his horse and tied the animal to a hitching post right outside.

It was surreal and unique in a way that Avery was sure to remember, even though there was no wedding photographer to capture the moment. No maid of honor or best man. No proud papa walking her down the aisle.

She glanced at Finn sitting beside her in the same hat and snakeskin boots he'd worn on the drive from Rust Creek Falls the day before. He'd changed into a fresh shirt, and she'd found a lovely white eyelet dress with ruffled sleeves in one of the boutiques in Great Gulch's recently revitalized downtown district. Paired with turquoise boots—her "something blue"—she looked more like a Miss Texas contestant than how she'd ever pictured herself on her wedding day, but the wildflower bouquet that trembled in her hands was a colorful reminder that she was indeed about to pledge herself to Finn Crawford for as long as they both should live.

What am I doing?

Her father had disowned her less than twenty-four hours ago. Shouldn't she give him a chance to change his mind?

Then again, why should she? She'd never heard her daddy say a single nice thing about the Crawfords, so he wasn't likely to start anytime soon. And now that she was pregnant with Finn's baby, she'd crossed over to the dark side. There was no going back.

Still, was this really the answer?

"Avery Ellington and Finn Crawford." The judge looked down at the papers in front of him and then peered out at everyone seated in the smooth wooden benches of the courtroom's gallery. "Please step forward."

Finn glanced at her and smiled as he took her hand and led her toward the bench at the front of the tiny space.

Avery took a deep breath as she walked beside him,

inhaling the rich scent of polished wood and the tiny
fragrant blooms beyond the opened windows. Finn had
told her the flowers were clematis, but most people called
them sweet autumn. They climbed the courthouse fa-
cade in a shower of snowy white, giving the old building a dreamy, enchanted air, despite its dusty wood floor
and the buffalo head mounted above the judge's bench.

Is this really happening?

Avery swallowed. This wasn't the way she'd always
pictured her wedding.

Not that she'd been dreaming of getting married anytime soon. But didn't all little girls dream of their wedding day when they were young? Avery always thought
she'd be married in a church, surrounded by friends and
family. She'd wanted a white princess dress with a train,
just like Kate Middleton. Like every other starry-eyed
teen, she'd been glued to the television for the royal
wedding back then. It seemed so perfect, a real-life
fairy tale. Never once had she imagined herself tying
the knot already pregnant and dressed like a cowgirl.

"Mr. Crawford and Miss Ellington." The judge's gaze
flitted back and forth between them. "You're here to
get married?"

Avery tried to answer him, but she couldn't seem to
form any words.

Beside her, Finn nodded. "Yes, sir."

"I see you've got your license." Again, the judge
sifted through his papers. Satisfied everything was
in order, he removed his reading glasses and smiled.
"Okay, then. Let's get to it."

Avery gripped her modest little bouquet with both
hands as if it was some kind of life preserver. She felt
like she might faint.

"We are gathered here in the presence of these witnesses to celebrate the joining of this man and this woman in the unity of marriage," the judge said.

Avery glanced at Finn, but he was staring straight ahead, so she couldn't get a read on his expression. Her pulse raced so fast that her knees were in danger of giving out on her.

It's not too late to change your mind.

No vows had been exchanged yet. She could apologize, turn around and walk right out of the courthouse. It wasn't as if anyone would stop her.

And then what?

She couldn't go home, but she wasn't completely helpless. She had an MBA, for crying out loud. Plus the Stricklands had become true friends. Maybe she could work out some kind of special arrangement to stay at the boarding house indefinitely. Surely she could pay them back eventually.

The more she thought about it, the more she liked the idea of staying with Old Gene and Melba. But if she walked away now, she and Finn would be over for good. There'd be no going back if she left him at the altar... even if the altar was technically a country courthouse with a shaggy buffalo head on the wall.

The judge droned on as her mind reeled, until finally he said, "Please face each other and hold hands."

The bailiff's spurs jangled as he stepped forward to take Avery's bouquet, prompting Finn to bite back a smile. At least he, too, seemed to appreciate the absurdity of the situation.

Once her hands were interlocked with his, though, fleeing seemed like an exceedingly difficult prospect. Could she really bring herself to be a runaway bride when he was holding her hands and looking at her as if she was the most beautiful woman he'd ever seen?

Beneath the amusement dancing in his gaze, there was something else—something that stole the breath from her lungs. Something that made her wonder if the vows they were about to exchange were indeed just words.

She bit her bottom lip to keep it from trembling as the judge said something about marriage being one of life's greatest commitments and a celebration of unconditional love.

Her heart drummed. *Love.* Did she love Finn Crawford? Did *he* love *her*?

Of course not. This wasn't about love. It was about the baby. But a small part of herself wanted it to be real, and that realization scared the life out of her.

"Finn, do you take Avery to be your wife, to have and to hold from this day forward, for better or worse, for richer, for poorer, in sickness and in health, to love, honor and cherish until death do you part?" The judge looked expectantly at Finn, and the moment before he answered seemed to last an eternity.

"I do," he said, and there was a sincerity to his tone that made Avery's fear multiply tenfold.

It's not real, she reminded herself. *It's all just pretend.*

She could do this.

But *should* she?

She placed her free hand on her growing belly to anchor her to the here and now. But when the judge turned his tender gaze on her and began to recite the same question, her throat grew dry and what she suddenly wanted more than anything—more than the wedding she'd dreamed about as a little girl, more than knowing that her father would eventually come around—was a sign. Nothing huge, just a small indication that she was doing the right thing. Everything within her longed for it.

Please.

It was a crazy thing to ask. She knew it was, but she couldn't help wishing…hoping…praying.

And then the most miraculous thing happened. Beneath her fingertips came a tiny nudge. At first she thought she'd imagined it, but then it happened again. The second time it was firmer, more insistent. She looked down at her belly, stunned.

Oh, my gosh.

Her pretty dress fluttered the third time it happened, and that's when she knew for sure—her baby had just kicked. *Their* baby.

"Avery, sweetheart?" Finn prompted.

She looked up and found her husband-to-be and the judge both watching her expectantly, waiting for her to say something.

She inhaled a shaky breath, and for the first time since the awful phone call with her father, she felt like everything might just be okay, after all. She'd needed a sign, and she'd gotten one. A sign more perfect than she could have dreamed of.

She fixed her gaze with the man who'd just pledged to love, honor and cherish her in sickness and in health, for richer and for poorer, and did her best to forget that she was definitely the latter at the moment. She was completely dependent on a man she barely knew, a man who just might have the power to break her heart.

"I do," she whispered.

And against all odds, she meant it, because the moment the baby moved, she'd stopped playing pretend.

They'd done it. After spending the past few months actively avoiding the altar, Finn Crawford was a married man.

He bit back a smile as he maneuvered his truck off Great Gulch's Main Street and onto the highway that led to Rust Creek Falls. There was no logical reason for the swell of elation in his chest. He'd practically been forced to beg Avery to marry him, and according to her terms, the marriage was hardly something to celebrate. Finn had no doubt that if Oscar Ellington hadn't acted like the world's biggest jackass, his daughter wouldn't be wearing Finn's ring.

But there it sat on the third finger of her left hand—rose gold, with a stunner of a center stone. He'd bought it on impulse at an antiques store across the street from the B&B. Avery's eyes had grown wide when he slid it onto her finger in the courthouse, but she'd yet to ask him where it came from. Finn wasn't altogether sure whether her silence was a good thing or a bad one, but every so often he glanced at her in the passenger seat and caught her staring down at the ring, toying with it with the pad of her thumb.

Married.

The beautiful woman sitting beside him was his wife, and she was pregnant with his child. Overnight, he'd gone from being free and single to being a husband with a baby on the way. He should be terrified half out of his mind or, at the very least, somewhat concerned about Avery's sudden insistence on a chaste relationship.

So why wasn't he?

From the moment she'd looked up at him with tears in her eyes and whispered the words *I do*, he'd felt nothing but pure, unadulterated joy. He'd worry about the details tomorrow. For now, he was content to let himself believe that he was ready to be a family man.

"Where are we going?" Avery frowned at the scene beyond the windshield as the truck rolled into Rust Creek Falls. "You just missed the turnoff for the boarding house."

Was she serious?

"That's because we're not going to the Stricklands'. We're going to the Ambling A," Finn said quietly.

Avery said nothing, but instead of toying with her wedding ring, she hid her hand beneath the folds of her dress.

Finn tightened his grip on the steering wheel. "I want to introduce my family to my wife."

Avery blinked at him. *"Now?"*

"Why not? The baby will be here in a matter of months. They may as well get used to the idea."

She shook her head. "We're still keeping the baby news to ourselves for now, right? I'm concerned that once the news is out, it will be all over town."

Finn's shoulders tensed, but she had a point. One thing at a time. Plus, he'd already given Rust Creek Falls enough to gossip about since he'd moved to the Ambling A. If the busybodies in town knew Avery was pregnant, their marriage would be reduced to nothing but a shotgun wedding.

Isn't that what it is?

Yes…no…maybe.

He wasn't sure of anything anymore.

"Okay, we still won't say anything about the baby." He took a measured inhale. "For now."

"Good." Avery nodded, but she was visibly nervous as they turned onto the main road leading to his family's ranch. She wrung her hands until her knuckles turned white.

Finn wanted to comfort her, but he wasn't sure how, especially when he caught sight of the numerous vehicles parked in front of the massive log home. Maximilian's luxury SUV was situated in its usual spot, as was Wilder's truck. But four more automobiles were slotted beside them, which meant Logan, Xander, Hunter and Knox were probably up at the main house, as well. What the heck was going on? Were they having a party in his absence?

He shifted his truck into Park. "It looks like we're about to kill six birds with one stone."

Beside him, Avery closed her eyes and took several deep breaths. When her lashes fluttered open, she glanced at him and shrugged. "Yoga breathing. It reduces stress and anxiety. It's also supposed to be good for the baby."

Finn smiled, then took her hand and gave it a squeeze. He also decided right then and there that they couldn't spend their wedding night at the Ambling A. Avery was right—they needed to be thinking about what was best for the baby. Staying under the same roof as his nutty father and the rest of his nosy family wouldn't be healthy for anyone, much less his unborn child. They'd get in, make their announcement and get out. Maybe they'd even head back to Great Gulch and that beautiful four-poster bed.

No sex, remember?

He sighed as he climbed out of the truck and slammed the driver's-side door shut. No sex. They had a deal. A completely ludicrous deal, but a deal nonetheless.

He had to give Avery credit—she put on a good show. When he pushed open the front door to the big log house, she greeted Maximilian with a big smile and a hug, just like a proper daughter-in-law. As luck would have it, not only were all five of his brothers situated around the big dining room table, but Xander's wife, Lily, and Knox's other half, Genevieve, were there, too. Hunter's daughter, Wren, had a bandanna tucked into the collar of her T-shirt and was digging into a big bowl of chili. Logan's wife, Sarah, sat beside her, bouncing a giggling baby Sophia on her lap.

Finn's attention lingered on the happy nine-month-old, and his chest squeezed into a tight fist.

"Son? Everything okay?"

Finn blinked and dragged his gaze back to Maximilian. "Everything's fine. Great, actually. What's going on? I haven't seen the main house this full in a while."

"We're all about to head down to the fall festival for pumpkin bowling, so Lily put on a pot of chili first." Maximilian planted his hands on his hips. "A few of us tried calling you, but your phone rolled straight to voice mail."

Right. Because he'd been a little busy getting married and all.

"Pumpkin bowling?" Avery grinned. "That's a thing?"

Logan nodded. "Sure it is. It's like regular bowling, only with a pumpkin instead of a bowling ball. It's taking place on the big lawn at Rust Creek Falls Park, and Dad has grand plans to beat us all to smithereens."

"Not going to happen." Genevieve shook her head. "I've been practicing."

"Seriously?" Lily laughed.

"Oh, she's dead serious." Knox slung an arm around

his wife and kissed the top of her blond hair. "G never kids about pumpkin bowling."

"Aunt Genevieve has been helping me, too," Wren said around a spoonful of chili. "She said we need to put Grandpa in his place."

"Oh, did she now?" Maximilian crossed his arms while the entire room collapsed into laughter.

"No worries, Dad. We have some news that might take the sting out of the fact that the family has been conspiring against you." Finn slipped his arm around Avery's waist and pulled her close.

The room grew quiet until the only sound was the scraping of Wren's spoon against her bowl and the pounding of Avery's heart as she nestled against Finn's side. Only then, at such close range, could Finn tell that her smile seemed a bit strained around the edges. Forced.

Because after all, they were only pretending to be happy newlyweds. The only thing real about their union was the baby on the way.

"We're married," Finn blurted.

So much for finesse.

He'd intended to say something more poetic, but Avery's stiff smile was messing with his head. What had happened to all the heat that had been swirling between them since she'd thrown herself at him in the pasture? He couldn't look at an ear of calico corn anymore without feeling aroused. He wanted her so much it hurt. And he knew…he just *knew*…that Avery still wanted him, too.

"You're *what*?" Logan glanced back and forth between Finn and Avery.

"Wait. This is a joke, right?" Hunter let out a nervous laugh.

Xander and Knox exchanged stunned glances.

Wilder and Hunter just stared, no doubt wondering if they must be next, considering that all of Maximilian's sons seemed to be falling like dominoes, one by one.

"Avery, sweetheart, is this true?" Finn's father set hopeful eyes on Avery. The pumpkin bowling conspiracy had apparently convinced him the entire family had it in for him. Probably because he deserved it after all the meddling he'd done in recent months.

Every head in the grand dining room swiveled in Avery's direction, and Finn's gut churned; he hoped against hope that none of his family members could see through the charade. He wasn't sure he could take it if they could, especially when Logan and Sarah, Xander and Lily, and Knox and Genevieve seemed so blissfully happy.

It was painful enough to know his wife didn't plan to share a bed with him, but it would be beyond humiliating for his brothers and his father to know it, too.

But in answer to Maximilian's question, Avery beamed up at Finn as if he'd hung the moon. Gazing into those warm brown eyes of hers took him right back to Oklahoma—the night that had changed both of their lives for good. And with a lump in his throat, he realized that if he could have gone back in time and done things differently, he wouldn't have changed a thing.

"It's true. Finn asked me to marry him last night, and we just couldn't wait. We went to the justice of the peace this morning," Avery said, the perfect picture of a blushing bride, radiant with happiness. Finn would have sworn on his life she was telling the truth. "I'm a Crawford!"

Chapter 10

I'm a Crawford.

The full consequences of what Avery had done didn't fully sink in until she said those words and watched Maximilian's face split into an ecstatic grin.

There was no turning back. The ring was on her finger, and now they'd shared the happy news with Finn's family. She was no longer Avery Ellington. She was Avery Crawford. *Mrs.* Finn Crawford.

"Well, I'll be." Maximilian let out a jubilant whoop that was so loud it shook the rafters of the extravagant log cabin his family called home. "Welcome to the family, darlin'."

He scooped her up in a big bear hug, and before she knew what was happening, Avery was being passed from one Crawford to the next, each one gushing with happiness over the surprise news. They were all so excited, so welcoming, that Avery had to remind herself that she wasn't truly a part of the family, despite the change in her last name. She and Finn were figuring things out, that's all. She'd married him to ensure that he would truly be a part of his baby's life, despite her father's attempts to cut him out entirely. He didn't honestly think of her as his wife, and she certainly wouldn't be standing in the grand main building of the Ambling A with Finn Crawford's ring on her finger if she weren't pregnant with his baby.

Her daddy would see things differently, though. The fact that she'd traded the name Ellington for Crawford would be an unpardonable sin, regardless of the fact that she'd been disinherited. Oscar Ellington had put something terrible in motion when he'd cut her off, but nothing that couldn't have been stopped. One phone call—that's all it would have taken to undo all the pain he'd caused.

But this...

This couldn't be undone.

"I must say, I'm surprised." Wilder narrowed his gaze at Finn. "You swore up and down that wild horses couldn't drag you to the altar."

Avery's ribs constricted, but she glued her smile in place.

"Things change, brother," Finn said, and his gaze found hers and he sent her a knowing grin.

Things change.

Did they? Did they really?

"How adept are you at bowling, Avery?" Genevieve arched a brow. "Do you have much experience handling pumpkins?"

Finn shook his head. "Don't get any ideas. The lot of you already outnumber Dad by a good amount. You're going to have to trounce him on your own."

He reached for Avery, and his fingertips slid to the back of her neck, leaving a riot of goose bumps in their wake. "Besides, it's our wedding night."

Her stomach immediately went into free fall.

Their wedding night? She hadn't thought that far ahead. Since telling Finn about the baby, she'd pretty much been operating on a minute-by-minute basis.

"Won't you two be taking a honeymoon? I can make a phone call and get the jet down from Helena in two shakes of a lamb's tail." Maximilian dug around in the pocket of his Wranglers for his cell phone.

"Oh, there's no need for that," Avery said before Finn could take him up on the offer. "We're not taking a honeymoon quite yet. Right...darling?"

She cast a pleading glance at Finn.

Darling? She was calling him darling now?

The corner of his mouth quirked into a half grin. "Right, love."

Love. As endearments went, it was a good one. A great one, actually. She practically melted into a puddle right there in the Crawford dining room, because again, she couldn't quite keep track of what was real and what wasn't.

"Maybe it's a good thing we're all heading out, then." Knox bit back a smile.

"Don't be an idiot. We're waiting on the honeymoon, but we're not spending our wedding night under the same roof as all of you." Finn rolled his eyes and punched his brother on the arm.

Knox winced as he rubbed his biceps. "Point taken, but where exactly are you going?"

Finn hesitated, because as Avery knew all too well, he was completely winging it. It was the briefest of pauses, but it gave Maximilian the perfect opening to swoop in with a grand, romantic gesture.

"You'll stay at Maverick Manor. The honeymoon suite!" He jabbed at the screen of his cell phone. "I'll take care of the reservation myself, pull some strings if I have to."

Panic shot through Avery. She couldn't spend the night with Finn in a *honeymoon suite*, of all things. Not if she had any chance of sticking to the arrangement they'd made.

"What's Maverick Manor?" she asked, even though she dreaded the answer.

"It's Rust Creek's newest hotel. Rustic, but upscale." Hunter grabbed a coffee carafe from the marble-topped kitchen counter where a huge blue Le Creuset enamel pot sat, surrounded by bowls of chili fixings. He gave a thoughtful shrug while refilling his cup. "It's quite beautiful, actually. The lobby has a stone fireplace that's so big you can stand upright in it, and the entire back side of the building faces the mountains."

"It's so romantic, Avery. Honestly, it's the perfect place for a wedding night." Sarah sighed. "You'll just love it."

Avery glanced at Finn—at his big broad shoulders, at his capable hands, at the mouth she couldn't seem to stop kissing at the most inappropriate times. Then she shifted her attention back to her father-in-law, grinning from ear to ear.

What bride would turn down the honeymoon suite at the most extravagant hotel in town?

A pretend one. That's who.

Avery was suddenly exhausted. She'd been married all of two hours, and reminding herself not to fall in love with her husband was already becoming a full-time job. Maybe it was a good thing she was unemployed.

"Thank you, Maximilian. That's so kind of you." She took a deep breath. How hard could it be to spend one chaste night in a luxurious room with Finn? It wasn't as if the bed would be heart-shaped. Would it? "Maverick Manor, here we come."

Avery had no idea what Maximilian had said to the staff at Maverick Manor, but whatever it was had everyone falling all over themselves to welcome her and Finn in grand romantic fashion.

"Congratulations, Mr. and Mrs. Crawford," the front desk clerk gushed the instant they'd set foot inside the lobby.

They hadn't even introduced themselves, which had Avery wondering if Maximilian had gone so far as to send photos in preparation of their arrival. Finn's father was definitely over-the-top, so she wouldn't put it past him. Then again, Rust Creek Falls was a small town, and everyone within a one-hundred-mile radius seemed to know precisely who Finn Crawford was... because they'd dated him at some point.

Avery forced a smile and tried not to imagine the effusive blonde with the Maverick Manor badge pinned to her cute denim dress sharing a candlelit meal with her husband.

"We've prepared a lovely stay for you," she said, and to her credit, she didn't seem overly familiar with Finn. *Thank goodness.* She must be new in town. "Tomorrow, we've got you booked for a special couples' massage overlooking the fall foliage on our new pool deck."

"A couples' massage?" Avery blinked. Apparently, a heart-shaped bed was the least of her worries. "That won't be necessary. We're checking out tomorrow morning."

"Are you sure, love?" Finn's hand slipped onto the small of her back, and a rebellious shiver snaked its way up Avery's spine.

"A couples' massage sounds quite—" his gaze flitted toward hers, eyes molten "—nice."

Avery knew that look. It was a look full of heat and promises. The same playfully wicked expression that she'd loved so much that night in Oklahoma. What woman wouldn't?

Damn him.

"Mr. Crawford booked the honeymoon suite for a three-night stay," the clerk oh, so helpfully said.

"If only we could stay that long." Avery batted her lashes at Finn, whose hand remained on her back, where it continued to infuse her with the sort of warmth she most definitely didn't need to be experiencing at the moment. "But we have an appointment tomorrow morning that we simply can't miss. Don't we, darling?"

They did, actually. Finn just didn't know it yet.

He angled his head toward her. "We do?"

Avery's first official prenatal appointment with an obstetrician was scheduled for the following morning at eleven o' clock. Her gynecologist back in Dallas had started her on prenatal vitamins once her pregnancy test had come back positive, but since she no longer delivered babies, she'd given Avery a referral. After a few days in Rust Creek Falls had turned into a week and a week into two, she'd finally broken down and found a doctor in Montana. She'd made the appointment last week, before Finn knew anything about the baby, so she'd chosen a doctor whose practice was situated a half hour away from Rust Creek Falls. That still seemed like a good call, since being in such a small town was like living in a fishbowl.

"Yes, we do." Avery nodded, hopefully putting a firm end to the idea of a couples' massage.

"So, just one night, then?" The clerk glanced back and forth between them.

"Just one night," Finn said with a sudden hint of regret in his gaze that seemed so real that Avery felt it deep in the pit of her stomach.

What were they *doing*?

"Well, the staff at Maverick Manor is here to help you make the most of it. Just let us know if you need anything. Anything at all." The clerk handed two keys to an attendant who looked like he'd arrived fresh off the rodeo circuit. "Kent here will show you to your room."

The congratulatory glint in her eye turned wistful, and it was then that Avery knew the young woman had indeed been one of Finn's many Friday night social engagements. Not to mention the other six days of the week.

She felt sick as she followed Kent, with his perfect felt Stetson and worn cowboy boots, to the top floor of Maverick Manor. The minute Melba had warned her about Finn's overactive social life, she should have turned tail and gone back to Dallas. She could have left him a note about the baby or written him an email. That would have been the chicken's way out, obviously, and Finn would have no doubt beaten an immediate trail to Texas. But at least then she would have been on her home turf. She might have stood a chance at escaping from their one-night stand with her dignity—and her heart—intact.

Now here she was. In Montana, of all places, with

a wedding ring on her finger and her heart in serious danger of cracking into a million pieces.

"Here we are." With a flourish, Kent gestured to the intricately carved door at the end of the hall. Then he unlocked it and held the door open, waiting for the "giddy" newlyweds to step inside.

A heady wave of fragrance drifted from inside the sumptuous room—something floral and sweet. Hyacinths, maybe. They'd always been Avery's favorite flower. And were those *rose petals* strewn on the floor?

God help her, they were. Where was a dust buster when she really needed one?

Avery stared at the petals, terrified to move. As luck would have it, she didn't need to, because before she could register what was happening, Finn scooped her in his arms and swept her clear off her feet.

She squealed in protest, even as her arms wrapped instinctively around Finn's thick neck. He laughed and it vibrated through her, sweet and forbidden.

Avery buried her face in the crook of his neck and whispered again the warmth of his skin. "What are you doing?"

"How would it look if I didn't carry my bride over the threshold? Just go with it, love," he murmured.

They were going to have words about this. They were also going to have words about his new nickname for her, because yes, they needed to put on a good show so their marriage was believable to the outside world, but she was only human. She had feelings, and right now, those feelings were in serious danger of throwing caution to the wind.

She blamed biology. Wasn't she chemically programmed to be attracted to the father of her baby?

*Right. That's it. Science. It has nothing to do with his
easy sense of humor or how sweet he is around animals
or his generous spirit.*

Or how he'd turned his entire life inside out for the
sake of their baby. Or how he'd been there for her at a
time when her own family had turned their backs on
her. Or how he looked at her as if he'd simply been bid-
ing his time with all those other women, waiting for her
to walk back into his life.

The list went on.

And on.

And on…

Kent tucked their bags away in the closet by the door
and slipped out of the suite, yet Avery's feet still weren't
touching the ground. The heat in Finn's gaze was suddenly infused with a tenderness that made it difficult to
breathe. She looked away, determined to collect herself,
but it was then that she noticed the trail of rose petals
led to a huge bed covered in pristine white bed linens,
facing a picture window with a stunning view of the
mountains. The sun was just beginning to dip low on
the horizon, bathing the yellow aspen trees in glittering
light. Their leaves sparkled like pennies, and it was all
so beautiful that Avery had to squeeze her eyes closed
against the romantic assault on her senses.

When she opened them, she found Finn watching
her…waiting. Was he ever going to put her down?

"If you make a crack about my weight right now, I'll
never forgive you." She gave him a tremulous smile.

It wasn't a test. She was merely trying to inject some
humor into a situation that suddenly seemed far too
intimate. Had it been a test, though, Finn would have
passed with flying colors.

"I wouldn't dare." His gaze narrowed and swept over her face, settling on her mouth. "You really have no idea how lovely you are, do you? Pregnancy suits you."

She had a sudden flashback of Finn moving over her, looking at her with the same reverence in his eyes as he pushed deep inside her, whispering sweet nothings. At the time, she'd attributed his words to the martinis and the darkness of the blackout, which had a strange way of making everything feel more real, more intense.

But maybe she'd been wrong. Maybe he really had felt those things. Maybe he still did.

"Thank you," she said stiffly, scrambling out of his arms and sliding clumsily to her feet. She took a giant backward step and pretended not to notice when Finn's expression closed like a book. "I'm kind of tired. I should probably get some rest."

"Right. Maybe we should take a nap." He scrubbed at the back of his neck and seemed to look anywhere and everywhere—except at her. "On top of the covers. Fully clothed."

This was the moment when she should have told him the truth—the moment she should have given up the pretense that she didn't have feelings for the father of her child. It would be so easy. She might not need to say anything at all. She could just rise up on tiptoe and kiss him gently on the mouth, and he would *know*. He probably already did.

But she couldn't do it. She couldn't open herself up that way. The past twenty-four hours had been more heartbreaking than she could have ever imagined. She'd lost her job. She'd lost her family. She couldn't lose Finn, too, and that's precisely what would happen if she tried to start something real with him and then realized he didn't love her. If he did, wouldn't he have led with that when he asked her to marry him?

"That sounds good." She nodded. Could this honeymoon get any more awkward? "I have a doctor's appointment tomorrow, at eleven if you'd like to come along. For the baby."

"For the baby," he echoed, and his tone went flat. Lifeless. "Of course I'll be there."

She nodded, because she didn't quite trust herself to speak.

"You okay, Princess?" Finn said, a bit of life creeping back into his tone.

"Yes." She nodded. "Just tired."

So very tired. Tired of dealing with her impossible father, tired of wondering what kind of mother she would be, tired of acting like the night in Oklahoma hadn't meant anything when just the opposite was true. But most of all, she was tired of pretending. Sometimes it seemed like that's all she'd been doing since the day she rolled into Montana—pretending she wasn't pregnant, pretending she didn't have feelings for Finn, and now, pretending they were like any other husband and wife. Suddenly, with Finn's ring on her finger, she wasn't sure she could do it anymore.

"Come on." Finn strode to the bed and gave the mattress a pat. "Lie down. I promise I won't bite."

He smiled, but somehow it was one of the saddest smiles Avery had ever seen. So she did as he said, kicked off her boots and curled onto her side on the bed with her hands tucked neatly beneath her pillow, lest they get their own improper ideas.

Her eyes drifted shut and just as she began to doze off, she felt the mattress dip with the weight of Finn's body. So solid. So strong.

Tears pricked her eyes, and she wasn't sure why she was crying. She only knew that it was almost physically painful to have him so close without actually touching her. The space between them felt heavy, weighted with all things they couldn't say or do to one another.

When they'd been together in Oklahoma, they'd fallen onto the bed together in a tangle of kisses and heated breath. Despite the martinis, she remembered everything about that night with perfect clarity. The thrill that coursed through her when she'd slid her hands up the back of his dress shirt. The way Finn's eyes had gone dark when looked at her bare body for the first time. His aching groan when he'd pushed his way inside her.

She remembered it all as clearly as if it had just happened yesterday. Did he remember, too?

Was he thinking about it right now, just as she was?

"Princess?" Finn's voice cut through the memories, but the ache in his tone was all too familiar. Too tortured to leave room for any doubt.

Of course he remembers. Of course he's thinking about it.

All she needed to do was turn to face him. She wouldn't even have to say anything. Everything she felt would be clearly written in her eyes—so much longing, and despite the craziness of their circumstances, so much hope.

She bit down hard on her lip to keep herself from answering him. And she didn't dare move. Instead, she squeezed her eyes shut tight and kept her back to her husband.

Then Avery Crawford let the heavy silence and the sweet smell of velvety rose petals lull her to sleep.

Chapter 11

Hours later, Finn lay stretched out on the sofa and stared at the ceiling, fully awake. He was either too mad or too turned on to sleep. Probably both, but he couldn't seem to figure out which bothered him most.

Avery wanted him. He knew she did, but something was holding her back. He just couldn't figure out what that *something* was, and he didn't want to push. She was his wife now, and she was pregnant. The burden of patience definitely fell on his shoulders in this scenario, hence his move from the bed to the sofa.

But they'd shared a moment earlier. He thought they had, anyway.

He glared hard at the rough-hewn wood beams overhead, wishing he could ask the room for confirmation. The space itself was glorious, with one wall completely made of stone opposite floor-to-ceiling windows overlooking the rugged Montana landscape. A fire blazed and crackled in the hearth. Hours ago, the air had been thick with longing, and now…

Now, nothing. Surely the walls remembered. Finn sure as hell did.

He sat up and raked his hand through his hair, tugging hard at the ends. Then he sighed, because in that moment, sleep seemed like the most impossible task in the world. He'd be better off spending half an hour under the cold spray of the suite's luxury rainfall shower head than continuing to lie on the sofa listening to the steady breath of his wife as she slept like a baby in the huge four-poster bed. Alone.

He stalked toward the closet, grabbed his duffel bag and slipped as quietly as he could into the grand his-and-hers bathroom. Through his sock feet, he could feel the warmth of the heated stone floor tiles. A Jacuzzi tub overlooked the darkening Montana sky, and like everything else in the suite, the enormous stone shower was built for two. He didn't need to close his eyes to dream of Avery, bare and beautiful, with water streaming down her changing body and droplets glittering on her eyelashes like stars. Sometimes it seemed as if she was all he saw, day or night.

It was making him crazy. They just needed to go ahead and sleep together so they could both get it out of their systems. Then they could go about dealing with the pregnancy with level heads. At least he hoped that's what would happen, because he wasn't sure how much longer he could go on the way things were.

Finn wasn't used to being so wrapped up in a woman like this. He was operating in strange and new territory, and he wasn't sure what to make of it. The baby had changed everything. Obviously.

Although…

Avery had been on his mind ever since Oklahoma, long before he had any idea she was carrying his child. On some primal level, he must have known. It was the only explanation.

The only one he was comfortable admitting to himself, anyway.

Get yourself together.

He glowered at his reflection in the bathroom mirror and hauled his duffel onto the natural marble vanity top. He'd been in such a hurry back at the Ambling A that he'd grabbed the first few articles of clothing he'd seen and stuffed them into his overnight bag along with his dopp kit. He wasn't even sure what all he'd brought.

But he was certain he hadn't packed the jewel-encrusted book that rested on top of his belongings and caught his eye the moment he drew back the zipper on his bag. He picked it up, turning it over in his hands. It was studded with colorful gemstones and looked like something he might see in the windows of one of the antique shops downtown. The jewels formed a swirling letter *A* on the front cover.

He squinted at it. The book definitely looked familiar, but how had it managed to get inside his bag, and what was he supposed to do with it?

Knox.

Finn sighed. He'd thought it was strange when his newlywed brother had insisted on carrying his bag to the truck so Finn could help Avery with her things. He definitely could have managed all their luggage on his own. But apparently Knox's helpful attitude had been a ploy to get his hands on Finn's duffel so he could tuck the book inside. Now that he knew where the gaudy thing had come from, he recognized it as the old diary that he and his brothers had found beneath the floorboards of the Ambling A when they'd been renovating the place a few months ago. Someone had finally managed to pry the lock open—Xander, if Finn was remembering correctly—and since that time, the old book had been making the rounds as each of his brothers had gotten married. Knox had been the most recent to walk down the aisle, so it made sense that the diary would still be in his possession.

Seriously, though? He was supposed to spend his wedding night reading an old book?

It's not like you're busy doing anything else at the moment.

True. So frustratingly true.

His jaw clenched as he moved to sit down, taking the book with him. Mildly surprised to find that the author was a man, he kept reading.

Oddly enough, the diary proved to be a pretty effective way of getting his mind off Avery and the myriad ways he'd rather be spending his wedding night than sitting on the bathroom floor with his legs stretched out in front of him, poring over the details of some poor sod from a different era. But as fate would have it, the author's girlfriend had been pregnant.

A child. A child! Unexpected, unplanned, but not for a moment unwanted. From the second I learned I was going to be a father, nothing else mattered. Only her— only the mother of my baby and the life we're bringing into the world.

Finn's pulse kicked up a notch when he came across

that notable detail. And his heart seemed to make its way to his throat as he read passage after passage about how happy the writer was about the baby. The writer never spelled out his girlfriend's name, but referred to her simply as W throughout the book. As Finn slowly flipped the pages, he realized why.

All this time...all these days we've lived and loved in secret. And now we can't tell anyone about the baby. Not yet. So we continue to go through life pretending, but it's getting more difficult by the hour. W is my whole heart, and I want the world to know how much she and our child mean to me. But as we both know, it's just not possible. Not now. Maybe not ever...

W and her sweetheart were keeping the pregnancy and their relationship under wraps for some reason. He wasn't sure why, but they wanted to keep the baby a secret.

That's when Finn slammed the bejeweled book closed. The similarities were beginning to freak him out a little bit. He felt for the poor guy and W, whoever they were. He really did, but most of all, he wasn't sure he wanted to know how their love story would end.

Avery slept like the dead. The turmoil of the past forty-eight hours had taken its toll, and once her head hit the pillow, she was finally able to escape the craziness that was now her life. She woke the next morning to sunlight streaming through the suite's massive picture window and a scowl on her husband's face.

"Oh." She winced as she sat up and caught her first glimpse of Finn slumped on the sofa. He was already fully dressed, cowboy boots and all. "Did you sleep at all last night?"

Finn looked terrible. He was still the same handsome

man who had the annoying habit of making her heart swoop every time she looked at him, but there were new dark circles under his eyes. Even the heavy dose of fresh scruff on his jaw couldn't hide the fact that his complexion was a good shade or two paler than normal.

"Good morning. I'm fine, don't worry about me." His voice was stiff as he closed the strange jeweled book in his hand. "I got you some coffee. It's decaf, so it should be safe."

He nodded toward one of the nightstands flanking the bed, where a steaming latte sat waiting for her with a heart swirled into the foam, and her guilt magnified tenfold.

He really should have stayed in the bed last night. For goodness' sake, it was so large that they each could have easily spread out like starfish and still not even touched one another.

Maybe.

Then again, maybe not. The last time she'd slept all night in a bed with Finn, she'd woken up convinced that she should marry him.

"Thank you." She reached for the latte and took a sip. Pumpkin spice, her favorite. She could still manage to drink it even though the smell of coffee beans sometimes made her nauseous.

But what didn't make her nauseous these days?

Finn stood and tucked the book he'd been reading into his duffel bag, then shifted awkwardly from one booted foot to the other. "You said your doctor's appointment is at eleven, right?"

She nodded.

He picked up his duffel, jammed his Stetson on his head and strolled toward the door. "We should leave in half an hour. I'll wait for you downstairs."

And then with a quiet click of the suite's carved wooden door, he was gone.

Okay, then. Clearly it hadn't been a magical wedding night.

But she'd been clear about the terms of their marriage from the very beginning. She didn't have a single thing to feel guilty about. Well, other than Finn's serious case of bedhead this morning and the fact that she felt perfectly rested. And maybe, just maybe, that she'd basically run for cover the night before at the first hint of sexual tension between the two of them.

That had been a very necessary moment of self-preservation, though. Surely Finn would get over it. He couldn't stay grumpy forever, could he?

Avery bathed, dressed and met Finn downstairs in half an hour, as requested. He smiled politely at her, carried her luggage and helped her into the truck, but something still seemed off. Despite every effort to dote on her, Finn barely looked at her. Avery should have been thrilled. After all, this was exactly the sort of arrangement she'd wanted. No risk. No pressure. No sex.

Absolutely no sex.

Yet she felt strangely hollow as they drove to her doctor's appointment. When they hit the open highway and Finn relaxed beside her, dropping his right hand to his thigh, she had to stop herself from reaching for it and weaving her fingers through his. She'd grown accustomed to his touch over their time together, and it felt strange now to be so close to him without feeling the brush of his skin against hers. She missed it more than she wanted to admit.

Be careful what you wish for.

The thought spun around and around in her mind as they wound their way past clusters of trees in saffron yellows and fiery reds. Bear's Paw, the town where her obstetrician was located, was situated halfway between Rust Creek Falls and Billings—close enough to a major medical facility in case something went wrong with her pregnancy, but still remote enough to guarantee a modicum of privacy. Avery only hoped Finn had never dated anyone who worked at the practice.

For the first time since their epic argument in Great Gulch, she considered what Finn had told her about his father's efforts to find brides for all six of his sons, to the tune of a million dollars. It sounded crazy. Then again, Maximilian Crawford was definitely the sort of man who got what he wanted, regardless of the cost.

Perhaps she shouldn't be so quick to judge Finn for systematically dating his way through the eligible female population of Montana. As he'd said, they'd been nothing but meaningless setups. Somehow, though, that almost made it worse. He'd been so intent on proving he couldn't be dragged to the altar that he'd acted like a kid in a candy store. And now here he was, right where he'd never wanted to be. Married.

She couldn't help but feel like the consolation prize. And still, all she wanted right then in the world was to hold his hand. Unbelievable.

"Almost there." Finn glanced at her, but his smile was stiff as he exited the highway and turned onto Bear Paw's quaint Main Street.

The town square, with its white gazebo in the center and surrounding mom-and-pop businesses, reminded Avery of both Great Gulch and Rust Creek Falls. There was certainly no shortage of small-town charm in Montana. Raising a family here would be so different than it would in a big city like Dallas. The thought put a lump in Avery's throat, and she wasn't sure why.

Finn's truck slowed to a stop in front of a redbrick building with an arch made of antlers hanging over the entryway.

"Here we are." He nodded.

"Yes, here we are." There was a telltale waver in her voice that had Finn's gaze narrowing in her direction.

For the first time since the night before when she'd leaped out of his arms, he looked at her...*really* looked.

"Hey." He cupped her face in one of his big, warm hands, and the simple contact was such a relief that Avery nearly wept.

Was she in for another five full months of out-of-control emotions? Because it was really getting old.

"You're not nervous about this, are you?" Finn said as his thumb made gentle circular motions on her cheek.

She was most definitely nervous about seeing the doctor. Terrified, actually.

Despite her recent success with the baby goat, she had no clue what she was doing. She'd been such a mess lately. What if the stress of keeping the pregnancy a secret from Finn for so long had somehow harmed the baby?

She'd never forgive herself if that were true. "I'm a little nervous."

"Listen to me." He leaned his forehead against hers, and as his gaze fixed with hers, the new frostiness between them thawed ever so slightly. "Everything is going to be fine. Okay?"

She nodded. "Okay."

With Finn there, it seemed easier to believe. And if anything was indeed wrong, at least she wouldn't have to handle it all on her own.

Her chest grew tight as she climbed out of the truck

and walked up the steps leading into building. Being cut off from her family stung now more than ever. If she had a difficult pregnancy or if her baby had health challenges, her parents were willing to let her handle things all by herself. She could hardly believe it. She'd never even set eyes on her son or daughter, and she couldn't imagine ever leaving them in this position. Totally and completely alone.

Except Finn was here, just as he'd promised. And he'd taken a vow to be by her side, no matter what happened.

The gravity of such a promise hit her hard as she checked in with the receptionist and filled out all the necessary medical forms. This was serious. There were pages and pages of questions to be answered and information to process. It all seemed to pass in a worrisome, overwhelming blur until at last she was wearing a paper gown and lying on an examination table beside an ultrasound machine.

After spending most of the morning in the waiting room, Finn now sat, stone-faced, in a chair facing the dark screen. Upon Avery's request, the nurse had gone to find him so they could both catch their first glimpse of the baby at the same time. There was still a layer of tension between them that hadn't been there before their night in the honeymoon suite at Maverick Manor. Although if she was truly being honest with herself, the strain in their relationship had raised its ugly head when she'd first told him about the pregnancy. It was just much more obvious since the tender moment they'd shared when he carried her over the threshold.

He was angry, and Avery could totally understand why. The secret had gotten away from her faster than she could figure out what to do with it, and now she was paying the price. Just because Finn was so eager to put a ring on her finger didn't mean he'd forgiven her.

Nor did it mean that he loved her.

Still, she was so glad to have him sitting there beside her that she could have cried.

"Okay, let's see what we have here." The doctor smiled at Avery and covered her belly with some type of gel.

Then she pressed a device that reminded Avery of a large computer mouse over her abdomen, and the screen lit up with moving shadows in various shades of gray.

The doctor confirmed what they both already knew—Avery's due date lined up perfectly with their night together in Oklahoma as the time of conception. But what Avery wanted most of all was a clear view of the baby, yet she couldn't make sense of the blurry images on the monitor.

And then all the breath in her body seemed to bottle up in her chest as a delicate profile came into view, followed by a glimpse of a tiny foot with five tiny, perfect toes.

"Are you two interested in having one of those trendy gender reveal parties? Or should I go ahead and spill the beans?" the doctor asked.

"Spill," Avery said. "Please."

There'd been enough surprises already. Besides, how could she have a gender reveal party when her own family wasn't even speaking to her?

"In that case, there she is," the doctor said, smiling.

Finn's gaze flew to meet Avery's, and all the things they couldn't seem to say to each other—all the hidden fears and insecurities, all the doubts, tempered by an aching, raw longing for connection—melted away.

There she is.

A little girl. Their daughter—hers and Finn's.

Chapter 12

Avery was relieved that seeing the sonogram alleviated some of the tension between her and Finn. A week later, they were still getting along well enough that the Crawfords seemed to genuinely believe they were in love. Even Melba and Old Gene had fallen for the ruse, showering them with congratulations and best wishes upon their return to Rust Creek Falls.

They'd moved into Finn's suite at the Ambling A, which so far had been spacious enough for them to move about in separate orbits. At night, Avery slept in Finn's king-size bed, with its rustic Aspen log frame and sheets that smelled of sandalwood, hay and warm leather. Of Finn.

Her husband camped out on the oversize leather sofa adjacent to the bed, far enough away to avoid any accidental physical contact, but close enough for Avery to grow accustomed to the rhythmic sound of his breathing in the dark. He hadn't touched her at all since she'd taken up residence in his home—not even a casual hug or innocent brush of his fingertips—and somehow hearing him sleep so close by made her feel a little less lonely. A little less like an outsider on Crawford territory.

They weren't going to get away with the lack of physical affection for long—not if everyone was going to remain convinced that they were actual, real newlyweds. But Avery was grateful for a little breathing room.

By the time she and Finn joined the rest of the Crawford clan at the annual Rust Creek Falls Halloween costume party, she'd foolishly begun to believe she had enough of a handle on her emotions to withstand a lengthy public charade.

She was wrong, of course.

So.

Very.

Wrong.

The party was held in the high school gym, which someone had spent a serious amount of effort transforming into a Halloween-themed delight. There was a maze made of hay bales off to the side, swags of twisted orange and black crepe paper and more fake spiderwebs than Avery had ever seen in one place before. As promised, Melba had made her famous caramel apples, and when Avery and Finn arrived, children dressed as ghosts, ballerinas and superheroes had clearly been enjoying the sweet treats, as evidenced by their sticky chins.

Avery couldn't help but smile. She'd never been to a party like this one before, not even when she was a child. She couldn't remember ever going trick-or-treating, either. Halloween night in Dallas always meant the mayor's posh Masquerade Ball, held at an exclusive hotel overlooking the city skyline. Invitations to the fancy masked ball were coveted, and Avery and her parents were always regulars. When she'd been a little girl, she'd stayed at home with the nanny and watched while her parents headed off to the party, dressed in opulent Halloween finery.

But this, she thought as she looked around the gym, *this is what a Halloween party should look like.*

She loved it all, from the happy children and homemade treats to the makeshift dance floor where an adult dressed as Frankenstein's monster was leading a group in a dance to the "Monster Mash."

"Wait a minute." Avery took a closer look at the face beneath the green makeup. "Is that your father out there on the dance floor?"

Finn shook his head and let out a wry laugh. "It certainly looks that way."

"Hey, it's about time the lovebirds arrived." Wilder, wrapped in bandages to look like a mummy, handed Finn a beer and gave Avery a peck on the cheek. "The gang's all here."

He wasn't kidding. The Crawfords were camped out at two adjoining picnic tables right in the center of the action. All five of Finn's brothers were there, accompanied, of course, by their respective wives and children—Logan and Sarah with baby Sophia, Xander and Lily, Knox and Genevieve, Hunter with Wren. Since Avery's surprise wedding to Finn, Wilder and Hunter were the only two remaining single brothers, and neither had dates for the costume party—unless Hunter's daughter counted. Avery certainly thought so. They looked like the perfect father-daughter Halloween duo, with Wren dressed in a puffy tulle princess gown and Hunter wearing a large cardboard rectangle covered in tinfoil strapped to his chest.

"What are you supposed to be, dude?" Finn cast a dubious glance at Hunter's cardboard accessory. Its tinfoil covering was starting to look a little worse for wear. "A robot?"

Hunter's face fell. "No."

"He's a knight in shining armor," Avery said, winking at Wren. "Obviously. You and your daddy match, don't you?"

"Yes!" Wren giggled and pointed at the plastic crown perched atop her silky blond hair. "I'm a princess, and Daddy is a knight."

"I totally see it," Avery said, struggling to keep a straight face as Finn shook his head at Hunter.

"Nope. That—" he pointed at Hunter's sad silver shield "—is weak. Don't tell me you couldn't come up with a more convincing knight getup."

Hunter glowered at him.

Avery thought it was sweet that Hunter had gone to the effort to try to make a costume.

"Cut your brother some slack." Avery gave Finn a playful little shoulder bump and then froze when she realized what she'd done.

She'd initiated contact—a clear violation of their unspoken agreement not to touch one another, because as they both knew, one thing could very well lead to another. Before the marriage, they'd agreed to no sex. But since the wedding night, they hadn't so much as kissed. Somewhere along the way, the no-sex rule had snowballed into something else. It was as if they were both going out of their way to avoid any physical contact whatsoever.

Avery crossed her arms, uncrossed them and then crossed them again, painfully aware of every part of her body relative to Finn's. Less than inch of space existed between her arm and his chest, and the air in that space felt electric all of a sudden.

A shiver coursed through her while she tried to concentrate on what Hunter was saying.

"I'm doing the best I can." He rested a hand on top of Wren's slender shoulder and gave it a squeeze. "You'll understand one day when you have kids."

Finn practically choked on his beer.

"When's that going to be, anyway?" Wilder grinned at Finn. "You were in such a hurry to put a ring on this lady's finger, I figure you'll be wanting to start a family sooner rather than later."

Avery didn't dare look at Finn. If she did, the truth surely would be written all over her face.

"Give us time" was all he said in response, but when the conversation turned to other, less panic-inducing matters, he slipped his arm around her waist and pulled her close.

Little fires seemed to skitter over her skin everywhere he touched her. Her brain told her to pull away, to save herself. But her body had other ideas. Every cell in her body seemed to sigh with relief at once again being so near to the man she'd married...the man she was afraid she was starting to care for far more than she'd ever intended.

Their eyes met, and then his gaze flitted to her lips. He quickly looked away.

It's all just for show. She needed that reminder. They were newlyweds. His family was watching…the entire town was watching. They needed to make it look real. After all, that's why they'd come to the party dressed in matching bride and groom costumes.

She just wished it didn't *feel* so real.

She did her best to shift her attention elsewhere. Maximilian seemed to be hitting the dance floor with a different partner every time the song changed. His partners ranged from small children he let stand on his feet as he spun them around to women his own age, and everyone else in between. Avery couldn't help but laugh. For a man who seemed so invested in marrying off his sons, he sure was a flirt. The biggest one in Rust Creek Falls, so it seemed.

"Avery." Little Wren tugged on the sleeve of Avery's white dress to get her attention.

"Yes, sweetie?" Avery took a seat on the picnic bench so that they were eye to eye. Finn's fingertips slid casually to the back of her neck, where he toyed languidly with a lock of her hair.

It's only make-believe, no more real than Hunter's tinfoil shield.

"You and Uncle Finn just got married, right?" Wren smoothed down the front of her pink tulle gown. Hunter had chosen the DIY route for his own costume, but he'd obviously steered clear of Pinterest for his daughter's. She looked like a mini Disney princess, all the way down to the petite velvet slippers on her feet.

"We did." Avery nodded, pushing the cheap tulle veil on her head away from her eyes.

Wren's little brow furrowed. "Why didn't you have a fancy wedding with a big white dress?"

"Oh. Well." Avery's heart was in her throat all of a sudden, and her simple bride costume made her feel more like a fraud than ever before. "Not everyone has a fancy wedding. What matters most is finding someone you care about, someone you know you'll love." She swallowed. Hard. "Forever and ever."

"Like happily-ever-after?" Wren said.

Avery nodded, not quite trusting herself to speak.

"Life is perfect when you're a princess or a bride." The little girl spun in a circle with her hands clasped in front of her as if she were holding a bridal bouquet.

Perfect?

Not quite. Avery was a bride, and her life was far from perfect. Sometimes she wished she'd never thought to make her marriage to Finn a business arrangement. Would it really be so terrible to try to make things work? They were having a baby together, after all.

"I can't wait until I'm a bride one day," Wren said, running her tiny fingers over Avery's short costume wedding dress.

And then she skipped away, a vision in tulle, and Avery couldn't help but feel like she'd just had a conversation with her younger self.

Had she really ever been as innocent and starry-eyed as Wren?

Yes, she had. And despite everything, a part of her— the wishful, hopeful part that seemed to rise from the ashes every time she looked at Finn—still was.

But she wasn't a child anymore. It had been years since she'd trusted in fairy-tale endings, and Finn had never tried to pretend he was her Prince Charming. He'd always been up front and honest about what they'd had. Not a lifetime, but a night. Just one…until the baby had come along. It was a shame little girls were set up with such high expectations.

Real life was so seldom as perfect as Wren believed.

Avery was gone.

One minute, she'd been chatting with Wren, and the next time Finn glanced in her direction, she wasn't here.

He frowned into his beer as his brothers continued their running commentary of Maximilian's efforts to charm Melba Strickland onto the dance floor. It wasn't going well for Max. According to town lore, she'd never danced with a man other than Old Gene, and by all appearances, it was going to stay that way.

"Denied." Wilder let out a laugh. "Again."

Finn glanced toward the games area of the gym, where Wren, Lily, Genevieve and Sarah were participating in a race in which they wrapped each other in spools of white gauze to look like mummies. Still no Avery.

"You're missing it." Hunter gave Finn a nudge with his elbow. "I swear Melba is on the verge of conking Dad in the head with one of her caramel apples."

"What?" Finn said absently as he continued scanning the surroundings in search of his wife.

"Hey." Hunter nudged him harder. "What's with you?"

"I can't find Avery."

Hunter shrugged. "She was here a few minutes ago. She probably went to the bar for a beer."

Wrong on both counts. Avery wasn't drinking because of her pregnancy, and it had been longer than a mere few minutes since he'd seen her last.

"I'm going to go look for her." Finn shoved his beer at Hunter.

He took it and shrugged. "Suit yourself, but if you're just looking for an excuse to run off and take your wife to bed, you could have just said so."

Finn grunted a noncommittal response and went to weave his way through the crowd, but he couldn't find Avery anywhere. Panic coiled into a tight knot in the pit of his stomach.

What if something was wrong, either with her or the baby?

She would have said something to him if she wasn't feeling well, wouldn't she?

He didn't want to worry his family or the Stricklands, so instead of asking Melba or one of his female relatives to take a look in the ladies' room, he knocked on the door himself. Still no luck. She wasn't anywhere in the gymnasium.

Adrenaline shot through him, causing a terrible tingle in his chest. He needed to find her. Now.

Finn fled the party without saying goodbye. If he told the other Crawfords why he was so desperate to find Avery, he'd end up outing her pregnancy when he'd promised her they would wait to tell everyone. But if she wasn't in the parking lot or right outside the building, he was going to have to get help from someone. She hadn't just vanished into thin air.

He pushed through the double doors of the gym, squinting into the darkness. The moon hung low in the sky overhead, so big and round it looked swollen. A harvest moon spilling amber light over the horizon.

And in the distance he saw her—Avery, so beautiful in the moonlight—sitting on a playground swing, looking even more like a bride than she had on their wedding day.

Stone-cold relief washed over him. He was too happy to see her to let himself be irritated at her for disappearing like that. He rushed toward her, swallowing the pavement with big strides, but then someone cut into his path. A woman.

"This must be my lucky night," she said, gazing up at him from beneath the brim of a witch's hat.

Finn had no clue as to the woman's identity, other than the generic naughty-witch vibe she was giving off in her skimpy costume. Didn't she know this was an old-fashioned family-friendly party?

"Sorry, I'm on my way…" He gestured vaguely toward the swing set, where Avery lifted her head and met his gaze.

"You're Finn Crawford," the witch said. "At long last. I've been trying to get ahold of you for days."

"What?" He dragged his attention away from Avery to look at the woman again. "I'm sorry. I don't think we've met."

"We haven't, but Viv Dalton assured me you'd be interested in making my acquaintance. I'm Natalie." The witch batted her purple eyelashes at him and laid a hand on his chest.

He gently but firmly removed it. "I think there's been a misunderstanding."

This must be the woman who'd been blowing up his cell a few days ago, the same woman who'd called the Ambling A and spoken to Maximilian.

"I'm not dating anymore," he said. "I actually just got married."

"So that's not just a costume?" The witch blinked in the direction of his tuxedo T-shirt and his adhesive "groom" name tag. Her face fell. "Oh. Too bad."

"Again, sorry. But I really need to go." He looked past her toward the playground, but the swing set was empty now. One empty, lonely swing moved back and forth.

Damn it.

She was gone again.

"Avery?" He called out, jogging toward the playground. She couldn't have gone far. "Avery! Where are you?"

He found her clear around the corner, stomping down North Buckskin Road, her costume bridal veil whipping furiously around her head.

"Avery, thank God," he said, breathing hard as he struggled to catch up. "You had me worried sick."

She rolled her eyes and kept on walking, and it wasn't until she passed beneath a streetlamp that he noticed the dark rings of mascara under her eyes. His gut churned.

She'd been crying.

"Where are you going? What's wrong?"

"Back to the boarding house." She sniffed and kept marching toward Cedar Street, where the old purple Victorian loomed at the intersection.

The panicked knot in the pit of Finn's stomach tightened until he was almost gasping for air. "What? Why?"

"I miss Pumpkin, and I don't want to be anywhere near you right now." She stopped abruptly and glared at him. "I'd much prefer the company of a baby goat to you at the moment."

"Because of the witch?" He glanced over his shoulder toward the high school and then fixed his gaze with Avery's again. She was angry—clearly—but somewhere beneath the glittering fury in her big doe eyes, he saw something else. Hurt.

"Avery." He shook his head and jammed his hands on his hips to stop himself from reaching for her… from plunging his hands in her hair and kissing her full on the lips in flagrant violation of their marital agreement. "Princess, she's no one. Just some woman Viv Dalton wanted to set me up with a while back. But that was after I found out you were here, so obviously I told her no."

Avery glanced up at him for a second, then resumed staring at a spot somewhere to his left. Clearly, she had no interest in even looking at him.

"If you'd stuck around back there, you would have heard me tell Viv's witch that I'd just gotten married and that I couldn't stop for a chat because I'd come outside looking for *you*."

Avery narrowed her gaze at him and squared her shoulders. "I wasn't jealous, if that's what you're thinking."

Liar.

Finn didn't dare laugh, but he was temped. "Is that so, wifey?"

"Okay, maybe I was just a little." She held her pointer finger and thumb a sliver apart. "An infinitesimal amount."

"Got it." He nodded, and the adrenaline flooding his body shifted into something else far more familiar, far more dangerous under the circumstances. Desire. "You're hightailing it back to the boarding house because you were jealous to see me talking to another woman."

He took a step closer, needing her softness. Her heat. "Even though you have no interest whatsoever in sleeping with me."

Her lips parted, and the tip of her cherry-red tongue darted out to wet them. Finn instantly went hard.

She lifted her chin, determined to stand her ground even though they both knew she'd just showed her hand. She wanted him just as badly as he wanted her. "I already told you why I was going back. I miss Pumpkin."

"So this wild-goose chase you've got me on is about a goat?" He wasn't buying it, not even for a second.

"Yes." She huffed out a sigh. "Mostly. Plus I was talking to Wren and she asked me why we didn't have a big wedding. She told me she couldn't wait to be a bride one day, just like me. And I just… I can't…"

Tears shimmered in her eyes, sparkling like diamonds in the moonlight. "What are we doing, Finn?"

He'd made Avery a promise when she'd agreed to marry him. She'd asked so little of him, and he'd been determined to keep his word, no matter how agonizing that promise turned out to be.

Did she have any idea how many times he'd nearly slipped up and reached for her? A thousand times a day, whether to simply hold her hand, spread his palms over her belly to feel the life growing inside her—the life they'd made together—or to touch her in all the ways he dreamed about every night when he slept alone on his sad leather sofa.

His gaze bored into her as though that's all it would take for her to understand. As if he only needed to look at her hard enough for her to know how badly he ached for her. Then…now…always.

She was his. She'd *been* his all along. Didn't she know that?

Screw it.

He couldn't do it anymore, and from what she was

telling him, neither could she. It was time to forget their silly rules and be honest with each other for a change.

"This," he said, lifting his hand to cup her chin between his thumb and forefinger. "*This* is what we're doing."

Then he touched his lips to hers with a gentleness in stark opposition to the riot taking place inside him. He wouldn't force himself on her—not now, not ever—and he needed some sort of confirmation that this was okay. That this was what she wanted, even though she'd been doing her level best to pretend otherwise.

That confirmation came in the form of a breathy, kittenish sigh and Avery's hands sliding around his neck, her nails digging feverishly into his back. Then she kissed him so hard he saw stars.

There's my girl, he thought. *There's my princess.*

And then there were no more thoughts, no more rules and no more walls as he scooped his wife into his arms and carried her to his truck in plain view of anyone who cared to look. Finn didn't give a damn about appearances. It was time to take his wife to bed.

Chapter 13

We shouldn't be doing this.

Those words kept spinning through Avery's consciousness as she and Finn fumbled their way up the stairs of the log mansion at the Ambling A, kissing and shedding articles of clothing along the way.

Thank goodness the rest of the family was still eating caramel apples and dancing to the "Monster Mash" back in the high school gymnasium. Because as desperately as she ached for her husband right now, she wasn't sure if she could have stopped for anyone or anything. Not even if Frankenstein's actual monster had been blocking their path to the bedroom.

We shouldn't be doing this.

Finn pressed her against the wall just outside his bedroom, and his lips moved away from her mouth, dragging slowly, deliciously down the side of her neck.

She sagged against the cool pine, hands fisting in his hair as he kissed his way from one breast to the other.

They definitely shouldn't be doing *that*.

Stopping wasn't an option, though. It no longer mattered what they should or shouldn't be doing. Desire was moving through her with the force of a freight train, bearing down hard. She needed this. She'd needed this so badly for so long. It felt like forever since the last time Finn had touched her like this, the last time he'd laid her down on the smooth sheets of his bed in Oklahoma and thrust inside her for the very first time.

The only time.

How was that even possible? She was made for this… made for him. They fit together like two halves of the same whole, and after they'd parted on that strange, sad morning in Oklahoma City, she'd never quite felt whole again. All these months it was as if she'd been walking around with a huge piece of herself missing, just out of reach.

And then…

Then she'd realized she was pregnant, and she'd somehow convinced herself that was the reason she'd been feeling so out of sorts. She wasn't in love with Finn Crawford. She couldn't be. They barely knew one another. The only thing she'd known for absolute certain was that he was a Crawford and that her father would probably drop dead on the spot if he ever found out they'd been intimate.

These were the things she'd told herself as she'd put away her pencil skirts, packed her yoga mat and headed to Rust Creek Falls. Love had nothing to do with her messy state of emotional disarray. It all boiled down to science. She was walking around with a piece of

Finn Crawford inside her, his DNA had gone and gotten itself all mixed up with hers, and now her body was confused. It was as simple as that. Three out of four biologists would totally agree with her.

Lies.

Lies, lies and more lies.

Had she really been so foolish as to believe that she could come to the Ambling A and not end up right here, with Finn slowly walking her backward until her knees hit the edge of the bed and they tumbled together, already losing track of where her body ended and his began? Had she honestly thought she could marry him and keep up the whole virgin-bride routine in an effort to spare her heart?

It seemed ludicrous now. Why should she forgo *this*? Finn was her husband, and she was his wife. There was nothing whatsoever wrong with the way he gently parted her thighs and kissed his way down her body, his tongue warm and wicked against the cool of her skin. On the contrary, it was exquisite. She was lost in the moment in a way that she'd never managed to achieve, no matter how many hot yoga classes she'd attended or how often she'd used the meditation app on her phone.

No one existed outside her and Finn. There was no embarrassment, no worry as her hips moved up and down, undulating in perfect rhythm with the stroke of his fingers, searching…seeking the release that only he could give her. She was free and open in a way that she'd never been able to be with anyone else. Because they were special. She could run all she wanted, but she'd always come back to this—to his hands sliding into her hair as his gaze burned into hers, branding her, soul-deep. To the flawless heat of his body perfectly poised over hers and the way he shuddered when he finally slid inside her. To the way she shattered around him instantly, crying out his name.

Finn.

It had always been him, and it always would be. Giving herself to him again changed nothing, because he'd captured her heart a long time ago.

Yet at the same time, it changed everything. Because somewhere beneath the honeyed heat of her desire, she remembered he'd never said it. The one thing she wanted to hear more than anything else in the world. *I love you.*

Her heart ached to hear it, but she managed to push her hunger for it down. Deep down to the place where it had been since the moment Finn slipped the ring on her finger and she realized she wanted it to be real. For *them* to be real.

And she actually thought it would stay there. She believed she could spend her nights in Finn's bed, touching him, loving him, pretending he felt it even though he never said the words. Because sometimes pretending was better than nothing. Sometimes pretending was as good as it got.

But after it was over—after he'd stroked her to climax again and again, after he'd groaned her name and shuddered his release and they lay beside each other with legs and hearts intertwined—he did something that finally broke the pretense beyond repair.

He leaned over and, with the softest brush of his lips imaginable, he kissed her growing belly. And with an ache in his voice that she'd never heard before, he whispered a word. Just one. The most profoundly beautiful one he could have said.

Mine.

If only she could have made herself believe he'd been talking about her. Or them—her and the baby both. But he hadn't. He'd meant the child, their child, and while it was sweet, it just wasn't enough. And it never would be, because sometimes pretending was better than nothing, but when it wasn't, it was the most devastating heartbreak of all.

I can't stay here anymore.

The thought started as a spark, and in the hours before the sun came up, it exploded into a wildfire, burning out of control and destroying everything in its path—every last hope for a future, charred beyond recognition. She'd repeated it to herself so many times in the night that it became a balm, a way to calm the panic that threatened to eat her alive at the thought of saying goodbye. By the time Finn opened his eyes, she was already dressed, packed and ready to go. All she had to do was tell him.

"I can't stay here anymore."

Finn was dreaming.

No, it wasn't a dream. It was a nightmare—the worst nightmare his unconscious possibly could have conjured.

He closed his eyes and willed the image of Avery, fully clothed with one of her slick designer suitcases in her hand, out of his head. His mind was playing tricks on him. That had to be it. Last night had changed everything. He and Avery had finally stopped pretending and been honest with each other about their feelings. They'd made love.

And that's exactly what it had been, too. Not just

sex. Things between him and Avery had never been just physical. He knew that now. On some level, he always had.

But no matter how hard he tried to keep his eyes closed and go back to the world from just hours before—the world where he and his wife were tangled in bedsheets—he couldn't. The space beside him was cold. Empty...

As empty as his heart felt when he opened his eyes and realized the sight in front of him wasn't a dream, after all. It was real.

"Excuse me?" he said, staring hard at Avery's suitcase.

When the hell had she packed it? Had she climbed out of his bed the moment he'd fallen asleep?

"I can't stay here," she repeated, a gut-wrenching echo.

He sat up, and the sheet fell away, exposing him. Avery took a sharp inhale and averted her gaze.

Seriously?

"Look at me, damn it," he growled. "What are talking about? You can't leave, Princess. You just..."

...can't.

What would he say to his family when they woke up and found out she'd left? What would he do? They were a family. She couldn't just leave.

But apparently she could, because she was already walking toward the door.

Out of his bed.

Out of his life.

"No." Finn jumped up and went after her. "Whatever's wrong, we can fix it. Let me fix it, Princess. Please."

He'd never allowed himself to be more vulnerable in his life. He was naked and begging, but he didn't care.

"We can take things slow, if that's what you want," he blurted as her hand gripped the doorknob.

She paused, just long enough to shake her head.

"Finn, we…"

"What happened last night doesn't have to happen again. We can wait. We can do whatever you want. Just don't leave."

"Can't you see?" She shook her head again. "I have to. I just need some space. Please."

Space.

He could give her that, couldn't he? Maybe a night or two at the boarding house would do them both some good.

No. Finn glared at her. He wanted her here, with him. He needed his wife and his baby. He needed them as surely as he needed his next breath.

"You're my wife. We had a deal, remember?" he said. Married…till death do them part.

God, what was wrong with him? He sounded as controlling and manipulative as his father.

"You're right." Avery looked past him, toward the bed. "And last night we broke that deal. So now all bets are off."

"Avery." He raked a hand through his hair, tugging hard at the ends. "I'm…"

He couldn't bring himself to say he was sorry. Because he wasn't. Not entirely. What had happened between them last night had been honest and real. Even more authentic than the band of gold around Avery's finger. She knew it as well as he did. Why else would she be running scared?

But even as he prepared to stand his ground stubbornly, he realized that somewhere deep down, he *was*. He was sorry for anything that made Avery hurt or made her afraid. Because all he wanted was to make her feel loved. And safe in his arms.

He took a deep breath and forced the words out. "I'm sorry."

It didn't matter. Nothing he said mattered, because she'd already made up her mind.

"Me, too," she said quietly.

And then she walked right out the door, taking Finn's baby and every battered beat of his heart with her as she left.

Avery's nonstop flight to Dallas felt like the longest two and a half hours of her life.

She did everything she could to make the time pass as quickly as possible, from her stack of glossy fashion magazines to the vast array of snacks she'd picked up at the airport gift shop. But living at the boarding house for so long had changed Avery's eating habits. She much preferred Melba's and Claire's home cooking to the quick grab-and-go fare and Lean Cuisines she'd lived on while she'd been so busy helping run Ellington Meats. And as it turned out, she'd even lost all enthusiasm for her beloved *Vogue, Elle* and *Harper's Bazaar* now that she could no longer wear any of the sleek, fitted clothes featured on their pages.

Or maybe she'd simply developed a sudden fondness for flannel and cowboy boots.

Good grief, what was happening to her? Tastes changed, she supposed. The delicate rose gold ring on her finger was perhaps the most glaringly obvious testament to that fact, from the ring itself to the marriage it represented. Her father would probably have a heart attack the minute he saw it.

She thought about removing the ring before the plane landed, but she just couldn't bring herself to do so. She'd told Finn she was leaving, but she hadn't said a word about ending their marriage. That was a given, though, wasn't it? Part of the condition of coming home had always been cutting Finn out of her life. As welcoming as her parents had been on the phone when she'd broken down and called them from the airport in Montana, she had no reason to believe that had changed.

Taking the ring off seemed so final, though. The ultimate ending to a book she wasn't sure she was capable of closing. She just knew she needed time away from Rust Creek Falls to clear her head and figure out what was truly best for her and her baby. But if sleeping with Finn had confirmed anything, it was that she wasn't built for a marriage of convenience. She'd been fooling herself thinking she could marry a man and not become emotionally attached, especially a man she was already head over heels in love with.

When her flight finally landed in Dallas, she deplaned with nothing but a lump in her throat and her lone carry-on bag. It seemed impossible that she would come home with so little physical evidence of a life-changing month away. Her time in Montana almost felt like a fever dream, too colorful and lush to be real. But that was the whole point, wasn't it? None of it had been real. And now here she was, back on Texas soil with her smallest Louis Vuitton rolling bag and more emotional baggage than she could possibly carry all on her own.

When she saw her mother and father waiting for her

just outside the security gate, she braced herself for a flood of emotions. But when her mother gathered her into her arms, Avery didn't even cry. Not a single, solitary tear. She'd come crawling home with her tail between her legs, but at the very least she'd expected to feel a small sense of relief.

After all, she was back in the fold. Her heart was safe now.

Then why did she feel nothing but a horrible numbness and the nagging sense that she'd just made the biggest mistake of her life?

It was a short ride from the airport to the Ellington family home in the moneyed neighborhood of Highland Park, and Avery's parents spent it getting her caught up on everything she'd missed while she'd been away.

Her mother told her about the latest happenings at the country club in lurid detail and suggested now that Avery was back, she might want to help cochair the upcoming Junior League charity fund-raiser. The lawn of the big gothic church on University Drive was a sea of orange now that the annual pumpkin patch was in full swing, and the mayor was throwing his annual Masquerade Ball. Avery had come just in time.

But the Masquerade Ball wouldn't be anything like the sweet Halloween dance she'd attended with the Crawfords. There wouldn't be any costumed children or fake spiderwebs or bobbing for apples. It would be a staid affair, perfectly planned, perfectly decorated and perfectly boring. She missed the small-town charm of Rust Creek Falls already.

Meanwhile, her father filled her in on what she'd missed at the office. He'd promoted one of the project managers in her absence, but her corner office was still ready and waiting for her. She could walk back into her old life just like nothing had ever happened. It would be as if she'd never gone to Rust Creek Falls at all.

Except she had.

She stared blankly ahead as the big iron gate at the foot of the driveway swung open and her father's Cadillac Escalade cruised past the security cameras. Neither of her parents had mentioned her pregnancy. Were they just going to pretend that she wasn't having Finn Crawford's baby in a few months' time? Was that how this strange homecoming was going to play out?

Her hand went instinctively to her baby bump, and a tiny nudge pressed against her palm, just as it had when she'd exchanged vows with Finn in the country courthouse in Great Gulch. Finally, something real she could grasp hold of. Her child. Avery was going to be a mother, and no amount of pretending could prove otherwise.

"I'm married," she said quietly as her father shifted the car into Park.

"Oh, dear." Her mother sighed. Finally she had something more pressing to worry about than the centerpieces for the next country club luncheon.

Her father's gaze locked with hers in the reflection of the rearview mirror. "I saw the ring and figured as much."

She bit her lip and nodded. Good. Perhaps their bizarre sense of denial wasn't as serious as she'd begun to think.

"That's what annulments are for. Our attorney can get this taken care of in a matter of days." Her dad shrugged one shoulder and then got out of the car and shut the door as if the matter had been settled once and for all.

All of Avery's breath bottled up in her throat. An annulment. Could she do that Finn? Did she even want to?

"Honey," her mom said, turning to rest a hand on Avery's knee. "Give your daddy time. We can talk about all of this later. The most important thing is that you're home now."

Avery nodded as she blinked back tears. Only they weren't the tears of relief she'd expected. They were something else, something too horrible and painful to name.

She climbed out of the car and went straight to her childhood bedroom at the top of the home's curved staircase. She passed the grand piano where she'd taken lessons as a little girl and the framed collection of photographs that lined the hallway—Avery as homecoming queen of her private high school, Avery dressed in a white satin gown and elegant elbow-length gloves at her debutante ball, her father spinning her across the dance floor at the father-daughter dance.

It didn't matter how old she was, how well she did at the office or even if she was pregnant, her father would always see her just like those framed images—as his daughter. Just a little girl, barely more than an extension of himself.

How had she never noticed this before? Sure, she'd always been a daddy's girl, following in her father's footsteps and working alongside him at the family business. Daddy's princess. But she'd always thought it had been her choice. *Her* path.

Had it? Had she ever been the one in charge of her own life?

It was all so confusing, and two hours later, once she'd showered, changed and gone back downstairs for dinner, she wasn't any closer to knowing the answer to the many questions spinning around in her head. She was only certain of one thing—the decision whether or not to end her marriage was hers and hers alone.

"Are you feeling better now, dear?" Avery's mom cast a surprised glance at the buffalo-checkered shirt she'd slipped into—one of her purchases from the general store—but refrained from asking why she hadn't dressed for dinner. Mealtime in the Ellington household had always been a rather formal affair.

"A little. I'm really tired." Avery took her seat, the same place she'd sat for every family meal of her life.

As usual, her father was already seated at the head of the table. "You'll feel back to your old self once you get some rest. Leave all the legal details to me. I'll meet with the lawyers first thing tomorrow and get the ball rolling."

Avery picked up her fork but set it back down. "Daddy, no. I'm not ready."

Oscar glanced at his wife, cleared his throat and then spread his napkin carefully in his lap. "Very well. We can discuss the legalities later."

"Absolutely." Her mother beamed. "Avery, I was thinking we could start decorating the bedroom next door to yours for the baby. Won't that be fun?"

Avery blinked. "What about my place?"

She hadn't protested when they'd taken her straight to the big Ellington mansion from the airport, but surely they didn't expect her to *live* here from now on. She was an adult, with her own townhome near the Galleria.

"We can get a crib for there, too, if you like. But

you're going to need help when the baby comes. We just assumed you'd want to stay here for a while." Her mother passed her a bowl of green beans.

Avery scooped some onto her plate and passed it to her father.

"We're just so glad you've finally come to your senses," he said. "Your child will have everything her little heart desires. She'll want for nothing."

Finally, they were talking about the baby. They were saying all the right things, making plans and acting like doting grandparents. Avery's childhood had been a happy one, and if her daughter grew up with the same upbringing, she'd no doubt be a happy, charmed little girl.

She'll want for nothing.

The words echoed in Avery's mind on repeat.

Right, she thought. *But what about what I want?*

Chapter 14

Finn parked his rental car at the curb in front of the Georgian-style columned mansion on one of Highland Park's most prestigious streets. The driveway was blocked by a black steel gate with scrolled trim and a crest featuring a single cursive letter. *E* for Ellington.

Was he really going to just walk up to the front door and ring the bell of Oscar Ellington's home when he knew good and well he wasn't welcome here? Hell yes, he was.

Avery had *left* him. And she hadn't simply moved back down the road to Strickland's Boarding House. She'd gone all the way back to Texas, and she hadn't even bothered to give him the news herself. Melba and Old Gene had broken it to him when he'd shown up, desperate to talk to Avery. Melba had even gotten a little teary-eyed. She sat Finn down and tried to feed him some fresh caramel snickerdoodle cookies she'd just made for her boarders, but he couldn't eat. If Avery had gone back to Dallas, it meant only one thing—she'd agreed to her father's ridiculous terms.

Finn hadn't just lost his wife.

He'd lost his daughter, too.

He climbed out of the car and slammed the door. If Avery thought he was going to let her go straight from his bed back to her father without trying to talk some sense into her, she was dead wrong. He had a good idea what this was all about, anyway. They'd broken her sacred no-sex rule. Their fake marriage had suddenly become far too real, and she was running scared.

It would be okay, though. *They* would be okay. They had to be, because if Finn had learned anything in the days since he'd exchanged vows with Avery, it was that he couldn't live without her. Their fake marriage had always been real to him.

He simply needed to talk to her and assure her they could take things as slowly as she needed to. He'd do whatever she wanted, save for one thing—he'd never, ever let her family keep him from seeing his child.

Every damn flight from Montana to Dallas had been booked solid. Avery must have gotten the lone remaining seat on one of the last flights out. Thank God he'd remembered Maximilian's offer to send them off on a private jet for their honeymoon. When Finn told his father why he needed it, he hadn't even hesitated. The plane had been all fueled up, ready and waiting when Finn got to the airport in Billings.

His first stop upon landing had been Avery's town house, but her doorman assured Finn she'd been gone for weeks. There was only one place else she could be—

the stately redbrick home in front of him. He gritted his teeth, pressed the doorbell and hoped against hope Avery would come to the door.

No such luck. *No one* came to the door. Instead, an older man's voice boomed through a small speaker situated next to the bell. "Sorry, son. This isn't a good time."

Finn's blood boiled at the sound of Oscar Ellington's condescending tone. He glanced around, trying to figure out how he'd already been identified. Sure enough, there were security cameras stationed in four different corners of the mansion's veranda.

He stared the closest one down. "I've come all the way from Montana. The least you can do is open the door."

"We're in the middle of dinner. Like I said, it's not a good time."

Seriously? He wasn't even going to come to the door?

Finn didn't know why he was surprised. The man had disowned his own daughter—his *pregnant* daughter, who'd always been daddy's little princess until she'd started calling the shots in her own life. Why would he suddenly be reasonable just because Finn had been on a wild-goose chase across the country?

He rang the bell again. Once, twice, three times.

"Am I going to have to call the police?" Oscar bellowed over the intercom.

If he wanted a screaming match, Finn was more than game. He yelled at the intercom, "Call whoever you want. I've come to take my wife home, and I'm not leaving here without her."

Across the street, a security guard's car rolled to a stop. Maybe Oscar wouldn't need to call the cops.

It looked as though the neighborhood watch had that covered.

He beat on the door with a fist. He was done wasting time with the stupid bell and the prissy little intercom. Oscar needed to come outside so they could discuss the situation like men.

But the next voice to come over the intercom wasn't Oscar's. It was Avery's.

"Finn? Is that you?"

He nearly wept with relief at the sound of her soft Texas twang. Less than twelve hours ago, she'd been naked in his bed, and now they were talking through a speaker.

He fixed his gaze on the closest security camera. "Avery, baby. It's me. I've come to take you home. Whatever is wrong, we can fix it. Please, you've got to let me fix it."

"Can't you see that she's made her choice? My daughter wants nothing to do with you. For the last time, I'm ordering you to vacate the premises." Oscar's tone wasn't any more sympathetic than it had been before Avery joined the discussion, and somehow Finn doubted what he was saying was true.

Avery was running scared, but had she really told her father she wanted nothing more to do with him? He didn't want to believe it, but despair had begun to tie itself in knots in the pit of his stomach. He needed to see his wife. He needed to look her in the eye and tell her everything would be all right if she would just come home.

Every muscle in his body tensed. If Oscar didn't open the door, Finn was going to tear it down with his bare hands.

"Daddy, stop," Avery pleaded.

She was crying again, damn it. What was her father thinking? She was pregnant. If he hurt her…if he hurt the baby…

Heat flushed through Finn's body. He felt like he was on the verge of some kind of breakdown, breathing in ragged gulps until he felt like he was choking.

And then, by some miracle, the door swung open.

His head jerked up. He wasn't sure whether to expect Avery or her father as hope and dread danced a terrible duet in his consciousness.

But it was neither of them. Instead, an older woman with Avery's kind eyes stood on the threshold. "You must be Finn. I'm Avery's mother, Marion."

"Hello, ma'am." Finn tipped his hat. "I'm sorry for the…ah…disruption. But—"

She held up her hands. "Don't apologize. I understand this is a volatile situation, and I want to invite you in so we can all discuss this like reasonable adults."

He nodded, wanting to trust her but fully expecting Oscar to appear out of nowhere and slam the door in his face.

"Please, Finn." She held the door open wide, and for better or for worse, he stepped inside.

Avery had never thought she'd see the day Finn Crawford would be standing inside the house where she'd grown up, but here he was…in the flesh. And much to her irritation, that flesh looked even better than she remembered it. Was it possible that her husband had gotten even more handsome in the twelve hours or so since she'd last seen him?

It wasn't, right? Which meant the reason the sight

of him sent shivers through every nerve ending of her body was because she'd missed him. She'd missed him more than she could fathom, but that didn't mean she was going to simply stand by and let the two men in her life argue over her as if she was one of their cattle.

At the moment, Finn and Oscar were staring daggers at each other with nothing but her mother's antique Chippendale coffee table between them to prevent an epic physical altercation. It was beyond ridiculous, and Avery was over it.

"Have you two completely lost your minds?" she spat.

They both started blaming each other at once, her father bellowing on about Maximilian, and Finn insisting that Avery pack her bags immediately and head back to the Ambling A. The crystal chandelier hanging overhead nearly shook from all the yelling.

Avery clamped her hands over her ears as tears streamed down her face. How was she supposed to make sense of anything when they were behaving this way? Maybe she should forget about Montana and Texas altogether and go raise her child on a desert island somewhere.

"Everyone, just settle down," her mother said calmly. "Or *I'll* call the police on *both* of you."

Oscar reared back as if someone had slapped him. Avery probably did as well, seeing as she'd never heard her mother speak to him like that before. Finn cast cautious glances all around.

Marion crossed her arms and continued, "Now that I have everyone's attention, why don't we all sit down? I told Finn we were going to have an adult conversation, and that's exactly what we're going to do."

No one moved a muscle. Finn and Oscar seemed to be engaged in some kind of alpha male contest to see who would comply first.

"That's it." Avery threw up her hands. "I've had enough of both of you."

Finn plopped down on the closest armchair so quickly it looked he was playing a game of musical chairs.

"I'm sitting. I'm ready." He fixed his gaze on her father. "Let's discuss this, Oscar. Man to man."

Her father sat, but not without commentary. "Fine, although there's not much to discuss. Avery left you to come home. I think that says it all."

Finn glanced at Avery, and the pain in his face was visceral. "With all due respect, sir. I'm Avery's husband, and her home is with me."

They were getting nowhere. Avery didn't know whether to cry or knock both their heads together.

"Enough," her mother said sharply. "This isn't for the two of you to decide. It's between Finn and Avery, no one else."

A tiny spark of hope ignited deep in Avery's soul. Finally, someone had said it. Whatever she and Finn felt—or didn't feel—for each other should be between them. She should have never agreed to marry him until the family drama had been sorted out, but she had.

She'd exchanged vows with Finn, all the while thinking she could protect herself from the feelings that came from a genuine relationship. So long as there was a wall between them, she'd be safe. In the end, though, it hadn't mattered how many bricks she stacked—she fell in love, anyway.

She *loved* Finn. Whether or not he loved her back no

longer mattered. Her heart belonged to Finn Crawford, whether he wanted it or not.

Her mother's gaze shifted from Avery to Finn and back again. "You are having a baby together. This baby will bond you together for life."

The vows from their simple country wedding ceremony echoed in her mind, beating in time with her heart.

Until death do you part.

Marion's eyes narrowed, and for a moment, Avery felt as if her mother could see straight into her soul. "I think I know how each of you really feels about the other, but this is not for me to decide. You two need to figure it out…together."

She was right. Of course she was, but they still hadn't tackled the biggest elephant in the room—the angry bull elephant more commonly known as Oscar Ellington.

"As for you." Marion squared her shoulders and turned to face her husband. "I've stood for your nonsense long enough. You had no business cutting Avery off like you did. She's our daughter, our own flesh and blood, and you've been holding on to some silly grudge against Maximilian Crawford for far too long."

Oscar's face went three shades of red. Maybe four. It reminded Avery of the bright leaves back in the maple forest near Rust Creek Falls.

He seemed to know better than to interrupt, though. Marion Ellington rarely criticized her husband. Almost never, as far as Avery could remember. But her patience had finally cracked, and she was apparently finished holding her tongue.

"Either you give Avery back her inheritance—and her job—or I will leave you, Oscar Ellington. This is no idle threat. I will walk right out that door." She pointed to the front door with a trembling hand.

All eyes in the room swiveled toward Oscar. Avery didn't dare breathe while she waited for him to respond.

The silence stretched on for a long, loaded moment until he finally nodded. "As you wish."

Oscar's voice was quiet. Contrite.

When he turned a tender gaze toward Avery, her heart gave a tight squeeze. But what she nearly mistook for heartbreak was something else entirely—it was her heart, and her family, mending back into one unified piece after weeks of shattered silence.

"Your mother is right, sweetheart. I love you no matter what. If you want to stay married to a Crawford, I might not like it, but I'll learn to live with it." With a deep exhale, Oscar faced Finn full-on. "You obviously feel passionately about my daughter. I love her with my whole heart, and if you do, too, then I suppose it's possible for us to find some common ground."

A surreal feeling of euphoria washed over Avery. It started in her chest and spread outward, leaving a tingling surge in its wake.

Her father had just said everything Avery had wanted to hear from the moment she'd first realized she was pregnant. Before she'd even set foot in Rust Creek Falls, she'd lain awake nights, wishing and hoping for something like this to happen. It just seemed so impossible, and once he'd called her with the devastating news that he was cutting her off, she'd given up every last shred of hope.

Thank God for her mother.

If she hadn't intervened, they might never have gotten here. But she had, because that's what mothers did.

They sacrificed all for their children. Avery was only beginning to understand the depth of that kind of unconditional love.

She rested her hand on her belly and fixed her gaze on Finn's. The feud was over. There was no longer anything standing between them. At long last, they could be together—*really* together—without the devastating heartbreak of being cut off from her family.

But now that all the obstacles had finally been torn down, Avery was no longer sure where she and Finn stood. A part of her—a very large, very real part— wanted to cross the room and throw herself at him the same way she had in the pasture at the Ambling A and in the cool quiet of the sugar bush at the syrup farm. Why shouldn't she? What her father thought no longer mattered.

But she'd left.

She'd finally given herself to Finn, and in the heady romance of the afterglow, she'd run away.

They could get past that, though, couldn't they? Everything had turned out for the best. Finn had followed her all the way here. And yet...

Finn was still sitting quietly on the rose damask sofa in the room where her mother threw tea parties. He hadn't uttered a word in response to what her father had just said.

I love her with my whole heart, and if you do, too, then I suppose it's possible for us to find some common ground.

This was the moment where Finn was supposed to confess his feelings. It was the only way to respond to that sort of statement, wasn't it?

I love Avery, too.

That's what Finn should be saying right now. Why wasn't he?

Please. Avery implored him with her gaze. Her feelings had to be written all over her face. Couldn't he see it? *Please, please say it.*

But suddenly Finn couldn't seem to look at her. The passion and fury that had driven him to fly all the way to Texas and practically beat down the door to the Ellington estate seemed to drain right out of him before her eyes.

He frowned down at his hands, folded neatly in his lap. Those hands had touched her in ways no one else ever had before. Those hands knew every inch of her body—every secret place, every soft, silken vulnerability. Avery couldn't look at them anymore without craving the exquisite pleasure of his skin against hers.

When Finn finally spoke, it was in a voice she'd never heard him use before. Quiet. Calm…terrifyingly so. "Can I have a word alone with Avery, please?"

"Of course," her mother said, rising to her feet as she shot a meaningful look at Oscar.

"Yes, yes." He stood as well, pausing to give Avery a kiss on the top of her head before they left the room. "I love you, honey. Remember that, okay? You have our support." He lingered for a moment, shifting awkwardly from foot to foot. "Whatever you decide."

It was strange seeing her father so unsure of himself and only underscored the gravity of what had just occurred. And what might happen next.

"I know." Avery reached out and squeezed his hand. "Thank you."

Finn's expression betrayed little as her parents left the room and closed the French doors, shutting them alone together inside. Avery no longer cared what exact words he uttered; she just wished he would say *something*. Anything.

"I—" She started to apologize for her disappearing act, but at the same exact time, Finn began talking, too.

"Avery—"

They both stopped abruptly and stared at each other. Another day, another time, they probably would have laughed. Neither one of them did so now, though. Avery's chin went wobbly like it always did when she was trying not to cry.

"This changes things," Finn finally said.

She blinked. "What does?"

"This." Finn gestured vaguely at their surroundings—the antique rotary telephone, the gilded wall mirror that had been passed down from generation to generation of Ellingtons, the grandfather clock with its familiar tick-tock that Avery would have recognized blindfolded.

The room they were sitting in hadn't changed a bit since Avery's childhood. She could have drawn a picture of it from memory and not missed a single detail.

"You're back in the fold," he said. There wasn't a drop of bitterness in his tone, and Avery was suddenly unsure whether that was a good sign or a bad one.

"I guess I am." She nodded. "But shouldn't that be a good thing? My father is finally letting go of whatever happened between him and Maximilian. He won't stop you from seeing the baby anymore."

"And you're no longer disinherited," he added with a sad smile. "Which means you no longer need me."

Wait, that wasn't what it meant at all. Was that why he was acting so strangely all of a sudden? He thought the only reason they were together was because she'd had no place else to go?

Isn't it, though?

No.

She tried to swallow, but her throat had gone bone dry. It wasn't the only reason—not anymore. Deep down, it had never been the only reason. Finn was the father of her baby, but it was more than that, too. She'd *wanted* to exchange vows with him in that dusty old courthouse. She'd just been too afraid to admit it because Finn had never been the marrying type.

Oh, no.

Avery's heart plummeted to the soles of her feet. That's what the sudden change in Finn's mood was all about. He didn't want to be married. He never had. He'd just proposed because of the baby and now that there was no feud standing between him and his child, he was trying to let her down gently.

"You don't need me to support you and the baby," he said, spelling things out in a way that hurt more than she ever thought possible. As if all along she'd only been interested in the Crawford money.

"That's not true." She shook her head.

Stop it, she wanted to say. *Just stop saying these things and tell me you love me.*

"I think you need some time alone to figure out what it is you want, sweetheart." The kindness in his voice almost killed her. She'd rather he yell and scream than look at her the way he was looking at her right then... with goodbyes in his eyes.

Sure enough, he unfolded himself from the chair he was sitting in and loomed over her. Just as Avery expected, he already had one foot out the door.

She stood on wobbly legs and forced herself to meet his gaze. Where was the man who'd pounded on the front door with his fists, insisting he wasn't going anywhere without his wife by his side? She needed that man, whether he realized it or not. She *loved* that man.

"You know where to find me when you make up your mind."

They were the last words her husband said to her, followed by a chaste kiss on the cheek and a walk through the foyer to the front door.

And just like that, he was gone.

Chapter 15

Avery couldn't seem to make herself move as the door shut softly yet firmly behind Finn. She wanted to go running after him. She wanted that more than anything in the world, but it was as if a physical force was holding her back, keeping her rooted to the spot.

He'd come all the way to Texas from Montana—for her. When she'd first spotted him on the security camera, she'd nearly wept with relief. If he'd chased her all the way to Texas, that had to mean he loved her.

Right?

She'd seen enough rom-coms to know that at some point, every good love story culminated in a grand romantic gesture. This was it. Finn had followed her to enemy territory so he could win her back.

But now that her mother had finally talked some sense into her father, Finn just up and walked away.

There'd been no declaration of love, no promise of a future together. He'd spoken about their marriage as if it was precisely what she'd set out for it to be.

A business transaction.

And then he'd left her alone to think things through. God, it was humiliating. Avery didn't need to think, and she sure as heck didn't feel like being alone. She wanted Finn, damn it. Couldn't he see that? She was in love with him. She'd been in love with him all along, which was precisely why she'd been acting so crazy—kissing him one minute and running away the next. Even marrying him when they hardly knew each other.

Her behavior had nothing to do with pregnancy hormones. She was head over heels, crazy in love with her husband.

And he'd just walked right out the door.

She'd never felt so alone in her life, not even when her father had so coldly informed her that she'd been disinherited. She pressed a hand to her baby bump, desperate for a reminder that she wasn't completely on her own. She still had her daughter, and she always would.

And she could still have Finn, too. He'd made it perfectly clear that the decision was up to her. But was there really a decision to make if he didn't love her? How could she have been stupid enough to believe that exchanging sacred vows could ever be anything remotely similar to a business deal?

"Avery?" Her mom walked tentatively into the entryway and looked around. "Where's Finn?"

"He's…" *He's gone.* Avery shook her head. She couldn't say it. If she did, she'd break and she wasn't sure she'd ever be whole again.

"Oh, honey." Her mom wrapped her arms around

Avery and hugged her tight. "Don't cry. Everything is going to be okay."

But it wasn't. There'd been no grand gesture, just a quiet goodbye, and now great heaving sobs were racking Avery's body. It was as if she'd been suppressing her real feelings for so long—since that fateful night in Oklahoma City—that she simply couldn't do it any longer. She was feeling everything at once. Joy and pain. Hope and fear. Love and loss.

So much loss that it nearly dragged her to her knees.

Her mother smoothed her hair back from her eyes, then cupped Avery's face in her hands. "Do you love him, sweetheart?"

She nodded as tears kept streaming down her face.

Her mom smiled as if she'd known as much all along. "Then it seems as though you have an important decision to make. Don't worry about your father. I'll handle him. You just do what you need to do."

Avery trembled all over.

Do what you need to do.

She took a ragged inhale as a terrible realization dawned—what she wanted to do and what she needed to do were two entirely different things.

The log mansion at the Ambling A was as quiet as a tomb when Finn walked through the door at three in the morning. He was immensely grateful for Maximilian's access to a private plane, just as he'd been the day before when he was in such a hurry to get to Dallas.

But at the moment, he was even more grateful for the fact that all of his family members were in bed and he wouldn't have to see their disappointed expressions when he walked back through the door without his wife.

The only thing that might have made him feel worse was the more likely possibility that they wouldn't have been surprised at all, that they'd have chalked up his short-lived marriage to Finn just being Finn. He never could commit to anyone or anything. Why should Avery be any different?

But she *was* different, damn it. She'd always been special. She was the one. She always had been, right from the start.

The baby mattered, obviously. Finn would lay down his life for his child, but Avery mattered just as much. He'd only fully realized how much she meant to him after she'd left him. And now...

Now it was too late. She was back in Dallas, back in the loving arms of her family. Finn had his own opinions about what sort of father would ever turn his back on his pregnant adult daughter, but at least Oscar Ellington had done the right thing in the end.

If anyone understood the importance of family, it was Finn. As maddening as Maximilian could be, he'd been the one to raise six boys all on his own after his wife had walked out and left him. There was no denying Finn's father was a difficult man, and there was plenty of blame on both sides where his parents' divorce was concerned, but Maximilian had always been there for his sons. Always would be. Which was why Finn had tolerated his meddling into his sons' love lives as best as he could.

It was also why he'd done an about-face and hadn't insisted Avery return to the Ambling A with him. He couldn't make that choice for her. The last thing he wanted was to come between her and her family yet again. If they had any hope of remaining together, she'd have to make that decision on her own. He didn't want to be the kind of husband and father she'd grown up with. As much as he loved Avery, as much as he wanted her, he refused to bully her back into his home…into his life.

In a way, he'd already strong-armed her into marrying him. Witnessing the effect Oscar's controlling behavior had on the people he loved most in the world had been a wake-up call. Finn loved Maximilian, but he didn't want to grow old and become his father any more than he wanted to become Oscar Ellington. He wanted Avery to come back to him on her own terms, no one else's.

He wanted her to *choose* him.

She would. She had to. They were meant to be together. Finn knew that as surely as he knew the sun would rise over Montana the next morning, filling Big Sky country with endless rays of hope and light.

Finn needed just a hint of that kind of hope right now. Desperately. Somewhere between Texas and Montana, a bone-deep weariness had come over him. He was too tired to think, too tired to hope, too tired to dream.

He just wanted Avery back in his arms and back in his bed. Until that happened, he was lost. He collapsed fully clothed onto his bed and closed his eyes against a darkness so deep that he felt like he was choking on it. And when sleep finally came, he dreamed of his daughter. He dreamed of Avery and the life the three of them could have together—a life filled with love and joy and as many children and baby goats as Avery wanted. He'd give her anything and everything.

But when he woke up, she wasn't there. Of course she wasn't. It was silly to think she'd chase him back to

Montana the moment after he'd left her daddy's mansion. She needed time. Of course she did. But she'd come back—she had to come back. Finn went about his day on autopilot, doing his best to simply get through the hours until Avery returned without breaking down.

For once in his life, Maximilian held his tongue. He must have sensed Finn's need for silence on the matter of his missing wife, because when he strolled into the kitchen to find Finn staring blankly out the big picture window at Pumpkin romping and playing in her new pen, he simply rested a single arm around his shoulder in a tentative one-armed man hug. The unprecedented tenderness of the father-and-son moment caused a lump to lodge firmly in Finn's throat. He nodded, then strode outside to feed the goat to keep the dam of emotions welled up inside him from breaking.

The day wore on, and he busied himself with the daily comfort of ranch work—mending fences, tending to cattle, filling the stalls in the barn with fresh water and hay. His brothers and the ranch hands steered clear, leaving him space and time to brood. In his solitude, Finn worked harder than he had in years, because that's what true cowboys did. They did what needed to be done, no matter what. When they made a promise, they kept it.

He brushed a few stray flakes of hay from his black T-shirt as the air in the barn shifted from soft pink light to the purple shadows of twilight. His back ached, and so did his heart. The day was done, the horses were locked up for the night and the cattle fed, but still there was no sign whatsoever of Avery.

Finn pulled his Stetson low over his eyes and pressed his fist into his lower back, seeking relief. Then, for the first time all day, he allowed himself to consider the possibility that he'd been wrong, that maybe Avery wasn't coming back to the Ambling A. Not today... not ever.

His throat grew thick again, and just like this morning when Maximilian had given him the closest thing to a true embrace they'd ever shared, he felt as if he was on the verge of tears for the first time in his adult life. But then he heard something that gave him pause—an excited little bleat coming from the direction of Pumpkin's pen. Finn's heart stuttered to a stop.

It was silly, really. Baby kids got excited about anything and everything. Just because Pumpkin was suddenly making a ruckus didn't mean the goat's—and Finn's—favorite person in the world had suddenly reappeared.

But hope welled up in his chest nonetheless. And when he bolted out the barn door and saw Avery's familiar silhouette framed by a perfect autumn sunset, he nearly fell to his knees in relief.

"Avery," he said, his voice rusty and raw. "Thank God."

He held out his arms, but instead of running toward him, Avery slowed to a stop and gave him a watery smile. It was the saddest, most lonely smile he'd ever seen, and that's when Finn knew. He knew it with every desperate beat of his battered heart.

His wife had come home to say goodbye.

The relief in Finn's weary face nearly shattered Avery's resolve.

Clearly he was happy to see her. Elated, even after she'd spent the duration of her travel day—two flights, one three-hour layover and the winding drive to Rust Creek Falls from Billings—convincing herself that she was doing the right thing. The *only* thing. As hard as walking away from Finn would be, it wouldn't be as torturous as building a life with a man who didn't love her, constantly waiting for the shoe to drop and everything she held most dear to crumble to the ground.

She was sure she couldn't do that to herself, and she was positive she couldn't do it to her baby. Better to develop some sort of reasonable, platonic co-parenting arrangement now than end up having to try to find her way once Finn remembered he'd never had any interest in marriage in the first place…to anyone, least of all her.

But she couldn't tell Finn what she needed to say over the phone. He'd been by her side since the moment she'd told him she was pregnant, which was more than she could say for her own flesh and blood. In the end, she'd been the one to run, not him. So he deserved to hear the news face-to-face.

First, though…

She sent a gentle smile to the baby goat bleating excitedly and butting her furry head against the hay bale in the center of her pen. "What is Pumpkin doing here?"

Finn removed his Stetson, raked a hand through his hair and replaced it. Avery tried, and failed, not to stare at the flex of his biceps as he did so. "You said you missed her, so when I went looking for you at the boarding house, I asked Melba and Old Gene if I could bring her to the Ambling A."

Oh. Wow. He'd gone looking for her at the boarding house? "I'm guessing Melba was delighted with that arrangement."

Finn nodded. "She said something about Pumpkin belonging to you already."

Once you name an animal, it's yours.

Avery could hear Melba's voice in her head as clearly as if she were standing right beside her.

How was she going to do this? She loved life in Rust Creek Falls. She loved everything about it.

"I think we should get an annulment," she said without any sort of prelude. If she didn't say it now, she never would. "Or if we don't qualify for one of those, then a divorce."

The *D* word. She barely forced it out. Her voice cracked midway through, turning it into three or four syllables instead of two.

Finn said nothing.

He just stood there staring at her as if she'd kicked him in the stomach. Behind him, the mountains shimmered in shades of red and gold. Never in her life had she thought complete and utter heartbreak could be surrounded by so much beauty.

She cleared her throat and forced herself to finish the speech she'd been mentally rehearsing for hours. "This is all my fault. I take full responsibility. I should have told you about the baby from the very beginning, and I never should have suggested our marriage be one of convenience."

It seemed so absurd now. How could she have ever thought a fake marriage was a good idea when, all along, her feelings for Finn had been heart-stoppingly real?

"It was just…" she continued while nearby, Pumpkin bounced on and off a bale of hay. *It was just the worst mistake I've ever made.* Avery swallowed hard. "It was wrong."

The set of Finn's jaw hardened. His soft brown eyes—eyes that usually danced with laughter and Finn's trademark devilish charm—darkened to black. "*Wrong?* That's the word you'd use to describe our marriage?"

Avery shook her head. This wasn't going at all how she'd planned. "Please, Finn. You know what I mean."

She was referring to the agreement they'd made not to become intimate, and he knew it. But neither of them could seem to acknowledge it out loud, probably because that arrangement had been nothing short of impossible. She'd fallen into bed with Finn almost instantaneously, and despite all the hurt feelings swirling between them, she still wanted him. She craved the weight of his body on top of hers, the velvety warmth of his skin, his searing kiss. She always would.

"I appreciate everything you were willing to do for me—" she paused for a breath, then forced the rest of the words out "—for the baby. But I should have never agreed to rely on you for money, no matter the circumstances. That's all sorted out now, and I'm not going to hold you to an agreement we never should have made in the first place."

There, it was done. Almost.

Finn deserved to know the whole truth before she walked away for good. "What the baby and I both need isn't money or security. It's love. *Real* love. And I can't let myself settle for a knockoff."

"What the heck are you talking about?" Finn's voice boomed louder than Avery had ever heard it before. It even startled poor Pumpkin into inactivity. She let out a mournful bleat. "Are you crazy? Of course I love you. Why would you think otherwise?"

Avery opened her mouth to yell right back at him, and then blinked, trying to wrap her mind around what he'd just said.

Surely she'd heard him wrong.

"But you..." She shook her head, and hot tears filled her eyes.

He couldn't be serious, but Avery didn't think he'd toy with her emotions. Not at a time like this. Finn had never once told her he loved her, though. How was she supposed to know?

"I love you, Avery! I fell in love with you the first night we were together back in Oklahoma!" He yelled it so loud that there was no way she could misunderstand. The entire population of Rust Creek Falls probably knew Finn Crawford loved her now.

Avery didn't know how to process it, though. It was too much, more than her fragile heart could handle after all she'd been through in recent weeks.

She burst into tears.

"Don't cry, love," Finn said, closing the distance between them and taking her into his arms. "I'm sorry for yelling. It's just that I've been tied up in knots, worried you weren't coming back."

He pressed a tender kiss to the top of her head as she buried her face in his shoulder. He smelled like hay and horses, farm and family...like all the things she'd come to love so much about life here in this wild, beautiful place.

"I love you," he said, gently this time. Like a whisper.

Avery closed her eyes, wanting to believe, but needing to be sure. What if this was still just about the baby?

She shook her head against the soft fabric of his T-shirt, fighting as hard as she could. But falling for Finn Crawford had always been as easy and sweet as falling onto a feather bed.

"You love me, or the baby?" she managed to murmur, even as she felt her heart beating hard in perfect harmony against his.

Finn pulled away slightly, took her face in his hands and forced her to meet his gaze. "I love both of you, Princess. I'll admit it threw me when you told me you were pregnant, and I definitely could have handled the news better. Our relationship hasn't exactly been traditional."

He sighed, and the corner of his mouth tugged into a familiar half smile.

Had Rust Creek Falls' most notoriously single Crawford just used the word *relationship*?

"But, darlin', there was always a part of me that connected with you right from the start. Didn't you feel it, too, Princess?" His gaze dropped to her mouth as the pad of his thumb brushed a tender trail along her bottom lip. "Don't you feel it now?"

Then her husband dipped his head and kissed her as the sun fell on another autumnal day in Montana, and while the horses whinnied in the barn and the trees on the horizon blazed ruby red, the last bit of Avery's resistance faded away.

She felt it, too—with every breath, every kiss, every captivated beat of her heart. She felt it.

This kiss, this place…this man she loved so much. Finn Crawford wasn't just the father of her baby. He was her home, and at long last, Avery Ellington Crawford was home to stay.

Epilogue

Hours later, Avery lay in Finn's bed, naked and sated. Once again, he'd scooped her off her feet and carried her upstairs, where he'd made love to her in the same bed where she'd somehow managed to convince herself that he didn't love her.

How could she have been so wrong?

The question nagged at her in the afterglow. Finn had told her why he'd been going on so many dates. He'd even admitted he hadn't slept with anyone since their night together in Oklahoma. How had she taken the beautiful moment when he'd kissed her belly and whispered *mine* as something else—something frightening and lonely? Something to run away from.

She wondered if the answer was somehow tangled up in the ugly episode of her disinheritance. She thought maybe so, but she didn't want to think about that now.

She'd made peace with her father, and in the end, her mother had stood up for her in a way she never could have imagined. On some level, she was glad it had happened. Being cut off from her family had taught her some important truths. It taught her she was capable of standing on her own two feet and making her own decisions. It taught her what kind of parent she wanted to be to her baby. And most of all, it taught her she could trust Finn Crawford. He was a keeper, and she had no intention of running again. Ever.

He ran tender fingertips across her baby bump, then pressed a hand to her heart and whispered her favorite word.

"Mine."

Her heart was his, now and forever. Past, present and always.

"I have an idea," he said, shooting her one of his boyish grins.

"Oh, yeah? Does this idea involve a goat?" She kind of wanted another one. Another baby, too, now that she was thinking about it. The more, the merrier. After all, the Ambling A had plenty of room.

"It does not." He arched a brow. "Unless you want Pumpkin to be part of our wedding. That could be arranged. Maybe she could be the ring bearer. Don't people do that with dogs?"

Avery shifted so she could get a better look at his expression. Was he serious? "Aren't you forgetting something, cowboy? We're already married."

He picked up her hand and toyed with the rose gold band on her finger. Someday Avery might pass it on to their daughter and tell her the story of how she'd married her father in tiny country courthouse in Great

Gulch where the bailiff wore spurs. And then maybe her daughter would pass it on to her own child, and so on and so on, so that generations of Crawfords would remember the fine man who'd won her heart against all odds.

"I know we're already married, but I'd like to have another wedding—a ceremony like the one Wren asked you about. A big celebration that both our families could attend." He bent to kiss her, warm and tender. "Think about it. How does that sound, Princess?"

She smiled at her husband. She didn't need to think about anything. The answer fell right off her tongue. "Perfect."

Just like a fairy tale.

* * * * *

"Now, I know the circumstances aren't ideal, but I'm looking forward to working with you."

She appeared to struggle, like she was thinking how to formulate her words. "I wish I was working with you by choice and not circumstance. Not that I would choose to," she said with a chuckle.

"I hear you. If it weren't for this situation, we would still be throwing daggers at each other during leadership meetings."

"Put yourself in my shoes. If you were going through this, how would you feel?" she asked, rubbing her toe into the carpet. "Honest answer."

"I'm not as brave as you are, and I have more pride than common sense."

She blushed and averted her eyes. "I would have resigned if I didn't have a mother and sister to consider. Pride is secondary to priority."

He felt ashamed and got to his feet. He went over to her. "You're right. I'm thinking like a single man. If I were married or had other responsibilities, I'd do what I'd have to and keep my job. I was hoping that Irene—" He stopped, unsure of the etiquette of bringing another woman into the conversation.

"No need to stop on my account. I know you had— have—a life."

Lynx wasn't about to talk about Irene, no matter how cool Shanna claimed she was with it. "I'm ready to fall in love, get married and install the white picket fence."

"How do you know you're ready?" she asked.

He rubbed his chin. "I'm at the brink of where I want to be professionally. I want someone to share my success with me."

"I get it," she said, doing that half-bite thing with her lip again.

Don't miss
Rivals at Love Creek
by Michelle Lindo-Rice,
available July 2022 wherever
Harlequin Special Edition books and ebooks are sold.

Harlequin.com

HSEEXP0522

Get 4 FREE REWARDS!

We'll send you 2 FREE Books plus 2 FREE Mystery Gifts.

FREE
Value Over
$20

Both the **Harlequin® Special Edition** and **Harlequin® Heartwarming™** series feature compelling novels filled with stories of love and strength where the bonds of friendship, family and community unite.

YES! Please send me 2 FREE novels from the Harlequin Special Edition or Harlequin Heartwarming series and my 2 FREE gifts (gifts are worth about $10 retail). After receiving them, if I don't wish to receive any more books, I can return the shipping statement marked "cancel." If I don't cancel, I will receive 6 brand-new Harlequin Special Edition books every month and be billed just $4.99 each in the U.S or $5.74 each in Canada, a savings of at least 17% off the cover price or 4 brand-new Harlequin Heartwarming Larger-Print books every month and be billed just $5.74 each in the U.S. or $6.24 each in Canada, a savings of at least 21% off the cover price. It's quite a bargain! Shipping and handling is just 50¢ per book in the U.S. and $1.25 per book in Canada.* I understand that accepting the 2 free books and gifts places me under no obligation to buy anything. I can always return a shipment and cancel at any time. The free books and gifts are mine to keep no matter what I decide.

Choose one: ☐ **Harlequin Special Edition**   ☐ **Harlequin Heartwarming**
(235/335 HDN GNMP)   **Larger-Print**
(161/361 HDN GNPZ)

Name (please print)

Address   Apt. #

City   State/Province   Zip/Postal Code

Email: Please check this box ☐ if you would like to receive newsletters and promotional emails from Harlequin Enterprises ULC and its affiliates. You can unsubscribe anytime.

Mail to the **Harlequin Reader Service:**
IN U.S.A.: P.O. Box 1341, Buffalo, NY 14240-8531
IN CANADA: P.O. Box 603, Fort Erie, Ontario L2A 5X3

Want to try 2 free books from another series? Call 1-800-873-8635 or visit www.ReaderService.com.

HSEHW22

Love Harlequin romance?

DISCOVER.

Be the first to find out about promotions, news and exclusive content!

f Facebook.com/HarlequinBooks

y Twitter.com/HarlequinBooks

O Instagram.com/HarlequinBooks

P Pinterest.com/HarlequinBooks

You Tube YouTube.com/HarlequinBooks

ReaderService.com

EXPLORE.

Sign up for the Harlequin e-newsletter and download a free book from any series at **TryHarlequin.com**

CONNECT.

Join our Harlequin community to share your thoughts and connect with other romance readers! **Facebook.com/groups/HarlequinConnection**

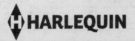

HSOCIAL2021